WICKED SPIRITS

A *BODIES FROM THE LIBRARY* BOOK

WICKED SPIRITS

Mysteries, Spine Chillers
and Lost Tales of the Supernatural

Selected and introduced by

TONY MEDAWAR

COLLINS
CRIME
CLUB

COLLINS CRIME CLUB
An imprint of HarperCollins*Publishers*
1 London Bridge Street
London SE1 9GF
www.harpercollins.co.uk

HarperCollins*Publishers*
Macken House,
39/40 Mayor Street Upper,
Dublin 1
D01 C9W8
Ireland

First published by Collins Crime Club 2024

1

Selection, introduction and notes © Tony Medawar 2024
For copyright acknowledgements, see page 343.

*These stories were mostly written in the first half of the twentieth century
and characters sometimes use offensive language or otherwise are described
or behave in ways that reflect the prejudices and insensitivities of the period.*

A catalogue record for this book
is available from the British Library

ISBN 978-00-0-856425-4

Typeset in Minion Pro 11/15 pt by
Palimpsest Book Production Ltd, Falkirk, Stirlingshire

Printed and bound in the UK using 100% renewable electricity
at CPI Group (UK) Ltd

MIX
Paper | Supporting
responsible forestry
FSC™ C007454

This book contains FSC™ certified paper and other controlled sources
to ensure responsible forest management.

For more information visit: www.harpercollins.co.uk/green

CONTENTS

Introduction   vii

THE LONELY HAMPSHIRE COTTAGE   1
Arthur Conan Doyle   13

THE VICAR'S CONVERSION   17
A. E. W. Mason   26

THE GHOST OF TRAVERS COURT   31
E. R. Punshon   42

DEAKIN AND THE GHOST   49
Ernest Bramah   53

A GOOD PLACE   55
H. C. Bailey   72

EXACTLY AS IT HAPPENED   75
E. C. Bentley   90

YE GOODE OLDE GHOSTE STORIE   93
Anthony Boucher   96

THE ATONEMENT   101
S. S. Van Dine   119

DISPOSSESSION   123
C. H. B. Kitchin   142

BLIND GUESS 147
Valentine Williams 168

MODERN ANTIQUE 173
Milward Kennedy 180

AN EXPERIMENT OF THE DEAD 185
Helen Simpson 196

WE ARE SORRY, TOO 199
Patricia Highsmith 210

VEX NOT HIS GHOST 215
John Dickson Carr 233

WRITER'S WITCH 237
Joan Fleming 245

THE SECURITY OFFICER 249
Val Gielgud 255

THE FRAUDULENT SPIRIT 261
Joseph Commings 290

THE LINE WENT DEAD 293
Leo Bruce 301

THE HOUSE OF THE LIONS 303
Desmond Bagley 314

THE HAUNTING MELODY 319
Christopher Priest 323

THE LAST WOLF 329
Reginald Hill 338

Acknowledgements 343

INTRODUCTION

'Yesterday, upon the stair,
I met a man who wasn't there.
He wasn't there again today.
I wish, I wish, he'd go away . . .'

Hughes Mearns

Do *you* believe in ghosts?

No more do I. And yet . . . we all know someone who claims to have seen, or heard, something they could not explain. The sound of banging coming from within an empty wardrobe. Or a little girl in a cream dress running in the corridor of a building where no child should be. Or, seated in the corner of the back room of a London pub, an elderly man nursing a pint and smoking a long pipe. A man who suddenly disappears . . .

So, while I believe *there's no such thing as ghosts*, I also believe I might be wrong.

In this volume of previously uncollected and unpublished tales, you will encounter a variety of spirits and other supernatural beings. Presented here in chronological order, some of the stories may make you smile and at least one will make you shiver. But in a few you will not find anything supernatural at all. After all, it would rather give away the game if you could always be certain of the outcome.

As in life, expect the unexpected . . .

Tony Medawar
April 2024

FOR NICOLA

THE LONELY HAMPSHIRE COTTAGE

Arthur Conan Doyle

John Ranter, ex-landlord of the 'Battle of Dettingen' public-house in Southampton, was not a man whom one would desire as a friend, and still less would one relish him as a foe. Tall and strong in his person, dark and saturnine in his disposition, the two-and-fifty years which had passed over John's head had done little to soften his character or to modify his passions. Perhaps the ill-fortune which had attended him through life had something to do with his asperity, yet this same ill-fortune had been usually caused by his own violent and headstrong temper. He had quarrelled with his parents when a lad, and left them. After working his way up in the world, to some extent, he had fallen in love with a pretty face, and mated himself to a timid, characterless woman, who was a drag rather than a help to him. The fruit of this union had been a single son; but John Ranter beat the lad savagely for some trivial offence, and he had fled away to sea as a cabin-boy, and was reported to have been drowned in the great wreck of the Queen of the West. From that time the publican went rapidly downhill. He offended his customers by his morose and sullen temper, and they ceased to frequent the 'Battle of Dettingen', until, at last, he was compelled to dispose of the business. With the scanty proceeds he purchased a small house upon

the Portsmouth and Southampton road, about three miles from
the latter town, and settled down with his wife to a gloomy and
misanthropic existence.

Strange tales were told of that lonely cottage, with its bare
brick walls and great, overhanging thatch, from under which
the diamond-paned windows seemed to scowl at the passers-by.
Waggoners at roadside inns talked of the dark-faced, grizzly-
haired man, who lounged all day in the little garden which
adjoined the road, and of the pale, patient face, which peered
out at them sometimes through the half-opened door. There
were darker things, too, of which they had to speak, of angry
voices, of the dull thud of blows, and the cries of a woman in
distress. However tired the horses might be, they were whipped
up into a trot, when, after nightfall, they came near the wooden
gate which led up to that ill-omened dwelling.

It was one lovely autumn evening that John Ranter leaned his
elbows upon that identical gate, and puffed meditatively at his black
clay pipe. He was pondering within himself as to what his future
should be. Should he continue to exist in the way in which he was
doing, or should he embark what little capital he had in some
attempt to better his fortunes? His present life, if unambitious, was
at least secure. It was possible that he might lose all in a new
venture. Yet, on the other hand, John felt that he still had all the
energy of youth, and was as able as ever to turn his hand to anything.
If his son, he reflected, who had left him fifteen years before had
been alive, he might have been of assistance to him now. A vague
longing for the comforts which he had enjoyed in more fortunate
days filled and unsettled his mind. He was still brooding over the
matter when, looking up, he saw, against the setting sun, a man
dressed in a long grey overcoat, who was striding down the road
from the direction of Southampton.

It was no uncommon thing for pedestrians of every type to
pass the door of John Ranter, and yet this particular one attracted
his attention to an unusual degree. He was a tall, athletic young

fellow, with a yellow moustache, and a face which was tanned by exposure to the sun and weather. His hat was a peculiar slouched one, of soft felt, and it may have been this, or it may have been the grey coat, which caused the ex-publican to look closely at him. Over his shoulder the stranger had a broad leather strap, and to this was attached a large black bag, something like those which are worn by bookmakers upon a racecourse. Indeed, John Ranter's first impression was that the traveller belonged to the betting fraternity.

When the young fellow came near the gate, he slowed down his pace, and looked irresolutely about him. Then he halted, and addressed John, speaking in a peculiar metallic voice.

'I say, mate,' he said; 'I guess I'd have to walk all night if I wanted to make Portsmouth in the morning?'

'I guess you would,' the other answered, surlily, mimicking the stranger's tone and pronunciation. 'You've hardly got started yet.'

'Well now, that beats everything,' the traveller said, impatiently. 'I'd ha' put up at an inn in Southampton if I dared. To think o' my spending my first night in the old country like that!'

'And why dar'n't you put up at an inn?' John Ranter asked.

The stranger winked one of his shrewd eyes at John.

'There ain't such a very long way between an innkeeper and a thief,' he said; 'anyway, there's not in Californey, and I guess human natur' is human natur' all the world over. When I've got what's worth keepin' I give the inns a wide berth.'

'Oh, you've got what's worth keeping, have you?' said the old misanthrope to himself, and he relaxed the grimness of his features as far as he could, and glanced out of the corner of his eyes at the black leather bag.

'Ye see, it's this way,' the young man said, confidentially; 'I've been out at the diggings, first in Nevada and then in Californey, and I've struck it, and struck it pretty rich too, you bet. When I allowed that I'd made my pile, I pushed for home in the Marie Rose from 'Frisco to Southampton. She got in at three today, but those sharks at the customs kept us till five 'fore we could get ashore. When I landed I let out for Portsmouth, where I used to know some folk; but you see I didn't quite reckon up how far it was before I started. Besides, this bag ain't quite the thing a man would lug about with him if he was walkin' for a wager.'

'Are your friends expecting you in Portsmouth?' John Ranter asked.

The young man laid down his bag, and laughed so heartily that he had to lean against the gate for support.

'That's where the joke comes in,' he cried; 'they don't know that I've left the States.'

'Oh, that's the joke, is it?'

'Yes; that's the joke. You see, they are all sitting at breakfast, maybe, or at dinner, as the case might be, and I pushes my way in, and I up with this here bag and opens it, and then ker-whop down comes the whole lot on the table;' and the young man laughed heartily once more over the idea.

'The whole lot of what?' asked John.

'Why, of shiners, of course—dollars, you understand.'

'And d'ye mean to say you carry your whole fortune about with you in gold?' Ranter asked in amazement.

'My whole fortune! No, boss, I reckon not. The bulk of it is in notes and shares, and they're all packed away right enough. This is just eight hundred dollars that I put to one side for this same little game that I spoke of. But I suppose it's no use trying to get there tonight, and I'll have to trust to an inn after all.'

'Don't you do that,' the elder man said, earnestly. 'They are a rough lot in the inns about here, and there's many a poor sailor found his pockets as empty in the morning as they were the day he sailed out of port. You find some honest man and ask him for a night's lodging; that's the best thing you can do.'

'Well, pard, I guess I've lost my bearings in this neighbourhood,' the gold-digger said. 'If you can put me on the track of any such berth as you speak of, I'd be beholden to you.'

'Why, for that matter,' John Ranter said, 'we have a spare bed of our own, and should be very glad if you would pass the night in it. We are simple folk, my wife and I; but as far as a fire and a warm supper go, you're very welcome to both the one and the other.'

'Well, you can't say fairer than that,' the traveller responded, and he walked up the little gravel walk with his companion, while the shadow of night spread slowly over the landscape, and the owl hooted mournfully in the neighbouring wood.

Mrs Ranter, who had been a comely lass thirty years before, was now a white-haired, melancholy woman, with a wan face and a timid manner. She welcomed the stranger in a nervous, constrained fashion, and proceeded to cook some rashers of bacon, which she cut from a great side that hung from the rafters of the rude kitchen. The young man deposited his bag under a chair, and then, sitting down above it, he drew out his pipe and lit it. Ranter filled his again at the same time, eyeing his companion furtively all the while from under his heavy eyebrows.

'You'd best take your coat off,' he said, in an off-hand way.

'No; I'll keep it on, if you don't mind,' the other returned. 'I never take this coat off.'

'Please yourself,' said John, puffing at his pipe; 'I thought maybe you'd find it hot with this fire burning; but then, Californey is a hot place, I'm told, and maybe you find England chilly?'

The other did not answer, and the two men sat silently watching the rashers, which grizzled and sputtered upon the pan.

'What sort o' ship did you come in?' the host asked, at last.

'The Marie Rose,' said the other. 'She's a three-masted schooner, and came over with hides and other goods. She's not much to look at, but she's no slouch of a sea boat. We'd a gale off Cape Horn that would have tried any ship that ever sailed. Three days under a single double-reefed topsail, and that was rather more than she could carry. Am I in your way, missus?'

'No, no,' said Mrs Ranter, hurriedly. The stranger had been looking at her very hard while he spoke.

'I guess the skipper and the mates will wonder what has become of me,' he continued. 'I was in such a hurry that I came off without a word to one of them. However, my traps are on board, so they'll know I've not deserted them for good.'

'Did you speak to anyone after you left the ship?' Ranter asked, carelessly.

'No.'

'Why didn't you take a trap if you wanted to get to Portsmouth?'

'Mate, you've never come ashore from a long sea voyage, else you'd not ask me that question. Why, man, it's the greatest pleasure you can have to stretch your legs, and keep on stretching them. I'd have padded on right enough if the light had held.'

'You'll be a deal better in a comfortable bed,' said Ranter; 'and now the supper's ready, so let us fall to. Here's beer in the jug, and there's whisky in that bottle, so it's your own fault if you don't help yourself.'

The three gathered round the table and made an excellent meal. Under the influence of their young guest's genial face and cheery conversation, the mistress of the house lost her haggard appearance, and even made one or two timid attempts to join in the talk. The country postman, coming home from his final round, stopped in astonishment when he saw the blazing light in the cottage window, and heard the merry sound of laughter which pealed out on the still night air.

If any close observer had been watching the little party as they sat round the table, he might have remarked that John Ranter showed a very lively curiosity in regard to the long grey coat in which his visitor was clad. Not only did he eye that garment narrowly from time to time, but he twice found pretexts to pass close to the other's chair, and each time he did so he drew his hand, as though accidentally, along the side of the overcoat. Neither the young man nor the hostess appeared, however, to take the slightest notice of this strange conduct upon the part of the ex-publican.

After supper the two men drew their chairs up to the fire once more, while the old woman removed the dishes. The traveller's conversation turned principally upon the wonders of California and of the great republic in which he had spent the best part of his life. He spoke of the fortunes which were made at the mines, too, and of the golden store which may be picked up by whoever is lucky enough to find it, until Ranter's eyes sparkled again as he listened.

'How much might it take to get out there?' he said.

'Oh! a hundred pounds or so would start you comfortably,' answered the man with the grey coat.

'That doesn't seem much.'

'Why anyone should stay in England while there is money to be picked up there is more than I can understand,' the miner remarked. 'And now, mate, you'll excuse me, but I'm a man that likes to go to roost early and be up at cock-crow. If the missus here would show me my room I'd be obliged.'

'Won't you have another whisky? No? Ah! well, good-night. Lizzie, you will show Mr—Mr—'

'Mr Goodall,' said the other.

'You will show Mr Goodall up to his room. I hope you'll sleep well.'

'I always sleep sound,' said the man with the grey coat; and, with a nod, he tramped heavily, bag in hand, up the wooden staircase, while the old woman toiled along with the light in front of him.

When he had gone, John Ranter put both his hands into his trousers pockets, stretched out his legs, and stared gloomily into the fire, with a wrinkled brow and projecting lips. A great many thoughts were passing through his mind—so many that he did not hear his wife re-enter the kitchen, nor did he answer her when she spoke to him. It was half-past ten when the visitor retired, and at twelve John Ranter was still bending over the smouldering heap of ashes with the same look of thought upon his face. It was only when his wife asked him whether he was not going to bed that he appeared to come to himself.

'No, Lizzie,' he said, in a more conciliatory tone than was usual with him. 'We'll both stay up a short time tonight.'

'All right, John,' the poor woman said, with a glad smile. It was many a year since he had ever asked her for her company.

'Is he upstairs all right?'

'Who? Oh, Mr Goodall? Yes; I showed him into the spare room.'

'D'ye think he's asleep?'

'I suppose so, John. He's been there nigh an hour and a half.'

'Is there a key in the door?'

'No, dear; but what queer questions you do ask.'

John Ranter was silent for a time.

'Lizzie,' he said at last, taking up the poker, and playing with it nervously, 'in the whole world there is no one who knows that that man came here tonight. If he never left us again no one would know what had become of him, or care to make any search after him.'

His wife said nothing, but she turned white to her very lips. 'He has eight hundred dollars in that bag, Lizzie, which makes over a hundred and fifty pound of our money. But he has more than that. He's got lumps of gold sewn into the lining of that grey coat of his. That's why he didn't care about taking it off. I saw the knobs, and I managed to feel 'em too. That money, my girl, would be enough to take the two of us out to that same country where he picked all this up—'

'For Heaven's sake, John,' cried his wife, flinging herself at his feet, and clasping his knees with her arms, 'for my sake—for the sake of our boy, who might be about this young man's age—think no more of this! We are old, John, and, rich or poor, we must in a few short years go to our long home. Don't go with the stain of blood upon you. Oh, spare him! We have been bad, but never so bad as this!'

But John Ranter continued to gaze over his wife's head into the fire, and the set sternness of his features never relaxed for one moment. It seemed to her, as she looked up into his eyes, that a strange new expression had come into them such as she had never seen before—the baleful, lurid glare of the beast of prey.

'This is a chance,' he said, 'such as would never come to us again. How many would be glad to have it! Besides, Lizzie, it is my life or this man's. You remember what Dr Cousins said of me when we were at Portsea. I was liable to apoplexy, he said, and disappointment, or hardships or grief, might bring it on. This wretched life has enough of all three. Now if we had the money, we could start afresh, and all would be well. I tell you, wife, I shall do it!' and he clenched his large brown hand round the poker.

'You must not, John—and you shall not.'

'I shall, and I will. Leave go of my knees.'

He was about to push her from him when he perceived that she had fainted. Picking her up he carried her to the side of the room and laid her down there. Then he went back, and taking up the poker he balanced it in his hand. It seemed to strike him as being too light, for he went into the scullery, and after groping about in the dark he came back with a small axe. He was swinging this backwards and forwards when his eye fell upon the knife which his wife had used before supper in cutting the rashers of bacon. He ran his finger along the edge of it. It was as keen as a razor. 'It's handier and surer!' he muttered; and going to the cupboard he drank off a large glass of raw whisky, after which he kicked off his boots and began silently to ascend the old-fashioned stair.

There were twelve steps which led up from the kitchen to a landing, and from the landing eight more to the bedroom of their guest. John Ranter was nearly half an hour in ascending those first twelve. The woodwork was rotten, and the construction weak, so that they creaked under the weight of the heavy man. He would first put his right foot lightly upon the board, and gradually increase the pressure upon it until his whole weight was there. Then he would carefully move up his left foot, and stand listening breathlessly for any sound from above. Nothing broke the silence, however, except the dull ticking of the clock in the kitchen behind him and the melancholy hooting of an owl among the shrubbery. In the dull, uncertain light there was something terrible in this vague, dark figure creeping slowly up the little staircase—moving, pausing, crouching, but always coming nearer the top.

When he reached the landing he could see the door of the young miner's room. John Ranter stood aghast. The door was on the jar, and through the narrow opening there shone a thin golden stream. The light was still burning. Did it mean that the traveller was awake? John listened intently, but there was no sound of any movement in the room. For a long time he strained his ears, but all was perfectly still.

'If he were awake,' John said to himself, 'he would have turned in his bed, or made some rustling during this time.'

Then he began stealthily to ascend the eight remaining steps until he was immediately outside the bedroom door. Still all was silent within. No doubt it was one of his foreign customs to leave the light burning during the night. He had mentioned in conversation that he was a sound sleeper. Ranter began to fear that unless he got it over soon his wife might recover and raise an alarm. Clutching his knife in his right hand, he quietly pushed the door a little more open with his left and inserted his head. Something cold pressed against his temple as he did so. It was the muzzle of a revolver.

'Come in, John Ranter,' said the quiet voice of his guest; 'but first drop your weapon, or I shall be compelled to fire. You are at my mercy.'

Indeed, the ex-publican's head was caught in such a way that it was difficult for him either to withdraw or to force his way in. He gave a deep groan of rage and disappointment, and his knife clattered down upon the floor.

'I meant no harm,' he said, sulkily, as he entered the room.

'I have been expecting you for a couple of hours,' the man with the grey coat said, holding his pistol still cocked in his right hand, so that he might use it if necessary. He was dressed exactly as he had been when he went upstairs, and the ill-fated bag was resting upon the unruffled bed. 'I knew that you were coming.'

'How—how?' John stammered.

'Because I know you; because I saw murder in your eye when you stood before me at the gate; because I saw you feel my coat here for the nuggets. That is why I waited up for you.'

'You have no proof against me,' said John Ranter, sullenly.

'I do not want any. I could shoot you where you stand, and the law would justify me. Look at that bag upon the bed there. I told you there was money in it. What d'ye think I brought that money to England for? It was to give it to you—yes, to you. And that grey coat on me is worth five hundred pounds; that was for you also. Ah! you begin to understand now. You begin to see the mistake you have made.'

John Ranter had staggered against the wall, and his face was all drawn down on one side.

'Jack!' he gasped. 'Jack!'

'Yes; Jack Ranter—your son. That's who I am.' The young man turned back his sleeve, and bared a blue device upon his forearm. 'Don't you remember Hairy Pete put that 'J.R.' on when I was a lad? Now you know me. I made my fortune, and I came back, earnestly hoping that you would help me to spend it. I called at the 'Battle of Dettingen', and they told me where to find you. Then, when I saw you at the gate, I thought I'd test my mother and you, and see if you were the same as ever. I came to make you happy, and you have tried to murder me. I shall not punish you; but I shall go, and you shall never see either me or my money any more.'

While the young man had been saying these words, a series of twitchings and horrible contortions had passed over the face of his father, and at the last words he took a step forward, raising his hands above his head, and fell, with a hoarse cry, upon the ground. His eyes became glazed, his breathing stertorous, and foam stood upon his purple lips. It did not take much medical knowledge to see that he was dying. His son stooped over him and loosened his collar and shirt.

'One last question,' he said, in quick, earnest tones. 'Did my mother aid in this attempt?'

John Ranter appeared to understand the import of it, for he shook his head; and so, with this single act of justice, his dark spirit fled from this world of crime. The doctor's warning had come true, and emotion had hastened a long-impending apoplexy. His son lifted him reverentially on to the bed, and did such last offices as could be done.

'Perhaps it is the best thing that could have happened,' he said, sadly, as he turned from the room, and went down to seek his mother, and to comfort her in her sore affliction.

Young John Ranter returned to America, and by his energy and talents soon became one of the richest men in his State. He has definitely settled there now, and will return no more to the old country. In his palatial residence there dwells a white-haired, anxious-faced old woman, whose every wish is consulted, and to whom the inmates show every reverence. This is old Mrs Ranter; and her son has hopes that with time, and among new associations, she may come to forget that terrible night when the man with the grey coat paid a visit to the lonely Hampshire cottage.

ARTHUR CONAN DOYLE

Arthur Conan Doyle, the most influential figure in the history of crime and mystery literature, was born in Edinburgh, Scotland, on 22 May 1859. His parents were Mary Josephine Foley and Charles Altamont Doyle, an artist and illustrator. From the age of eleven, Doyle studied at a Catholic school, Stonyhurst College, where as well as playing a full part in school sports he founded, edited and largely authored a single issue of a magazine, *The Stonyhurst Figaro*. Doyle also studied at Stella Matutina, a Jesuit school in Austria. However, rather than inspire him, these religious educational establishments convinced him to become an agnostic. At Edinburgh University, he underwent five years of 'drudgery' as he studied for his intended future profession as a doctor, and he would later immortalise two of his tutors, Professor William Rutherford and Doctor Joseph Bell, as the rumbustious explorer George Challenger and Sherlock Holmes respectively.

While studying, Doyle wrote fiction and his first short story, 'The Mystery of Sasassa Valley', was published in *Chamber's Journal* in September 1879. A few months before his 21st birthday he took up a position as doctor on the *Hope*, a whaling ship, but this gave him little opportunity to hone his developing skills as a physician. On returning to Edinburgh he completed his degree and in 1881 enlisted for a four-month tour of duty as a surgeon on the *SS Mayumba*, a passenger ship sailing between England and the West

Coast of Africa. Doyle next moved to Southsea where he established himself as a general practitioner while playing a full part in the social and sporting life of the town. He was a keen footballer and a strong cricketer, although he was once bowled out for 15 by the great W. G. Grace. He was also a founder member of the Portsmouth Literary and Scientific Society; at its first meeting in November 1883, Major-General George Evatt lectured on his life as an army doctor in the second Anglo-Afghan war, which would later inspire the creation of Dr John Watson. At the Society's second meeting, Doyle spoke on 'The Arctic Seas' and at a later meeting on the life and work of Thomas Carlyle.

In 1885, Doyle married Louisa Hawkins, a widow whose brother was one of his patients. He and Louisa, whom he called 'Touie', had two children: a daughter Mary and a son known by his middle name, Kingsley. Doyle also continued to write. In the late 1880s, one of his near neighbours in Shaftesbury Road, Southsea, was a Mrs Sherlock of Holm Leigh, and she may have provided part of the inspiration for the name of Sherlock Holmes, whose first 'adventure', *A Study in Scarlet*, would be published in *Beeton's Annual* in November 1887. This was followed by *Micah Clarke* (1889), *The Sign of Four* (1890) and *The White Company* (1891); and he also secured publication of an earlier manuscript, *The Firm of Girdlestone* (1890).

Increasingly specialising in the eye, Doyle undertook further studies in Vienna in 1891 and on his return he and Touie moved to London where they eventually settled at 12 Tennison Road, Upper Norwood. He took rooms in Wimpole Street as an oculist, dealing with patients in the morning and working at a hospital in the afternoon, leaving only part of the evening for writing. Eventually something had to give and in 1892 Doyle resolved 'to throw physic to the dogs' and become a professional writer, juggling the commercially advantageous adventures of Sherlock Holmes with historical novels, writing at a mahogany desk surrounded by his father's drawings and souvenirs of his own youthful adventures, including a bear's skull and a seal's paw brought back from the Arctic. His work appeared in countless newspapers and magazines—from *London Society* to *The Boy's Own Paper*. He also supported novel literary endeavours: together with Bram Stoker, Grant Allen and others, he co-authored a round-robin novel, *The Fate of Fenella* (1891) and in 1892 his story 'The Major's Card' was published in the first issue of *Sword and Chatelaine*, a new but short-lived Southsea literary magazine for the forces.

In 1893, Doyle decided to kill off Sherlock Holmes after 23 successful short stories, in 'The Adventure of the Final Problem', a case set in Switzerland which the author Silas Hocking had identified as the ideal resting place for the detective. In the same year, Touie was diagnosed with tuberculosis and Doyle decided that the family should move away from London and settle in Hindhead, Surrey. While Touie recuperated in Switzerland, he oversaw the building of their new home, 'Undershaw', completed in the late autumn of 1897. While Doyle had killed off his creation, Holmes was uneasy in his grave. Pressured by his publisher and mindful of the financial benefits, Doyle produced *The Hound of the Baskervilles* (1901), before reviving him properly in 'The Adventure of the Empty House'. Much as he regretted the fact, Holmes is unquestionably Doyle's greatest achievement. Excluding ephemera, the character appears in 58 short stories, four novels and one stage play by Doyle, but his fame can be measured in the innumerable pastiche adventures authored by hundreds of writers including Agatha Christie, J. M. Barrie, P. G. Wodehouse and even John Lennon.

As well as writing fiction, Doyle served briefly as a war correspondent and as a doctor in the Second Boer War which he chronicled. He also became interested in politics and over 20 years campaigned on many issues. He was in favour of a Channel tunnel but against free trade and uncontrolled immigration. He also joined the Liberal Unionist Party and stood for Parliament, losing to a Liberal Party candidate for the seat of Edinburgh Central in 1900 and again in 1906 at Hawick Burghs. In 1902 Doyle was knighted by King Edward VII, an honour declined by Sherlock Holmes in a later story.

After Touie's death in 1906, Doyle married Jean Leckie, with whom he had maintained a platonic relationship since their first meeting in 1897. They had three children together, their second son Adrian later collaborating with his father's biographer, John Dickson Carr, to produce *The Exploits of Sherlock Holmes* (1954). Over the next ten years he also published two of his most popular books: *The Lost World* (1912), forerunner of Michael Crichton's *Jurassic Park*, and *The Valley of Fear* (1914), the last of Sherlock Holmes' four novel-length adventures.

After the death of his first son in the 'flu pandemic of 1918, and the death of his mother two years later, Doyle began to display signs of the mental health issues that had affected his father and other members of his family. He published outlandish theories on the existence of fairies and made extravagant claims about spiritualism. But he also published his autobiography, *Memories and Adventures* (1924) and in March 1927 'The Adventure of Shoscombe Old Place', Sherlock Holmes's final 'final problem'.

Prodigiously active to the end, Arthur Conan Doyle suffered a heart attack and died at home on 7 July 1930.

'The Lonely Hampshire Cottage' was first published anonymously in *Cassell's Saturday Journal*, 2 May 1885.

THE VICAR'S CONVERSION

A. E. W. Mason

'These are fancies,' said the vicar.

The vicar was fresh to the parish, and had come straight from a college lecture room. The peasant with whom he was walking on the trim gravel path between the lych-gate and the church door had heard that clock strike six on every morning of his seventy-two years.

'These are fancies, Jan, and reprehensible. It is disheartening to notice how the traditions of ignorance still live in distant villages. In olden times there was more excuse, and to be sure instances were more common. An unexpected draught of wind on a calm day and a rustle of the trees, and at once it was the fairies calling 'horse and hattock,' as they were transported from place to place. To see oneself in a dream divided into a two-fold person was a sign of death, doubtless because such a vision had happened to a man in a delirium and near his end. Superstition was an excuse, too, for quacks, and by them encouraged. There was a miller in Norfolk who owned a beryl set in a circle of silver, on which were engraved the names of four angels—Ariel, Raphael, Michael, and Gabriel—and in his beryl he professed to see prescriptions written on the images of herbs, and so to cure the sick.'

Jan shook his head in admiration of the vicar's harangue.

'There's book-larnin' in every word,' he said.

'Then there are the phantasmata proper,' continued the vicar, 'such as corpse-candles, which, rightly understood, are no more than will-o'-the-wisps or marsh fires and exhalations of the soil, and when seen in churchyards are indeed an argument for cremation.'

The vicar was enjoying his lecture too much to remark the look of dismay on Jan's old, wrinkled face, or to pay any heed to his expostulation against that or any argument for cremation. He bore Jan down with knowledge.

'Besides these, there are the apparitions, reserved, it would seem,' he continued, with a severe look at Jan, 'to those who have the second sight. The Scotch are the chief offenders in claiming that gift, and they tell many ridiculous stories about meeting people on the high road with winding sheets up to their knees or necks, according as they are to die immediately or only soon. There is a legend told of the Macleans, whose child's nurse began suddenly to weep when she saw Maclean and his lady entering together. She wept, it seems, because she saw between them a man in a scarlet cloak and a white hat, who gave the lady a kiss. And the meaning of that rubbish was that Maclean would die and his lady marry again, and marry a man in a scarlet cloak and a white hat.'

'An' did she?' interrupted Jan.

'Did she?' said the vicar with scorn. 'Would any woman marry a man in a scarlet cloak and a white hat?'

'She might be daft loike,' said Jan.

The vicar waved the suggestion aside.

'The Scotch, indeed, make the most absurd pretensions. Aubrey writes that in the Island of Skye they offered in his day to teach second sight for a pound of tobacco.'

'They couldn't do that,' said Jan. ''Tisn't to be larned. 'Tis born in the blood so to speak. My father had it afore me—'

'Now, Jan,' interrupted the vicar, 'I cannot listen to you. It is mere presumption for you to speak in that way.'

'Be sure, vicar,' replied Jan. 'Oi aren't proud o' the gift. Would get rid of it if Oi cud. "Tisn't pleasant to sit suppin' your ale with them as you knows are corpses already, so to say, and many years Oi've never been near churchyard at all on New Year's Eve, so as Oi' moighn't knaw. But when Oi do come, sure enough all who are goin' to doi durin' the year comes down the lane, through the gate, and on the path into the church. An' those who'll doi first comes first. They don't wear no sheets or trappin's, but they comes in their clothes, opens gate, and so into church. An' Oi'll prove it to you, vicar.'

'How?'

'Oi'll watch tomorrow, bein' New Year's Eve, and Oi'll wroite down the names of the three who first go through the gate. Then Oi'll put the names in envelopes and mark 'em outside, "1", "2", "3", and give you the envelopes. Then, when the first person doies you open the first envelope, and there you'll find the name, and same wi' the second and the third.'

The vicar was in a quandary. It was undignified to accept the challenge; it would seem cowardly to refuse it. He compounded with his dignity and accepted.

'Not because I have any doubts myself,' he said to Jan, 'but in order to convince you of the absurdity of your pretension.'

On the first day of January the three envelopes were delivered to him by Jan. They were sealed and numbered. The vicar tossed them contemptuously into a drawer, and locked them up. He forgot them altogether until the end of the month, when he was summoned hastily to the bedside of a labourer who was ill with influenza. The man was very old—eighty-four, the doctor said.

'Is there a chance of his living?' asked the vicar when he came out of the cottage with the doctor.

'Not one in ten thousand. He has been breaking for months. Last autumn I didn't think he would see another summer.'

The vicar met Jan in the street, and remembered the envelopes. He shrugged his shoulders at the recollection of the ridiculous challenge, and went home to his study. His uncompleted sermon lay on his desk, and he sat down to it. In a minute or two he went to his bookcase for a reference, and, standing before his shelves, forgot why he had risen from his chair. He was thinking, 'After all, old Peter Stewer's death was an easy guess.' He went back to his table and unlocked the drawer. 'It wouldn't be proof if Peter Stewer's name was in envelope No. 1.'

He took out envelope No. 1. 'Anyone, it seemed, might have known in the autumn that Peter Stewer was breaking.' And his next thought was, 'Those envelopes are very thick.' He woke up with a start, to realise that he was holding the envelope up to the light of the window, and he tossed it back impatiently and snapped the drawer to. Peter Stewer died at three o'clock in the morning. The vicar heard the news at nine, as he was walking to the cottage, and he suddenly turned back as though he were going home. He changed his mind, however, and turned again, continuing his walk to the cottage.

'He was eighty-four,' said Peter's daughter, phlegmatically.

'A ripe age,' replied the vicar.

He repeated, 'Eighty-four,' to himself more than once as he went home.

'Eighty-four. Very likely his name's in the envelope. There's no proof in that.'

And he felt himself grabbed by the arm. It was the doctor who had caught hold of him.

'You're in a great hurry,' said the doctor.

'Am I?' said the vicar, colouring red. 'I did not notice. My thoughts were busy.'

'On tomorrow's sermon, eh? Well I won't spoil it.'

The vicar, however, now would not let the doctor go. He loitered; he had word for everybody he passed in the street and it was not until the evening that he opened the envelope. He opened it with a great show of carelessness all the greater because he was conscious that his heart was beating a little quicker than usual. He was prepared for the name and yet the sight of it written there in black and white, 'Peter Stewer,' was a shock to him. He tore the paper into fragments and tried to thrust the matter from his mind.

But Jan was at the funeral, and after the ceremony he said: 'What did I tell 'ee, vicar?'

'Peter was old,' said the vicar, 'and breaking fast. It was easy to guess his name.'

'Wait to the next, vicar,' said Jan. 'Oi'm not proud o' the gift. Oi wish oi hadn't it. But wait to the next.'

Now, the parish was situated in a healthy upland district and the winter was mild. One or two of the elder people suffered the usual ailments in February and March, but there was no serious illness. More than once the vicar was inclined to tear up his envelopes during that time, for he had come to live in an expectation of a summons to a death-bed. But it would have seemed almost a confession that he gave in, that he admitted the possibility of second sight, and the possession of it by Jan.

He did not. He assured himself often that he did not. Indeed, it would after all prove nothing if all three envelopes contained the correct names. For there were extraordinary flukes; they happened every day. The vicar had read in his newspaper of their happening at gambling saloons. Jan was just gambling on the names as a player on numbers. No, the vicar did not object to the letters because he shirked the challenge, but because they kept him, in spite of himself, speculating who of his parishioners would be the next to go.

Half-way through March he knew. A servant from the great house on the hanger above the village came to fetch him. A runaway horse, a collision with a cart and the daughter of the house was seriously hurt—this was the footman's story. The vicar hurried up the hill. The envelopes in his drawer were at that time swept clean out of his mind. He had no thoughts but thoughts of dread and pity. The girl who had been injured was barely nineteen, and she had all her acquaintances for her friends.

The doctor was already upstairs. The vicar waited in the great hall with the girl's father, hearing over and over again a broken narrative of the accident. At last the doctor descended, and neither of the two men waiting below had the courage to put the question. The doctor replied to their looks, and replied cheerfully. He recommended that a telegram should be sent for a specialist.

'There is a chance, then?' asked the father, in a voice he could not raise above a whisper.

'More than a chance,' replied the doctor, and the vicar was at once, in spite of himself and against his will, certain there was no chance—not one in ten thousand. Perhaps it was that he remembered a similar question put by him outside old Peter Stewer's gate. At all events the envelopes were recalled to his mind. Jan had as much as told him that the next of his parishioners to go would be young. And a conviction, which he could not shake off, stood fixed in his mind that 'Gertrude Leslie' was the name written within the envelope.

He seemed, as he stood there in the hall, listening to the interchange of hopeful words, to be actually reading the name through the envelope, and it was with a start almost of guilt that he roused himself to take his leave. In three days' time he had occasion to open the second envelope. 'Gertrude Leslie' was the name inscribed in it, and he opened it on the day of Gertrude Leslie's death.

'What did I tell 'ee, vicar?' said Jan.

The vicar hurried away without answering. He could not argue that Jan had merely made a lucky guess. Apart from the other circumstances, it hardly seemed natural that Jan should have guessed at the squire's daughter at all, when there were all his cronies and acquaintances to select from. The vicar from that moment took an aversion to Jan as to something repellent and uncanny, and it became a surprise to him that the villagers regarded the peasant with indifference, and almost with pity, as being endowed with a commonplace but uncomfortable gift.

The vicar no longer disbelieved in Jan's second sight. He owned as much frankly to himself one evening, and took the third envelope from the drawer.

'I may as well burn this, then,' he debated, 'since I am already convinced.' And even while he was debating he replaced it in the drawer. His disbelief was replaced by curiosity—curiosity to know not so much whose name was in the envelope, but rather which of his parishioners would be the next to die, a point upon which the breaking of the seal would surely illumine him. He felt that it would be weak, however, to break the seal. He had a sense, too, that it would be wrong. It seemed to him almost that it would he an acknowledgment of a submission to the powers of darkness.

But he kept the envelope, and it tormented him like a forbidden thing. It called him to break the seal and read; it became permanent in his thoughts. His parishioners began to notice a curious, secret look of inquiry, which came into his eyes whenever he met or spoke with them. He was speculating, 'Is it you?'

And the spring came.

The vicar threw up his window one morning, and felt his blood renewed. He drew in the fresh morning air, with a consciousness that of late he had been living in and breathing a miasma. The trees in his garden were living and musical with birds, there were sprouts of tender green upon the branches, the blackbirds were pecking at his lawn, and between the blades of grass he saw the shy white bells of snowdrops. He determined to brush all this oppressive curiosity from his mind, to forget the envelope lurking in his drawer.

He breakfasted and went out to make a call. On his way to the cottage he was visiting he passed the post office. By the letter box the schoolmistress was standing with some letters in her hand. She raised her hand and slipped one of the letters into the box just as the vicar came up to her. The vicar was a keen-sighted man, and it chanced that his eyes fell upon the envelope. He read the superscription, and recognised the handwriting. The envelope was addressed to Jan's son, a yeoman with the South African Field Force, and the address was written in the same handwriting as the names in the enveloped marked '1' and '2' which he had opened.

'So you are posting Jan's letters?' said the vicar, who was a trifle puzzled.

'Yes,' explained the schoolmistress. 'Jan's an old man, and there was no school here when he was a boy. So he never learned to read or write. He tells me what he wants to say to his boy, and I write it for him.'

'Then you know the name in the third envelope?' cried the vicar.

The question was out and spoken before he was aware of what he said. Then he flushed with shame. It was humiliating, it was most undignified to betray such vehement curiosity. The vicar was so disconcerted that he barely paid heed to the confusion and excuses of the school mistress.

'I did not know why Jan wanted the names written,' she pleaded. 'He never told me. I would not have done it if I had known that this was one of his heathenish tricks. I did not guess until the squire's daughter died. I don't believe it, sir, even now, any more than you do.'

'Well, well!' The vicar cut her short, anxious to escape from his undignified position! 'You were not to blame, since you did not know. But it is not right to encourage Jan in these'—he cast about for an ambiguous word, and found it—'in these devices.'

The vicar hurried home in a turmoil of indignation against Jan, and more particularly against himself. He would put an end to the obsession of this sealed envelope which was daily engrossing more and more of his life. He went straight to his study, unlocked the drawer, and pulled out the envelope. He tore it open, shutting his eyes the while unconsciously, so that he might read the name at once and have done with it. Then he opened his eyes and read.

The name was his own!

The vicar looked out of his window upon his garden, but the spring morning had lost its charm for him.

A. E. W. MASON

Writer, spy, politician and actor, Alfred Edward Woodley Mason was born in South London in 1865. He attended Dulwich College where he excelled in modern languages. He also took part in the school's theatrical productions, acting in French and German plays as well as Shakespeare, including playing Oliver in *As You Like It* (1883). On leaving Dulwich, Mason went up to Oxford, studying at Trinity, and he joined the Oxford University Dramatic Society. Among many roles, he played Heracles in 1887 in a production of Euripides' *Alcestis*; in the same production the character of Death was played by Arthur Bourchier, who in 1920 would portray the French police officer Gabriel Hanaud in Mason's adaptation of his own novel *At the Villa Rose* (1910).

In 1888, after graduating, Mason joined Sir Frank Benson's repertory company but he was not with them long. He moved to the Compton Comedy Company and then Ben Greet's Company, with both of which he toured the British Isles, fulfilling minor roles in plays like Sheridan's *A School for Scandal* in 1890 and Sydney Grundy's *A Village Priest* in 1891. Mason was not a particularly good actor—at an Old Playgoer's Dinner in 1928, Sir Frank Benson commented drily that, while Mason didn't always know his lines, those he improvised were often better than the original; at the same event Mason acknowledged his own shortcomings, noting his appearance in the first production of George Bernard

Shaw's *Arms and the Man* (1894), at which—on the opening night—
Shaw had taken to the stage and panned it as a comedy rather
than the tragedy he had written.

While acting, Mason produced his first play, an adaptation in
1894 of the famous French comedy *Frou-Frou* by Ludovic Halévy
and Henri Meilhac. He also began writing short stories which
appeared in provincial newspapers as well as in journals like
Cassell's Family Magazine, the *English Illustrated Magazine* and the
Illustrated London News. Mason completed his first novel, *A
Romance of Wastdale* (1895), and then, buoyed by its reception,
The Courtship of Morrice Buckler, which he would go on to adapt
for the stage in 1897, co-authoring the script with the actress Isabel
Bateman with whom he had appeared in a production four years
earlier.

When his theatrical career came to an end, Mason became a
political agent for the Conservative Party and later joined the
staff of the Church Defence Society—both undemanding jobs
that allowed him to pursue his writing. It was with his ninth
novel that his career as a novelist took off. *The Four Feathers*
(1902) is a thrilling adventure set during the Mahdist War in
North Africa. The book has been filmed six times, most memo-
rably in 1939 under the direction of Zoltan Korda and with a
screenplay by R. C. Sheriff, author of the classic anti-war play
Journey's End (1928).

In 1903, in the wake of the success of *The Four Feathers*, Mason
was invited to take up a career in politics. Always up for a challenge, he accepted and, despite living in Queen Anne's Mansions
in Westminster, London, he was selected as the Liberal Party's
candidate for Coventry, a city in central England. At the General
Election in 1906, he won the seat, overturning a massive majority
and taking more than half the votes cast. As a politician Mason
championed equality and the rights of the individual, arguing
against racist exclusionary laws in South Africa and in favour of
women's suffrage at home, as well as pushing for free school meals

and the provision of land for allotments, arguing that 'the desire for a piece of land was the one sure sign of a healthy mind'.

Although Mason was a tremendous success as a member of Parliament, the pressure of maintaining two careers was enormous. He stepped down at the January 1910 election, at which the Liberal Party's new candidate was another author, Silas K. Hocking, who lost narrowly; other than for the eight years following the December 1910 election—when another man called Mason (but no relation) was elected—the Liberal Party never again won a Coventry constituency. As always, Mason made practical use of his political experience, which he drew on for a play, *Colonel Smith* (1909), and a novel, *The Turnstile* (1912); in later years he would criticise the idleness of minor politicians who 'haven't a moment to spare, they do nothing with so much energy and persistence'.

After leaving politics, Mason decided to move into crime fiction and to create a detective who would be a professional, in contrast to the likes of Sherlock Holmes and Father Brown, and credible in his methods rather than a super-normal expert like Dr John Thorndyke. In a profile broadcast on the BBC Empire Service in 1935, Mason explained that while Inspector Gabriel Hanaud was in part a portrait of a detective friend, he had also drawn on the memoirs of several senior French police officers. Like Holmes, Hanaud has his Watson—a retired London banker called Julius Ricardo—but the ebullient Hanaud's investigations focus more on psychological rather than physical clues. Mason had been inspired to write Hanaud's first case, *At the Villa Rose* (1910), by the chance observation of two French names scratched on the window of an English inn, names connected with the real-life double murder and robbery in 1903 of Eugénie Fougère and her maid Victorine Giriat at Aix-les-Bains in France. The book was an enormous success and has been filmed five times. Hanaud would go on to appear in four more novels (he is mentioned in a fifth but does not appear), the last of which was Mason's final book, *The House in Lordship Lane*, published in 1946.

In 1914, with the advent of what would come to be called The Great War, Mason and his friend Sir James Barrie travelled to America on a 'mission of truth' to combat German propaganda. In 1915 he was gazetted a temporary captain in the 21st battalion of the Manchester regiment; and in 1917 he was appointed an honorary major in the Royal Marines and served in the Intelligence department of the Admiralty, working to frustrate the German military in Morocco and Spain and even in Mexico, where Mason helped to destroy an enemy transmitter.

With the war behind him, Mason resumed writing and engaged a secretary, a young woman called Muriel Stephens. In the early 1920s, he published three books, including the second Hanaud novel *The House of the Arrow* (1924), but by the mid-1920s Muriel was ill with 'consumption', or pulmonary tuberculosis. Mason took the unusual step of adopting his secretary and funding her treatment at a sanatorium in the New Forest. Muriel's health did not improve and in 1929, she died in Arosa, Switzerland. She was 27 years old.

Shattered, Mason threw himself into writing and his hobbies—mountain-climbing and sailing his 50-ton ketch *Mannequin*. In 1936 he produced what many regard as his finest novel, *Fire over England* (1936), an Elizabethan romance of espionage that drew in part on his own experiences during the First World War. An enduring classic adventure, the novel was filmed in 1937, featuring Laurence Olivier and Vivien Leigh, with William K. Howard directing and Zoltan Korda's brother Alexander heading production. The same year, Mason renamed *Mannequin* the *Muriel Stephens* and he sailed from Brixham to Gibraltar with the hope of finding inspiration for a novel about the Spanish Civil War. Despite spending three months moored off the coast he did not find it and, on returning to Britain, he decided to resume writing historical fiction.

In 1941, Mason had published a biography of Sir Francis Drake and, at the time of his death from heart trouble and asthma in

November 1948, he was working on another biography about the seventeenth-century naval commander Admiral Robert Blake. In his will, Mason left the bulk of his estate—the equivalent of £2.5 million (about $3 million)—to his alma mater, Trinity College, Oxford. As well as large bequests to his secretary and manservant, Mason left a sum 'to be applied for the care or relief of consumption', the disease that nearly twenty years earlier had taken the life of Muriel Stephens.

'The Vicar's Conversion' was first published in *The Grand Magazine*, November 1908.

THE GHOST OF TRAVERS COURT

E. R. Punshon

When Mrs Bertram and her three daughters, Mary, Beatrice and Connie, of New York City, NY, learned from an article in the *Weekly Illustrated Paper* that Travers Court, the house in Hampshire of which they had just taken a three years' lease, possessed a widespread celebrity as the home of the famous Travers ghost, it is quite impossible to describe their interest and their delight.

To them, as bustling Americans, England's air of reposeful age had been singularly impressive; and the idea that they were to occupy a house supposed for many generations to be haunted, seemed somehow to link them at once with the ancient orders of things they found surrounding them.

'One feels so dreadfully new over here,' Mary Bertram had remarked with a sigh one day, 'just as if one were a crude experiment that might just turn out any old way, and it's perfectly horrid to feel like that.'

Her sisters had shared this feeling, and even their placid and tranquil mother acknowledged to an impression that one ought to be at least a century old before landing in England. So that to all of them, this link of association with the historic past that the ghost offered, was full of delight, relief and joy.

'I shall begin to feel old and respectable myself soon,' said Beatrice, with a sigh of pleasure.

The three sisters posted off in hot haste to interview Mr Isaacs, their landlord; and they nearly broke that astute gentleman's heart when he found how they regarded the ghost, and that instead of letting them have the place cheaper on account of the story, he might have valued the alleged haunting at £50 per annum extra.

However he had no information to give them on the subject, so the girls had to retreat disappointed. But from another source they learned that the ghost was supposed to be that of a Travers of the sixteenth century who had expiated the crimes of a wicked life by cutting his throat in the west attic. At intervals his spirit appeared in this same attic and was to be heard heavily descending the stairs, to the accompaniment of a clanking chain, to the hall where it was accustomed to vanish. They also learnt that the house had been recently in the possession of Miss Travers, who had borrowed money from Mr Isaacs, the present owner, and failing to repay it in time, had lost her ancestral home.

'There was some sharp practice about it on Isaacs' part,' remarked their informant, 'and I understand he had quite a stormy scene with young Anthony Travers, Miss Travers's nephew. Everyone is expecting the ghost to be particularly active now that the house has passed out of the hands of its family; so you may quite reasonably expect to see it.'

The Misses Bertram expressed sympathy with the dispossessed members of the Travers family, but were too excited over the prospects of meeting a genuine ghost to be able to spend much thought on the ill fortune of such complete strangers. They returned and imparted the information they had obtained to their mother, who received it in her usual placid and tranquil manner; and in due course they arrived at Travers Court, all very eager to catch the first sight of the ghost.

The first two nights nothing happened. On the third night Mrs Bertram went to bed a little earlier than usual, while the three girls, preparatory to following her example, were enjoying a final chat in Connie's room. The question they were debating was one of some interest and importance—it concerned Connie's new hat, in point of fact—and they were all so hard at it as to have quite forgotten the ghost when they distinctly heard a faint sound upon the stairs outside.

'What can that be?' wondered Mary; 'all the servants went to bed long ago.'

Connie opened the door and went out on to the landing.

'Is that someone calling?' she asked; 'is that someone on the stairs?'

Then she heard a faint, low moan, and the merest echo of a rattling chain. She stared, fascinated, and distinctly saw approaching her through the gloom of the landing towards where she stood at the head of the stairs a tall figure, all white, that as it came nearer groaned again and very softly shook a chain it seemed to drag behind it.

Connie clasped her hands.

'Oh, mother! Oh, sisters!' she cried at the top of her voice, 'I do believe that here is the real, real ghost at last.'

Mary and Beatrice came out with a run and ranged them-selves beside Connie at the head of stairs, so that if the ghost wished to continue it progress to the hall it would have to pass right through them. It paused, however and stood at a little distance, a tall, white, shapeless form in the darkness that was only faintly illumined by the light from the gas in Connie's room, of which the door was but half open. As if resenting the way in which its further progress was barred, the ghost now groaned much louder than before and at the same time shook its chain with tremendous vigour; and Connie fairly yelped with delight.

'A real, live, lovely ghost,' she cried excitedly, 'just think of it.'

'You talk such nonsense, Connie,' complained her oldest sister, Mary; 'how can a ghost be alive?'

'Well, a real, dead ghost,' said Connie, 'just look.'

More hideously, more terribly than ever groaned the ghost, more threateningly did its chain rattle; and from the three Misses Bertram came a simultaneous murmur of delight and gratification.

'Isn't it real bully?' demanded Connie, giving herself all the airs of a pioneer.

'Yes, indeed; and where will Jane Hands be now with her stuffy old Mayflower ancestors,' said Beatrice, the second sister, 'when we have a house with a real, live—no, dead—a real, dead ghost in it?'

'Girls,' said Mary solemnly, 'this is a great and serious occasion and we must make the most of it.'

Apparently this remark somewhat troubled the ghost, for its tall white form seemed to shiver, and then it groaned and shook its chain once more, and once more a simultaneous sigh of delight came from the three sisters.

'What is all this noise about?" called a voice just then from a neighbouring room, and Beatrice pushed open the door.

'Oh, mother,' she said, 'here is the ghost, and it is all true, and isn't it just a lovely experience, and won't all the folk at home he just real jealous, and won't the papers give us a write up?'

'A genuine British ghost in a genuine British mansion,' said Connie with a happy sigh; 'it is more than I ever dared hope for.'

'I wonder if it can understand us,' said Mary excitedly; 'oh, please,' she said to the ghost, 'if you can understand, will you rattle your chain once for yes, and twice for no?'

The ghost moved slightly and certainly its chain rattled once. The girl took this for an answer in the affirmative to Mary's questions, and once more they sighed with delight. 'What shall we say to it?' asked Mary eagerly; 'I wonder what it wants. Are you happy?' she asked the ghost.

The chain rattled twice with some vigour. Whatever else the ghost was, it seemed certain that it was not happy.

'Poor thing,' said Connie compassionately.

'I wonder where it is now?" observed Beatrice with an air of deep meditation; 'if it is not happy, it can't very well have gone to heaven when it died, and—er—'

'I don't like to ask it that,' said Mary hesitating; 'it seems so personal somehow.'

'But then everyone knows it was awfully wicked when it was alive,' urged Connie; 'so it is only to be expected . . .'

'Girls,' came Mrs Bertram's voice from her room, 'you must never hurt any creature's feelings, not even those of a poor disembodied ghost.'

'Let us ask it about ourselves,' suggested Mary; 'something interesting about our future lives.'

'Oh, yes,' agreed Beatrice, 'ask it when we shall be married.'

'Oh, how lovely,' cried Connie, delighted. 'Oh, please,' she asked the ghost, 'shall I be married soon?'

The chain rattled twice.

'Will any of us be married soon?' inquired Mary.

The chain rattled twice.

'Will any of us be married after a long time?' inquired Beatrice.

The chain rattled twice.

The three girls exchanged pale glances.

'Will any of us ever be married?' inquired Mary, rallying for a last effort.

The chain rattled twice.

The three girls were silent. They breathed rather quickly and they held each other's hands hard.

'Horrid, silly old thing,' said Connie in a murmur.

'I don't believe it can do anything but rattle its stupid old chain twice over,' declared Beatrice.

'Do you mean I shall die an old maid?' asked May, bravely putting into words the awful doubt that had assailed them all.

The chain rattled once.

A silence of great horror brooded upon the scene like some material thing. The girls held each other's hands very hard, and Connie wiped away a tear.

'I just don't believe,' cried Mary at last, 'that the mean old thing knows one single thing about the future.'

The chain rattled once.

'But perhaps it only means we shall always refuse all proposals made to us,' suggested Beatrice, seeking a glimmer of hope anywhere.

'We shall have proposals anyway, shan't we?' asked Connie, clasping her hands.

The chain rattled twice.

'Gracious!' gasped Mary; 'this is more horrible than anything anyone could ever possibly have imagined.'

'It is some consolation at any rate,' said Beatrice viciously, 'that we know where this horrid old ghost was sent when he died, and I just hope they keep him in a good hot corner.'

The chain rattled twice.

Connie suppressed a sob, but another escaped her, quite startlingly loud in the darkness.

'Girls,' said Mary, 'we can't put up with this . . . something has simply got to be done.'

'Not even a proposal,' sighed Beatrice, quite crushed.

'But why not?' demanded Connie, hot with the injustice of the thing; 'are we not as pretty as other girls? Don't we dress as a nicely? Don't men like us just as much?' she demanded of the ghost.

The chain rattled twice.

'Well,' said Mary thoughtfully, if men don't like us . . .'

'. . . It is certainly rather strange,' agreed Beatrice, 'that . . .'

'They may do it out of pity,' said Connie, sniffling; 'only when you get hugged as hard as—'

'Connie!' came Mrs Bertram's voice from the room nearby.

'I mean "when" in the future sense, mother,' exclaimed Connie hurriedly.

The chain rattled twice.

'You horrid, mean old spook, you,' cried Connie in a rage, 'what do you know about it?'

The chain performed a perfect fanfare of rattles.

'Gracious!' said Mary, appalled.

Her two sisters were unable to utter a single word.

With a stately, gliding motion the ghost turned and went in the direction of a small room at the end of the corridor, originally used as a gun room.

'Oh, it's going,' said Mary.

The chain rattled once.

'Good thing, too,' said Beatrice.

'Only hope to goodness,' said Connie resentfully, 'that they have been stoking up good and hot for it, while it has been on the loose around here.'

With a last reproachful double rattle of the chain the ghost vanished into the gun room, closing the door behind it. The three girls followed and stood hesitating on the threshold without.

'We ought not to have let it go like that,' said Mary.

'But perhaps it is still there,' said Beatrice; 'I don't think ghosts can vanish till cock crow, can they?'

Mary opened the gun-room door and peeped cautiously in.

'It has gone,' said Beatrice, looking round carefully.

'Mean old spook,' said Connie half crying, 'I don't believe it knows any more about the future than we do.'

'This has been a trying, even an awful experience,' said Mary; 'I was just thinking that perhaps a cup of tea . . .'

'I should just love it,' said Beatrice.'

'Shall I light the oil stove?" asked Connie.

'No, no,' said Mary, 'we will light the fire here . . . There is coal in the bucket and, Connie, you might just get some wood and my copy of this month's parish magazine out of my room, will you?'

With considerable dexterity and rapidity a fire was laid in the large grate of the huge, old-fashioned fireplace, over which yawned a chimney that was like a cavern.

'Use plenty of wood,' Mary said, 'we want a big fire so as to make the water boil soon.'

'I will put the oil out of this lamp on, to make it burn up,' said Beatrice.

'Where are the matches?' asked Connie.

A rustling, a weird and unearthly rustling was heard within the cavernous depths of the chimney, and then a weak but clear voice called:

'Don't light it, I'll come down.'

There succeeded a shower of soot and a sound of scrambling, and then there appeared and sat sadly in the fireplace a figure that was no longer white. Not another word did it speak, and in equal silence the girls stood round and watched intently.

'If this isn't just the funniest ghost,' said Mary at last.

'There seems to me,' murmured Beatrice, 'more soot than ghost.'

'Strange,' mused Connie, 'that that should have brought it down—I should have thought a little fire would only have seemed homelike and comforting.'

The ghost continued to sit in profound silence and the three girls continued to regard it.

'If you please,' said Mary after another prolonged pause, 'do you mind telling us who you are?'

'I am Anthony Travers,' said the ghost meekly.

'Oh, we know all about you,' said Beatrice encouragingly. 'You cut your throat in the west attic after just being as wicked and mean as you knew how all your life, and ever since you have been coming around haunting . . . I suppose you can't rest in your grave?'

'At any rate,' said Connie, 'it is evident it cannot foretell the future very well, for I am sure it never expected, when it set out to do its night's haunting, that it would end the evening up a chimney.'

'I should not have believed it,' said Anthony with fervour, 'not if a dozen ghosts had sworn it to me."

'Well, and we don't believe you about us either,' said Mary. 'So there.'

'Neither about the marriages nor the proposals,' declared Connie.

'That I was wrong about the marriages is probable,' said Anthony; 'that I was wrong about he proposals is certain, for I said you would never have one, and now I venture to propose to all of you myself.'

'Dear me,' said Mary.

'This is so sudden,' said Beatrice.

'Well, it counts as one, anyway,' said Connie with some satisfaction.

'A third of one, you mean,' Mary pointed out.

'Not at all,' said Anthony, 'it is a whole one to each of you.'

'But supposing we all accepted you?' said Mary.

'That, I fear, is not probable,' returned Anthony; 'your objection is merely theoretical, not practical.'

'Well, I don't think I want him myself,' said Beatrice candidly.

'If there were pound of tea or something of that sort,' said Mary, 'one might consider it, but as it is . . .'

'Girls,' said Connie, 'do not let us act rashly . . . for one thing he ought to be washed first.'

'Scraped,' said Mary.

'Peeled,' suggested Beatrice meditatively. 'I don't think anything else would be much use.'

'In the meantime,' said Mary, 'what are we to do with him?'

'The police,' observed Beatrice, 'would be but a tame ending to such an evening, I suppose?'

'Let's ask him to explain,' said Connie. 'I suppose really he is that Miss Travers's nephew we heard about, and he has been trying to play the ghost to scare us so badly that we wouldn't stop, and Mr Isaacs wouldn't have any tenants . . . I'm sorry,' she added politely to Anthony, 'that we could not scare more.'

'Then he is not a genuine ghost at all?' exclaimed Mary disappointedly. 'I do call that real mean when we had been looking forward so.'

'It is awful disappointing,' sighed Beatrice; 'let us ask mother what we had better do.'

Mrs Bertram decided immediately that the young man must forthwith be shown out of doors.

'But don't be hard on him, girls,' she said; 'he has done his best to provide you with your ghost.'

So Anthony was allowed to depart, and the next afternoon there appeared Miss Travers, the late occupant of Travers Court, and Mr Anthony Travers. She came somewhat unwillingly but driven by her nephew, a tall, good-looking and wonderfully clean young man, in whom hardly a resemblance to the midnight ghost could be now perceived. Mrs Bertram was very pleased to see Miss Travers, and highly interested to meet a represent-ative of the family who had inhabited the old house for nearly seven centuries. Anthony volunteered on his account to point out to the ladies the chief features of interest in their new abode, and showed himself an expert guide. Later on, he offered his apologies in private to Mrs Bertram and to each of the Misses Bertram, and they on the whole decided to forgive him, though Connie confessed it was with a pang she realized he was not a ghost. But in private they all agreed that Mr Isaacs was a mean old man who did not deserve ever to have any tenants; and they also decided that if one were a maiden aunt, it would be nice to have a nephew to stick up for one, however hot-headedly. Since then, Anthony has repeated his apologies to Connie rather frequently, in rather long and very private interviews, and there appears some probability that may achieve the success his first lacked.

And for the genuine ghost of Travers Court, it has never been heard of from that day to this, so presumably it has, like Anthony, decided to haunt no more.

E. R. PUNSHON

Ernest Robertson Punshon was born on 25 June 1872 at Ivy Bank in Underhill Road, East Dulwich, to which his parents Selina, a teacher, and Robert, a commission agent, had moved from Newcastle-upon-Tyne a few years after their marriage. When Ernest was only fifteen years old, his mother died and, shortly after, he got his first job, working as an office clerk. Four years later, he left Britain for Canada with the intention of becoming a farmer, a career for which he quickly realised he was not well suited. After a variety of other jobs there and in the north-western United States, Punshon worked his passage from Boston to Liverpool serving as a deck hand.

On returning to England, Punshon moved in with his aunt Sarah and decided to try his hand at writing, claiming in later years to have begun what would be a long career by using a toy typewriter. His first published short story was 'The Solitary', a religious parable which appeared in *Black and White* in 1898. Over the next five years, other stories were published in a variety of magazines including *Chambers's Journal*, *Crampton's Magazine*, *The Echo* and *Pearson's*. His first novel, *Earth's Great Lord* (1901), dealt with gold digging and murder in Australia and it was positively received, as was his second, *Constance West* (1905). In 1905, Punshon married Sarah Houghton in Chorlton, Lancashire, and the couple moved to Poynton and into South Cottage, which he would later draw on for *The Cottage Murder* (1931). In 1906, his career took off when his third novel, *The Choice* (1908) won the modern-day equivalent of £10,000 in a competition run by a newspaper, *The Morning Leader*. In the novel, which was widely syndicated before publication in hardback, a young woman commits bigamy as part of a scheme to raise money to pay to free her parents from a Russian prison.

Ernest and Sarah moved to Streatham in south London where they would live for the rest of their lives: first at 123 Welham Road; and later at 23 Nimrod Road. They both became active in local politics, campaigning for the local Liberal Party, but he was now writing full-time and over the next twenty years he published countless short stories and novelettes as well as a score of novels. Often his work had strong elements of melodrama and romance which led a reviewer for the *Daily Chronicle* to suggest that 'E. R. Punshon' was a woman, a misunderstanding the author gently corrected in a letter to the editor. Increasingly, his novels became more criminous and thrillingly suspenseful, as reflected in their titles such as *Ensnared: The Mystery of the Iron Room* (1906), *The Mystery of Lady Isobel* (1907), which when serialised was accompanied by a competition, and *The Diamond of Death* (1925), published four years later as *The Blue John Diamond* (1929). As well as romance and mysteries—and a stage play *Learning Business* (1928)—Punshon also wrote many comic pieces for magazines like *Punch* and short stories featuring fantasy or the supernatural, sometimes light-hearted and sometimes distinctly less so, as in his very popular novel *The Solitary House* (1918) which features a wood haunted by a strange and murderous creature.

During the First World War, Punshon served as a Special Constable and he was actively involved in local defence against air raids. After the war, he remained a member of the Special Constables Association, attending concerts at which Sarah sometimes gave recitations, and playing competitive whist, a game that he and Sarah would enjoy on and off for the next thirty years. By the mid-1920s, the public appetite for crime and detective stories was enormous and Punshon responded, creating two police officers, the quicksilver Inspector Carter and his more stolid partner, Sergeant Bell, who would appear in five novels between 1925 and 1932. The main character in his second and more sustained series of mysteries is Bobby Owen, an Oxford graduate who becomes a police officer and, despite being slow on the uptake in several cases, nevertheless rises through the ranks across thirty-five novels and a single radio play.

As a writer of detective stories, Punshon's work is uneven. Some were highly praised, like *Proof Counter Proof* (1931) and the anti-Axis Bobby Owen puzzles *The Cross-word Mystery* (1934) and *Dictator's Way* (1938). Others fared less well, with the novel *Genius in Murder* (1932) being eviscerated by one reviewer as 'the dullest, least interesting, slowest and most unconvincing detective mystery ever written'; ironically, *Genius in Murder* had initially been announced as being by the journalist John V. Turner and Punshon had had to get an injunction to prevent its publication under that name. Like Turner—better known as 'David Hume'—and many other crime writers, Punshon also wrote under a pseudonym, in his case drawn from his mother's family name. As 'Robertson Halkett' he authored *Where Every Prospect Pleases* (1933), a slightly bizarre thriller in which a man investigates the death of his brother in Monaco. Three years later *Documentary Evidence* (1936) appeared, as by 'Robertson Halket' [*sic*]; in presenting a mystery as a set of documents, the book follows a broadly similar pattern to *The Documents in the Case* (1930) by Dorothy L. Sayers and Robert Eustace, and Philip Macdonald's *The Maze* (1932).

Complementing his political activities, Punshon was also an avid correspondent, writing regularly to the press on subjects such as the need for something more practical than compassion in response to the Nazis' persecution of Jewish people, British naval policy, the case for freer trade and Russian obduracy. He also addressed less serious issues such as the facts of the Battle of

Hastings, the seventeenth-century mystery of the Campden Wonder, *Hamlet* as a detective story, the case for subsidised theatre and the deficiencies of the artist Graham Sutherland. Between 1935 and 1942 he also reviewed books for the *Manchester Guardian* under his own name and as 'ERP'.

During the Second World War the Punshons remained in Streatham where Ernest served as the day guard at the Mitcham Lane headquarters of the local battalion of the Home Guard, Britain's civilian army for those too old—or too young—to serve in the regular forces. When on duty and while waiting in the guard room for the inevitable air raids, Punshon conceived and wrote one of the best Bobby Owen mysteries, *Ten Star Clues* (1941), which drew inspiration from the celebrated Tichborne claimancy. Other Bobby Owen mysteries were also inspired by real cases, including *Comes a Stranger* (1938), based on the forgeries of Thomas J. Wise, and *Murder Abroad* (1939), whose origins lie in the brutal killing of Mrs Dora Hunt at Cannes in 1936.

After the war, the Punshons resumed their involvement in local politics and Ernest became treasurer of the Detection Club, the convivial dining society founded by Anthony Berkeley Cox—in the words of Freeman Wills Crofts, 'so that writers of detective stories might meet each other'. Punshon had been accepted as a member in 1933 and he provided a chapter on the French serial killer Henri Landru for *The Anatomy of Murder* (1936), a set of true crime essays by Club members, and a radio play featuring Bobby Owen, 'Death on the Uplift' (1941), to the Club's first series of radio mysteries for the BBC. In 1945 he took part alongside other members such as Dorothy L. Sayers and John Dickson Carr in *Detective Quiz*, a popular celebrity gameshow for BBC radio. Curtis Evans, the American historian of the Golden Age of crime fiction, has written extensively on the Club and Punshon's battles with its founder in his fascinating and invaluable 2011 booklet on *The Detection Club and Fair Play* (*CADS* Supplement No. 14).

Punshon also enjoyed the regular meetings of his Home Guard

battalion's Old Comrades' Association, taking part in a *Brains Trust* programme in 1945 where he and other members of the battalion answered questions about the value of fiction, which Punshon championed, and 'suburban snobbery', which he defined as 'excessive respect for wealth and position'. Unsurprisingly, he also supported the Liberal Party's calls for a statutory minimum wage, which would eventually be introduced in Britain in 1998, and for membership of a European federation. More controversially, he suggested that the amount of wealth one might inherit should be set at the modern-day equivalent of £200,000, and he criticised women's fashion, in particular slacks, suggesting that women 'wouldn't wear them if they knew what they looked like from the rear'. In the same year, Punshon stood unsuccessfully as a Liberal Party candidate for election to the borough council, and in 1946 was made vice president of the party's local association, sitting on its executive council while Sarah served as secretary and later chairman. He and Sarah also enjoyed the association's monthly whist drives at the White Lion Hotel in Streatham and he took part in other local activities. In November 1948 he gave a talk on 'The Detective Novel and Real Life' at Streatham Secondary School, during the course of which he revealed that, while travelling in the United States, he and a friend had been arrested on suspicion of involvement in a woman's death and that they had only been released because the local police could not believe a detective novelist would be capable of committing murder.

Throughout the 1940s Punshon had continued to produce a steady flow of Bobby Owen mysteries and several non-criminous plays for the BBC, and as the decade came to an end he continued to campaign vigorously for the Liberal Party. In 1950, he mounted a personal campaign against the local Conservative Party in its efforts to encourage Liberal supporters to defect. However, Punshon's health was failing and in the early 1950s he fell down a flight of stairs at a meeting of the Detection Club in Kingly Street, Soho—providing another member, the mischievous Christianna

Brand, with an anecdote about 'blood in the stairwell' which she would never tire of telling. Ernest and Sarah withdrew from civic life and in 1954 he collapsed in Kensington Gardens, where he was found by a member of the St John's Ambulance. He later sent his Samaritan a copy of the 33rd Bobby Owen novel, *Dark Is the Clue* (1955), inscribed 'as a small memento of an incident in Kensington Gardens'.

Ernest Robertson Punshon died in a nursing home on 23 October 1956. An eclectic selection of his many short stories was published by Ramble House in 2015 and, more recently, all of the Bobby Owen books have been reprinted by the much-missed Rupert Heath for his imprint Dean Street Press. And in 2025, almost a century after their original publication, his pseudonymous novels will at last be reprinted.

'The Ghost of Travers Court' was published in *The Weekly Scotsman* on 13 May 1911.

DEAKIN AND THE GHOST

Ernest Bramah

When Deakin first came to Roland House School he might have been anything between five and fifty. Actually, I believe that he was then twelve, but he was very small for his age. His infantile face was wizened and lined to an extraordinary degree, his expression one of ancient cunning, his manner self-reliant within proper bounds. Obviously a boy to be left alone, at all events until we had seen something more of him, but Megson was not a creature of deep intellect, and Megson tried it on.

In the dormitory that first night of a new term there was the usual mixture of openness and intrigue. Old friendships had been dissolved, and eternal new ones were in the process of being sworn. At one end of the long bare room Megson was in whispered confabulation with the boy who had bagged the bed next to his: he himself had bagged the best one that there was—the one that was hidden from anyone who suddenly opened the door. Deakin, who was the smallest boy in the dormitory, and the only new one, had been told to take the bed at the other end of the row. It creaked horribly, and we all knew it.

Presently everybody was settled, and the wildness of the jabber-talk died down. Megson suggested that someone should tell a story. We all liked listening, but the office of narrator was not a sought one. On this occasion, however, the boy next to

Megson at once volunteered. It was a ghost story that he at once launched off into, and whatever it lacked in the subtler qualities, it was plainly his intention to make our flesh creep. The plot was concerned with boarding-school and a murdered boy—a new boy—and a dark stain on the floor of one of the bedrooms—coincidentally almost incidental with the one that we were in—that no amount of scrubbing could ever obliterate. Just when he had got to 'Then with an unearthly moan that echoed through the haunted chamber and froze Cuthbert's blood at its source' there was an unearthly moan. At the other end of the dormitory a nebulous figure in white, with a face vaguely outlined in phosphorescent vapour, had appeared. Even we seniors experienced an unmanly tremor before we satisfied ourselves that it was only Megson in his sheet. As for the new boy, whose bed the apparition was now slowly approaching with outstretched hand, we all expected him to shriek aloud.

Instead, he spoke.

'If that's phosphorus that you've put on you,' he said sharply, 'I hope that you won't touch me with it. I don't want to be poisoned.'

There was an astonished pause throughout the room for a few seconds. The groan that the ghost essayed, to save the situation, sounded doubly hollow. Then someone asked:

'What's phosphorus?'

'The stuff that's at the end of matches,' replied Deakin.

'Is it poison?'

'I should just rather think it was! It's what they call one of the seven deadly poisons because it acts on your vitals direct."

'But that's only if you eat it,' interposed another.

'No,' replied the authority firmly, 'it's more dangerous externally. It's bad enough if you get it on your hands—that's why the ends of matches have to be painted red by law—but it's the worst of all on your face because there are more pores there.'

'I suppose it's all right if you wash it off soon?' said Megson's voice tremulously from the neighbourhood of the washstand. The ghost had faded out.

'You can't wash it off: it only drives it deeper into the pores. Washing is the very worst thing you can do.'

There was what one might call an awkward moment. Then the story-teller rallied.

'How do you know all this?' he demanded.

'I know because my father is a doctor, and what is called a specialist,' replied Deakin. 'He is always consulted in fatal cases of poisoning. Just before I came here a boy was brought into the surgery who had got phosphorus on his face. He was raving.'

'Did he die?'

'Yes, in agony. My father said he could have saved him if they had taken it in time, but it was too late then, because the poison had worked into the system, where it corrodes the tissue.'

'How long would it take to be too late in?'

'Oh, about ten minutes.'

I think it was at this point that someone was heroic enough to handle a match and to light the gas. Megson was lying at full length on the floor, and if pallor is the correct attribute of a ghost, he required no make-up.

'Did your father say what would have saved the boy's life?' he asked faintly.

'He said the only thing to do was to throw yourself into a healthy perspiration. Then it comes out again.'

'How do you do it?'

'You take something, but I forget what. Or you run round and round until you are very hot, and then jump into bed.'

Megson got to his feet unsteadily. We supported him.

'Would it do to run round and round in here?' he asked, surveying the narrow space between the bed and the wall.

'No, there isn't enough room here for the circulation to expand properly. It ought to be somewhere outside.'

There was no difficulty in getting outside, as we all knew.

But it was not a pleasant adventure for a cold winter night. Megson cast himself on the mercy of the room, and two of us undertook to stand by him. I suppose that I could not have been one of them, because I distinctly remember hearing Deakin's bed creak occasionally during the next twenty minutes. But he was right: we had to acknowledge that, for, in proof of it, Megson did not die, but recovered completely under his treatment. I say 'completely', for of course a particularly bad cold doesn't count in view of the seriousness of the case. As Deakin said, it only showed that the pores had been properly opened.

Alas, poor Deakin, he was too clever! He amused us in a variety of entertaining ways when we came to know him better. Then later in the term coins and other things began to disappear. Deakin's property was among them, you may be sure, but in the end he was caught red-handed. He put up a very ingenious defence, I believe, but the fates were against him, and he had to go.

ERNEST BRAMAH

Ernest Bramah Smith was born in 1868 and brought up in Lancashire where he attended Manchester Grammar School. After leaving school in 1884 he worked on a farm, an experience that provided the material for his first book, published that year as by Ernest Bramah. Smith next took up journalism, first working alongside Jerome K. Jerome at *Today Magazine*. He also started writing short stories, and in the late 1890s he created the character that was to make him famous, Kai Lung, an itinerant storyteller whose tales and proverbs help him to outwit brigands and thieves in ancient China. While many modern readers would dismiss these stories as literary yellowface, they were immensely popular and, although Smith never visited China, his portrayal of the Chinese and their customs was accepted as a guide to a country about which most of his readers and contemporary reviewers knew very little. However, the character has dated badly and Smith's purple prose, replicating what he and others considered 'Oriental quaintness' and 'the charm of Oriental courtesy', means that the Kai Lung stories are seldom read today.

In 1913, Smith created his other great character, Max Carrados the blind detective, for a series of stories for the *News of the World*. Carrados was immediately hailed as something new and the stories were extremely popular. While he owes something to Sherlock Holmes, Carrados's nearest contemporary would be the preternaturally omniscient Dr John Thorndyke, the creation of R. Austin

Freeman, and there are many similarities between the characters of Carrados's household and their equivalents in Freeman's Thorndyke stories. More than one contemporary critic also suggested that Carrados might have been inspired by the career of Edward Emmett, a blind solicitor from Lancashire, who achieved some celebrity towards the end of the nineteenth century. As well as Carrados, Smith's stories feature some economically drawn but memorable characters, such as the detective's amanuensis, Parkinson, who has an eidetic but erratic memory, and the self-described 'pug-ugly' Miss Frensham, once known as 'The Girl with the Golden Mug'. And the stories often feature contemporary concerns like nationalist terrorism, Christian Science and suffragacy. However, Carrados's hyper-sensory brilliance can sometimes appear unconvincing, no more so than when he is able to detect by taste traces of whitewash on a cigarette paper that has been fired from a revolver.

A little after the outbreak of the First World War, in 1916 Smith enlisted in the Royal Defence Corps. This led to his writing non-fiction pieces for various magazines on a wide range of subjects but he continued to write stories about Kai Lung and Carrados and also completed a few stage plays, including adaptations of two of the Carrados stories as well as an original play, *Blind Man's Bluff*, written in 1918 for the actor Gilbert Heron. The previous year Heron had had great success with his own adaptation of another Carrados story; *In the Dark* had been very successful not least for its 'great surprise finish' when the final scene was performed in absolute darkness. Both plays originally featured on a variety bill and, as well as detection, Smith's play accommodates an on-stage demonstration of ju-jitsu.

The final stories about Max Carrados appeared in the 1920s, followed by a single full-length novel, *The Bravo of London*, in 1934—but Smith would continue to write from time to time about Kai Lung, up to his death in Weston-super-Mare in 1942.

'Deakin and the Ghost' is previously unpublished.

A GOOD PLACE

H. C. Bailey

In the presence of Mrs Clare Montacute, it is reported, duchesses and actresses quail. Such is the prestige of her registry office. But Jane Cummins, called from the servants' waiting-room that Mrs Montacute might speak to her, turned not a hair of her neat head.

Mrs Clare Montacute looked and dressed like the late Queen Victoria. She surveyed Jane Cummins, a trim, buxom person, majestically, and said that Jane Cummins must think herself exceedingly fortunate, considering that she was so young and inexperienced. Jane had no reason to expect so good a situation, a very responsible situation. Mrs Montacute had not expected that Jane would satisfy Mrs Lyndishoe. Still, Mrs Lyndishoe had decided not to look further for the moment. And she hoped—emphatically hoped—that Jane would do her best to give satisfaction.

'If the place doesn't suit me, I'll drop you a line,' said Jane.

Many capable nurses, it was pointed out, would be proud to take the situation. Some with high recommendations had failed to please Mrs Lyndishoe.

Jane smoothed down her grey cloak. 'And she took me. That's all there is to it.'

Mrs Montacute was surprised. The Lyndishoes she wished Jane to know, were one of the oldest families in England

and the little boy was the only son. A very important responsibility.

'I dare say he don't bite,' said Jane quietly.

And Mrs Clare Montacute was left wondering.

It seemed to Jane Cummins entirely natural that Mrs Lyndishoe should have chosen her. She was young, she had only been an under-nurse before, but she suffered from no doubt of her superiority to an older woman. She approved of Mrs Lyndishoe, who had plainly seen it at once; in return Jane recognized her as 'the goods,' a lady of blue and ancient blood. The one doubt which disturbed Jane was whether she could live in a place off the map. Jane is country bred, but of the home counties, and the Lyndishoe estate is in the western midlands, which seemed to her as remote as Siberia.

This feeling was strengthened by the tedious railway journey and the long drive over wooded uninhabited hills which are the means of approach to Bransmere Abbey. The last stage, a mile or more from the lodge gates across the park, which is a wild place with many thickets and an expanse of black water, brought dismay to her cheery mind.

'Nice and homely, I don't think,' said Jane to the solemn groom who drove the waggonette.

He replied in a dialect unknown to her.

'Darkest England and no way out,' said Jane, and shuddered into her cloak. The groom pointed his whip and made more strange sounds. Bransmere Abbey rose before her. It is a noble place, a medley indeed, Tudor work built on to and out of older stuff, but a mellow mass of stone, beautiful as a whole and infinitely interesting. Jane was not interested. She wanted her tea.

She had it in the housekeeper's room and found the housekeeper a formal old dame, anxious to be civil. Mrs Lyndishoe had given particular orders notice was to be made comfortable. Nurse could be sure everything would be done. The housekeeper was only too glad to have her.

Jane went warily. She suspected that somebody was not glad to have her and made investigations. The child she had come to nurse, the small heir of Bransmere was Mrs Lyndishoe's grandson. Mrs Lyndishoe, long widowed, had two sons, Charles and George. The elder went to France with his yeomanry, came back, married in haste, went to Palestine and was killed. After his death Mrs Charles bore him a son. She was not, Jane saw, approved by the family of Lyndishoe. She was a nobody. It was even whispered that she had worked in an office. She showed no proper feeling. She did not want to bring her son to Bransmere. She had tried to set up house for herself. All the authority of the family was required to induce her to come to Bransmere and take her place as the mother of the heir and have him reared as became one of the dynasty of the Lyndishoes. 'Poor little soul,' said the housekeeper.

'What's the matter with him, Mrs Edwards?' said Jane.

'The poor boy is well enough if he had the chance, my dear.'

'And what's worrying him?'

Mrs Edwards pursed her lips and looked wise. She asked if Jane had ever had to deal with a spoilt child. 'Bless you, I never had any other sort,' said Jane cheerfully.

'And yet I don't know that I could say Mrs Charles spoils him,' the housekeeper reflected. 'It's not so plain as that, if you understand me.'

Jane did not and said so.

'You will,' said the housekeeper grimly. 'You'll understand a lot before you're done . . . Well, it's not for me to say, to be sure, but Mrs Charles don't act like any other lady I ever knew that was a mother. Why, if you'll believe me, she wouldn't have a nurse for the boy till now. Mrs Lyndishoe had all the trouble in the world to make her take you.'

It seemed to Jane that Mrs Charles had not pleased the servants at Bransmere.

Mrs Lyndishoe then rang, and to Mrs Lyndishoe Jane was

taken. The old lady looked the grandmother but not less the mistress of a great house. Jane found her benign. She hoped that Jane had had a good journey, that she had been made comfortable, that she would ask for anything she wanted. Very well. Then she wanted Jane to understand that she would be entirely responsible for Master Julian. They had been rather anxious about him. There was nothing about actually the matter with the child, but his health had not been satisfactory. He wanted looking after. He wanted taking out of himself. He must be made to feel that he was quite safe. 'Do you understand me, Cummins?'

'Well, no, ma'am, not wholly,' said Jane.

Mrs Lyndishoe's brown eyes looked through her. 'That's right. Always say what you think to me. You will understand. Now you are to be responsible. If anyone interferes with you or there is anything that disturbs you, come to me at once.'

Jane's answer was lost in the coming of a man, plainly a son of Mrs Lyndishoe by the glance she gave him, by the likeness. He was a smaller edition of her and in that, in some softening of feature, in a shy look more feminine than she. But the straight lines of her face were in his, and the dark eyes. 'This is Nurse Cummins, George,' his mother said.

'How do you do?' he smiled all over his face. 'Lucky fellow, young Julian. He's really a jolly kid, you know, nurse. I'm sure you'll take to each other.' He had been looking at her and looking away again in a shy fashion which amused Jane.

'You might fetch Phyllis, George,' his mother suggested and then he went out. 'My daughter-in-law has been giving us some anxiety, nurse,' Mrs Lyndishoe explained. 'She is—I fear she is not—' she stopped and in a moment or two her daughter-in-law came in.

'Oh, temper,' was what Jane said to herself. Mrs Charles was a frail, fair woman, little more than a child, very pretty in a photographer's fashion, but of such a worn and petulant expression that another woman could hardly allow her prettiness.

'Here is our nurse, my dear,' said Mrs Lyndishoe.

'Oh, very well,' the daughter-in-law sent Jane one glance of contemptuous dislike.

'What a cat,' said Jane to herself, and aloud. 'Good evening, ma'am.'

Mrs Charles did not choose to answer. Mrs Lyndishoe said placidly, 'We must show Cummins the nursery, Phyllis: and introduce her to Julian.'

'I suppose you know he'll hate you,' Mrs Charles flashed upon Jane.

'I hope,' said Mrs Lyndishoe slowly as she rose to lead the way, 'I hope he will live to be very grateful to Cummins.'

Jane stood aside to give place to Mrs Charles but was impatiently waved on. Yet Mrs Charles went with them.

'Talk about the silent tomb!' Jane said to herself as she looked round the nursery. It was a vast room with walls and floor that seemed to be black and for some time Jane mistook the old oak for stone. A fire on the open hearth, under a chimney-piece like a huge extinguisher, was incredibly remote. One lamp giving little light in proportion to its bronze mass was drearily incompetent to break the solid gloom. Where its rays fell on the floor a small boy sat and made patterns with coloured beads.

'Julian,' said Mrs Lyndishoe.

'Go away,' said the small boy. 'Don't want you. Don't want anybody.'

Jane knelt down beside him. She is a wholesome-looking creature. The small boy gazed at her. She saw a frail body, a thin pallid face comically and calm. He saw jolly pink and white cheeks and a buxom young woman who was very much alive. He put out a thin and grubby hand and stroked her dress, then patted her face. Jane laughed.

'This is Cummins, your nurse, Julian,' said Mrs Lyndishoe.

'I don't mind,' said Julian and returned to his beads.

'Julian!'

'We understand each other, ma'am,' said Jane. She went over to the fire and put another log on. 'But we want some more light in here. It isn't what you call a bright room, is it?'

'It has been our nursery for two hundred years, Cummins.'

'Yes, it looks it, ma'am,' said Jane.

Mrs Lyndishoe swept away. Jane went back and sat on the floor with the boy. After a moment he held out for her admiration a large and purple bead.

His mother drew nearer and nearer, watching jealously. 'Come and help me dress for dinner, Julian,' she said. Julian looked up and shook his head. The door banged behind her so that the beads jumped. 'Oh ee,' said Julian and soothed them.

'Home sweet home, I don't think.' said Jane to herself. But she and the boy got on very well together. He was the most self-contained child in her experience, yet he seemed to want her. Jane was satisfied with him: 'But this place, it's a bad dream,' said she as she went to bed in the night nursery, another vast and shadowy room. And she had some difficulty in going to sleep. Perhaps she had not gone when she was roused by a rustle, a consciousness that someone had come in. She sat up and in the faint gleam of the night-light made out a figure bent over the child. She sprang out of bed: 'And what can I do for you, ma'am?' she said.

'Do pray mind your own business,' Mrs Charles said, and hurried away.

'What a look!' Jane murmured. 'I'm making friends, I am.' And she examined Julian carefully. He was not damaged. He was still asleep. It appeared that his mother had only kissed him. But Jane slept badly.

She got up with her mind in some disorder. It is not her habit to take much notice of what people say, but she was not able to forget the odd things that had been said to her at Bransmere, the obscure warnings from Mrs Lyndishoe, the enigmatic malice of Mrs Charles, and with the quaintness of the child and the dreary old rooms these things were worked up into such a medley of alarms that (as she told herself) she didn't know what was what. Things were not healthy. For two pins she would tell the old dame that she was not suited. Some have said that Jane is hard as nails. But she looked at the unnaturally calm child talking to himself on the floor and decided that she couldn't leave the kid alone in that place.

He was, she soon discovered, a handful. At breakfast he ate enough honest food for a sparrow and then teased her for sweets and wailed. His mother rushed in, gave him many chocolates and stormed at Jane. Jane made pungent answers. At the din of battle, the small Julian dropped his sweets and retired into a corner and silently wept. Jane left his mother vainly trying to persuade him to eat them and went to complain to Mrs Lyndishoe.

The great lady was oracular. 'Now you begin to understand me,' said she. 'You must do your best, Cummins, you must do your best.'

'So must others, ma'am,' said Jane, with her little nose very high in the air. But Mrs Lyndishoe ignored her.

Jane retired with a high temperature, saying bitter things about her sex. Some she opined were solemn donkeys and some were spiteful cats. Coming to particulars she decided that mamma would be the death of the poor kid and grandma for all her high and mighty ways was too feeble to stop it. 'Balmy, all balmy.'

The small Julian was found telling his mother to go away and stating that he wanted Cummins. At the sight of Jane and Jane's triumphant smile the mother fled. She also was crying. But having got his Cummins Julian was difficult as ever. He did not want to go out, he would not go out. Jane stands no nonsense. Soon a miserable small boy was being towed out into the park.

This achievement was watched with smiles by his grandmother and his uncle George. Neither he nor his nurse was in any temper to reply to their patronising congratulations.

The park, like the house, is a glorious place, but no doubt you have to be in the right mood to admire it. Jane was not.

In a little while she was aware that they were being followed and saw the slight figure of his mother. 'Spying cat,' said Jane to herself, and talked loudly and brightly to Julian and loitered. But Mrs Charles did not catch them up. She vanished.

It was on the way back that they saw her again. She was in eager conversation with a man, a smart young man in riding-breeches.

'Oh, quite a nut, aren't you?' said Jane to herself. The hand of Mrs Charles was on his arm. He was laughing and making her laugh. 'Oho, that's it, is it? Looking after a number two, ma'am, I see. I've got your measure now,' said Jane with bitter satisfaction. 'You're a merry widow, aren't you? Not half!'

She looked at the small Julian. It had been possible to explain his condition by his mother's folly. What if she was something worse than a fool? What if he stood in her way? The mysterious hints of Mrs Lyndishoe acquired a grim importance. 'The poor little morsel,' said Jane to herself and became very gentle to Julian.

He did not seem to know what to make of it but clearly he liked her. He would not, if he could help it, let her out of his site. She was little harassed, for he did not want her to play with him or amuse him; he occupied himself in his odd way; her presence was all that he required and the day went well enough.

The catastrophe came at bed-time. With solemn promises that she would not be long, she obtained leave of absence on official business about bedclothes. She was not long, but while she was in the linen closet with a housemaid she heard a cry, a thud. She fled back along the corridor to the nursery. When she came to the head of the great oak staircase, she saw something white on the landing below which was Julian's face. Julian lay there silent and still.

Others were with him almost as soon as she. Uncle George calling out as he came down six stairs at a time, 'Good God, what's the boy done?' Mrs Lyndishoe majestically ascending. But the mother did not come. She leaned far out over the balustrade above, her hand at her thin side.

Jane gathered the child in her arms. 'What is this, Cummins?' said Mrs Lyndishoe severely.

'It's concussion, that's what it is,' said Jane.

'My God, he's not dead?' George Lyndishoe cried.

'Not yet,' said Jane.

'Pray, how did it happen, Cummins?' Mrs Lyndishoe frowned.

'I don't know how things happen in this house.'

'You will kindly explain yourself.'

'I left him half a minute to see that he had another blanket. And here he is thrown downstairs on his precious head.'

'Thrown!' Mrs Lyndishoe exclaimed.

'Oh, be quiet! That's what he wants now. Quiet. And you'd best send for your doctor, and get him here quick.'

'By Jove, she's right there.' George ran off and Jane bore the child away.

She put the little still body to bed and sat by it, watching. She had never been so glad in her life to see any man as she was when at last the doctor came. And he pleased her. Both George and Mrs Lyndishoe attended him in state. He turned them brusquely out of the room. He let Jane stay. When he had done with the child he turned upon Jane, pulled her into the light, stared at her and grunted, 'I want to know how he fell so far and so hard,' he said.

'So do I,' said Jane.

'H'ump' He still stared at her. 'You're new. Like the place?'

'It's a bit weird,' said Jane.

'D'you like the boy?'

'He's never had a chance, poor mite.'

'Well, stick to it. I will send over a couple of nurses as soon as I can. Divide up the time with them. One of you must always be with him. See? Always. It's a bad concussion.' He shook hands with her emphatically and was gone.

The next morning, while Julian still lay unconscious, there was a little sound at the door, not so much like a knock as a cat scratching. Jane opened it and saw Julian's mother. She looked wretchedly ill. She whispered, 'I must see him. I won't do anything else, indeed I won't. I must see him.' Jane was astonished, and what is rare for her, bewildered. The mother stole into the darkened room and looked long at her son. 'He is alive still,' she murmured. 'Is he alive?' Jane nodded, and she went out.

He continued to live, and he recovered consciousness at last, a forlorn little person, like a spirit which has wandered back to put on a strange body. He knew Jane, he knew where he was, he had really decided to live but he did not know much about it. He knew nothing about his accident.

However, as the days went by he grew stronger and the hospital nurses departed. Jane watched the boy jealously, but she had no more alarms. His mother would steal in often and sit with him for a time, but she always knocked at the nursery door; she asked meekly if she would be in the way. She made no attempt to interfere with Julian's precisely ordered life. She was miserably anxious to please Jane. And Jane's contempt for her became more bitter.

'Scared of me, are you, my lady? You don't know how much I know. Cowardly cat,' said Jane to herself. 'And you think you can get round me with your sly, smooth ways. Not much!'

The rulers of Bransmere, Mrs Lyndishoe and George, paid

an occasional state visit to the child but now that he was well, think of little interested in him as he in them.

Jane believed in open air. Julian did not. Julian never wanted to go out, but he was docile and they spent much of the shortening winter days in the park. Jane came to enjoy wandering away among the coverts to the lake, and when the sun gleamed on the black water of the lake would pronounce that the queer old place was not so bad.

She was sitting one morning on an outcrop of rock, while Julian skirmished looking for goblins' holes. (He would talk of such things in spite of all she could do.) Jane's nose went up. She beheld that young man with whom Julian's mother had been discovered. His gaiters were glossy as ever, his riding-breeches as baggy, his cap even more on one side; it was not to be doubted that he waxed his moustache. Flashy, beyond dispute and equally beyond dispute, no class. Mighty pleased with himself he was, too. He smiled at Jane, he lifted his cap, and said that it was a nice morning.

'The morning's all right,' said Jane. 'I don't care so much for the company.'

'Speak your mind,' the young man had the impedance to laugh at her.

Jane looked up at the sky. 'I'm waiting for you to go,' she remarked.

'Why?'

'So that I can go the other way.'

'I say, don't be stuffy. I don't bite. How's the young one doing?'

Jane sprang up. 'Julian!' she called. 'Come along, ducky.'

Julian in the distance look up rather earthy, like a terrier who has been digging. 'Hello, major!' he called out began to run.

'Good morning, captain,' said the young man—clicked to attention and saluted.

Jane stared at him. 'Major, indeed!' she said.

'Sergeant-major, miss.'

Jane visibly relented. 'Oh, a sergeant.'

'Squadron Sergeant-major Dunster,' he smiled at her. 'Sounds almost respectable, don't it? Commonly called Bill.'

'I must say you don't look it.'

'That's my deadly beauty.' Julian arrived and shook hands. 'How are you feeling, sir?' said the sergeant-major.

Julian was quite well, thank you, Dunster; and how was the major and his mother and father? He walked some distance, talking gravely, and ran off again.

'Quite a man, isn't he—some ways?' said the sergeant-major. 'Captain Lyndishoe was my officer, you know. One of the very best. I was with him when he was killed. Gives me a kind of feeling for the boy. And Mrs Lyndishoe.'

'The old lady?' said Jane.

He slashed at a gorse bush. 'Not much. Mrs Charles. Poor young lady. She's been through it. My oath, she's been through it. My father's the bailiff, you know, up at the farm. We've been on the land about as long as the Lyndishoes. And the young one's the heir. Gives you a kind of feeling—about things.' He stopped and looked shrewdly at Jane. 'You've had a hard job by what I hear.'

Jane blushed. This is unusual. 'He's all right now,' she said in a hurry. She was uncomfortable. She was struggling with new facts. The flashy nut as a solid sergeant, the guileful adventurer as a faithful retainer; these transformations disturbed Jane. Not less disturbing was the transfiguration of Mrs Charles into an ill-used woman, a woman with a right to pity and devotion. Jane couldn't make it fit.

'He would be all right with you,' the sergeant-major was saying, and he looked at her with respectful admiration 'Anyone would be. They need someone as'll stand by 'em, him and his mother. Proud to have met you, Miss.' He saluted, turned off, and vanished in the covert.

A little way further on Julian came back to her and they met

George Lyndishoe sauntering with dogs and gone. He smiled
at her; he was always civil, and told her that the weather suited
her, and Julian and she were running wild. But Jane had never
been interested in George Lyndishoe.

Winter made itself out at Bransmere. Easterly weather set in,
ice spread out from the shallows over the lake. With vast fires
Jane could hardly make her nursery warm, but Julian throve
on the cold, and there was no need to keep him in. He was
vastly more vigorous and happier; he was something like a
normal boy. But though they ranged the park hither and thither
Jane saw no more of her sergeant-major. She was annoyed with
him. There were a good many things she wanted to ask him.
But nothing disturbed the peace of the old house.

A day came when they wandered down to the lake. It was
frozen over from end to end, for all its fabled depth, and the
ice glittered in the sad December sun. Julian was vastly interested, and with Jane holding his hand, was permitted to test it
by the edge of the shallows. George Lyndishoe came up.

'Hello, found your way here young man?' He greeted Julian
cheerily. 'The ice looks well, doesn't it, nurse? Good stuff. Are
you a skater?'

'Only rollers, sir. And that was enough for me.'

'Pity,' he said carelessly. 'It seems rather a shame to see no
one on all that ice. I must ask some people.' He stepped off the
bank, took a run and stood laughing at himself. 'I'm rather old
for that sort of thing. I wish I was your age, young sir.' He made
another slide.

'Let me,' Julian cried. 'Let me,' and tugged at Jane's hand.

'You? You've hardly found your legs yet, have you?' George
slid again.

'I can. I know I can,' Julian protested.

'Is the ice safe, sir? Will it bear him?'

'Great Scott, yes. It's bearing me. I should make six of him, shouldn't I?' George laughed . 'And three of you, I suppose. Let's see what I can do.'

Jane came down to the ice and holding Julian, let him try, and, of course, he tumbled over his own feet. Jane demonstrated. He began to get the knack of it, but still tumbled and was fearful. Jane towed him. 'I am sliding. I am, aren't I?' he cried in triumph.

'Oh, you're a great man,' George laughed, and gave another demonstration.

They spent some time so, and Julian was learning, undeniably learning, but Jane, with a mind on his tea, announced that they must go. Julian protested, argued, wept. 'I'll tell you what,' said George amiably, 'we'll take you home along the lake young man.' That brought joy, and off they went, Julian in turn experimenting by himself and being towed by one or the other.

This brought them, you see, away from the shallows over deep water, but the ice looked sound enough, and they kept together and kept to the edge. Who fell first or how they felt Jane never knew, but they all went down and with a cracking and sucking in her ears she screamed, and for a moment knew nothing but the shock of the cold water.

She was in the dark, she was stifling, she felt the ice press upon her head. She struck wildly with one hand, the other held to Julian's, to Julian somewhere down in the black depths. The ice broke to her bleeding fingers, her head surged out of the water and she plunged for the shore. There stood George Lyndishoe. She called to him, she stretched out her hand; he stooped and she saw his face. She knew what he meant to do. As he struck at her she clutched him. He swore, he struggled, he kicked her hand, her arm, but she held fiercely and the two bodies in the water dragged him down.

As he fell upon her, and long she remembered the moment's sight of him between earth and water, she struck out to swim away. He grasped at her but could not reach her—he vanished. She felt him underwater against her feet and kicked furiously in a moment she was at the bank again and still Julian at her side.

Hands reached down and caught her under the armpits and hauled her out. She stood, her knees weakened; she sank down to the ground in a heap, hugging Julian to her bosom.

'I saw you,' said the sergeant-major. 'I saw that—' (Never mind what he called George Lyndishoe.) 'My oath, I was always watching you two when he was out. That accident up at the house made me more careful.'

'He—he tried to kill us,' Jane gasped, shaken with cold and fear. 'Oh, where is he?'

The sergeant-major pointed down. Somewhere in the weeds, somewhere under the ice lay George Lyndishoe. Again the sergeant-major pointed down.

'He's paid,' he said. He jerked Jane to his feet. 'Come on, take hold of yourself, my girl, or you'll be gone too, you and the young one.' He tore off his coat and wrapped it round Julian and wrapped the shivering child to his body. 'Run, my girl, run. You've got to get some life into you. Come on to the farm, that's nearer—and better, too.' And he ran on with the child, and Jane toiled after him.

While Julian and Jane lay between the blankets and his mother fussed faithfully over the small heir of Bransmere, the sergeant-major's father and he mustered men for the grim business at the lake. As twilight was falling the body of George Lyndishoe came back, borne on the hurdle to the old house.

Julian's mother was pacing to and fro before the door, it was long past Julian's time and fear was quick in her. Mrs Lyndishoe sat at a window above watching and smiling. She saw the little party coming heavily and went down to meet them.

'My dear Phyllis!' she said benignly, 'I think there must've been an accident. What can they be carrying there? '

Julian's mother gave one glance at the placid, cruel face and ran forward crying, 'What is it? Oh, what is it? Where is my boy?'

The sergeant-major's father, the bailiff was marching ahead of the bearers. He waved her away. 'It's not for you, indeed. Your boy is safe at the farm.'

'Pray what has happened, Dunster?' said Mrs Lyndishoe, a note of alarm in her voice now. 'What is it there?'

'It's Mr George has been drowned, ma'am.'

Mrs Lyndishoe thrust him aside and dragged the rug from the hurdle.

'George!' she screamed. She stood a moment staring at the dead, distorted face then flung herself upon Julian's mother, striking her. 'You beast!' she said, 'You beast! '

'Now, ma'am, now,' old Dunster thrust himself between them and his son drew Julian's mother away. And still Mrs Lyndishoe abused her, her and her brat who lived, whose part it was to die . . .

When there was an end of that, when the scared, horrified servants had laid hands on their mistress and drawn her in to be safe with her dead, when Julian's mother was safe at the farm. 'It had to be. Praise God 'tis done, Bill,' old Dunster said. 'Ay, 'tis well done.'

'That girl's a rare plucked one,' said the sergeant-major.

'Ay, surely. A brave wench. Ay,' he pondered. 'It will be the mistress put it into Georges head first and last. I'll always believe that, Bill. It was never George of himself. Not but what he was greedy. All his life he was greedy, but he was nought. And she is a dark masterful woman.'

'We'll never know,' said the sergeant-major. 'My oath, she's paid, too.'

'Ay, George was always her boy.'

In the bedroom in the farm, Julian's mother fell on her knees by Julian and hugged him. 'Oh my darling, my darling, I have you. I really have you, haven't I?' she whispered.

'Course you have,' said Julian.

Jane, overwhelmed in a vast flannel dressing-gown, stole away and sat herself down by the fire and gently but steadily cried.

After a while Julian's mother came and stood before her. 'You!' she said. 'Oh, and I hated you so.'

'I'm just—just a fool, ma'am,' Jane gulped. They went into each other's arms.

'What are you crying for?' said a contemptuous small boy.

H. C. BAILEY

Henry Christopher Bailey (1878–1961) created one of the most popular detectives in Britain in the 1920s, Reginald Fortune, referred to by his friends as 'Reggie' and by others as 'Mr Fortune'. Between 1919 and 1948, Reggie appeared in nine novels and over eighty carefully plotted long short stories that are peppered with humour and full of originality. Fortune is a gentleman detective, a surgeon who acts as a medical consultant to Scotland Yard in the shape of, for the most part, the Honourable Stanley Lomas, chief of the Criminal Investigation Department, and Superintendent Bell. While the stories have become damaged by the detective's mannerisms, as well as by some regrettable racist and anti-Semitic references, Fortune is a likeable, well-rounded character and his cases tackle themes that rarely occurred in crime fiction of the period. As well as Fortune, Bailey created Joshua Clunk, a Dickensian lawyer, who has a cameo in one of Mr Fortune's novels, while Fortune plays a minor role in two of Clunk's cases. And, less unusually than might be thought would be the case for detective fiction of the Golden Age, both Clunk and Fortune are prepared to take the law into their own hands.

After graduating from Oxford in 1901 with a first-class honours degree in 'Greats', Bailey became a journalist, joining the *Daily Telegraph* where he stayed for over forty years fulfilling a variety of roles including drama critic, crime journalist, war correspondent and editorial writer. While at University Bailey had begun writing well-regarded historical novels, often set in the Middle Ages and sometimes with criminous elements, but in the late 1910s he turned to detective fiction. While Bailey continued to write historical fiction until the 1930s when his thirtieth book, *Mr Cardonnel*, appeared, he is best known for his richly atmospheric and entertaining detective stories in which Fortune—or Clunk—unravels a crime, and sometimes a conspiracy, from apparently insignificant clues.

Though they do not always conform fully to the 'rules' of fair play, Bailey's detective stories explore psychology and detection, unusual for the genre, and they often probe themes that are considerably darker than those investigated by Fortune and Clunk's contemporaries, for example corruption among politicians and the police, child abuse and miscarriages of justice. Such originality won Bailey the admiration of his peers as well as readers. Despite— or perhaps because of—his career, working for the most conservative of Britain's newspapers, Bailey also used detective fiction gently to satirise class-consciousness and other 'traditional' values, thereby mildly lampooning precisely the kind of person who might be thought to read the *Daily Telegraph*.

'The Good Place' was first published in *Pan: The Fiction Magazine* in January 1922.

EXACTLY AS IT HAPPENED

E. C. Bentley

Mrs Margetts and the niece Beryl, who shared with her the work of the house, had hurried off by eight o'clock, and James Ringrose was left alone. He was feeling unsettled.

For one thing dinner had been too early, and they had hurried him over it at that. Still, he couldn't complain. They would be gone just for the one night, they had promised to be back early in the morning, and it had been clearly understood from the first that nothing on earth would induce them to stay in the place through the hours of darkness on the anniversary of the Captain's death. That would be a silly thing to do—all the village was agreed about that. Mrs Margetts had said that it would be tempting Providence; and even Beryl, a less devout Christian, had said that it would be 'asking for it'. Not once, but twenty times, they said, folk had been terrified into fits who stayed in the house that one night in the year, and for ten years past no one had taken the risk. Old Dyson, from whom Ringrose had bought the place, had said nothing about this little detail; and Ringrose had learned afterwards that Dyson always shut up the house and went away for his holiday when the uncomfortable date drew near.

But Ringrose, his mentality moulded by twenty years' practice at the Bar, was what he called 'not superstitious', and he had warmly declared it to be high time that this damned nonsense was knocked on the head. His resolve to sleep that night in the house had been announced by him with a contemptuous emphasis which he now felt to have been a little unnecessary. He could not possibly back out of it. That it was damned nonsense he was wholly convinced; but he had reminded himself, on reflection, that one's nerves could play one tricks sometimes, and he had been glad enough when Dr Verrill had offered to come over and sit out the night with him. The doctor had said nothing of any motive he might have in making the offer; but Ringrose had assumed Verrill to be, like himself, an impatient sceptic. Also he was, as Ringrose now found it a relief to recollect, a man of singular courage. So Ringrose sat by the window and waited, studying his brief in an impending case; and as the light failed, he glanced up from his papers again and again.

Twilight was far advanced when at last he raised his eyes to see the well-known, long, lean face regarding him humorously through the open casement. 'Here I am,' said the doctor. 'Stay where you are, old man; I know my way.' He passed on to the house door, and soon was in the room with Ringrose, who now set about lighting the two big lamps on table and sideboard, and drawing the curtains upon the falling darkness without.

The two men, old schoolfellows now reunited after many years by the accident of Ringrose's choice of a country retreat, were well matched. Both were tall and vigorous; both had managed, in spite of their professions, to be active, open-air men; both were unaffected, unromantic and unencumbered. But the barrister's life had been passed in terms and vacations, with the High Court and the Temple never very far away. Verrill, as a young medico, had knocked about the world a good deal, and could, when he chose, tell of strange adventures and tight places. There was about him a touch of piratical hardihood and boldness that his friend found attractive always and deeply comforting now.

They discussed in a matter-of-fact manner the conditions in which they should pass the night. It was agreed that they should stay in the comfortable sitting-room where they were. The two deep armchairs before the fire, as their owner observed, were made for sleep, if sleep there was to be.

Dr Verrill concurred. 'Though, mind you,' he added, 'I don't expect to drop off, myself. I never felt more keyed-up in my life.'

Ringrose looked at him, a little startled. 'Surely you don't suppose that—that anything is going to happen?'

'On the contrary, I think it very likely,' the doctor answered. He spoke with a touch of hesitancy. 'You see, I've been in this neighbourhood for a considerable time. I know that things have happened in this place on this night of the year. I don't express an opinion about what caused them, but happen they did. People have been terrified—yes, and sometimes injured, too. When I heard you say you meant to stay this night in the house, I decided to offer to join you, but that was because I am interested in this business, not because I think there's nothing in it.'

Ringrose thought it over. After all, this action of Verrill's, believing as he did, was very like the man. As to his half-admission of acceptance of the local myth, Ringrose told himself he had been hasty in assuming that a medical man must be a sceptic in such matters. His own disquiet, he felt, was increased; and it grew as he began to note certain evidences of nervousness in his guest. Usually a man of deliberate habits, the doctor this evening was plainly fidgety. He moved about the room, he fiddled with this object and that, he opened books and shut them after a glance within.

With an effort Ringrose regained his self-command. 'I wish,' he said calmly, 'you would tell me something about the late lamented Captain. Up to now, I confess, I've never had the patience to go into the story attaching to these premises. Who was he? What was he? When was he?'

Dr Verrill smiled. He appeared to be relieved at having something to fix his attention. He sat down for the first time.

'Yes,' he said, looking musingly at the floor, 'I can tell you about him. He was a very interesting man. To begin with, he wasn't a captain at all. Perhaps he should have been; he would certainly have made a fine soldier, for he was absolutely without fear, had all his wits about him, and was a devilish handsome man into the bargain. His name—perhaps you have heard his name at least—was Robert Halliday, and he was well-known about town for some years as "Mad Bob". He was born in 1743. He was a younger son with a small patrimony, which didn't last long when he came of age; for Bob lived like a gentleman—a little free, that's to say, as gentlemen did in those days. What with cards, and hazard, and women, and wine, and what with Bob's having a heart of gold, so that he could never refuse anything to a friend, the day came when, for a lad of spirit, there was nothing for it but the toby.'

'The what?'

'The toby—robbery under arms on the King's highway. I dare say you've heard that in those days many a man of family, who had had his misfortunes, took to the mask and pistols. Bob was resolved to do the thing in style, as most, of that class of tobymen did; but he soon surpassed them all in reputation for courteous and considerate dealing, and for several years he was acknowledged on all hands to be the best-behaved man on the road. He had, of course, to move among a very low lot, and it was they who gave him the courtesy title of captain. They used to give it, you know, to a 'wayman who had distinguished himself and who was what they called "a rank nib".'

Ringrose's eyebrows rose enquiringly.

'That,' continued Dr Verrill, 'was their low expression for a real gentleman. Well, for nearly two years the Captain worked the roads north and west of London, and did very well for himself. He bought this little place, where he lived part of the time under the name of Lawrence, with a young woman who passed as his wife, and not a soul in the neighbourhood suspected how he made his living. At last the thing happened that he might have expected, seeing how often he had known it happen to others. The she-devil who lived with him grew tired of him; the price on his head was a big one, and she sold him to the traps. One May morning the Captain, waking earlier than usual, heard the sound of horses stirring and champing in the road in front there. He slipped out of bed and peeped through the curtains. There were a dozen nags tethered to the fence-posts at the end of the garden, with one fellow in the saddle with a pistol in his hand; and standing there talking to him was Hailes, the riding officer, with the crooked grin on his knocked-about face that every "cross cove" in London knew so well. There were men, too, moving off to left and right through the orchard and kitchen-garden to surround the place.

'The Captain ran to the door. It was locked from outside. He caught up his pistols from the dressing-table. The charges had been drawn and his powder-flask taken away. Even his razors and his clasp-knife had been removed.

'There was only one chance for him, he thought, and that was desperate enough. He hurried into his clothes, and as he drew on his riding-boots he heard Hailes tapping lightly at the front door below. The bolts were quickly drawn, and someone stepped out—he knew well who it was. "It's all bowman," he heard her whisper—for the two were right beneath his window, which he had now set a little open, without drawing the curtains. As Hailes began growling some questions, the Captain drew the curtains back, making no sound, and climbed on the sill, with a pistol held by the muzzle in each hand. Then, at the same instant that the man with the horses gave a shout, he kicked open the casement and leapt right on top of the pair below. Fanny Bolder's scream was the last sound she ever uttered, for her neck was broken. Hailes got a crack on the skull from a pistol-butt that laid him senseless, and the Captain made a rush for the horses. The mounted man, still shouting, fired at him and missed, and the Captain, who was fighting mad, dragged him from his horse and doubled him up with a kick in the midriff. Next moment he was in the saddle: but it was no good. The traps were running from both sides of the house, and as he galloped off he got two bullets in his body and then a third in the head that finished him.'

Doctor Verrill, who had told his tale with evident relish, lay back in his chair with his hands in his pockets and stared at Ringrose, as if to say, 'What do you think of that?' Ringrose gratified him with a gasp of genuine admiration.

'What a story! By Jove! Doctor, you know how to pitch a yarn.'

'All the country people about here know it,' his guest answered. 'There's a pretty detailed account of the business, too, in a book of local history written by one of the vicars of the parish. Well! Now you know who and what the Captain was, and that's your ghost, if there is one.'

Ringrose replied with what he hoped would be taken for a sceptical grunt. His imagination had been excited, and the picture of the desperate robber trapped in the bedroom was somehow before his mind in much more vivid detail than Dr Verrill had given to it. An actual living face, white and set and dangerous—a face quite strange to him—seemed to flash into his consciousness and then vanish. Again it happened; then again. He got abruptly to his feet.

'I mean,' he said, 'to do the regular thing, and go right through the house from top to bottom to make sure there's nobody and nothing that could play us tricks. I'd be glad if you would join me.' The Doctor readily assented. Anything, he said, was better than sitting still and fancying things. With Ringrose leading the way with a hand-lamp, they carried out a very thorough examination of the little house; first the ground floor, then the upper rooms.

'And this,' Ringrose said, as he threw open the door of one of the bedrooms, 'is where I sleep. It's also the room, judging from your description, where the departed highwayman—' He stopped and listened, the light in his hand quivering visibly.

'I thought,' he said in a low tone, 'I heard a—a suppressed laugh; a sort of snigger. It was a horrible sound.'

'Damn it! So you did hear it,' answered Verrill irritably. 'I laughed—a little nervously, I dare say, but I don't know what you mean by horrible. I couldn't help it—I was thinking of what happened, some years ago, in this very bedroom. It's the Captain's bedroom, of course, as you were saying. But it wasn't of the Captain's last moments in it I was thinking. It was of Mr James Higginson's experience, which really was amusing—though not for him. But I'll tell you about it downstairs; it's too infernally creepy in this room to stand yarning up here.' The search of the bedroom and the others still unvisited was soon completed, and the two men returned to the sitting-room below.

It occurred to Ringrose that the cheerfulness of a fire would not be out of place. He remarked that the nights were chilly for the time of year, and the doctor, to the slight annoyance of his host, frankly said that a bit of a blaze might help to keep off the horrors. A match was put to the ready-laid fire, and both men produced their pipes.

'I was going to tell you about Higginson,' Dr Verrill began as he settled himself in his chair. 'Now I come to think, he was the last person before yourself to take the risk of staying in this house on this night of the year. Higginson was one of those self-made fellows who do nothing but brag about themselves, and he made a great parade, as that kind sometimes do, of never believing anything on any other man's account of it. About ghosts in particular he was a blatant and contemptuous sceptic. He took this place for the summer ten or twelve years ago.

Kenny, the village postmaster, asked him point-blank one day if he wasn't afraid of the ghost. "Afraid of the goat?" says Higginson, pretending to misunderstand him. "I said ghost," says Kenny. "Oh, ghost!" says Higginson. "I thought you said goat. Yes, I'm as much afraid of one as I am of the other"—and he went off guffawing like a jackass. His wife didn't like it, though; she insisted on clearing out before the Captain's invariable date came round. So did the servants, of course, and Higginson was left vowing that he would put an end to the silly story—like you.'

The doctor glanced mischievously at Ringrose, who affected a stolid unconcern.

'He meant to have no trickery, so about his usual time for going to bed he searched the whole place, just as we've done. When he came to his own bedroom—the same that you sleep in now—he found it all as usual. He put his candle on the mantelshelf, looked under the bed and behind the curtains, then crossed the room and looked inside the cupboard where he kept his clothes hanging. No sign of anybody or anything wrong. Then, just as he was leaving the room to finish his inspection, he heard a queer noise behind him—a sort of snuffling noise, he called it, when telling the story afterwards.'

At this point Dr Verrill paused, set as if listening intently, and then glanced quickly over his shoulder. Ringrose, who could see that there was nothing unusual in that direction, gripped the arms of his chair and said, rather loudly, 'Well?'

'Higginson spun round, as you may imagine,' the doctor went on, 'and there by the light of the candles he saw, lying in the bed that he had actually been touching a moment before—what do you suppose?'

'I can't guess,' replied Ringrose irritably, 'what the fool thought he saw, or chose to say he saw.'

'A great, black, long-horned goat was lying in the bed with the clothes drawn up to its chin and its beard sticking out over the coverlet. Its eyes were shut, and the slight noise of its breathing was what Higginson had heard. Then, as he stood glaring at the creature, it suddenly opened its eyes—you know those yellow eyes with strange flattened pupils that goats have—and glared back at him. It gave a loud, discordant bleat, and then'—here Dr Verrill broke into a chuckle which Ringrose did not find infectious.

'And then?' he said.

'It asked him to have the goodness to shut the door.' The doctor burst into a shout of laughter, laying his head back and clutching at his ribs; again and again he fetched his breath and roared. Then, his speech broken with gusts of subsiding mirth, he went on, 'Higginson took his oath—that those were the very words—the goat said to him—"Will you have the goodness"'— here Dr Verrill's merriment again overcame him completely.

Ringrose looked at him with impatience. 'I don't really see much to laugh at,' he said, 'in such a preposterous lie. But perhaps the fellow was out of his mind. Or was he suffering from delirium tremens? Surely you don't imagine there's a word of truth in his silly story.'

The doctor ceased laughing abruptly, as if taken in an indiscretion. 'Well, I don't know so much about that,' he declared soberly enough. 'Queer things have happened here—I believe that. And there Was some pretty unpleasant truth about the rest of his story, for Higginson was found early next morning lying in the road half-dead with fright and exposure and pain, his right arm being broken. He broke it, he said, in his flight from the house, trying to take the staircase in two jumps; but even so he got outside and fifty yards down the road before he fainted with the pain. That's all I know about Higginson, old man; and now suppose we change the subject. In one way it's a devilish funny story, but it must have been a ghastly experience for a man in a nervous state—and no man can help being in such a state in such circumstances.'

Ringrose was too honest a man to demur to this. He knew himself to be thoroughly on edge. When a coal snapped lightly in the glowing fire, he started and caught his breath; and it chilled his spirit to see that Dr Verrill did the same. They avoided each other's eyes for a time, until Ringrose spoke again.

'Well, I don't believe,' he declared bluffly, 'that a ghost can do me any harm. Supposing that such things as ghosts are permitted to exist, it's quite beyond belief, to my mind, that a ghost should have the power to hurt me. I'm not a monster of wickedness, hang it all! One doesn't discuss such things as a rule, but I suppose you'd say, doctor, that I was a fairly decent sort of devil. I don't know that I ever did anyone an injury knowingly. If there are ghosts, they belong to the spirit world, and if there's a spirit world, it must be under Divine direction, and not a source of danger to people who do their best to keep straight and do their duty.'

He had gazed into the fire while putting words to his thought, and now glanced up with sudden irritation as his friend began to chuckle in the manner which Ringrose had already found so disagreeable.

'That's what you want to believe,' said Dr Verrill, ' but, my dear fellow, look at the thing in the light of common experience! What has the excellence of your personal character got to do with it? Perfectly blameless men are getting undeserved hard knocks and fatal blows every day. You may be an absolutely unspotted saint, but if you take a walk through the Indian jungle you are just as likely as any other man to be killed by a tiger or a cobra—I suppose you'll admit that. And if dangerous wild creatures are what you call "permitted to exist", why shouldn't dangerous ghosts be "permitted to exist", too? The one world, you know, is as much "permitted" as the other to go on in the way it does. If a spiritual being can hurt you, it's no more and no less of a mystery than it is if you get horned by old Penruddock's bull . . . See what I mean?'

Ringrose had risen and begun to pace the room. 'Yes, I see what you mean. But . . . one doesn't, as a matter of fact, get gored by Penruddock's damned bull.'

'No: because you take jolly good care to keep out of his damned field.'

Ringrose stared at him. 'Then you think—what you're leading up to is that we are a pair of fools to be in this house at the present moment.'

'Something like that.' The doctor leant back in his chair and stuck his hands in his pockets. My belief is that you're doing a very risky thing—there you have it.'

'And what about you?'

'Well,' the doctor answered slowly, 'it isn't I, you know, who have been by way of putting the local phantom's back up. *I* haven't gone about saying he didn't exist, and that he couldn't hurt anybody if he did, and that all the stories about his proceedings were rubbish. The captain, while he lived, always had the reputation of being a little bit touchy, and if you look into his record after death, I think you'll find that the only cases where he made himself actually unpleasant were cases in which there had been doubting, and sneering, and turning up of noses—as in that affair of Higginson's that I was telling you about . . . But perhaps you'll think I only take that view to keep up my own courage. Well, I won't say you're wrong. I haven't pretended that I'm feeling comfortable.'

Ringrose, who considered that he had put a decidedly better face on his emotions than Verrill had done, admitted this with a touch of emphasis. He continued to pace the room, uneasily turning over the other's argument in his mind; then he stopped before a small cabinet on a side-table.

'How about a game of cards to pass the time away?'

Dr Verrill accepted the proposal with alacrity. 'What shall it be? I'm pretty fair at the usual two-handed games.'

Ringrose was fond of piquet, and said so. He was relieved to hear that the doctor would have suggested that very game. The cards were produced, the little table was drawn out, and the two men cut for the deal.

Ringrose had never played cards with his guest before, and he was a little surprised to find that he had met his match in a game which he knew himself to play uncommonly well. But it was a strange contest. Ringrose's was the sound game, largely based on study of its minor and better balanced chances. Verrill, on the contrary, systematically neglected these, challenged his luck by dashing and precarious play, and would be satisfied with nothing less than 'pique', 'repique' or ' capot.'

Both became absorbed in the game; an hour slipped by unnoted, then another hour. A time came when the doctor, after a run of irresistible hands, had a long lead in points. Then the cards took to falling more evenly, and Ringrose's more sober method began to tell. His guest's advantage diminished rapidly, and it gradually became apparent to Ringrose that the doctor did not like it. By the time that his lead was wiped out, he was scowling at his cards and swearing under his breath.

All at once, as he was about to deal a new hand, he jerked himself upright in his chair and stared at Ringrose. 'Did you hear?' he whispered. His face had gone quite white.

The almost-forgotten terror flooded back upon Ringrose's mind in redoubled volume. His palms were suddenly moist, his mouth dry. Not trusting himself to speak, he shook his head as he returned the stare.

'Didn't you hear—something—a kind of dragging noise— outside the door?' stammered Verrill. Almost in a moment the man's appearance had become ghastly. His forehead was beaded with sweat, his colourless face pinched, his mouth set in a grimace: his eyes, wild as a cornered beast's, were fixed upon the door. His straining fingers clutched the pack of cards; and as Ringrose, fascinated by such a spectacle of moral torture, watched him, he slowly, and as if unconscious of his action, *tore the pack in two.*

The sight shocked Ringrose into violent movement, and gave him back his voice. He sprang to his feet. 'Good Heavens, man!' he exclaimed, stretching out an arm across the table to seize Verrill by the shoulder.

And at the instant when his clutching hand should have felt the contact—there was nothing! His fingers closed on empty air; before his eyes were the torn cards, the table, the chair, the background of the room. Just as a candle is puffed out, Dr Verrill had been snatched out of visible and tangible existence . . .

Ringrose stood swaying on his feet; a heavy groan broke from him, His roving stare, passing over the objects before him, lighted upon the clock on the mantelshelf. And as his brain mechanically noted that it was half-past two o'clock, the little oscillating bracket of the visible escapement faltered in its motion and stood still.

With the cessation of the clock's faint ticking, there was now complete silence in the room. The fire was noiseless in the grate. From without came no stirring of leaves, or nocturnal sound of any kind. The phrase 'silent as the grave' came into Ringrose's mind as he stood in agonised expectancy.

A slight sound, a barely audible creak, came from behind him. He spun round, his hands clutching at his breast. Was it from the door that the noise had come . . . ? It came again; he saw that the door-handle was being slowly and stealthily turned from without.

And as his brain received the appalling message of his senses, the end came. All consciousness was instantaneously blotted out.

When Ringrose came to himself he was lying where he had swooned, with a great cushion from one of the armchairs beneath his head. His nostrils were tingling and smarting, and his head ached violently. Dr Verrill, looking pale and fatigued, knelt beside him, holding a squat green bottle in one hand and fingering the prostrate man's pulse with the other.

'You'll do,' said the doctor. 'Lie there a bit and keep quiet. I'll get you upstairs to bed presently.'

The morning sun poured a glory of light into the room. Through the open window came a ceaseless singing of birds.

'What's the time?' asked Ringrose faintly.

The doctor glanced up to the mantelshelf. 'Your clock's stopped,' he said. Ringrose shuddered. The doctor produced his watch. 'Nearly seven-thirty.' He went to the sideboard. 'Rather early for a drink, but it's doctor's orders . . . Here, swallow it down . . . B'Jove, I could do with one myself after the night I've had . . . ! Aha! That's better.'

Ringrose's brain was beginning to clear. He raised a hand and felt the wet bandage round his head. 'What's happened?' he inquired in a stronger voice.

'Slight concussion is what's happened, I should say,' the doctor replied, finishing his drink. 'Fell over and cut the back of your head open on the fender How you did it, you know best. Mrs Margetts found you stretched on the hearthrug when she got here at seven. I should say from the look of the cut that you had been unconscious quite a long time.'

Ringrose thought it over. 'Yes, but,' he persisted, 'you know what I mean. What happened when you disappeared?'

Verrill stared at him. 'When I what?' Then his look of puzzlement faded. 'Oh! You mean when I didn't appear. You're still a little bit woolly in the head, old man—it'll soon pass off. Why, what happened was that just as I was thinking of walking over to join you as arranged, I was sent for in a hurry to attend old Henry Parsons' wife in her confinement, and there I had to stay till daylight. I wanted to send you a message, but no one would take it, of course. I got back feeling tired out, and I hadn't been asleep an hour when your maid routed me out to come and look after you. Come now!'—the doctor's voice changed—'Pull yourself together, man! It's all right now. I believe you *have* had a fright, too. Tell me about it later on. Here, let's see if we can get you on your legs and into the armchair.'

With the doctor's arm about him, Ringrose got shakily to his feet. His glance fell on the little table, and on the litter of torn playing cards, giving back from their glazed surfaces the sane, sweet light of the sun.

E. C. BENTLEY

Edmund Clerihew Bentley was born in West London on 10 July 1875, the son of John Bentley, a civil servant, and his Scottish wife Margaret, whose maiden name was Clerihew. Edmund attended St Paul's School and was elected to a Modern History Exhibition at Merton College, Oxford. He enjoyed university life and, as well as writing for university magazines like *Isis* and *The J.C.R.*, he was a keen oarsman. He was also an effective debater and, in November 1897, was elected president of the Oxford Union Society. In 1936, he and Dorothy L. Sayers would lose an O.U. debate on the motion 'That the present excessive indulgence in the solution of fictitious crime augurs ill for our national future', in which Sayers noted that Oxford dons were clearly devotees of crime fiction given how many wrote to tell her about the mistakes in her books.

After coming down in 1898, Bentley began studying to become a barrister. He was called to the bar in 1901 and, on 14 June the following year, he married Violet Boileau, with whom he would have three children. Never wholly comfortable with what he described as 'the shifts and compromises of the law', he decided to become a journalist. He joined the *London Daily News* where, working alongside his schoolfriend G. K. Chesterton, he wrote political and social commentaries under his own name and, as 'Edmund Clerihew', comic vignettes with titles like 'Things Seen by a Dentist', 'The Truth about Toys' and 'The Importance of the Zoo'.

Under his own name, Bentley also wrote comic verse for *Punch*, and under his pen-name short stories for *The Bystander*. With *Biography for Beginners* (1905), a volume illustrated by Chesterton, Bentley immortalised the 'clerihew', a form of poem to which he would return to in *More Biography* (1929) and *Baseless Biography* (1939). His definition of a clerihew was:

A short four-line verse of which the first and second lines are expected to rhyme, more or less, and also the third and fourth. The hero, so to speak, should be a well-known person, alive or dead, whose name should terminate the first line. A certain rhythmic quality should be observed.

The form was easily copied and in 1949, Bentley judged a competition run by the *Sunday Times* to write a clerihew about two famous people, picking from a list of six. This attracted 6,000 entries, among which Bentley particularly enjoyed the following 'ghoulish' but ineligible entry:

Incidentally,
Mr Bentley,
Have you a clerihew
For the stone when they berihew?

By 1908, Bentley had risen to assistant editor of the *Daily News* and, with his journalistic career and family life progressing nicely, he decided to try to write a detective story. He began *Trent's Last Case* (1913) by writing the final chapter and, with its sensational twist ending, the hitherto moderately amusing journalist became one of the most respected names in crime fiction, surpassed only by Conan Doyle and perhaps Chesterton, to whom he dedicated the book in reciprocation for G.K.'s dedication to him of *The Man Who Was Thursday* (1908). More than a century after its publication, it is hard to exaggerate the importance of *Trent's Last Case* in sustaining and fuelling the popularity of crime fiction into the so-called Golden Age. However, it is important to recognise that Bentley planned the novel as a satire first and as a detective story second. In the same vein, despite the book's success, he would always consider himself a journalist rather than a writer. In 1912, to further his career, he moved from the left-leaning London newspaper the *Daily News* to the right-leaning national newspaper the *Daily Telegraph*, where he remained, on and off, for twenty-two years, writing political commentaries and reviewing books, mainly crime fiction.

Despite pressure to write more mysteries of his own, Bentley was well aware of his limitations. He did revive Philip Trent for a series of short stories, *Trent Intervenes* (1938—reprinted in 2017 with the inclusion of the previously uncollected Trent story 'The Ministering Angel'), and in 1943 he wrote 'The Body in the Heather', a brief non-series puzzle-play for BBC radio. Bentley's only other novel, *Elephant's Work* (1950), is a thriller, while the second detective novel to feature Trent, *Trent's Own Case* (1936), was written with his friend and fellow journalist Herbert Warner Allen, whom Bentley had hired at the *Daily News* back in 1908. Warner Allen had already written several crime novels including *Mr Clerihew, Wine Merchant* (1933), and in *Trent's Own Case*, Bentley's Trent works with Warner Allen's detective, the eponymous wine merchant and president of the Junior Clerihew Club of oenophiles.

In 1947, Edmund Clerihew Bentley retired from journalism and his final short story, an uncharacteristic piece of science fiction called 'Flying Visit', appeared in 1953. He died after a short illness at his home, 10 Porchester Terrace, Paddington, on 30 March 1956.

'Exactly As It Happened' was first published in *Cassell's Magazine*, December 1926.

YE GOODE OLDE GHOSTE STORIE

Anthony Boucher

'But there ain't no sech thing!' said Jed Hoskins' old man forcefully.

'No such thing as what?' queried the stranger with the black bag, who had just seated himself near the group.

'Ha'nts,' Jed hastened to explain. 'Grandad Miller there, he says the old Lawrence home's ha'nted, and my dad, he says it can't be, 'cause there ain't no ha'nts.'

'Aren't there, though?' said the stranger, half to himself.

'Ye believe there be, don't ye?' asked Grandad Miller hopefully.

'Yes, I do. I had a horrible experience once over in England . . .'

'England?' (This from Jed, who thought it a place only geography teachers could be familiar with.)

'England it was. Would you like to hear about it?'

'Yes!' came a chorus of assent, even from old man Hoskins.

'All right.' And so he began.

'It must have been about two years ago that Lord Fantomheath invited me to spend the weekend at Fantomheath Fields, his ancestral domicile. I accepted with pleasure—and promptly forgot all about it. I was to have left London on the . . . on the

. . . well, I don't exactly remember the train, but it was some-where about noon on Friday. I didn't remember my engagement until about 6.00 Friday evening. Then I hurried down *lo más pronto posible*.'

'Low mass?' asked Grandad Miller, the only Catholic in Higginsville.

'*Lo más pronto posible*. It's a Spanish phrase meaning "as quickly as possible".'

'Oh!'

'Percy—that is, Lord Fantomheath'—a gasp of surprise went round—a man who could call a lord by his first name!—'was awfully angry at my being late. "Harry," he said, "if we weren't such good friends, I'd cut you altogether."

'"Well, Perce," said I, "as long as you don't cut me all apart, it's all right."

'"But that's just what might happen," he explained. "If you stay, you will have to sleep in the Chilling Chamber, otherwise known as the Bloody Bedroom. It was there that my revered ancestor, Lord Felix of Fantomheath, committed suicide by slitting his throat with a razor. Since then, every guest that has slept in the Beastly Boudoir has been found next morning with his throat cut!"'

A shiver ran around the little circle, even though the fire was blazing gaily away. 'Didja sleep there?' asked Bob Hill.

'Of course. Would I be afraid of the ghost of a long-dead Englishman? Never! So Percy had Barracks, the butler, show me upstairs to the Horrible Haunt of the Suicidal Spirit.

'Feeling marvellous, I began to dress for dinner. Now, if it hadn't been for Percy's sister, Alicia, it might never have happened. But I was hopeful of persuading her someday to marry me. She was pretty, rich, and of one of England's best families. Can you blame me?

'I'd already shaved once that day but the thought of Alicia inspired me to shave twice in one day for the first time in five years. I had lathered my face, and was all set to begin. Then I saw in the mirror a horrible *form* at the other end of the room. It was absolutely and indescribably horrible. It was one of those things that are unmentionable, that *should not be*. It had a slight semblance of human form, but it was horribly distorted. It was unholy, sacrilegious . . . It is not healthful for a man to see such things . . .

'Slowly it advanced on me. I was helpless, spellbound, standing there motionless with the razor in my hand. An arm appeared from nowhere on the *shape*, seemingly projected like the pseudopod of a protozoan.'

'Like the which of a what?' asked Jed.

'Never mind. Anyway, an arm appeared. The *thing* was now standing directly behind me. Slowly *it* reached out and seized my hand. I could not move. Still more slowly *it* drew my own razor, in my own hand, across my throat!'

'But you're not dead!' Bob Hill objected. 'How come?'

'Wait a moment and you'll see. I came to in Alicia's arms. She was supporting me while Barracks poured brandy down my throat to revive me. "My hero!" cried Alicia. "You've freed the family of its curse. It has been foretold that if anyone survived the Gruesome Ghost's attack, he—I mean the ghost, of course—would never be able to appear again."

'"Alicia," I said, "I claim but one reward. Will you marry me?" And Barracks discreetly turned his head. And so we lived happily ever after.'

'But I don't see,' Hill reiterated, 'how come *it* didn't kill you?'

'Very, very simple.'

'But how?'

'I was using a safety razor!'

'Now, gentlemen,' he went on, opening the black bag. 'I have here a very fine assortment of Burham-Triplex safety razors at very reasonable prices.'

ANTHONY BOUCHER

William Anthony Parker White, who would become one of the most important figures in American mystery fiction, was born on 21 August 1911 in Oakland, California. His parents were doctors and after his father's death in 1912, White was raised in the Catholic faith by his mother with the support of his grandfather.

A voracious reader, White soon tried writing himself and at the age of only fifteen sold a supernatural short story to *Weird Tales*. Nevertheless, writing was a hobby; his passion was the theatre. At Pasadena Junior College he became president of the Players' Guild, the college's junior dramatic society for which he acted in numerous productions, such as *Phaedra* (1932), *The Merchant of Venice* (1931) and *The Royal Family* by G. S. Kaufman and Edna Ferber (1930). He also directed and sometimes acted in his own plays, including *Erlkönig*, a translation from Goethe. As well as German, White was or would become fluent in French, Italian, Russian, Spanish and, to a degree, Sanskrit.

After leaving Pasadena in 1928, White went to the University of Southern California to study for a Bachelor of Arts degree, and in 1932 he went up to the University of California in Berkeley to study for a Masters. At UC he wrote plays for the Experimental Theater Company, including the supernatural mystery *To Remember Me* (1933) and two campus comedies, *Kaleidoscope* (1933) and *Second Semester* (1933). It was at Berkeley that White met Phyllis

Price, the daughter of his German professor, and the two bonded over a shared love of opera. While he achieved his masters, with a thesis entitled 'The Duality of Impressionism in Recent German Drama', he shelved his original idea of becoming a teacher and decided instead to pursue a career in journalism.

White's career as a journalist took off quickly with a stint as arts critic for the *United Progressive News*, a short-lived Los Angeles newspaper. The job required him to do what he liked to do anyway—attend theatre and concerts—and it also gave him time to try his hand at writing a novel. Rather than use his own prosaic, and far from uncommon, name, he decided to adopt a pen name, the first of several. He became 'Anthony Boucher', the name by which he is most familiar to crime fiction readers; the pseudonym combines his middle name and his grandmother's maiden name. In June 1937 Simon & Schuster announced that Anthony Boucher's first novel would be *Death of a Publisher* and it would be published that year. Autumn came and White's first book duly appeared, although it had a different title and no publisher was harmed as part of its plot. *The Case of the Seven of Calvary* is a campus mystery, set in Berkeley, and the case is investigated by White's alter ego, Martin Lamb, and Dr John Ashwin. Ashwin also features in an unpublished short story, 'Death on the Bay', and a second novel— as revealed in the most authoritative overview of White's life and achievements, *Anthony Boucher: A Biobibliography* by Jeffrey Marks (2008).

In 1938, White and Phyllis Price were married. They had two sons and, juggling family life with writing, White published six more novel-length detective stories by 1942. These included two under another pen name, 'H. H. Holmes', itself the pseudonym of an appalling serial killer whose real name, Herman Mudgett, White would also use for short stories and verse.

White's novels are archetypal Golden Age puzzles peppered with impossible crimes, unusual clues and arcane references, which also feature in his shorter fiction published in *Ellery Queen's Mystery*

Magazine and elsewhere. White was an innovator and more than any other writer he sought to blend mystery with other genres, particularly horror, espionage and science fiction. By contrast, other than where a campus provides the setting, there is little overtly biographical in his work, although his Catholicism is shared by his best-loved characters, Sister Ursula of the Order of Martha of Bethany, and the California police detective Fergus O'Breen.

Despite—or perhaps because of—never being in full health, White's energy was simply phenomenal: he translated the work of others, including Georges Simenon and Jorge Luis Borges; he edited anthologies, the first of which appeared in 1943; and in collaboration with others, he wrote dozens of radio plays for series such as *The Adventures of Ellery Queen*, for Sherlock Holmes, and for his own creation, *The Casebook of Gregory Hood*. When not at his desk White was gregarious, and as well as helping to set up a California chapter of the Baker Street Irregulars, he was a founding member of the Mystery Writers of America, which awarded him the first of four Edgars in 1945.

Like a number of other writers, White receded from writing fiction when he found that reviewing was less arduous and more remunerative. Over the course of his career, he reviewed for— among others—the *San Francisco Chronicle*, the *Chicago Sunday Times*, the *Los Angeles Daily News*, *Opera News* and, in New York, the *Herald Tribune* and the *Times*. He also became increasingly active in local politics, and in 1947 was elected chair of the Berkeley Democratic Club. A year later, he was elected to serve as the member for Alameda County and as a representative for the Democrats on the party's state central committee. A passionate libertarian, White was one of the many who campaigned—success-fully—against Richard Nixon and Karl Mundt's infamous bill to 'protect the United States against un-American and subversive activities'.

In 1951, with White as its President, the Mystery Writers of America published a collaborative novel on similar lines to *The*

Floating Admiral, published twenty years earlier by the MWA's British counterpart, the Detection Club. As often with such round-robin novels, the majority of the contributors to *The Marble Forest* by 'Theo Durrant' (named for another infamous murderer) were lesser lights and other than White are largely unknown today.

During the 1950s, White also edited *Fantasy and Science Fiction Magazine* and *True Crime Detective* while continuing to review books, write stories and edit anthologies and even appear on the radio. But, despite a formidable work ethic he remained a strong family man and found time to relax with Phyllis and the boys, to listen to his extensive collection of early opera recordings, and to cook and play poker with friends.

White's life was to be cut short at the age of 56. After a very late diagnosis, he died from lung cancer on 29 April 1968 at Kaiser Foundation Hospital in Oakland, California. He lives on, in reputation and in the annual crime and mystery fiction convention 'Bouchercon', established in his honour in 1970.

'Ye Goode Olde Ghoste Storie' was first published, as by William A. P. White, in *Weird Tales*, January 1927.

THE ATONEMENT

S. S. Van Dine

'It's utter rot!' declared Wyman. 'One would think we were still in the dark ages.'

The speaker was a Johns Hopkins M.D. who, though barely thirty, had begun to attract national attention with his researches in glandular secretions.

He glanced, as if for approval, across the table to Grier, for years a staff member of the Rockefeller Institute. Grier acknowledged Wyman's look with a thoughtful nod.

'I see,' he rejoined, 'that the Sorbonne, after attempting an analysis of ectoplasm, has declared it non-existent.'

'No court of law would admit any of this so-called evidence of spiritualism,' threw in Coberly, a dignified, middle-aged lawyer, who sat at Grier's right.

A brief silence ensued and Wyman at length turned to the fourth member of the group, who, during the discussion, had scrupulously refrained from any comment.

'Don't you agree, Dr Saville,' he asked, 'that all this talk about the materialization of the dead is rank nonsense?'

These four friends met once a week in this same secluded corner of the Knickerbocker Club grill.

Dr Saville, being the oldest and wisest in the ways of life, had assumed a sort of intellectual leadership.

Slowly the old doctor took his pipe from his mouth and with

a gentle smile said: 'The tenets of spiritualism do seem at variance with the specific laws we have been taught to respect. But somehow, as I grow older, I feel more and more disinclined to call any sincere human belief "rank nonsense".'

At this moment a well-built, serious-looking young man passed close to the table on his way from the room and bowed to Dr Saville with a friendly, intimate smile.

When he was out of hearing Coberly remarked: 'Felton's a lucky man. District attorney at 36 and headed on up the ladder. Old Trask's money was certainly a godsend to him. Before Trask died Felton hadn't a nickel—and no prospects. Funny thing, too—that will. Everyone thought Trask disliked him.'

'You're his physician, aren't you?' Wyman asked casually, turning to Dr Saville.

'Yes,' the other replied. 'And I attended old Trask, too, during his last illness.'

'Another funny thing about Felton,' Coberly continued. 'He married a girl beneath him—I remember the talk at the time. But she has certainly made good. Has done wonders for Felton and is received everywhere.'

Dr Saville drained his glass and, setting it down decisively, leaned over the table.

'I'm going to tell you something about Daniel Felton,' he announced. 'I have a particular reason for wanting my young friend here to hear it.' He turned and smiled with gentle quizzicality at Wyman. 'Felton did not marry beneath him. I was with Amos Trask the night he died, and I know why he changed his will at the last minute and left everything to Felton. In many ways it is an amazing tale—from Wyman's purity materialistic viewpoint, at least . . .'

Felton, as you know, was a westerner. That is, he came from California, where he had studied for the law. When he graduated his father sent him east here with a letter to old Trask, who at that time was one of the biggest and shrewdest lawyers in New York.

Felton Senior and Trask had grown up together as youngsters. When Trask's parents died old Mrs Felton practically adopted the boy and mothered him for a number of years. So, naturally, Felton did not hesitate to ask a favour for his son.

Well, Trask gave Young Felton a place in his office, and for a long time things went well with him—as well, that is, as things could go with anyone who had to associate constantly with a crabbed, bitter old creature like Trask.

I needn't recall his reputation. People who had known him as a young man said life had soured him.

He had no reason for disliking Felton except that Felton was young and optimistic and clean minded. Felton was sensitive— an idealist and generous. Several times he had been on the point of quitting the firm and returning to California. But, for his father's sake, he stayed on.

This went on for several years. Then Felton met the girl. She was singing in a musical comedy at the time—filling a small, inconspicuous part; but her beauty rather marked her out. She disliked going about on parties, but her position meant a great deal to her and in order to hold it she had to make occasional compromises. However, she was always mistress of herself.

Felton met her one night at a late and rather gay supper party given by old 'Pop' Seldridge in his apartments. Seldridge was one of Trask's most valued clients, and Felton went to the supper largely as an act of business diplomacy. He was somewhat stunned, therefore, at finding a girl like Ruth Wallace among the guests. To him she seemed entirely different from the others.

Anyway, Felton looked into the girl's eyes and neither one moved or spoke for several seconds. But they felt something— some subtle, dim recollection, as it were—pass between them; and when their fingers touched in the unconsciously prolonged handshake that followed they were both trembling a little and their pulses were beating fast.

Later in the evening Felton managed to get the girl alone in an alcove.

'What are you doing here?' he asked her, with the candid concern of an old acquaintance.

She smiled a bit rudely and looked at him with tender gravity. 'I might ask the same question of you,' she rejoined, a bit eagerly.

'I came wholly as a matter of business,' he told her, in that honest, straightforward manner which had carried him so far.

She dropped her eyes. 'In a way, that is just the reason I also came,' she murmured. Then she added, with a tinge of bitterness: 'A girl must go through much more even than a man when she has her living to make.'

Felton succeeded in taking her away that night before the others left. They rode home in silence, and at the door of her flat—which, by the way, was in Harlem near the East River—he kissed her on the forehead.

This was Saturday, and as she did not have to go to the theatre the next evening she had given him permission to call. At eight o'clock, accordingly, he was there. She was living with her father and mother, and when Felton met them he received a shock which would have shattered the romantic enthusiasm of a less idealistic nature.

Her parents were obviously common people, and, worse, they were vulgar. They appeared to Felton like lowly, simple working people who had been insidiously corrupted by poverty and misfortune.

But, on the contrary, there were many evidences about them of an ample income.

As he sat in that gaudy living room comparing the sensitive, beautiful girl with the coarse, inferior man and woman, he found it difficult to accept the fact that she was of that same flesh and blood. She seemed to belong to a separate and distinct world. Furthermore, he felt that there existed between the girl and her parents some subtle lack of sympathy amounting almost to antagonism.

The next morning he encountered 'Pop' Seldridge in Trask's office.

'Rather took a fancy to my little singer, didn't you?' Seldridge grinned.

At the mention of the girl's name old Trask had turned sharply and given Felton a searching, supercilious look. Later, when Seldridge had gone, he summoned Felton to his private office.

Then, without taking his eyes from the other's face, he asked: 'What's this I hear from Seldridge about you and this Wallace woman? Do you think I care to have one of my associates entangled with a notorious chorus girl?'

Felton felt the blood leap to his throat and suffuse his face. He was incensed, but he held himself under admirable control.

'I assure you sir, he began, 'that Miss Wallace—'

'I know all about this Ruth Wallace,' Trask cut in sharply. 'She's a chorus girl in a musical show, and you met her at a drunken orgy in Seldridge's apartments—didn't you?'

The boy, abashed and angry, muttered some faltering defence of the girl, but Trask interrupted him with a sneer.

'Who is she? Who are her people? Have you seen them? My orders to you are to keep clear of her. Get a woman in your own class. If I hear any talk about you in connection with her—'

He paused, and turned menacingly upon Felton, but before he completed his threat the other rejoined with tense dignity: 'You need have no fear of that, sir!' And he went resolutely from the room.

But old Trask's remarks had their effect on him. He had met the girl at Seldridge's. And she was a chorus girl. And her parents—they were the most disturbing feature of the whole situation. Yes, the boy suffered considerably.

However, something in the girl's appeal—some sweet allure in her forlorn loveliness—had reached his heart, and he went on seeing her. He was, however, discreet and cautious about it, lest gossip of the affair reached old Trask, for his work and his position began to mean more to him now.

Gradually, beautifully—with the pure ardour of an idealist— he felt the miracle of love creep into his life. It was a fresh, virginal, wholly idolatrous love that came to him.

There was also a certain pity intermixed with his emotion; for he could sense that the girl was not happy. He could not help but attribute it to her life at home. Once he protested gently about some unpleasantness connected with her position at the theatre and had urged her to give up the work.

'I can't, Daniel,' she had answered, sorrowfully, on the verge of tears. 'You will not understand, perhaps, but I must—I must go on. There is something deep down within me—something I don't understand myself—which won't let me accept the support of my parents any longer.

'Sometimes I feel vaguely that I don't belong to them—that the real bond is missing. I don't mean that they are unkind. They have given me an education and advantages far beyond their own station, and they are willing to help me now. But they seem to act merely from a sense of duty. That's why I can't accept anything more.'

One Sunday afternoon in late spring Felton had taken her for a walk in Central Park. The warm twilight found them seated in a little secluded arbour.

Their hands touched accidentally, and, as he closed his fingers over hers, she impulsively responded to the pressure.

'Ruth—Ruth!' he whispered, drawing closer to her.

But she placed her free hand lightly over his lips and said beseechingly: 'Not now, Daniel! I know what you want to tell me—but please wait just a little while.'

'Why should I wait?' he exclaimed with passionate earnestness.

'I love you. I want you to marry me. There won't be much for us just yet, but I am just beginning. After a while—'

Again she turned to him, a despairing appeal in her look. 'Dan,' she implored, 'don't urge me—now. Oh, it isn't that I don't care,' she added quickly, seeing the stricken look which came into his face. 'It's for your sake, dear.'

She knew how impulsively young and idealistic he was. 'It would break my heart if I should ever cause you a moment's regret or unhappiness. That's why I want you to wait a little while. I want you to be sure—to see things just as they are. Then—if you love me—' Her voice faltered and her head fell forward on her breast.

Felton's idolatry was such that even this request was like a sacred command to him.

Felton was very busy the next two days. Trask had turned over a civil case to him and he was in court most of the time. He had no opportunity to see the girl, but there was some compensation for this in the fact that he won his case in particularly brilliant fashion and secured judgement for the entire amount sued for.

The case had been accepted partly on a contingent basis and the morning after judgement had been rendered Trask called him to the office and presented him with a cheque for $1,200—a percentage bonus for having won the suit. It was an unusual thing for Trask to do, but Felton was too happy to question it. It was a beginning of the things he had been hoping for.

Late that afternoon he hastened to the girl's home. He was met at the door by Mrs Wallace, who received him in so tragic a manner that he immediately became apprehensive and frightened.

'Oh, Mr Felton,' the woman began, 'Ruth has been taken sick—it's the theatre that did it. The doctor says she's worked too hard.'

'Tell me—about it,' the boy blurted, his heart now in his throat. 'Where is Ruth now?'

'She's in bed,' Mrs Wallace informed him, sorrowfully. 'But she can't see no one. The doctor says she ought to go away—to the country somewheres. These places in the country are awful expensive, Mr Felton. They're for rich folks—that's what they are.'

'If there's anything I can do . . .' Felton began falteringly. He thought at once of the money he had just received.

'That's what Ruth said,' Mrs Wallace answered him, ostentatiously stifling a sob. 'She said you'd help her if you could. Oh, Mr Felton, it's so good of you to offer. The poor girl was afraid maybe—that is, that you mightn't be able to do anything for. But she said it wouldn't do no harm to ask you.'

'No—of course not,' he murmured, eagerly. 'I can't do a great deal, but—how much do you need?'

'Well, Mr Felton,' the woman began, glancing at him furtively, 'would a thousand dollars be too much for you? . . . You see, these places are awful expensive . . .' She paused, her words suspended, and narrowed her eyes expectantly.

Felton did not hesitate. He took out his chequebook and filled in a blank for one thousand dollars. The woman's face beamed as he passed it over to her, and her grief gave way immediately to smiling and voluble thanks.

'Can't I see Ruth—just for a minute?' Felton begged distractedly.

'She's too sick—poor girl,' the mother informed him resolutely. 'And the doctor says nobody was to see her. Anyway, she's sleepin' right now. But she said to tell you she'd write to you.'

And she did write. After a week of torment, Felton received a letter from a small sanatorium in the Adirondacks. It was a tender, solicitous letter, bidding him not to worry, and holding out hope for their future.

He received two other letters, and then the news that she was nearly well, and was returning within a week or so. At just this time Trask sent for him.

'I'm naturally interested in the future of my employees,' he began, giving the boy a cynical smile, 'and I like to know how they spend their money . . . Now, what have you done with the commissions you received from the Arnheim case? Put it away—eh?'

Felton, despite himself, started slightly.

'No, sir,' he rejoined, 'I did not put it away. Such was my intention; but an emergency arose, and—I lent it—to someone who needed it more than I.'

A silence followed. The smile on Trask's face was supplanted by a shrewd, disdainful look. 'Lent it?' he repeated mercilessly. 'To a woman, perhaps?'

A hot wave of colour surged to the boy's cheeks. 'Yes, to a woman—the woman I love!'

Trask narrowed his eyes. 'Was it, by any chance, that Wallace woman?'

'It was Ruth Wallace,' Felton replied.

Trask regarded him for a moment with sardonic amusement. 'So!' he sneered, with an inquisitional inflection. 'She landed you, too! . . . Did the old woman do the string pulling, as usual? I know a damned sight more about Ruth Wallace than you do. I've got her whole record. Maybe I'll show it to you some day.'

'I don't want to see it,' Felton flung back, hotly. 'Whatever Miss Wallace wants me to know she'll tell me herself.'

The old man studied him sharply for a few seconds, and then dismissed him with an ironic shrug.

That night, tortured by the memory of Trask's words, Felton sat for hours in his study fighting with a vague sense of worry which had crept into his mind.

The following morning at the office dragged interminably. Shortly before noon Seldridge emerged from Trask's private office and passed him with a curt bow. An undefined nervousness came over Felton as the time passed and he was unable to eat any lunch.

When he returned to his desk he found a brief summons from Trask.

Trask greeted him with a malicious smile.

'I've a case here, Felton,' he began, indicating several documents on his desk, 'which I particularly want you to handle. Although, on the surface, it is merely a suit to recover monies and valuables obtained by unfulfilled promises, both verbal and written, the case is in reality one of extortion.

'The items sued for were obtained by deliberate deception and fraud. There is ample evidence, in the shape of letters, documents and records, to prove this point; and you are to bring out the true character of the defendant and to emphasize the nature of the fraud perpetrated.

'This suit is being brought by Seldridge.

'Briefly, the facts are these: He has been mixed up with a woman for some months. She has been leading him on under pretence of affection, promising marriage, and, in the meantime, bleeding him. Her parents are mixed up in it, too; and between them they have gotten into Seldridge for a considerable sum. The woman pretended illness recently, in order to make a final touch, and left the city for a while.

'She broke the engagement by mail so as to avoid a scene; and when Seldridge went round to see her people they laughed at him and practically told him she had never had any intention of coming across . . . It seems she has worked the same game a couple of times before and fortunately we've got the complete records here in the office . . .

'I'll turn over everything to you in the morning—Seldridge is bringing in his cancelled cheques then. In the meantime, here's a copy of the suit. The woman's still away, but she'll be back in a few days; and I want you to attend, also, to the service of the summons.

'You may be interested when I tell you who the woman is

that has swindled Seldridge . . . It's your friend, Ruth Wallace.'
And he dismissed Felton with a wave of the hand.

For the remainder of the afternoon the boy sat at his desk
in a daze, the document spread out before him. He did not
remember exactly how he got home; but when his brain began
to clarify he found himself sitting on the lounge of his study,
holding his head in both hands.

A great revulsion swept over him, and he was caught in the
clutches of an irresistible desire to get away—far away—where
he would never, by any chance, see the girl again.

The next morning he went directly to Trask's office.

'I regret, sir,' he announced, calmly, 'that I shall not be able
to undertake the case you turned over to me yesterday. I am
leaving for the west as soon as I can get ready . . . Here's my
resignation.'

He laid the paper on Trask's desk, and before the other could
make further comment, had turned and walked away.

On his own desk he found a letter from the girl. It was more
tender and solicitous even then the others, and it ended: 'Oh,
dearest, to think that in less than a week I shall again be with
you!'

Felton read it with a grim smile, but despite the anger in his
mind there was an ache in his heart. Nevertheless, he sat down
and wrote this reply:

'I shall not be here when you return. It may interest you to
know I am fully cognizant of your affair with Seldridge. He
intends to bring suit to recover the money you have obtained
from him by promises of marriage; and the case was given to
me to prosecute. But I am resigning from the firm. At least I
shall not be the one to expose your shame.'

It was a cruel, bitter, and unforgivable thing to do; but the
boy was in such pain he was scarcely rational.

After posting the note he went home and began putting his

affairs in order. There were many details to be attended to—odds and ends to be straightened out—and it was several days before he was able to get away. He had not returned to the office—there was no need. His few personal letters had been forwarded to his apartment.

Nor did he hear from the girl.

The night of his departure he was alone in his apartment, putting a few things in his handbag. He was to go on the early morning Limited which left at one o'clock, and it was now past midnight. A taxicab was already waiting at the door.

He was standing in the centre of the living room when the doorbell of his apartment rang. It startled him somewhat.

It was exactly twenty minutes past twelve—only forty minutes before train time . . . Again the bell rang.

With a slight sensation of apprehension, he went into the hallway and opened the door. To his amazement, there before him stood Trask, his gaunt, old body but dimly distinguishable in the deep shadows.

'Thank God, I'm not too late!' the old man exclaimed.

'What can I do for you, sir?' Felton demanded curtly and a bit irascibly.

'I must see you at once,' Trask returned in an eager, almost appealing, voice . . . 'And there's no cause now for anger, Daniel,' he added, gently.

Felton hesitated, completely taken aback.

'I haven't much time,' Felton returned, with an effort at civility. 'I'm making the one o'clock train.'

The old man came humbly forward and seated himself in a great armchair near the centre table, watching Felton with grave, expectant eyes.

'There's no hurry, my boy,' he announced, in a calm, even tone. 'You're not going to take that train tonight.'

Felton wheeled and stared at him.

'No,' Trask went on, calmly. 'You're going to stay here in New

York . . . And instead of going to the station tonight, you're going to Ruth. She returned today. And do you know where she is now? . . . She's all alone in that little arbour in the park where you once told her you loved her. And she's broken hearted—because of you, Dan. She loves you, and you're going to her—now.'

When he had managed to collect himself sufficiently he stammered incredulously: 'How do you—happen to know these things—about the arbour—about Ruth? . . .'

An inscrutable, faint smile spread over Trask's wizened face.

'I know, he answered, simply. 'I know many things tonight . . . That is why I am here, Dan. And you must heed what I tell you. Ruth loves you—and you are not going to wreck her life and yours, too.'

'No!' he exclaimed, feverishly resuming his packing. 'She lied to me, deceived me, and—used me . . . I've made my decision.'

'You can't go, Dan!' Trask remonstrated in an agonized voice. 'Don't you understand—don't you see? She has done nothing to you—she's as innocent as you are.'

Felton swung around, his face white and distorted with suffering.

'You tell me that!' he cried, bitterly. 'You, who poisoned my mind against her—you, who only a few days ago handed me the proof of her guilt! . . . You tell me she has done nothing to me!' A great sob shook him. 'She has trampled on everything worthwhile in my life—'

'Stop!' the old man broke in. 'I tell you she is innocent. You are condemning her and rejecting her love without a hearing . . . It is you who have wronged her, Dan.'

Felton moved a step forward. 'What of the money she took from me? And why did she reject my love? What of your own accusations and warnings? And what of Seldridge's suit, and the documentary evidence? . . . Condemned without a hearing?' He gave a dry, mirthless laugh.

The old man gazed sadly for a moment at the grief-stricken, angry boy. Then he said, gently: 'They were all lies, Dan—lies told you deliberately in order to wreck her happiness. They were the lies of hate and vengeance. And—God help me!—they almost succeeded.'

'Lies?' the boy repeated, in a husky whisper, his mind in a turmoil.

'Has it ever occurred to you, Dan,' the old man continued, softly, 'why I have always avoided my own kind—why I was bitter and selfish and merciless? . . . Twenty years ago I was like you—idealistic, believing. I, too, loved someone who meant the entire world to me.

'She was the symbol of everything beautiful and holy; she took the place of my own soul . . . And then—she deserted me, humiliated me, robbed me. A child had just been born to us, and she even deserted that child.

'I broke down, and was out of my mind for a week. When consciousness returned I was another being. I was poisoned with a deadly hatred. From that day to this I have lived in a world of venomous shadows.

'I hated the child as I did the mother; all the awful bitterness in my nature was focused on this offspring of the woman who had wronged me. I paid a poor family to adopt it and raise it as their own. I could not bear the sight of it, but I wanted the child to suffer, as I was suffering.'

He raised his eyes to the boy, who stood watching him in a dazed wonderment.

'Now you know, Dan,' he added, brokenly. 'Ruth is my daughter . . . And when I saw happiness coming to her through your love, I hated you, too, and planned to turn that happiness into tragedy—to make you both suffer.' His voice trailed off and his head fell forward on his breast.

After a tense silence old Trask looked up again. 'I planned it all,' he went on humbly. 'I knew your nature—it was so like mine in the old days. I knew what the purity of the girl meant to you, and how you would react to my insinuations. I even gave you the money so that the woman who you thought was Ruth's mother could take it from you as I had instructed her.'

'And—Seldridge's suit?' faltered the boy.

'It was another girl he was suing,' the old lawyer explained. 'I had the papers copied, with Ruth's name substituted. It was those I gave to you.'

'But—how did you dare?' Felton demanded, incredulously. 'How did you know I wouldn't go to her and discover your—deception?'

'I knew you too well, Dan,' the other told him. 'And I had already carefully sown the poison seed of doubt in your mind. Moreover, when she was ill I myself had her sent away. I knew what the effect of it all would be on you—that you'd go, too, before she returned. Hadn't I myself once passed through the same horror?'

'But why—why didn't she answer my letter?' the boy cried, in an agony of despair. 'Why didn't she explain?'

Trask drew himself up.

'Explain!' he retorted. 'After the accusing, terrible note you wrote her? What of her pride, Dan? Could any girl explain after those words of yours?'

'God!' breathed the boy. 'Of course not! But how I must have made her suffer.'

'It was I who did it all, Dan,' the other confessed. 'But, thank God, I was able to tell you! Last night I was afraid I couldn't do it. Now you see why you must go to her.' He rose unsteadily and stood before the unhappy boy, his wrinkled old face radiant with a new light.

'How can I go to her,' Felton groaned, 'after what I have done? How can she ever forgive me?'

'She will forgive you, Dan,' the old man told him. 'She loves you—and she will understand.'

'But why did she refuse my love weeks ago?' the boy persisted, fearing to accept too fully the wonder of this new and unexpected revelation.

'She didn't reject it,' the other answered. 'She knew how young you were and she wanted you to be sure—so that you would never suffer. It was the unselfishness of her love.'

'How can you—know about—these things?' Felton breathed, wonderingly.

'I know many things tonight, Dan, that I never knew before,' the other answered. 'That's why I had to come—to tell you the truth—to atone.' He moved towards the door. 'Come, Dan,' he urged, gently. Felton no longer hesitated. His sense of bewildered amazement now turned into nervous eagerness. A great longing for the girl took hold of him. Hurriedly crossing the room he held the door open for Trask to pass out and followed him down the stairs, his heart beating violently.

On reaching the pavement the old lawyer paused. 'Try to forgive me, Dan,' he said, and with a last appealing look at the boy he turned and walked away down the shadowy street.

When Felton reached the arbour he found the girl with her head bowed in her arms. She heard him approach and looked up in startled and incredulous wonder. He moved towards her, trying to speak, but no words would come, and he fell on his knees, hiding his face in her lap and sobbing like a child.

'Ruth—forgive me!' he whispered, looking up at her through a mist of tears. 'I know the truth—at last. And, oh! Try to love me—to forget the wrong I have done you.'

The girl drew him up beside her, and the silence that followed was pregnant with the tenderness of love and forgiveness.

They walked home in silence, and even when she lifted her lips to his for a last goodnight kiss, no word was spoken. Yet each knew the things which the other's heart was saying.

The following morning Felton returned to the office.

Approaching Henderson, the chief clerk, he enquired casually if Trask had come in yet.

'You—haven't heard?' the other asked, in a slightly incredulous tone. 'Mr Trask is dead. I thought, of course, you knew. It was his heart.' He hesitated a moment. 'Then perhaps you don't know, either, that he left you everything he had.'

'I—didn't know,' Felton stammered. 'Thank you, Henderson.' And he at once hastened out of the office.

He stood in the street for several minutes trying to adjust his mind to this unexpected and tragic turn of events. Then he hailed a taxicab and drove at once to Trask's residence.

He was admitted by the old butler, who, without a word, solemnly led him upstairs. In the upper hallway he was met by a nurse; and a moment later he was standing with her beside the old-fashioned canopied bed whereon lay the man who had so long been his enemy. Trask appeared merely to have fallen into a peaceful slumber.

Felton stood for a moment looking down at him. Then he remarked softly to the nurse: 'It's hard to believe he is dead when I saw him only last night, apparently well.'

'You are mistaken about seeing him last night,' the nurse rejoined. 'He was stricken at the office two days ago and has been confined to bed ever since.'

A chill ran over Felton. 'But—I thought—I saw him—late last night.'

'Mr Trask lapsed into a coma early last evening,' the nurse informed him in a matter-of-fact tone. 'I was here at the time. He died without regaining consciousness.'

Felton did not move, and it was several moments before he could speak.

'Just—what time,' he asked, 'did Mr Trask die?'

He was trembling as the nurse picked up the chart from the

small table at the head of the bed and run her eye down the entries.

'He died,' she announced, 'at exactly 12.20 this morning.'

Several minutes of silence followed Dr Saville's story. At length Coberly turned towards the doctor.

'I just don't understand about the will,' he said. 'How did Trask happen to change it before—before he—found out?'

'That was the crux of the whole affair,' Dr Saville answered. 'When I arrived that last evening—about eight, I should say— Trask beckoned me to him. He was sinking pretty fast. It was an aneurysm; and he had already entered a little way into the shadows—perhaps just far enough to see and understand certain things.

'"Doctor," he said, "I've got something I must straighten out before it's too late. I've done a great run and I must set it right."

'Then he made me send for Henderson, and he drew up a new will. The effort tired him, and he lay for a while barely breathing. I thought it was the final coma, but his lips began to move slightly and I bent over him.

'"The will was only part of—my atonement," he murmured, faintly. "The rest—you must do for me . . . I—can't go myself— and the boy must know—the truth. Go to him, doctor—tell him I sent you—and explain to him—"

'But he never finished telling me what it was he wanted me to do. The shadows had to come too quickly, and he dropped into unconsciousness.'

Dr Saville paused a moment and then added:

'As I see it, Trask passed out of this life without being able to tell me just how I could help him right this great wrong he had done. And so he had to do it himself—somehow.'

S. S. VAN DINE

'S. S. Van Dine' was the pseudonym of Willard Huntington Wright (1887–1939), art critic, philosopher and champion breeder of Scottie dogs. Wright was born in 1888 in Charlottesville, Virginia, the son of relatively wealthy parents. He was fiercely intelligent and in 1906 he went to Harvard. However, he came down a year later, claiming that 'they had nothing more to teach me'. His first story had been published in 1906 and, after studying art for a year in Paris, he returned to America where in 1907 he married Katharine Belle Boynton, with whom he would have a daughter, and also became literary editor of the *Los Angeles Times*. Three years later he was among the journalists who escaped when the newspapers' offices were destroyed with dynamite, killing 21 staff.

As well as conducting interviews and delivering a regular column on 'New Books and Book News', Wright wrote for the *Times* on all sorts of literary subjects, the most significant of which was undoubtedly a piece lauding a book by H. L. Mencken: it was subsequently through Mencken's influence—and an incendiary essay on Los Angeles—that in 1913 Wright became editor of the prestigious *Smart Set* magazine at the age of only 25. A precocious talent, he was also in demand as a public speaker on literary matters and, more contentiously, on subjects such as the advantages of stupidity in dramatic censorship and England's continuing 'intellectual colonisation' of

America as well as women's suffrage, which Wright vehemently opposed. He also reviewed books and theatre for *Town Topics* and other journals like the *North American Review* while remaining editor of the *Smart Set* until he was sacked in 1914.

1914 also saw the publication of *Europe after 8:15*, in which he wrote about Vienna and London while other cities were considered by his co-authors, H. L. Mencken and George Jean Nathan, then the *Smart Set's* theatre critic; the three had collaborated before for the *Smart Set* under the pen name 'Owen Hatteras'. Other books followed, including *Modern Painting: Its Tendency and Meaning* (1915) and *What Nietsche Taught* (1915), as well as an unpleasantly misogynistic novel *The Man of Promise* (1916) and a series of short crime stories under the pseudonym 'Albert Otis', named for General Harrison Otis, former editor of the *Los Angeles Times*. Another book *Misinforming a Nation* (1917) criticised America's entry into the First World War, prompting some of his former colleagues to shun him, and towards the end of the decade this and various other issues led him to take up drugs.

While Wright worked as literary editor of the *New York Evening Mail* and wrote for magazines such as *Harper's Bazaar* and *International Studio*, his health declined. In 1923, after the publication of his book *The Future of Painting*, he suffered a complete breakdown and the story goes that his psychiatrist— or was it his doctor?—allowed him nothing more stimulating than detective stories which the patient read avidly for the next two years—or was it three?—before deciding that he could do better.

For what would become an immensely successful series of books, Wright adopted a pen name because he felt that 'detective stories come under the head of froth and frivolity' and so might damage his reputation as a serious critic. And so 'S. S. Van Dine' was born. When *The Benson Murder Case* (1926) was published—on the 13th of October, as all of the Van Dine novels would be—the publishers stated that Van Dine was a Harvard graduate, which Wright most certainly was not, and that Van Dine was also 'not only an expert in criminal psychology and in the various Continental and American methods of crime detection but a thorough student of the literature of crime both historical and fictional . . . for many years . . . collecting material and adapting it to detective form for his new series', which at least was partly true.

An untiring self-publicist, Wright made public appearances as Van Dine and also used the name for numerous newspaper and magazine articles in which the fictional Philo Vance analysed notorious non-fictional crimes such as the infamous Hall-Mills murders of 1922. In parallel, under his own name, Wright edited *The Great Detective Stories* (1927), an excellent anthology whose publication fuelled speculation that the famous critic and the reclusive author were one and the same, which was revealed in 1928 by Harry Hansen of the *New York World* not long after Wright, as Van Dine, had prescribed a set of rules for detective stories in *The American* magazine.

In 1929, with the popularity of the Philo Vance stories fuelled by William Powell's portrayal in the films *The Canary Murder Case* (1929) and *The Greene Murder Case* (1929), Wright took self-promotion to a new level when, as Van Dine, he agreed to serve as Police Commissioner of Bradley Beach, New Jersey. Expecting a sinecure, he was shocked when, not long after his appointment, a local man was murdered and he found he was expected to lead the investigation. With newspapers challenging S. S. Van Dine to solve what they termed 'The Pajama Murder Case', Willard Huntington Wright stepped down.

In 1930, not long after the divorce from his first wife, Wright married again, this time to the painter Eleanor Rulapaugh. As Van Dine, while continuing to write the Philo Vance novels, Wright also produced scenarios for twelve 'two-reel detective stories', which were developed into scripts by Burnet Hershey.

The films feature the bullying Inspector Carr and Dr Amos Crabtree, a psychology professor; and the scripts of some were published in cartoon form with Philo Vance as the sleuth.

Almost one hundred years after the publication of the first of Philo Vance's twelve murder cases, the detective's affectations have dated badly and even as early as 1931 the character was ridiculed—Ogden Nash spoke for many when he joked that 'Philo Vance needs a kick in the pance'. Undoubtedly, the quality of the books diminishes, albeit erratically, and the last two—*The Gracie Allen Murder Case* (1938) and *The Winter Murder Case* (1939)—are little more than padded scenarios for films starring, respectively, the comedienne Gracie Allen and the ice skating champion Sonja Henje.

Nonetheless, the novels of S. S. Van Dine—at least the early titles—remain classic puzzles of Golden Age detection and Willard Huntington Wright one of the most important figures in the history of the American detective story.

Wright's health continued to decline through the 1930s and he died of a heart attack in New York in April 1939.

'The Atonement' was first published, as by Willard Huntington Wright, in *The Toronto Star Weekly*, 9 March 1929.

DISPOSSESSION

C. H. B. Kitchin

I

July. Two hours after midnight. The small windows of the first-floor room of 15, Cherry Lane, Chelsea, were wide open, but the blue curtains, closely drawn behind them, were shaken by no breeze. The night was hot in the street, and even hotter in the dark bedroom. Flat on its back, on the middle of an old four-poster bed, lay the body of Harry Duke, still as a corpse, and almost as cold.

Suddenly a muscle twitched beneath the sheets. The body grew warmer. A leg stirred, then a hand. The spine and loins shuddered. Drops of sweat crept through the skin. The mouth opened and gasped. An eyelid fluttered. Then the whole body heaved, while two brown hands jerked upwards over the chest and with one strong movement flung the bedclothes aside. The head shot forward. The unseeing eyes opened widely. The breath came quickly and violently.

Meanwhile the buried mind had taken shape, and struggled painfully upwards like a seed lying deep down in the earth and putting out a frail shoot past strata of peculiar perils. Each moment new visions pressed upon it, while old fears, writhing in sudden coils from a limbo of the brain, would have encircled it and dragged it down, had not the steady impulse of a growing will urged it onwards. Half an hour later, the man got out of bed and, tottering to the door, switched on the light. At the sight of himself in a long mirror he stood for some minutes in bewilderment, and then, stripping off the silk pyjamas still drenched in sweat, looked with hesitant pride at his naked body, felt one hand with another, caressed with a lover's fingers his lips, moustache and eyes, and turning himself this way and that, as if the glass had never before reflected such an image, stroked trunk and arms and legs. Yet even while he surveyed himself and rejoiced so strangely in his strength, a dizziness came over him, and scarce had he staggered on to the bed, before the whole room swam round him and his eyes shut as if never to open. In vain he grappled with his wandering mind, summoning all his wits to consider where he was, and the plans which were still to be made. His senses ebbed away, and left the body as it had been before, quiet and untormented and almost dead.

II

Harry Duke woke at eleven. By five minutes past, he had realised that the electric light was burning, that his pyjamas were lying on the floor and that he was hungry and unaccountably tired. He wondered, also, why the alarm clock had not roused him at eight. He had not expected to be called, as the couple who attended to him had gone for their holiday and he had counted on being well able to look after himself for one night. But it was irritating to have missed the boat train, even though there were other services which he could take, and the hour of his arrival at Wimereux was of no great importance.

He went to the bathroom and lit the geyser. While the water was being heated, he felt so ravenous that he went downstairs in search of food. There were some biscuits in a canister in the sitting-room, and he ate them greedily, deciding to have a proper meal in a restaurant as soon as he had dressed. On his way back through the hall, he noticed two newspapers in the letter-box. He expected one; but why two? He hoped the Dennisons had remembered to stop the papers while he was away. He couldn't bother to go himself to the newsagent that morning. After all, a penny a day for ten days is only tenpence. Still, tenpence wasted . . . Whatever had possessed the boy to leave two papers? With a jerk he pulled them through the slit in the door, and looked at them on the way upstairs. A glance showed him that they were different issues of the same paper. The headlines were not the same. July 25, and July 26. He'd had yesterday's paper— but July 26—what could it mean? There must be a mistake. July 26 was tomorrow—Friday, July 26. Today was Thursday. On Wednesday, the night before, the Dennisons had left. This was Thursday, the day he was to go to Wimereux. On Friday he'd arranged to play golf with Grimwade's party.

After a little time, it dawned on him that he had overslept not by a few minutes, but by more than twenty-four hours.

He lay in the bath and groaned. This time there was no escaping it. He was not well. He was—a moment's horror seized him. What could he do? How could he go on hiding it? What would be the end? He was unused to mental suffering, and longed suddenly for someone to give him sympathy, for contact with another person, for an almost bodily comfort. Only one person had seemed able to understand his trouble, even to guess that he had one—that spectacled girl, Joan Averil, a damned inquisitive little fool. So far, she had been the only one to take him at a disadvantage, to realise the crisis when it came. He used the word 'crisis' to describe one of a series of events which lay outside the process of his normal life. It was only lately that he had classed them together as a series. Having no gift for introspection, he had been very slow to notice any progress or similarity in the accidents which for the past eight months had been pursuing him. But now he was forced to 'look facts in the face', to try to understand himself, to learn what it was that had to be cured, if cure there was.

He dried himself and, as he dressed, looked at tomorrow's paper. 'Still no sign,' he read, 'of missing architect. Thousand pounds reward offered by solicitors.' In his bedroom, he unlocked a drawer and brought out a bundle of manuscript, the very writing of which seemed full of fear and shame. The composition dated from his most serious attempt to take stock of himself—after the last crisis. At best, writing did not come easily to him.

The first page was headed *October 26th*, and the record was as follows:

'Dined with Embley and his wife and Mrs Pole. About 10.30 went to party given by man called Grover (?) in St John's Wood. Dancing and charades. E. said it would show me what Bohemian society was, though I must be careful not to use the word. I soon got too drunk to be shocked—not that I should have been if I'd kept sober. At 1.30 a good many people left and a man and a woman, whose names I never caught, proposed we should go round to a party in the Adelphi. Got separated from the E.s and Mrs P., and faintly remember driving in a taxi with three women and another man. My head was rather clearer on arriving and I jibbed at going in, but it seemed rude to back out of it. The people at the new place were a very odd crew. I didn't know any of them and shouldn't recognise them again. There was some gambling, in which I felt too drunk to join, and some of the people seemed to be dressing and undressing and acting charades on their own. More drink. I was completely knocked out, and the last thing I remember is falling flat on a kind of divan, and someone saying, "Come on, old chap, I'll see you home."

'I awoke in my own bed the next day—feeling like death. My latch-key was on the dressing-table. I was too ill to get up, and as I felt even worse at night, I told Dennison to fetch a doctor. God knows I'd been drunk often enough before, but never like this. I thought I must have been poisoned—or doped. The doctor—a breezy fool—said there was nothing the matter with me except the obvious, and gave me some medicine. That night I had awful nightmares, which I can't remember. The day afterwards I felt better, and got up. For about a week I had appalling dreams every night, though there seemed nothing the matter with me by day. I called in the doctor again, and he still didn't take me seriously. "Constitution of an ox," he said, and then murmured something about burning the candle at both ends. I paid him off, and decided to get better by myself. For a time I did.'

December 2nd.

'I'd been living very soberly—nothing in the nature of a binge for weeks, no worries to speak of. Physically quite fit. Dennison called me as usual, he said, and couldn't awaken me. I slept till three, and woke up in a sweat, feeling that something had happened. All the energy seemed to have been sucked out of me, and there was a kind of whirling at the back of my head, as if I was a corkscrew being drawn backwards through putty. I didn't want to eat, or read, or see anyone, and yet was terrified of going to sleep. When I did fall asleep, nothing happened. Awoke the next day feeling weak but better. Day after, quite well.'

December 15th.

'Same as December 2nd, but worse. Went to specialist to be overhauled. Cheered up on hearing there was absolutely nothing wrong with me.'

December 23rd.

'Went to the Partingtons for Christmas. The usual crowd, except for a Miss Averil whom I hadn't met before—somebody's odd relation. Spectacles, no S.A., and very intelligent. She seemed to find me interesting.'

Christmas Eve.

'After dinner we had some bridge and then all sat round
the fire talking and drinking punch. A cheery scene, holly and
all that. Somebody told a ghost story or two, rather poor ones,
and then it was suggested that we should take turns in telling
what we thought was the most thrilling event in our lives.
Edgar P. began with his old yarn about the bomb at the Gare
du Nord. Phoebe produced an affair with a burglar, Jimmy
Hale another ghost, and so on. Then it came to my turn, and
I was racking my brains to see if I couldn't improve on my
story of the puff adder, when the room swam round in circles,
and I had the corkscrew feeling again, but somehow reversed.
I managed to get out a few words, and then everything became
a blank.

'N.B. The punch was fairly strong, and the room pretty hot,
but I'll guarantee I've as good a head as most people, and I've
never before found myself sensitive to heat or cold.

'I was naturally rather upset next day, and apologised to P.
after breakfast. He seemed surprised and said he hadn't noticed
anything unusual. "How did I get to bed, then?" I asked. "Why,
by walking upstairs, I suppose," he said. I pressed him a little
further, but he seemed so convinced, in his dull way, that I
hadn't done anything out of the ordinary, that I let the matter
rest. He suggested I'd been having a nightmare as a result of
the punch, and I half agreed with him.

'On Christmas afternoon I found myself alone with Miss
Averil in the library. She made me feel uncomfortable, and I
tried to escape, but couldn't.

'"What regiment were you with during the war?" she asked
me suddenly. I told her, and she went on to ask if I'd ever been
attached to the Third Middlesex Rangers. I said I hadn't, and
more than that, that I'd never even come across anyone who
had. I was a little annoyed by her curiosity, and was afraid she
was going to bring out some appallingly sentimental memory,

or tell me that I was the image of her dead fiancé. But she hadn't finished yet, and asked me several other questions. Where was I during the war? Partly in England and partly in France. Whereabouts in France? All over the place: Loos, Vimy, Arras, Fauquissart, Ypres, Cambrai, etc. Was I ever at Miraumont? No, never. It was one of the few bits of the line I'd given a miss to. "But in your story," she said, "on which I congratulate you, you specially mentioned a dug-out beyond the front line between Miraumont and Grandcourt." "I was never nearer either than Albert," I said, and went on to ask her what kind of a story I'd told. "D'you mean to say you don't remember?" "I don't. I'm afraid the punch must have gone to my head. I suppose it was absolute rot." "Not at all," she replied. "Well then, what was it?" She seemed unwilling to tell me just then, and before I had time to get it out of her we were interrupted. She had to go to London that night, and all she managed to say to me before she left the house was: "Give me your address and I'll write to you." I gave her my card, and said good-bye, hoping that I should neither see her nor hear from her again.

'The rest of the visit was quite ordinary, and I tried to put the business of Christmas Eve out of my mind.'

Next in the bundle of manuscript came some sheets of blue note-paper covered with a careful and feminine hand.

January 4th.

Dear Mr Duke,

In case you have really forgotten the amazing story you told us on Christmas Eve, I send it you now. I have a good memory, and have tried to use your own phrases. You told it well. Indeed—forgive me—I think you will find the style hard to recognise.

I feel I understand something about you that you don't. If I can help you at any time, I shall be very glad to do so.

I live normally with my parents in Flat 50, Clarence House,
Park Lane.
　　Yours sincerely,
　　Joan Averil.

Mr Duke's Story

'In January 1917, I was a junior subaltern with the 3rd Middlesex Rangers. The battalion had charge of a vast and vague area of mud in the Somme district. The whereabouts of the enemy's lines was hardly known. All landmarks had been destroyed, and what with the mist that overhung the desolate region and the absence of all tracks, means of communication were hazardous and primitive.

'With a few men, I was in charge of an outpost, the position of which was at the time recorded on none of our maps, some-where between two ruinous areas which had once been the villages of Miraumont and Grandcourt. Apart from visits to my chilled and sodden sentries, I had little to do—or rather, I did little; for I dare say I could have found many duties had I sought them. The deep dug-out left to us by the retreating enemy, in which I spent my idle hours, was divided into two parts, separated by a hanging blanket. My men lived in the larger and I in the smaller, which was so small that, though they were eight or nine, and I was only one, I was almost as cramped for room as they.

'One morning, before daybreak, my sergeant was shot in a sudden burst of machine-gun fire while on patrol. The men with him brought the body to the dug-out and I told them to let it rest in my cell till night; for it was impossible to carry it back to our headquarters during daylight.

'The body lay on the floor, covered by a waterproof sheet, and I on a wire trestle beside it. I had no horror of corpses that had met with a clean death. Indeed, it seemed companionable to have it there, and before long I lifted the waterproof sheet and looked at what lay beneath with sad curiosity. The only sign of the wound was a little stain on the tunic near the heart. Except for the absence of all breathing, you would have taken the body for that of a man who was asleep.

'It was a fine sergeant we had lost—a little stupid, but brave and magnificently strong. I remembered having seen him stripped at the baths, and noticing his healthy skin and well-built powerful limbs. And now, as I looked at his calm face, it was not without a sense of jealous inferiority that I thought of my own poor body, stunted and thin, never free from some ache or uneasiness. You laugh as I say this, *but perhaps I am not the man I seem.* How wretchedly unjust, I thought, that I should go through life burdened with this corpse of mine, this miserable mass of nerves and skin perpetually hampering the exercise of my will and brain, and destined one day to harry me to death. Why could I not fall asleep and find myself rid of it, wake up as a new creature with a body equal in vigour to my mind? Must it be that these legs and arms beside me—and as the thought came to me, I stroked them gently—that firm flesh, those splendid muscles, still fully fit for living, even though dead, should moulder into decay and no use be found for them? So great was my disgust with Nature's law, so intense my despair at falling so far short of a perfection which, strangely enough, seemed almost attainable, that a mood of reckless agony came over me, and, hardly knowing what I did, I stretched myself out over the sergeant's body, my mouth on his mouth, my legs along his legs, as Elisha stretched himself upon the Shunammite's son whom he raised from the dead . . .

'When I opened my eyes, it was my own face, pale and horrible, that I saw above me, my own body that lay on the top of me, but when I thrust it away, it was the sergeant's hand that moved. Triumphant in my new form, I stood up, and, gazing with hatred at the prostrate body that had been mine, I kicked it heavily in the ribs and covered it with the waterproof sheet that had covered the sergeant's body. Then, being still somewhat unsteady on my new-found legs, I sat down on the floor, lay back and laughed with joy.

'An hour later, my servant found me, bruised and numb, under the waterproof sheet.'

III

At this point Duke pushed the bundle of papers aside, and lit a cigarette with nervous fingers. The story, not being written by himself, still moved him. When he had first received it, he had almost been amused. Later, when chastened by the next 'crisis', he had written a short note to the sender, begging her not to bewilder him any more. Her reply, from the South of France, assured him that the story was substantially as he had told it. Then why, he had wondered, if by any strange chance this was the truth, had none of the others spoken to him about it? Of course, they were a dull and stupid crowd. Perhaps they had all, except for the one attentive listener, been half asleep, half drunk, and hadn't understood what he was saying—or if they had, disliked it and did not wish to mention it again.

One thing reassured him. The story was objectively untrue. Apart from regimental records, there were many living people who could vouch for his never having been near Miraumont and Grandcourt. At the beginning of 1917, he had been a company commander in a battalion stationed near Merville. This was a crumb of comfort, but his telling of the story, and its reference to himself, if any, was still mysterious. Was it a dream? Had he talked in his sleep? Perhaps. But he had had too many strange dreams to feel easy about even them.

Forgetting the need of breakfast, he walked round his bedroom in agitation. The newspaper— 'tomorrow's' news-paper—was lying on a chair, and caught his eye. He picked it up and read it as he walked.

'Still no sign of missing architect. Thousand pounds offered by solicitors . . .

'The whereabouts of Mr de Milas are still unknown. He was last seen at his residence, 22, Amboyne Road, Adelphi Terrace, by his housekeeper, Mrs Garley, about half-past two on Wednesday afternoon. He was then going upstairs to rest in his bedroom. Mrs Garley first became uneasy at nine o'clock, when a manservant, sent to the bedroom, reported that it was empty.

'Mr de Milas is a gentleman of considerable means and somewhat eccentric habits. He is described as an architect, but it is not known when or where he exercised that profession. He served with the infantry during the war, and his age is now about forty-five. For some time his health has given cause for anxiety.'

Anxiety, anxiety, anxiety, thought Duke, throwing the paper down in disgust. Was there no escape from trouble, other people's and one's own? Was he never to get back to ordinary life, cheerful society, cards, games and horses? How had this blight come upon him, this train of odd symptoms that seemed to pursue him from within, drawing him inwards, making him think too much about himself? Yet it had to be faced. He was worse, not better. With a sigh, he sat down and turned again to the manuscript:

February 16th.

'I was to ride Lady Foyle's Halsettia in the Lauderbrake Steeplechase. A year ago I came in third on Diamond Claw, and this year hoped to win. The evening of the day before the race I had a feeling that something was wrong. A bad night, but no dream that I can remember. Felt very low at breakfast. Took my temperature. Normal. Very angry with myself. Wondered if it was simply funk, though I'd never been taken that way before. Decided to force myself to carry on, even if I broke my neck. Anything's better than being out of things.

11 a.m. violent headache. Had to go to bed, in great pain. Wired unwell. Headache easier by 4 p.m. Fit as a fiddle by 6. Johnson, who rode instead of me, was thrown and killed at the second jump. Outcry in papers about course being too dangerous.'

March 25th.
'Awoke very late. Dazed. Felt like a sleep-walker. Early to bed.'

March 26th.
'Too feeble to get up. Dozed most of the day. Refused to have doctor sent for.'

March 27th.
'The same. At night an extraordinary dream. These are the only bits I can remember.

'I seemed to be in a kind of orderly-room—bare boards and tables, and army forms, etc. Through holes in the wall, I could see wild flowers bending in the wind. The sun was setting, and I got caught in a long red ray, which made me unable to turn round. Suddenly a voice—behind me or in the ceiling—said, "Is it impossible for us to get on better?" "Who are you?" I asked. "Can't you see?" I made a great effort and turned round, but could see no one.

'I went out into the fields, and all at once the voice said again, "You must take me for granted without seeing me, then. You laugh, *but I am not the man I seem.* After all, what have I done to you? I have caused you really so little pain. Of course, I apologise for the Christmas joke. But I saved your life, though you may not know it. Oh, don't think I'm a clairvoyant. You are a good rider and might perhaps not have been killed. But you were too valuable for me to take the risk."

'The voice went on speaking for a long time, till I found myself alone with someone in the room in the Adelphi where the party of October 26th was given. "If ever you want a refuge," the voice said, "you can have what I can provide. Even you might be ill, or in trouble. Look!" At this point I felt as if I was going to learn an amazing secret, but the room was suddenly draped in thick red curtains, which opened and closed, showing me little pieces of something and blotting it out again. I can't remember what it was that I was so eager to see, but each time I looked, I had the sensation that I was escaping from my body. Then the curtains swooped down on me and smothered me till I died. After my death, which wasn't painful, I looked into the orderly-room, and saw myself lying on the table. I longed terribly to be alive again, and took my body in my arms, intending to carry it home, but wherever I went, I found red curtains in the way. Then the voice spoke again, but I have forgotten what it said.

'Woke up very late the next day, weak, but better.'

April 2nd.

'To Vinton, nerve-specialist. Talked a lot about dual personalities and psycho-analysis. Don't trust him.'

April 6th.

'Hear that Phillips—poor chap—had been to Vinton for two months before he committed suicide. Panicked, and decided not to go to V. again.'

May 18th.

'No crisis, but since I've decided to keep notes on my "case", had better put this down. Met Miss Averil, at the Jordans' party— only for a few minutes. She asked me if I had been telling any more stories. I felt very awkward, and she saw it. Suddenly I blurted out, "Do you think I have a double personality?" She said, "No, not exactly, in the ordinary sense of the words. Won't you tell me more about your trouble?" Then we were interrupted, and feeling a fool, I managed to slip away.'

June 4th and 5th.

'Very like March 4th, 5th and 6th, but no dream. Worried on "recovering", whether I'm becoming different from what I was. In my body, I feel as well as I ever did, but I can't be so certain of my mind. Remembered Jekyll and Hyde, which frightened me. If I have a "double personality", can anything be done about it? But Miss A. seemed to think it wasn't that. What does she know about these things?'

IV

For luncheon, he had gone to a quiet restaurant near his house. He had given up all intention of going to France, but had made no other plans. He could think of nothing but himself, his mind and his body, and something that seemed to be occurring in both of them. As he walked back home, he noticed the newspaper placards. 'Missing architect still untraced.'

When he reached his house, he had a strong impulse to go to bed, but was afraid to do so. He felt himself to be in a state receptive of extraordinary influences. There was a continual drag on his brain, paralysing his capacity for action and urging him to look inwards. More and more, he seemed to be dreaming, and wondered how it is that we ever know the difference between drams and waking life. Some of his thoughts seemed to be his own, and others the product of an alien mind. These would come suddenly, in the midst of his own mental sentences, interrupting them as a heckler might interrupt an orator. '*Give in, give in. Cease to struggle,*' an inner voice kept saying, and again with an insidious sweetness, '*Come with me. Follow me. Find where I am.*'

At four o'clock, when for a few moments the tension relaxed, he looked out Miss Averil's number in the telephone book.

'Miss Averil?'

'Yes.'

'My name is Duke.'

'I remember. What is it?'

'I'm in great trouble. I need someone to help me, badly. I'm slipping away—slipping out of myself. Can you help me?'

'I'm in bed, recovering from measles—not ill, but infectious. Tell me everything from the beginning.'

'Wait a minute then. I've got some stuff written down, which I could read you.'

He put down the receiver, and went upstairs.

'Come with me. Follow me. Find where I am.'

He looked for his manuscript in the wrong drawer.

'Give in. Give in. Let yourself go. Sleep, while I wake.'

At length he found the manuscript, and went downstairs: 'Miss Averil?'

There was no answer. He looked hurriedly in the directory and rang up again.

'Can Mr Duke speak to Miss Averil, please?'

'Speak to whom?' asked the voice of an old woman.

'Miss Averil.'

'I'm afraid you've got the wrong number. This is Mr de Milas's house.'

'Is there any news of Mr de Milas?'

'Who is that speaking, please?'

Horrified, he rang off.

A newspaper boy was shouting in the street. Duke went to the door, bought a paper, and took it with him to the telephone. 'Three o'clock results.' ... *'Follow me. Find me* ... 'Missing Architect . . . Mrs Garley admitted that she had been surprised by her master's absence from the house on one or two previous occasions, and on being pressed for the dates of these, identified one of them with February 16th, which she remembered because it was the day of the Lauderbrake Steeplechase. Her nephew had persuaded her to put five shillings on Halsettia, the ill-fated horse which was killed with its rider, Captain Johnson. But her master had walked into the dining-room. at about nine o'clock that evening, and she had thought no more of the matter . . .'

'*Follow me. Follow me. Follow me home.*'

'Mr de Milas also, it seems, disappeared towards the end of March. It is true he had told Mrs Garley that he might find it necessary to be absent from the house for a time, but as he seemed far from well, and gave no instructions about his luggage, she was uneasy till she saw him sitting in the drawing-room at tea-time three days later . . .'

'*Sleep, while I wake.*'

'He was also away on the 4th and 5th of June, but as he had packed a small hand-bag, she felt no anxiety. The strangest part of the mystery is that on none of these occasions did Mrs Garley see her master leave his house or return to it . . .'

'*You laugh, but you are not the man you seem.*'

Very quietly, Duke picked up the telephone receiver, and asked for a number.

'Can I speak to Miss Averil, please?'

'This is 22, Amboyne Road, Mr de Milas's house. Who is that speaking please?'

'I am the missing architect, Mr de Milas.'

'Oh, sir, is that you? This is Mrs Garley speaking, sir. Dr Polder made me notify the police the day before yesterday, that you were missing from home. We've all been very anxious about you, sir.'

'I shall soon be home.'

'I'm sure I'm very glad to hear that, sir. We've—'

He put down the receiver, went up to his bedroom, and lay on the bed. A force seemed to be entering him, in spiral fashion like a corkscrew, while at the same time his normal will drained away, leaving the body without resistance. And yet at that very moment he had a sense, that he had never had before, of the preciousness of his body, its vigour and the perfection of all its organs. 'This is your treasure,' a voice seemed to murmur, 'this is what you can give me. Forget your foolish little mind with its racing debts, its games of golf, its dances. Be generous to me, and give all you can freely. I have great need of you.'

Then, after a period of silence during which Duke opened his eyes and saw the familiar things in the room shrinking and dwindling away, a rhythmical whisper seemed to flow gently along his spine. At first the words, if they were words, were too indistinct for him to catch, and sounded like a mere pulsation in common time. But soon the beat quickened, and became more staccato and articulate. 'Go and find me. Go and find me. Leave this body. Go to mine. Go to mine. Leave this body free for me.' The words were repeated monotonously, and at the same time Duke seemed to assent of his own volition and to be persuading himself to yield. 'After all,' he thought, 'why shouldn't I do as he asks, poor devil? Why shouldn't I give him a chance? He may make better use of me than I can. Come! I'm ready.'

But as if even this generous submission were not enough, the rhythm of the summons grew suddenly more imperious, irregular and desperate. 'Let me in. The time is so short. Let me in Your place is in the black box, in the cupboard. Go and hide there, in what I'm leaving you. Five minutes! Only five minutes! Give me yourself for five minutes! The black box in the little room. You've been there before. Go again now, just this once, and save me. Save me, and give me peace. Help! Help! I'm choking . . .'

The last word went through Duke's body as if a claw were tearing him apart. For an instant, he seemed poised on the edge of an unfathomable void, while the smell and touch of clammy flesh came over him and squeezed him together in a small and narrow space. 'The grave,' he thought, 'the grave!' and with a convulsive movement, he threw out his arms and legs.

All at once the rhythm ceased, and he was filled with a sane and miraculous calm. A distant lorry rumbled towards the river. The clock on the mantelpiece ticked gently. Duke opened his eyes and looked at it. Five minutes past six. Then urgently the telephone bell rang downstairs.

'Hello. Is that you at last, Mr Duke? Joan Averil speaking. I've tried eight times to get you.'

They had a long conversation, in which, full of wisdom, she told him what to do.

V

'Missing Architect found.
'Mrs Garley's Extraordinary Story.

'The mystery of the disappearance of Mr de Milas was solved yesterday evening in an amazing and tragic fashion. Mrs Garley states that she was disturbed several times during the afternoon by telephone calls from persons who had, as they thought, recognised Mr de Milas from his photograph in the Press, and were eager to give information as to when and where they had seen him. In each case, Mrs Garley requested the speaker to communicate at once with Mr de Milas's solicitors or the police. Two of the calls, however, were of an unusual nature. On both occasions a man's voice began by asking to speak to a lady, whose name Mrs Garley did not catch. On Mrs Garley's suggestion of a wrong number, the speaker did not ring off at once, but, in his first call asked for news of Mr de Milas, and in his second call announced that he was Mr de Milas himself. It is now thought that the inquiry was a piece of facetiousness on the part of some irresponsible person who had accidentally been given Mr de Milas's number instead of the number he required, and that on a repetition of the same accident, the unknown was so far exasperated as to be guilty of a joke in exceedingly bad taste, pardonable only on the assumption that he was ignorant of the circumstances into which he was intruding.

'No further incident occurred till shortly after seven, when

Dr Polder, who had attended Mr de Milas during his illness, called at the house and asked Mrs Garley if she knew of a black box belonging to her master. It seems that the doctor had been rung up about a quarter to seven by a man who purported to be speaking for Mr de Milas. The speaker had requested him with great urgency to visit Mr de Milas's residence and search it for a black box, which he was to open immediately. He was assured that the opening of the box would throw a light on Mr de Milas's disappearance, and that circumstances might arise in which medical skill would be essential. Garley replied that there was such a box in a big cupboard opening out of Mr de Milas's bedroom. To her knowledge the box-an old-fashioned leather trunk—had not been used or opened for some years. She accompanied Dr Polder to the cupboard in question and saw the box in its usual position. The doctor attempted to lift it into the light, but could not do so owing to its great weight. He then asked Mrs Garley to bring him a candle or lamp, and when she had left the room, he raised the lid of the box, which was unlocked. *Inside, huddled up on some blankets, was the dead body of Mr de Milas.* The body was fully clad, and covered in part by a waterproof sheet such as was used extensively by soldiers during the war . . . It is the opinion of Dr Polder that death occurred about six o'clock the same afternoon, though the body might have been in a trance or state of catalepsy for several hours beforehand.'

Stop Press

'Call to Dr Polder traced to Piccadilly subway.'

So ran the account of the finding of the missing architect as given to the public. Two people alone could have added substantially to it—Harry Duke, who was playing golf at Wimereux, and that devotee of psychical research, Joan Averil, who was recovering from measles in Park Lane. But neither of them cared to do so.

C. H. B KITCHIN

Clifford Henry Benn Kitchin was born at Harrogate in Yorkshire on 17 October 1895. His third name was for his mother, Sarah Ellen Benn; and his first for his father, a prosecution barrister and, in his spare time, a keen chess player and amateur gardener. Both of Clifford's parents wrote: his father had been a journalist and wrote poetry, and Nellie wrote and performed monologues for performance at church events.

Their son, 'Master Cliffie', first appeared in the newspapers aged just three when he was page of honour at the wedding of his aunt Florrie, at which he and the bridesmaids wore 'cream satin frocks, trimmed with lace, and carried bouquets of lilies of the valley'. Around the turn of the century, the family moved to Goyfield House in Felixstowe, Suffolk, and in 1907 they moved again to Bristol where they lived at Cabot House, 50 Clifton Down Road. Clifford and his younger brother John attended Braidlea School in Goodeve Road, Stoke Bishop, before moving to Clifton College. It was at Clifton that Kitchin met the future novelist Leslie Poles Hartley, who would become a lifelong friend and almost invariably give his books an ecstatic review.

Kitchin did well at Clifton, winning an open scholarship in Classics to Exeter College at Oxford University. Aside of his studies and officiating at the annual sports day, he did a little acting, appearing in June 1914 as the gatekeeper of Hades in a scene from

Aristophanes' *The Frogs*, presented as part of the College's annual Guthrie commemoration. After he left Clifton, Kitchin's mother—who was by now a widow—moved with both sons to *Holmwood*, a house in Boar's Hill, Berkshire. Clifford helped John with his education in the expectation that they would both go up to Oxford. However, the First World War intervened and the brothers enlisted. After a brief spell in the Officer Training Corps of the Inns of Court, Kitchin joined the Royal Warwickshire Regiment, serving as a second lieutenant until January 1917 when he was wounded in France. John had joined the Royal Air Force as a lieutenant but on 21 June 1918 he was accidentally killed when starting out on a patrol. The impact on Kitchin of his younger brother's tragically early death, as well as his own war experiences, is clear from his first book. This was *Curtains*, a slim volume of poetry published in 1919 by Blackwell's.

After the war, Kitchin completed his studies and came down in 1920 with a Bachelor of Arts degree. A second volume of poetry followed, entitled *Winged Victory* (1920), which won him praise and favourable comparisons with the French symbolist poets. In 1924, he was called to the Bar at Lincoln's Inn, forty years after his father. While practising, he also began writing in earnest. As well as poetry, he had written several short stories under his own name, and anonymously, for the *Oxford Outlook* and the *Oxford Chronicle & Reading Gazette*. In 1925 he published *Streamers Waving* (1925), an enigmatic novel about an androgynous woman, her love for a mountaineer and her death from a broken heart, worsened by pneumonia. The presentation of the story through a female character was a feint for Kitchin's homosexuality, which became less ambiguously disguised in several of his later, equally elegaic novels.

Kitchin became a stockbroker and moved to London. His next novel *Mr Balcony* (1927) was inspired in part by a childhood encounter at Bexhill, but reviewers drew unfavourable comparisons with the work of Virginia Woolf and Aldous Huxley. Perhaps it was this that led him to attempt a detective story. The result, *Death of My Aunt* (1929) introduced Malcolm Warren, a timid stockbroker who shared his creator's temperament and profession. Warren would go on to appear in three more novels including *Crime at Christmas* (1934), but his first case was his best—in the words of a contemporary reviewer, 'there is a human, ordinary motive for the murder, which still has a touch of surprise in it'. The book was widely praised but Kitchin would come to hate it, balefully referring to as 'that wretched book' and bemoaning the fact that his small output of crime fiction overshadowed the work of which he was genuinely proud. In one of his ten 'serious novels', he sought to satisfy both his muse and the market. This was the excellent *Birthday Party* (1938), wherein a death—which might be an accident, suicide or perhaps even murder—is described in retrospect by four different characters, emulating Wilkie Collins and anticipating crime writers like Agatha Christie and her mystery *Five Little Pigs* (1941).

After Nellie's death in May 1930, Kitchin bought two houses: *The Byletts* in Pembridge, Herefordshire, and *Chiddinghurst*, a smaller house in Chiddingly, Sussex. A frequent visitor to both was Clive Preen, an accountant nine years Kitchin's junior. In Chiddingly, the two men enjoyed village life both serving as vice presidents of the football club, while Kitchin helped to revive the moribund annual flower show, run by the Women's Institute. He was a keen gardener, specialising like his father in roses. He won many prizes for his flowers and vegetables, with his roses and dahlias winning first prizes, as well as his cauliflowers, celery, gooseberries and cooking apples; his 'tinted eggs' fared less well, coming only third.

At the start of the Second World War, Clive Preen's firm moved to Leominster, within easy reach of *The Byletts*, and the two men also spent periods at River House in Mawnan Smith near Falmouth, Cornwall. They planned to retire to the South-West but in 1944, Preen died while staying at the Adelphi Hotel in Liverpool. He left quarter of his estate to. Kitchin, who was by now a very wealthy man. Heartbroken, Kitchin threw himself into local life, taking part in the Mawnan show of garden and farm produce, once again winning prizes, and he served as vice president of the Mawnan Cricket Club. He also belonged to the Falmouth Philatelic Society for which he ran quiz nights, setting and asking the questions as well as providing the prizes. As he had before the war, Kitchin spent time in London where, among other things, he could indulge his eclectic passion for collecting, whether Dutch flower paintings, George II silver, French paperweights, Meissen teapots, books or stamps—his own collection was sold at auction in 1953. Kitchin was an excellent pianist and he enjoyed playing bridge, algebraic puzzles and gambling.

While he spent most of the time in Cornwall or London, Kitchin continued to own *Chiddinghurst* until the early 1950s, when he sold it to the father of the Oscar-winning scriptwriter and novelist Julian Fellowes, who lived there as a child and was told by his parents of Clifford and Clive's 'tremendous parties, one taking the theme of a ship going down . . . Men were hired to stand round the house throwing water against the windows, in rhythm, for the entire evening'.

Kitchin moved to Brighton, where he lived on the King's Road, first at *Embassy Court* and then at *Abbotts*, another block of purpose-built apartments. During the 1950s and '60s, he produced arguably his best books: *The Auction Sale* (1949) is very much a collector's novel, dealing with the lives that lie behind the different lots at the eponymous auction; *The Secret River* (1956) is a story about a tyrannical mother and her daughter; and *The Book of Life* (1971) harks back to Kitchin's childhood holidays in Bexhill and, with echoes of his own inheritance, focuses on a small boy who will one day inherit a fortune.

C. H. B. Kitchin died in Brighton on 2 April 1967 (not the 4th, as misstated in some sources). He left £360,000 (equivalent to over £4,000,000) to Lord Ritchie of Dundee, deputy chairman of the

Stock Exchange, his osteopath John Bond and the author Francis King. His final book *A Short Walk in Williams Park* was published posthumously.

'Dispossession' was first published in Lady Asquith's anthology *Shudders* in 1929.

BLIND GUESS

Valentine Williams

Young Timmie Herron, I decided, was asking for a thick ear. Ever since Sara Carshill's arrival that afternoon, he had scarcely had a word for any of us, least of all for Antonia, his wife. He was whispering to Sara now and making her giggle as she sat crouched on a low stool before the flaming hearth, her tawny head pillowed against his knee.

Timmie would explain that Sara was his guest, that it was his duty to make her feel at home at Herron Place. But that was no excuse for the way he was cutting up, as I could see Antonia was also thinking. Perched on the arm of Jack's chair, she affected to be smiling over an argument that was in full cry between Virginia and Isobel Sprote, on the one hand, and Mark Bendall and the three Air Force youngsters, brother officers of Jimmie's—I knew them only as Bill, Kenneth and Geoffrey—on the other. But I was aware that Antonia was watching her husband and Sara through her long lashes. Her proud and lovely face gave me no clue, but I had known her fiery temper since her childhood, and I asked myself how much of this sort of thing she was willing to put up with. There was Roger Carshill, too; sodden hulk though he was, I wondered what he thought of his wife's carryings on.

Around eleven o'clock, after the Christmas tree in the Long Gallery and some osculatory rough-and-tumble under the mistletoe, we had trooped off to Jack's study to drink punch. We put out the lights and piled in round the elm logs blazing in the huge Tudor fireplace of old rosy brick. It was young Isobel Sprote who started Jack off on the legend of Tiffany's Walk.

Tiffany's Walk is the distinctive feature of Herron Place. It is a covered arcade dating back to the late 17th century, which, in the shape of an E with the central bar missing, makes three sides of a parallelogram at the back of the house, to which it is joined through two small lobbies situated in the north and south wings respectively. With its low, deep-eaved roof carried on massive cross-beams, it affords adequate protection against almost all varieties of English weather, notwithstanding the fact that it is open, through a succession of wide bays, to the air. Within, it is lined with majolica tiles representing, with pleasing *naïveté*, birds and beasts, fishes and flowers, and floored with old red brick.

'I bet you've got a ghost in this topping old house of yours, haven't you, Major Jack?' Isobel piped up—'Major Jack' was what they all called him.

'Indeed we have,' Jack retorted, with proprietorial pride. 'And, what's more, it's a lady and a relative of mine!'

There was an immediate clamour of 'Tell us about her!' Said Antonia, lackadaisically, 'Oh, Jack, you're not going to make us listen to that old story again?'

'Shut up, Antonia!' Virginia cried indignantly. 'Just because you live here . . . Go on, Major Jack,' she encouraged our host. 'Make our flesh creep!'

'You all know Tiffany's Walk,' Jack began. 'It's called after Theophania Herron, an ancestress of mine—Tiffany is an old diminutive of Theophania. She was born in the reign of Charles the Second as an only child, and the legend runs that from birth her face was covered with fine, silky hair, like a spaniel's . . .'

An eruption of 'Ughs' and little feminine squeaks ran round

the circle. 'So that she never appeared in public,' Jack's quiet voice overtoned the hubbub, 'without a thick black veil. When her parents died and she became mistress of this house and estate, she grew more and more sensitive of her horrible disfigurement. To avoid the necessity of showing herself in public, she got a Bologna architect named Bonaventura to build her this arcade. Here it was her habit to promenade the greater part of the day. Then the catastrophe happened. A new steward was engaged, a handsome, strapping fellow, with an eye to the main chance. At any rate, he made up to Aunt Tiffany . . .'

'A-ha!' knowingly. This from Geoffrey, who had his arm about Virginia.

'You can imagine,' Jack pursued, 'the tumult in that maiden breast. She had reconciled herself to the prospect of lifelong spinsterhood, believing that, even with the Herron Place rentroll, no one would want to marry a dog-faced lady of uncertain age. And here was the dashing steward kissing her hands and bringing her posies and pestering her to lift her veil and let him see her face, vowing that his love was proof against anything. Well, she let him have his way at last. But when he looked upon that terrible face, his heart failed him and he fled away and was never heard of again . . .'

'And what happened to poor Tiffany?' Sara Carshill enquired in her caressing voice.

'She became more of a recluse than ever, spending the whole of the day and often half the night in the arcade, the scene of her broken romance. One morning, when the servants went to look for her, they found her, in the long black cloak and veil she always wore, hanging from a beam . . .

'O-ooh!' A shudder rippled through the audience.

'And ever since that day'—our host's voice was deliberately dramatic now—'they say that poor Tiffany walks the arcade by night, sighing and wailing and ringing her hands. And if she encounters any human in her path, she parts her veil and reveals her face, and, so the story goes, the sight is so bloodcurdling that anyone who looks upon it drops dead on the spot . . .'

'Have you ever seen her . . . ?' Isobel broke off, her cheeks aflame. 'Oh, I'm sorry, Major Jack . . .'

He laughed good-humouredly, 'My dear child, I'm spook-proof. No ghost is going to waste her time on me, especially when her trick is mainly visual. But all my family firmly believe in Aunt Tiffany. My great-aunt Ada had a grisly tale about a Swiss valet, whom my great-grandfather brought back with him from the grand tour, being found dead early one morning in Tiffany's Walk with his features convulsed with horror . . .'

'B-rr!' ejaculated Roger Carshill, suddenly waking up—he had drunk a lot of champagne at dinner. 'You give a feller the creeps, Major!' 'Pretty grim!' said Kenneth. 'What a rag if one met her!' murmured Isobel ecstatically. 'Good for you, Isobel,' Bill cried joyously. 'You and I'll go out some night with a dog biscuit and see what happens.' He snapped his fingers and began to prance about. yelling 'Here, Tiff! Tiff, Tiff, Tiff! Good dog! Come and kiss the steward!' They all started ragging and the party broke up in a turmoil.

It was Jack's habit to stroll for a while in Tiffany's Walk before turning in. That night I accompanied him. 'Tell me about this Mrs Carshill that Timmie's so stuck on,' he said suddenly.

As a novelist who has his office under his hat and can drift about the world at will, I had known Sara Carshill for several years. She was the Honourable Mrs Banksley when I first ran into her at Biarritz: then Banksley let her divorce him as the easiest method of getting on with his polo undisturbed, and soon after I encountered her at the Villa Igeia at Palermo with a somewhat moth-eaten Italian duke in tow. Carshill was new to me; all I knew about him was that he had some hazy connection with the Turf and a virtually unassuageable thirst.

I gave Jack these facts baldly. 'She's an attractive baggage, a man-eater. She'll grab Timmie if she gets half a chance . . .' Jack grunted. 'Running her rather hard, isn't he? I mean there's an inflection in his voice when he speaks to her . . . Or am I wrong?'

'I wish you were, for Antonia's sake. She hasn't said anything yet. But she was watching them tonight. If I know anything about it, she's blowing up for one grand old row . . .'

My host sighed. 'Poor Antonia! They're tremendously fond of one another really—after all, they've only been married two years. But they're going through a difficult period—separate rooms and so forth. I wish to God she'd have a baby, Ned. This old place is something to hang on to in these changing times. Timmie will have it after me and his son after him, if only the young ruffian and Antonia would buck up and do their duty by the family . . .' He broke off. 'You know, I can't help feeling that I've met Mrs Carshill before. And that she recognises me . . .'

'My dear old boy,' I protested, 'I don't see how you can possibly tell that.'

'That crooning voice of hers, her laugh, is it? Anyhow, there's something about her personality that's familiar. I can't explain what I mean exactly, but blind people are receptive towards such influences . . .'

When Jack Herron, after twenty-two years of soldiering, walked into a German machine-gun barrage on the St Quentin Canal, he retired to the ancestral seat in Wiltshire and, with characteristic pluck, proceeded to make the best of a desperately bad job, For a man of forty to lose his sight is bad enough; in the case of a fellow like Jack, well off, handsome, a keen soldier and good all-round sportsman, it might well have proved a tragedy.

But Jack would not have it so. I had not seen him since the Hindenburg Line, for I was out of England when my young friend Antonia married his nephew, until I came across him at a regimental dinner in London. His eyes were not disfigured and he camouflaged his disability and bore himself with so much confidence that, but for a certain halting deliberation in his movements, you would scarcely have guessed that he was stone-blind. He was not in the least sensitive about his affliction; on the contrary, he was eager to talk about the new existence he had built for himself. 'No dog and string for me, Ned,' he laughed. 'I may still be a bit at sea in town, but come down to Herron Place and I'll show you some gadgets that'll knock you cold!'

It did my heart good to behold old Jack strolling up through the gardens to welcome me as though he had never lost his sight. Of course he had lived at Herron Place all his life and knew every stick and stone on the property; and fourteen years of darkness had quickened his remaining senses. But, apart from this, he was out to help himself. The whole estate was a mass of 'gadgets', as he called them, to help him find his way around without mishap, from life-lines in the gardens, and a row of posts kept freshly creosoted to warn his sense of smell that he was approaching the lake, to bosses on drawers and cupboards in his apartments to enable him to locate his things.

He would not let his old batman, Sims, now installed as butler-valet, do a hand's turn for him beyond his ordinary duties. He gloried in his independence, shaving himself, even tying his own tie. He had learnt to read Braille and use a typewriter. He fished. He spoke of taking up shooting again, assisted by Sims and a range-finding system of his own invention. He was even trying to devise a safe means of driving his car.

His only crotchet was a dislike of strange presences about him. Visitors to the house had to be brought to him immediately so that he might thereafter identify them by their voice or footstep—he was extraordinarily sharp about this. Walking with him in the arcade the afternoon I arrived, I drew his attention to the fact that a row of bricks in the flooring were loose—they had clanked under our feet as we strolled along.

Jack chuckled. 'Just another gadget, old son. I often sit out in Tiffany's Walk and I like to know who's approaching. I've come to be pretty good at spotting people by their tread, and those loose bricks help me—my detector, I call 'em. You've no idea of the variations in sound. I don't make many mistakes . . .'

Although maids waited on guests in the bedrooms, no servant, with the exception of Sims, ever appeared on the ground floor at Herron Place after 7 a.m. Jack's rooms were on this level, looking out upon Tiffany's Walk and communicating with it by a side door leading into the south wing lobby. Under the above arrangement he could wander about the ground floor and out into the arcade as he liked without fear of encountering an unfamiliar presence in the shape of a new maid.

The back part of Herron Place was the oldest. The south wing, Tudor, incorporated the original dwelling house, with a turret in rear, built under Elizabeth, which had later been pierced, as to its lower part, to give access to Tiffany's Walk. The bachelors of the party were in this wing, sharing a bathroom, myself in the upper room of the turret, Mark Bendall next door, Bill and Geoffrey doubling up across the way, and Kenneth at the end of the passage. A corkscrew stair descended from our corridor to the little lobby in the base of the turret leading into the arcade. Off this lobby was a minute bedroom to which Timmie had moved, surrendering his bedroom, next to Antonia's in the north wing, to Virginia and Isobel so that they could share Antonia's bathroom, Timmie using Jack's, across the lobby. In the north wing also, at the head of a small flight communicating with the north entrance to Tiffany's Walk, the Carshills were lodged, in separate rooms with a bath between. Christmas was two days gone, and I was sitting up late over a set of proofs which I had overlooked until a frantic wire from my publisher at dinner-time reminded me of my neglect. It was two o'clock in the morning; the rowdy gang in the Long Gallery had long since broken up and the house was plunged in silence. The night was so mild that I sat, wrapped in my old camel's-hair dressing gown, at the open window. When I raised my eyes I could see Tiffany's Walk spread out in a dark rectangle below.

I was absorbed in my task when my ear caught a faint sound outside. I glanced out. The night was moonless, but the tiled walls of the gallery reflected the faint light in the sky. Under its broad roof the arcade ran its length in obscurity and emptiness. Jack's excellent ghost story seeped into my mind and, although I am completely incredulous about the supernatural, I remained gazing out, thinking about poor Miss Tiffany and her unhappy fate. And so it happened that my glance was directed at the farther end of the arcade, where it was joined to the north wing, when I saw a flutter of white and heard a muffled scream.

There was nothing spectral about the sound—it was a girl, Antonia or one of the Sprotes, I concluded, who had cried out in terror. In two seconds I was down the winding stair. Cutting across the garden to save time, I dashed into the north wing lobby.

Light fell dimly from the corridor above and I recognised Isobel. Her teeth were chattering with fear. 'Ned,' she panted, 'I've seen her . . . Tiffany's ghost . . . Oh, gosh! I've had such a fright . . .' She clutched me. Her hands were dead.

'My dear Isobel,' I soothed her, 'what on earth are you talking about? You've been walking in your sleep . . .' Then I perceived that she was in her nightdress. I may be old-fashioned, but really, what girls consider clothing nowadays! I slipped my dressing gown about her shoulders—at least my pyjamas were not diaphanous.

'Virginia was cold and went to sleep in my kimono,' she explained, still trembling, 'and I didn't want to wake her up. Bill bet me I wouldn't go into Tiffany's Walk at night. I was to leave my hanky there as a proof . . .' She broke off, her eyes round with terror. 'Ned, you've got to believe me! I saw her, as plainly as I see you . . .'

'Saw whom?'

'Poor Tiffany . . .'

'Oh, rot, Isobel! You've been dreaming.'

'I haven't, I tell you. Just as I came out of the lobby I saw her, all in black, just as Jack described. She was walking away from me when she suddenly stopped. I thought she was going to turn and show me that terrible face and . . . and I screamed. Then you came . . .'

There was a step on the stairs. Antonia, her flaxen hair flowing down her shoulders, looking as slim and as ghostly as a young birch in her white kimono, stood behind us. 'Ned,' she vociferated, 'what on earth are you doing here? And Isobel?'

'Isobel's been having nightmares,' I explained. 'She thinks she's seen the ghost . . .'

'But I did, Antonia, I did,' the girl broke in. 'I saw her with my own eyes, all in black, walking down the arcade . . .'

At that moment I heard a door close softly in the corridor above, and I recollected that the Carshills were sleeping in that wing. I wondered whether Antonia had heard it too. I looked at her, but her expression was unrevealing.

'Never mind about that now, Isobel, but come to bed,' she said gently, and put her arm about the girl. 'Sorry you were disturbed, Ned!'

Bewildered and rather chilly, I returned to my chamber. As I crossed the lobby something was glittering on the flags. It was a bronze hairpin. I realised that it lay outside Timmie's door.

Coming from breakfast next morning, I bumped into Sara in the hall. She was going to play eighteen holes before lunch with Timmie, she informed me.

'Yours, I think, Sara?' said I, and handed her a bronze hairpin.

'Thanks, Ned!' Unsuspectingly her deft fingers tucked it in

her clustering Titian hair. She was a fascinating hussy—a formidable rival for any young wife. Clearly she had marked down Timmie as her unlawful prey. I remembered that one day he would inherit Herron Place and all Jack's money. Knowing Sara, my heart misgave me.

A klaxon honked, and Timmie called from the drive. Sara ran out to him. I turned to find myself gazing into Roger Carshill's yellowish eyes. I recalled the fuddled and rather quarrelsome state in which I had left him on the previous evening. He cast a rancid look after the departing car.

'What's this I hear about you and the Sprote kid seeing ghosts last night?' he rumbled.

I laughed. 'Isobel obviously ate something that disagreed with her, and walked in her sleep . . .

'A woman in black, eh?' he grunted. His lizard eyes rested unpleasantly on my face. I walked away.

Going up to dress that evening, I found that Isobel had not returned my dressing gown. So I went across to the north wing, where in the corridor I met Antonia, who fetched it. Then 'Come into my room for a minute,' she begged. 'I want to talk to you.'

'Ned,' she said abruptly, but very earnestly, 'I'm going to lose Timmie, and I don't know what to do about it. No, you don't have to sympathise with me. Timmie and I haven't been hitting it off, but I love him and he loves me. Only he's weak and easily led. That Carshill woman means to steal him, and the damnable thing is that I can't see how I'm to prevent it . . .'

I murmured something about temporary infatuations. 'Oh, Ned,' she burst out impatiently. 'I'm not a fool. Timmie's room is just off the arcade. Don't you realise it was she who was in Tiffany's Walk last night?'

I thought of that bronze hairpin, but said nothing. 'The only reason she didn't go to Timmie last night was because Isobel scared her off,' Antonia went on tensely. 'I can see her game.

She means to compromise Timmie so that Roger will have to divorce her and she can marry Timmie.' The young face flamed suddenly. 'But she's not going to get away with it, if I have to kill her first . . .' Her voice was harsh with passion. 'I have a pistol and I shan't be afraid to use it . . .'

A pallid woman in shiny black looked in at the door. It was Sara's French maid. She had a small jar in her hand. 'I bring Madame back the cream she lend Madame,' she said impassively.

'All right, Jeannette, stick it down anywhere,' Antonia told her.

'That woman heard you,' I said reprovingly, when the maid had gone. 'How can you say such crazy things?'

Antonia's shrug was stubborn.

'Why not talk to Timmie?' I suggested.

'Do you think I have no pride?'

'Jack, then?'

Her expression softened. 'Poor darling, he has his own cross to bear . . .' She gave me her hand. 'Thanks, Ned. I wanted to tell someone. But I must work this out for myself . . .'

After dinner that evening, however, I had a word with Jack. I told him everything I knew, excepting only Antonia's foolish threat, which I did not take seriously. Jack was very calm about it. 'Thanks for letting me know, Ned,' he said. 'But leave this to me—do you mind?'

He must have spoken to Timmie. The next afternoon he sent for me. I found him with a rug over his knees in his accustomed seat at the south end of the arcade. 'The damned young fool wants Antonia to divorce him so that he can marry Mrs Carshill,' he grumbled.

'He ought to be horsewhipped,' I declared. 'What does Antonia say?'

'I haven't spoken to her. But Timmie has. He says she refuses. And she's right.'

'Look here, Jack, do you want me to have a word with Sara?'

He shook his head. 'No. I'm the one to do that, but it'll be in my own time . . .'

In the Long Gallery that evening after dinner, I noticed that Jack made Sara sit beside him, and they had a long chat.

It was not my business to interfere between husband and wife. But I resolved to be on the watch, and if I caught Sara again at her nocturnal prowling to tackle her and read the Riot Act. The night after Isobel's adventure there was much whispering and giggling in Tiffany's Walk, and I gathered that the gang was out ghost-hunting.

Two nights went by without any spectral manifestation. Sitting up was no hardship for me. On the third night, the household had retired a good two hours, and it was getting on for three when, casting one of my periodic glances towards the north wing, whence I knew the 'ghost' must emerge, I descried a figure standing motionless at the entrance to the lobby.

In a flash I was on my feet and down the stairs. The figure had not budged. Preferring to challenge her under cover of the house, where we should not be overlooked, I made across the garden, keeping well in the shadow of the house. The night was dark as only the midwinter night in the country can be, with a touch of frost in the air. As I neared the far end of the gallery a shadow seemed to detach itself from the gloom of the lobby and went flitting past the first bay of the arcade. I realised then that I had missed her. If I wished to confront her, I should have to head her off.

I pointed half-right and darted swiftly over the flower-beds, following with my eye that dark form slipping from bay to bay. Then, looking towards the turret entrance whence I had emerged, I was brought up short, my blood freezing in my veins.

What happened thereafter was the affair of split seconds. From where I was halted, panting, I had a clear view of the turret entrance. A shape lurked there, a shrouded, amorphous shadow. As I gazed, it moved forward, its hands, which were clasped beneath its robes, rising and falling in a gesture of despair.

At that instant I heard a clanking sound in the arcade and knew that Sara had passed over Jack's 'detector'—that row of loose bricks. They lay a little more than halfway along the walk, nearer the south than the north end, and I realised that as soon as the second figure I had seen had turned the corner of the gallery, she would meet it face to face. Scarcely had the thought come to me than I heard a dreadful, blood-curdling shriek. Its echo was swallowed up in the ear-splitting crash of a shot.

I was aware of an orange flash that had split the darkness, of a stealthy footfall within the arcade. But I paid no heed to these. I sprang forward, vaulted the nearest bay into the gallery and recoiled in horror.

A dark mass lay on the ground. It was Sara. A dark kimono covered up her black nightgown and she wore black slippers. It did not take me a moment to discover that she was past help—the doctor told us afterwards that she was shot through the heart and killed instantaneously.

A light footstep and Antonia in her white robe gazed down on me where I knelt. 'Ned,' she gasped, 'what is it? There was a shot . . .' Then she saw what lay in front of me. She had an electric torch and flashed the beam on the dead woman.

'She's dead,' I said.

'Dead?' Her eyes were wide with fear. 'Oh, Ned . . . !'

'What did you do with the gun, Antonia?'

She stared at me in tearful dismay. 'Ned, you don't think . . .' She seized my arm and shook it. 'Ned, I never even saw her go out. I left my door ajar, meaning to follow her if I heard her leave her room. But I fell asleep. It was the shot that wakened me. Ned, you've got to believe that . . .'

Two pyjamaed figures broke from the south wing—Timmie and Sims. Timmie raised a haggard face to me from beside

Sara's dead body. 'Who killed her?' he demanded, with a sob in his voice.

I took him aside. 'She's dead, Timmie, and we can't do anything about it. We shall have to send for the police and they'll ask questions. You've got to pull yourself together and stand by Antonia . . .'

'Antonia?' blankly.

'Don't you realise that she'll be the first the police will suspect?'

'Good God.' His glance sought his wife, but she had disappeared. 'Find her,' I told him curtly. 'And don't leave her. And listen, let me have that gun of hers . . .'

'Ned,' he cried, horror-stricken, 'you're not suggesting . . . ?'

He went off. Jack was at my elbow, telling Sims to ring up the county police. 'Just a minute, Jack,' I interposed. But he shook me off. 'I heard what you said to Timmie,' he remarked gruffly. 'Nevertheless, the police must be notified. Is Roger Carshill anywhere about?'

'He went to bed tight as usual,' I rejoined. 'I was just about to wake him. But he'll keep. Jack, I've got to talk to you before the police arrive . . .'

He let me take him a little way along the arcade and tell him what I had seen.

'So you were out prowling, too, were you?' he remarked, mildly curious. 'Policemen are material beings, Ned. I shouldn't start telling them ghost stories if I were you . . .'

I glanced at him sharply, but his sightless orbs robbed his face of all expression.

'But, old man,' I cried, 'you don't understand. It's Antonia I'm thinking of. She threatened to shoot Sara Carshill, and, what's more, that French maid of Sara's heard her . . .'

He frowned. 'I didn't know this. Even so . . .' He broke off. 'Go and wake Carshill now and bring him to me. I must wait here for the doctor . . .'

'Is there nothing we can do to shield Antonia?' I persisted.

'We shall clear Antonia, never fear!'

He spoke with so much assurance that I gazed at him, a dread suspicion clutching at my heart. His apartments were but a step from the arcade: he might well have conceived the plan of dressing up to frighten Sara out of her little dodge to confront Roger and Antonia with the accomplished fact. Had Jack heard the shot? Impossible. How could he, a blind man, have recognised her, seen to aim? Even when I remembered his detector and his boast that he could identify any footstep once heard, I could not believe that old Jack could have murdered a woman in cold blood.

One glance at Superintendent Smith of the Medford police, and I decided that Jack's advice was good. I told this heavy, plethoric person, therefore, merely that, writing late, I was disturbed by a noise in Tiffany's Walk, and, going down to investigate, was accidentally an eyewitness of the fatality, With regard to the direction from which the shot came, I was unable, in all honesty, to help him; but I apprehended from the drift of his questions that the bullet had struck Sara from behind, passing through the lung and lodging in the heart—the suggestion was that she had been shot down from a distance of about 25 yards by someone who entered the arcade behind her. This cleared Jack; but it made things look blacker than ever for Antonia.

It was the evidence of Roger Carshill and Jeannette between them that first turned the Superintendent's mind towards Antonia. Carshill had seemed dazed when I awoke him with the news of the shooting, and remained in the same confused state when confronted with his wife's dead body. But the arrival of the police roused him from his stupor, and in hysterical tones he blurted out, in my presence, the whole story of his wife's love affair with Timmie.

Colonel Masser, the Chief Constable, arrived towards dawn.

He was personally acquainted with Jack as a prominent resi-
dent of the county. When Carshill's statements were
communicated to him, he at once sent for Antonia. The examination took place in the Long Gallery. She threw me a pathetic,
hunted glance as she passed me at the door—poor child, I
pitied her from my heart. The next I heard they were searching
her room—for the gun, of course; and then Jeannette was
fetched.

Soon after, Timmie, white to the lips, came out. Jeannette
had told her story. The gun that had killed Sara had not been
found—Antonia's pistol was unaccountably missing. It was a
small Browning he had given her when they were motoring in
France. Antonia was quite frank about it, Timmie said. She had
come across it in a drawer a few days before and might have
left it out—at any rate, it had disappeared.

I was brought in and asked to corroborate the maid's story.
The first person I saw was Jack, seated at the table with Colonel
Masser and the Superintendent. Antonia, pale but composed,
faced them in a chair, and Carshill, who kept mopping his face
with his handkerchief, lounged on a settle.

It was no good lying about it. I made light of Antonia's remark,
saying it was merely an outburst of childish temper. But I saw
by the expression on Masser's hard face that his mind was made
up. After questioning him closely for particulars of Antonia's
appearance after I had reached Sara's dead body, he turned to
Jack. 'I'm sorry, Major,' he said, 'but I shall have to ask Mrs
Herron to accompany us back to Medford.'

Timmie bounded forward, 'You're not to arrest her, surely?'
he faltered.

'She will be detained on suspicion pending enquiries' was
the dry rejoinder as the Chief Constable stood up.

Jack's arm went out groping and detained him. 'One moment,
Colonel. There's yet another eye-witness to be examined . . .'

'Oh, and who might that be?' Masser demanded.

'Myself . . .'

The Chief Constable cleared his throat and cocked an eye at the Superintendent. 'An *eye*-witness, Major?' he said.

'If you'll defer action with regard to Mrs Herron for a very few minutes,' Jack offered delicately, 'and will come down with me to the arcade, I'll show you what I mean.' He rose to his feet. 'Ned, are you there? Give me your arm. And, Carshill, I heard your voice just now. Be a good fellow and lead me on the other side. All these strange people confuse me! Are you there, Antonia? You come too!'

We entered Tiffany's Walk from the north wing and traversed its whole length as far as the bench in front of the south lobby, which was our host's favoured retreat. Guided by Carshill and me, Jack sat down.

'Last night,' he said, 'as often happens, I could not sleep. So I came out here and sat down on this bench, which, as every-body in the house knows, is my particular pitch. In this way, I happened to be here in the arcade when Mrs Carshill was shot . . .

'Of course, I'm not an eye-witness in the accepted sense,' Jack proceeded. 'but when a fellow can't see, his ears must serve him for eyes. And now for a little experiment to explain my meaning. Let anybody who is staying in the house go to the far end of the arcade and approach me, and I'll guarantee to tell you, by the footstep, who it is!'

With a supercilious smile the Superintendent consulted the Chief Constable's face. But it was evident that Masser was impressed. Silently he signed to Carshill. But the latter shook his head sullenly. With an enquiring glance at Masser, Antonia proposed herself. But the Chief Constable's headshake negatived the suggestion, and he signed to me.

I began to see old Jack's game. He had dressed up to frighten Sara, and as he advanced along the gallery had heard the foot-step of her murderer approaching from the other end and recognised it. But who could it be? Timmie? As the result of some bitter and dramatic lovers' quarrel?

Taut with suspense, I threaded the garden to the north wing and went in under the arcade. I walked briskly along it, striking with my heels, and when I reached Jack's detector you may be sure I made it ring. 'It's Ned,' Jack cried, when I was but a few yards from him.

But apparently Masser was not entirely satisfied. I saw him draw Carshill out of earshot and argue with him strenuously, with the result that, with obvious unwillingness, the latter slouched off across the garden towards the other end of the covered way. 'Once more, Major, if you please,' the Chief Constable commanded curtly.

Carshill's footsteps approached. My eye sought out Jack. He was leaning forward in his chair, his head canted forward and sideways, listening intently. Tense and erect, Antonia stood beside him, her hand resting protectively on his.

The sloppy footfalls came nearer. *Clank-clank* went the detector. Jack's face was stony. But as Carshill rounded the angle of the gallery and halted sheepishly within a few paces of our little group, the man on the bench shot out an accusing finger and cried harshly 'Carshill!' Then, moving his head from side to side, he said querulously, 'Colonel, where are you?'

'Beside you, Major,' said Masser.

'Take him,' Jack rasped. 'He's your man!'

There was an angry growl from Carshill. He recoiled a pace, casting suspicious glances about him. 'What's this nonsense?' he snarled. 'The fellow's off his chump!'

'Last night as I sat here,' Jack declaimed, in a swift, triumphant voice, 'I heard someone coming along the arcade. I knew it was a woman, by the lightness of her tread, and that she was hurrying. Standing up and going forward, I discovered from her footstep that it was Sara Carshill. I suppose my unexpected appearance scared her, for she screamed. At the same instant my ear picked up another tread, heavier and stealthy, approaching along the gallery. As it drew nearer I identified it as her husband's. Then I heard the shot . . '

'It's a lie!' roared Carshill. 'I was asleep when it happened. Ask him!' He pointed at me.

'If you'll search his room, Colonel,' Jack went on evenly, 'I've no doubt you'll find the gun—the gun he took from Mrs Herron's dressing-table . . ' He broke off and called out in alarm, 'What's happening?'

A savage scuffle had broken out between Carshill and Timmie. While Jack was speaking, Carshill had suddenly sprung backward, brandishing a pistol. Without hesitation Timmie leapt at his throat, bearing him to the ground. With a crash that awoke a thousand echoes under the vaulted roof the pistol went off. But the Superintendent had hurled his 200 pounds into the mêlée, and Carshill, sullen and enraged but unhurt, was overpowered.

Superintendent Smith held out his hand to Colonel Masser. The Browning looked very small in that immense palm. 'Here you are, Colonel. With two cartridges missing from the magazine!'

'Why, it's my pistol!' Antonia shrilled.

'And the gun that killed Mrs Carshill,' Jack put in.

Carshill, slumped in a chair, was babbling out a lachrymose confession. Jeannette had told him of Antonia's threat: he had seen the gun in Antonia's room and abstracted it as a measure of precaution. He hadn't meant to kill his wife. He was drunk: he had only fired to frighten her. Twice before she had left him for other men.

They took him away on the first stage of his progress towards the five years' penal servitude he got at the assizes on the manslaughter charge.

The house party broke up incontinently. Jack was in Medford with the police all day. But that evening we dined alone together before the fire in his study.

'Jack,' said I, raising my glass, 'I looks towards you. You're a marvel!'

He laughed. 'That rat,' he pronounced deliberately, 'always gave me a bad feel!'

'There's one thing I don't understand,' I put in. 'You told the police you identified Carshill by his footstep when he followed Sara into the arcade. But when he shot at her he can't have been within 20 yards of your detector, as you call it. How did you spot him, then?'

Jack chuckled. 'Pure bluff, old boy!'

'Bluff? Then that experiment in the gallery . . .'

'Fake. Not with you—I'd know your elephantine tramp anywhere, and you sounded those bricks like a good 'un. But with Carshill. You see, he'd always steered clear of me, and I wouldn't have known his footstep from the Queen of Rumania's . . .'

'Then how did you work it?'

'Antonia. She Morsed his name on the back of my hand. Yours, too, only with you it wasn't necessary. Antonia and I have been practising for ages. It saves all kinds of explanations in public. I got the idea from Edison and his wife, though Edison was deaf . . .'

'That's all right for the experiment. But how did you know it was Carshill who followed Sara into the gallery?'

'I didn't. It was a blind guess.' He chortled. '"Blind guess" is good. You see, Sara and I were old acquaintances, though her name was Stella Young when I knew her in Egypt. She never dreamed that I, blind as I am, could possibly have known her again. But I'm pretty sure she recognised me: the way she kept her boy away from me proves that . . .'

'Then you'd met Carshill before, too?'

'Rather. The pair of them were playing the badger game—blackmail, you know—in Cairo, way back in '15. The Provost Marshal ran them out, and I was the A.P.M. that put them on their ship at Port Said . . ' He raised his head sharply. 'Who's that outside in the arcade?'

I stepped to the window. 'Two young idiots making a fresh start,' I said.

As I turned back to the table I saw, hanging behind the door, a black domino, relic of some old masquerade, and with it a black silk handkerchief large enough to serve at a pinch as a veil. I glanced accusingly at Jack; but he had settled himself back in his chair, his clear-cut face illuminated by the look of inward peace that comes to a man whose day's work is done.

VALENTINE WILLIAMS

George Valentine Williams was born in London on 20 October 1883. In later life he preferred to be known by his unusual middle name, which he owed to his Irish grandfather on the side of his mother, Tilly Skerrett. She had been raised in Florence during the protracted unification of Italy and this in part may have inspired her son to witness for himself what he would later describe as 'the world of action'. Inspiration would also come from his father Douglas, a journalist with the news agency Reuters, where he eventually became chief editor. Many years later, Valentine Williams would draw on his father's reminiscences when writing the script for the film *A Dispatch from Reuters* (1940), in which Edward G. Robinson played the agency's founder, Paul Reuter.

Valentine Williams was educated at Downside Abbey, a Catholic school in Somerset, and in 1901 he spent a year at Kleve in Germany where he became fluent in German. In 1902, at the age of eighteen, he joined his father at Reuters as a sub-editor and from 1904 to 1909 he was the agency's Berlin correspondent. In 1907, Williams met the woman to whom he would become engaged four years later. Alice Crawford was an Australian actress, in Germany with Sir Herbert Beerbohm Tree's touring company, and after falling while alighting from a train at Berlin station she was introduced to Williams on the platform by another journalist, E. C. Bentley, then with the *Daily Telegraph*. After five years in Germany, Williams joined the *Daily Mail* as its Paris correspondent, but he also reported on various European crises, including the overthrow of the Portuguese monarchy in October 1910, the creation of Albania and the first and second Balkan wars. As well as writing short stories for *The London Magazine* and other journals, and a handful of 'sentimental' revue songs, Williams made a translation of Arthur Schnitzler's popular Viennese play *Liebelei* under the title *Light O' Love*. The play opened in May 1909 at His Majesty's Theatre in London and two years later his translation of *Le Typhon* by Melchior Lengyel was produced in Paris.

On the outbreak of war, Williams became the *Mail*'s chief war correspondent and he was the first accredited journalist to be embedded at the general headquarters of the British Expeditionary Force in Belgium. His reports for the *Daily Mail* appeared in the *London Evening Standard* and were widely syndicated in Britain and abroad, but Williams became increasingly frustrated with what he saw as the stupidity of censorship. He decided to enlist and in December 1915 was commissioned as an officer in the 1st Battalion of the Irish Guards. He was wounded and then worked in London where he assembled the official account of the Battle of Neuve Chapelle, which appeared in his book *With Our Army at Flanders* (1916).

In August 1916, he and Alice were finally married. After the wedding Williams returned to the front in France where he was wounded for a second time, this time more seriously after being blown up in what would now be termed a friendly fire incident. He was well-connected and Princess Louise, Duchess of Argyll and daughter of Queen Victoria, lent him and Alice a shooting lodge on the shores of Loch Gare. This was where, while recovering from his physical injuries and shellshock, he was awarded the Military Cross 'for conspicuous gallantry' and where he wrote a roman à clef for *Blackwood's Magazine* entitled *The Adventures of an Ensign* (1917) and published as by 'Vedette'.

At this time works of this kind were subject to censorship and among those tasked with reviewing Williams' manuscript was John Buchan, then director of information at the Foreign Office and best known today for his thriller *The Thirty-Nine Steps* (1915) which had been published in *Blackwood's* in 1915 as by 'H de V'. Buchan advised Williams to follow his lead and write what he termed, rather oddly, 'a shocker'. Williams took Buchan's advice and wrote *The Man with the Clubfoot* (1918), subtitled 'A romance of the German Secret Service'. The book was serialised in *Answers* and was published as by 'Douglas Valentine'—the pseudonym probably necessitated by the fact that the idea of journalists writing fiction was anathema to the proprietor of the *Daily Mail*, Lord Northcliffe. The 'man' of the title was Dr Adolph Grundt, a German spy whose origins lay in real people, including a bumptious German journalist and a Scottish tailor who had turned out to be a German spy. However, Grundt's club foot was inspired by Sir Mansfield Smith-Cumming, the head of the British Secret Intelligence Service, who had had a foot amputated after being injured in 1914. Despite the times, the anti-hero Clubfoot was an immediate success and a few years later the character and his arch enemies a Secret Service agent called Desmond Okewood and his brother Francis, would be among the characters parodied in the *Partners in Crime* series of detective stories by Agatha Christie.

Although Williams found writing books hard—harder even than newspaper work—he found it easy to write dialogue and decided to adapt *The Man Who Was Clubfoot* for the stage. Alice Crawford was cast as the leading lady, although there is no record of the play being produced. A second Clubfoot volume followed—*The Secret Hand* (1918), again first published as by 'Douglas Valentine'—and Williams began to consider the possibility of writing fiction full-time. By this time he was the *Daily Mail*'s foreign editor and he led the newspaper's team at the Paris Peace Conference in January 1919. In the same year, the Belgian King conferred on Williams the title of Chevalier in the Order of the Crown.

With the death of Northcliffe in 1922, Williams no longer needed to use a pseudonym and from then on his fiction appeared under his own name. He also remained with the *Mail* and, among other reports, covered the discovery of Tutankhamun's tomb, breaking the exclusive arrangements secured by *The Times* newspaper. In 1923, he and Alice moved to Cannes where every morning he would sit in what he described as 'a small kiosk, built on the site of a Napoleonic battery' and type two or three chapters. As well as more Clubfoot stories, Williams wrote the very entertaining thriller *Mr Ramosi* (1926), which drew on a nine-week journey he and Alice made across North Africa in 1925.

While he continued to write novels such as the slightly Ruritanian thriller *The Three of Clubs* (1924), Williams also wrote shorter fiction including his best-known short story, 'The Witness for the Defence', which was collected in *The Knife behind the Curtain: Tales of Crime and the Secret Service* (1930). He also wrote the script for a documentary film *Land of Hope and Glory* (1927), occasional short articles on all manner of subjects for the *Daily News* and the *Sunday Graphic*, and a rather odd series on English spa towns—'a vital national asset'—for the *Sunday Times*. Like every good news-paperman, he carried a notebook at all times; as he said in an interview published in 1930, 'ideas come to those who are looking for them. I find them everywhere, at all sorts of time and in all sorts of places'.

In 1931 the Williamses went to New York where Valentine's brother was Reuters' correspondent. Enchanted, they decided to make America their home for the next six years. There were further Clubfoot novels including *The Gold Comfit Box* (1932) and *The Spider's Touch* (1936), and Valentine and Alice adapted one of them, *The Crouching Beast* (1928), for the stage, which under the title *Berlin* was produced at the George M. Cohan Theatre in 1931 with Sydney Greenstreet as Dr Grundt. While in America, Valentine and Alice also wrote and starred in four half-hour radio plays for NBC: 'Moon Maiden', 'The King's Messenger', 'Mata Hari the Spy' and 'The Mummy's Hand', about the opening of Tutankhamun's tomb. Williams also wrote and narrated a series of 'Portraits of Famous Britons' and in 1931 also featured in a demonstration of television at the Radio Electrical World's Fair where '10,000 people sat in Madison Square Gardens and saw his head appear six times larger than life size, and heard his voice reproduced in stentorian tones through loudspeakers'.

After the Williamses returned to London in the mid-1930s, Williams worked for the Foreign Office before moving at the start of the Second World War to the British Embassy in Washington, where he represented the Special Operations Executive and carried out what one obituarist opaquely described as 'valuable work'. Williams worked closely with members of Britain's Secret Service but, contrary to what is stated in some sources, he was not involved in the recruitment to the Service of the writer Malcolm Muggeridge and Kim Philby, who would be unmasked as a Soviet spy; this reflects confusion with the similarly named deputy head of the Service, Colonel Valentine Vivian.

Towards the end of the war, Valentine Williams went to California where he worked with Alexander Korda at the Metro-Goldwyn-Mayer Studios. However, Williams' health was poor and after a brief visit back to the UK he returned to America on the maiden peacetime passenger voyage of the *Queen Elizabeth*. On the liner's arrival in New York, Williams was taken to Gotham Hospital where he died on 20 November 1946.

'Blind Guess' was first published in *Britannia and Eve* in February 1933.

MODERN ANTIQUE

Milward Kennedy

One day, a week before the end of our holiday, I was alone; that happens quite easily when one is on holiday. My wife and the children had gone off in the car to expect a battleship, and I had cried off on the grounds that I had to write. I was so anxious to avoid the fatigue of climbing up the insides of masts and trying to ask intelligent questions about paravanes and donkey-engines that I did not blench when my wife told me that she had promised the servants the day off. After all, a lunch of beer and cold pie and fruit is the kind of meal which any man can get ready for himself.

And so as soon as they had all departed and I had the bungalow to myself I decided that I would postpone work until I had had a stroll. Up the village I went (preferring that to the sandy shore), and in I went to an antique shop against the window of which we had once or twice flattened our noses on our way to buy the day's provisions: it being the local custom to collect one's own food from the shops—a custom created by the inability of the shops, during the August rush, to deliver your lunch before about 10.30 p.m.

It was a surprising shop to find in such a place; for though one window was full of the trumpery junk (Chinese bowls and brass ashtrays and pen-holders in the form of penguins) that would serve nicely as souvenirs of a summer holiday and ultimately fail to sell at a rummage sale, the other had the sort of stuff that would draw a collector. Bristol glass, blue and white and magenta and amethyst and the rare green, and some pieces of Waterford, and superb pewter dishes; and beyond this one could see lovely, unfashionable mahogany. There was, for instance, a big bureau; its front was open, and its cunning interior was obviously full of secret drawers. But what had caught my wife's eye and mine was a little oak chest which was exactly what we wanted to go in the big, open-down fireplace at home.

No harm to ask its price. Well, it was cheap, but—no; it would be an extravagance unjustifiable when there was the rent of the bungalow, and . . . I switched to a fire-bucket, and that was dear and I did not want it. And just as I was wondering whether I must retreat with ignominy, I noticed a big glass ball: green, with white serpentine lines in it, like a vast specimen of the marbles with which I and my sisters played solitaire in my youth.

The old lady who kept the shop was rather scornful: the thing was not authentic—she doubted, even, whether it was solid, it was so light; and it was mine for seven shillings. Such was her scorn that I swore to myself that I had to go straight back and write a short story and devote the proceeds to the purchase of the chest. I almost said as much to the old lady; I felt, somehow, that I should regain my prestige if I told her that I was an author.

I carried the glass ball back to the bungalow, wondering why on earth I had wasted seven shillings, and wondering also whether it was wise to embark on a short story when I was already behind-hand with a novel, and making very slow progress with it.

I went into the bungalow, put the globe on the table, collected my materials and set to work, but with no success. My mind was a blank. I stared at the glass ball and cursed myself for having gone to that shop; to write to order seemed utterly impossible—to write for an oak chest.

Suddenly I felt—I knew—that I was not alone in the bungalow. I had not heard anyone knock or ring, and as far as I knew there was nothing for tradesmen to deliver—no laundry due back; and in any case, a tradesman would not walk in. And I was sure that there was someone inside the bungalow.

I told myself that it was absurd. Thieves don't break into holiday seaside bungalows; there was certainly nothing to steal in ours. I felt that it was ridiculous even to look. In fact, I would not look . . .

But it was no use. I could not write. I felt more and more aware that there was someone else in the place. Once even I thought I saw something—some movement—reflected obscurely in the glass ball in front of me. Probably, I told myself, a curtain behind me swaying in the light breeze.

Well, I got up and made a tour. I even looked in the cupboards and had half a mind—no, I'll confess: I did look under the beds.

Of course, there was no one. I knew there would not be, I told myself. And just as I was going back to the sitting-room I stopped short. The sense of a presence was strongest in the hall. Really, it was absurd; it was as though the bungalow was haunted; and I could think of nothing more improbable than that such a modern bungalow (it was as new as it was flimsy) could be haunted or that I of all people could see or feel a ghost. Besides, it was a glorious day of bright sunshine, and the hour was about noon.

The hall was little more than a long, narrow passage; I had hardly noticed it before. I had certainly *not* noticed that there was a little oak chest in it. I was so surprised that I forgot all about my imaginary ghost. I stared at the chest, and for a second I believed that it was the very one I had seen in the antique shop: the one to buy for which I ought at that moment be writing a short story. It was nothing of the sort, I need hardly say; it was a reproduction, quite modern, an obvious fake. Yet not so obvious. I went and looked at it more closely and decided that someone had made quite a good job of it. Still, no one, even as inexpert as a I, could be deceived at close quarters.

I wondered whether it was locked. I put my hand on the lid—and instantly I was the victim of an overwhelming emotion which I can hardly describe. It was partly fear—almost panic: I felt that I was on the edge of the most deadly danger; that if I opened the lid something beastly would spring out—no, ooze out—at me. If it touched me—touched even my little finger . . . All the same, I felt a most disgusting excitement, a desire to see what was inside, to seize it in my hands and squeeze and squeeze it . . .

Half of me prayed that the chest was locked; the other half compelled me to try. And try I did.

Locked. Try harder.

The lid flew up.

Inside the chest, crammed in (and how it had been possible to cram it in I could not imagine) was a naked body. A young woman. Her head was forced down, so that I could not see her face. Somehow I lifted it up. It was the girl who lived in the next bungalow. Young and pretty, I had admired her, and her generously displayed figure; and I had wondered how she had come to marry the sullen, stout, dark, evil-looking man who lived there with her. They had no maids, by the way, and few visitors. A young man had driven up once in a car, but the husband had appeared and the young man had driven on, and I noticed afterwards that the girl's eyes were red.

But I did not think of those details when I had opened the lid and raised her head. I did not even wonder how she—it— could have got into my bungalow, into the chest in my hall; perhaps if I had I should have cursed myself again for my walk up to the village. But I thought of nothing—nothing. For the frightful thing was that when I lifted the head, it—well, I lifted it. I mean, it was not joined to the body. It had been cut off. Hacked off. And there was a sticky—my hand . . .

And at that precise moment the front-door bell rang. You know the sort of bell. You press a button in the door and it rings on the other side. Very startling when you ring it; but on that occasion far more startling to me, who had not rung it.

Even now I hardly know what I ought to have done. The chest, remember, was in full view from the front door: it was a little low chest . . .

I doubt whether anyone could have left the chest open, held that grisly, pretty head in his hand, gone to the door, and said: 'Look what I've just found.' What could I do but what I did—jam the poor head back against the poor, white, red-smeared body, shut the lid, and walk—no, stagger—to the door?

At the door stood an ordinary man, in shirt sleeves, wearing a peaked cap with some name or other on it, and a brown apron. He said something—I hardly heard him; he repeated it, aggressively, and still I could not make head or tail of what he was saying. He more or less pushed past me into the hall, and stood—his leg was touching that chest.

'For God's sake,' I said, wildly I expect, 'come in here!' and led the way into the sitting-room. It was easier in there; and yet I felt that someone was laughing evilly and silently at me.

'Now, tell me, *what* d'you want?' I asked the van man.

What he said almost restored me to my normal self; no, not quite that, I hope—it made me extremely angry.

'But—but look here. It's fantastic! I'm the tenant. I've taken this place furnished for a month. I can't help it if the owner hasn't paid for the furniture. I don't even know whether he has or hasn't paid for it. All I know is that you can't remove the furniture—any of it—'

The man said that he was sorry; he also said something or other about what the law was.

I protested, with growing vigour. He repeated that he was sorry, but that he would have to take certain pieces. We should be all right, he said; the beds would stay and . . .

I became almost speechless with indignation.

'Come on, Bill,' said the man over his shoulder, and I realised that a companion had followed him into the bungalow.

He backed out into the hall, and I thought that I had won. But I hadn't—I had lost.

''Ere, Bill.'

My God, they were going to take the chest! And they were going to try to lift it by the lid!

I shouted something—I don't know what. I suppose that my manner was nearly lunatic. The two men stared at me; in the eyes of Bill's companion there was a queer look—he was staring at my left hand. I stayed at it, too—it was red, sticky . . .

The man's mouth opened as if he was shouting. He pointed at my hand. And at the same second Bill jerked up the lid . . .

I can't think how I had come to pick up the green glass ball from the table in the sitting-room. I am sure I did not know that I was holding it, or what it was that I threw . . .

Crash! Splinters of glass . . .

And there I was, sprawled in the chair in the sitting-room, and the unauthentic glass ball on which I had just squandered seven shillings was in fragments on the floor. And there was no one in the hall, and the chest there—it was nothing like the one which I had seen in the antique shop.

There was just one odd thing. When I picked and swept up the bits of green glass I found that the carpet—an Indian rug, mainly cream in colour—was stained: a little pool of thick black stuff that smelled abominably. How it got there, even if the ball was hollow, I can't think.

Well, my seven bob was wasted, but I suddenly found that I could write, and here's the story—and the authentic oak chest from the antique shop is over there by the fire. I bought it just before we came home, a week ago.

The really queer thing, though, is about the people next door. In the course of that afternoon which I spent all alone, the stout, dark, unpleasant man loaded up his car with luggage and belongings and drove off—by himself. He left the bungalow all shut up, and during the rest of our stay we never saw him again, or the girl. I like to think that she drove off first with the young man, but—well, I can't help wondering whether in the hall of the bungalow next door there's an imitation antique chest and whether one day a furniture van will drive up and . . . But you can read the newspapers just as easily as I can: keep your eyes open.

MILWARD KENNEDY

Milward Rodon Kennedy Burge was born on 21 June 1894 in Matfield Grange, Matfield in Brenchley, Kent. In time the family would move to Westgate-on-Sea in the same county and to a house called *Ingleton*, which in later years became a hotel where—coincidentally—the editor of this volume frequently spent his childhood summer holidays.

Burge's parents were Theodora Vessey and Gerard Rodon Burge (whose father was Milward Rodon Burge). They had married six years earlier in St James Church, Piccadilly and were a very close couple, giving musical recitals together in Blean, where Dora's father was vicar. However, it was not to last. In November 1902 Dora died and her son was only seven years old. Gerard was a private tutor but the following Easter, rather than home-tutoring him, Gerard sent Milward to the Reverend Vernon Royle's school at Stanmore Park in North London, where he would follow in his father's sporting footsteps and play cricket, which he would continue to play on and off for over forty years.

In September 1907, despite having won a scholarship in the same year to Harrow, Burge went up to Winchester College where his uncle, the Reverend Hubert Burge, was Headmaster. He excelled academically and won many prizes, including the Warden and Fellows' Prize for Essay Writing with 'How Far Is Civilisation Progressive?' as well as the King's Gold Medal for English verse with 'England in India'. In his final year he was made Prefect of Hall and also organised the College's annual sports day. Throughout his school years, and despite a weak heart caused by childhood diphtheria, Burge played cricket; he was a useful bowler and a solid if unspectacular middle order batter which led to his playing for the first eleven in matches at Lords cricket ground. He also captained the College's fives team and played as a rugby forward.

In 1913, Burge won a Classics scholarship to New College, Oxford. After coming down in July 1916, he enlisted as a lieutenant in the East Kent Regiment. This was swiftly upgraded to Acting Captain, a rank he retained for the rest of the war. After being wounded, he joined the War Office as a General Staff Officer, where his work with Military Intelligence won him the Croix de Guerre. Part of his role included compiling a history of the Secret Service's operations in Holland and Russia, and he served as a member of the British delegation to the Paris Peace Conference in 1919. After this, he worked briefly in the Egyptian Ministry of Finance.

On 7 May 1921, Milward Burge married a young woman called Georgina Lee and in that October they moved to Switzerland where he joined the International Labour Organisation at the League of Nations in Geneva. Initially private secretary to the ILO's then deputy director, he was appointed director of the London Correspondence Office in January 1924, a post he would hold until he resigned in June 1945. After Georgina's tragically early death, Burge met Eveline Schreiber, who became his second wife in April 1926. He began writing short stories and in 1925 two appeared in magazines under the pen name 'Evelyn Elder', in humorous tribute to his wife, who was known as Lina. He decided to see if he could develop a story at novel length. The result was *The Bleston Mystery* (1928), published as by 'Robert Milward Kennedy' and co-authored with 'Robert Keaver', one of many pseudonyms of A. G. Macdonnell, another Winchester alumnus and fellow Sherlock Holmes enthusiast who would go on to write other detective stories under the

pen names 'Neil Gordon' and 'John Cameron' as well as the celebrated satire *England, Their England* (1933).

In *The Bleston Mystery*, which was published by a New College
alumnus Victor Gollancz, three amateur detectives—two men and
a woman—and a blackmailer set out to locate a cache of money
and a packet of compromising material, and the story climaxes in
a tunnel beneath an internment camp. Like Macdonnell, Burge
also decided to become an author full-time; half a dozen novel-
length detective stories followed in quick order, all published as
by 'Milward Kennedy', the name by which Burge is generally known
today. Two feature Inspector Cornford—the neatly deceptive *The
Corpse on the Mat* (1929) and *Corpse Guards Parade* (1929) in
which a man, who might be called Henry Dill, is found with a
bullet hole in his forehead—which wasn't the cause of death—and
a man admits killing Henry Dill—who turns out not to be dead.
Burge also revived the pseudonym 'Evelyn Elder' for two mysteries
and, after becoming a member of the Detection Club, he contributed to the Club's most celebrated collaborations *The Floating
Admiral* (1931) and *Ask a Policeman* (1933).

In common with many writers of crime fiction, Burge sometimes
drew inspiration from the press. The brutal murder in 1929 of Alfred
Oliver, a Reading tobacconist, inspired *Death to the Rescue* (1931),
which was described in a prefatory note as 'a novel of detection with
a detective who is wholly amateur and has no knowledge of shellfish
or fingerprints or cigar ash'. In the novel, a louche lothario called
Gregory Amor investigates an unsolved crime and fixes on a debauched
actor, Garry Boon, as his prime suspect. The book attracted positive
reviews and when a cheap edition was published in 1934 it came to
the attention of a man called Philip Yale Drew, an actor who had been
the prime suspect in the Oliver case. Yale Drew promptly brought a
libel action against Burge as well as Gollancz and even the printers;
this ended in an out-of-court settlement and a commitment to withdraw all editions of *Death to the Rescue*.

Curiously, it was an American review of another novel by

'Milward Kennedy', *Half-Mast Murder* (1930), that—according to the Oxford English Dictionary—coined the term 'whodunit' in relation to detective stories, notwithstanding that that term had already been used to describe films in the genre.

A year after the birth of their son Rodon in 1931, and while remaining in his role with the ILO, the Burges moved to Rudgwick, West Sussex, where they lived in a house called *Cousens* on Cox Green. It seems reasonable to suppose that the disreputable amateur sleuths Sir George and Lady Bull—who appear in two of his novels—were based, at least partly, on Milward and Lina. Theirs was a close marriage and they were keen gardeners, which led to Burge's only non-fiction book, *An Innocent in the Garden* (1933), which was published as by 'Joseph Cabot', a pseudonym he also used for two novels of village life. At Rudgwick, Burge captained the cricket team and was an active member of the Overseas Comrades and the War Memorial Club as well as, in 1937, the Rudgwick Coronation Committee. He chaired the parish council and among other duties ran a successful wartime campaign to recycle waste paper. Lina also became a councillor, though not at the same time as her husband, and she was very active in the civic life of the area, raising funds for the Rudgwick Queen's Nurses Fund and representing Rudgwick on Horsham's Hospital Committee and the War Weapons Week Committee, which raised thousands of pounds for Britain's war effort.

In 1934, Burge began reviewing books for the *Manchester Guardian* as 'Milward Kennedy', moving after a year to the *Sunday Times*, for which he would review on and off until 1942. A year later he became Director of the UK's Information Office in Ottawa, in which capacity he attended the Second Quebec Conference which, among other matters, agreed plans for the atomic bombing of Japan. After they returned to Britain, he became the London editor of the *Empire Digest* in 1945, which he remained until 1949 when he retired for the second time.

In 1945, Burge also resumed reviewing for the *Manchester*

Guardian and returned to writing; in the main this was shorter fiction but there was also *Escape to Quebec* (1946), a thriller inspired by the 1944 Conference in Canada. From 1950 to 1951 he served as chairman of the Oxford & Cambridge Club, where he had played a vigorous role in various committees since joining in 1917. As well *Golden Gates* (1950), a fourth and final book from 'Joseph Cabot', an at-times brutal historical romance set in the Caribbean in the eighteenth century, he wrote two more thrillers as 'Milward Kennedy'. In the first, *The Top Boot* (1950), a Canadian Mountie tackles criminals in a London night club, which gives the novel its unusual title, as well as in a Sussex village not unlike Rudgwick. The second, and Burge's final book, was *Two's Company* (1952), which deals with what one reviewer described as 'the hazards of being a rich and lonely Australian girl in London'.

In the early 1950s, Milward and Lina made a 20,000 mile 'motor tour' of America with two American friends during which they stayed in Wyoming and visited thirty-eight other states. This led to *Behind the Dollar Curtain*, a series of interviews broadcast on the BBC in 1955, in which the Burges described their impressions of America. After this, they both retired and, once again, threw themselves into village life, hosting events at their home *Cousens*, as well as, in Lina's case, judging flower and produce competitions and raising funds for the village church, while Milward watched cricket and helped to raise funds for the local Conservative Association.

On 20 January 1968, Milward Burge died at home, four years after the birth of his granddaughter Josephine, who would go on to marry the British actor Oliver Reed. Burge was buried in the grounds of Holy Trinity Church at Rudgwick; tragically, his and Lina's only son, Rodon, would be buried there only four years later after being electrocuted in the kitchen of *Cousens*.

'Modern Antique' was first published in *The Bystander* on 11 November 1936.

AN EXPERIMENT
OF THE DEAD

Helen Simpson

It was a most shocking surprise to that highly respectable firm of solicitors, Messrs Walker, Paradise and Walker, when Lady Paula Lidyard went off the rails, causing almost as much confusion and loss of life as might an express train similarly fated. She had been in the habit of drinking too much, spending too much, and risking her neck in swift vehicles far too lightly; but she had somehow kept clear of scandal, which to the legal mind (and indeed to most other minds) meant lovers. Then, at forty-six, what must she do but fall in love with a boy of twenty-three, a young soldier, and announce that she intended to marry him.

Alaric Lidyard, who had been married to her for twenty years, and was a little sorry for the young man, refused flatly to give her her freedom. Mr Percival Walker listened, nodding comprehension, to his reasons.

'She'll get sick of him, y'know. And it's not fair to young Ninian. He'd have to send in his papers—they don't care for this sort of thing in the Brigade. He won't take her on, if it means blowing all his prospects sky-high. We'd better sit tight till she quiets down.'

Mr Walker agreed heartily with this solution, which was well within the traditions of his firm.

'Quite,' said Mr Walker, 'quite. We may safely leave the whole matter to Time.'

With which words, followed by a smile as of parchment cracking, he sent Alaric Lidyard to his death.

For Lady Paula, caught in their trap of inaction, sought escape as an animal might. There was an accident; the car in which she was driving her husband to a dinner-party on the other side of the county turned over into a granite quarry. Lady Paula, bleeding and exhausted, was picked up by a passing motorist as she stumbled, in her evening shoes, towards the nearest village for help. Alaric Lidyard lay at the bottom of the quarry with the car on top of him. When they recovered his body, the head was found to be smashed in.

All very natural, given the weight of the car, and the thirty-foot drop. But an alert young doctor noticed one or two things. He observed that the head wounds, under their mask of blood, were numerous, smallish and deep. A blood-stained spanner was found, hidden under a pile of stones. There were inexplicable stains on the grey upholstery of the car. In short, the conclusion was inescapable. Lady Paula had halted the car, struck her husband repeatedly with the spanner, killing him; then, getting out and putting the car in gear, had sent it with its freight straight at the fence that railed the quarry.

The Coroner's inquest, and the trial at the Assizes, took their course. Messrs Walker managed with despairing skill the only defence on a criminal charge that had ever come the firm's way. In vain. Paula Lidyard, daughter of one of those earls whose names in white paint adorned Messrs Walker's deed-boxes, was to die, hanged by the neck, on a given date in November.

The day after the announcement that her appeal had failed, an odd-looking figure called upon Mr Percival Walker. He had the look of a not very exemplary clergyman, grossly fat, and of an appearance disturbing to confidence. He spoke well, however, and made an extraordinary request in very seemly language.

Briefly, he wished for an interview with Lady Paula in prison; an interview with her alone.

'Impossible,' said Mr Percival Walker with finality. 'Apart from the technical impossibility of introducing a stranger at this time, I may say it is not likely that a gentleman of your cloth would meet with a good reception.'

'Is she bitter?' asked the clergyman, eagerly. 'Terrified? Reluctant to die?' Mr Walker regarded him stiffly, and the visitor resumed, more calmly: 'The fact is, I am a relative of Lady Paula, and I have a communication of some importance to make to her.'

Mr Percival Walker looked at the visitor's card, which read: 'The Reverend Dionysius Luan', and turned his eyes towards the red volume of *Burke's Landed Gentry*. Mr Luan followed the glance, smiling.

'By all means,' said he; 'you will find me there. Her first cousin. No cure of souls—at present.'

Mr Walker did not consult the volume. Recollection stirred in him; this was the son of Lady Paula's only uncle; a recluse, the author of books on certain occult subjects, a practitioner of certain odd and mystical experiments. Certainly, he was the nearest relative of the firm's unfortunate client. All the same— 'May I know your purpose in wishing to see her?' enquired Mr Walker.

'I can only inform you that it is a private matter of the first importance—to me, at any rate,' the clergyman answered; and there was a kind of urgency, almost a glitter, in his small, sunken eyes.

Mr Walker turned the matter over. Taking into consideration his visitor's cloth, with his relationship to the condemned woman, he thought it might be done. The clergyman beamed and swallowed, clasping his fat hands together in gratitude. Would Mr Walker be so good as to approach the proper author-ities? And communicate their decision? Mr Luan could not really express his obligations. And the date of the execution—so soon? Unhappy woman, poor Paula!

With this lamentation the clergyman heaved up from his chair, shook hands with a clinging pressure, and went rolling and labouring out through the old-fashioned high doorway. Mr Walker, moved by a need for air, opened the window a little wider after his departure.

Ten days later he sat opposite Mr Dionysius Luan in a railway carriage. Both men were reading; but while Mr Walker deplored the Gadarene course of British politics as revealed in the pages of *The Times*, Mr Luan was deeply intent upon a red leather book which had the appearance of a manual of devotion. He seemed to read always the same few pages, turning back again and again, as though committing some passage to memory. Once, when moving lips and half-shut eyes showed him engrossed, the book slipped to the floor. Mr Walker, active and polite, bent quickly to recover it, glancing as he did so at the open pages; he observed that one was devoted to a diagram in black and red, which might have been an astrological design except for certain symbols which had no obvious connection with astrology. He had time only to notice this, and to read a few words in large type which headed the opposite page, when Mr Luan took the book from him, eyeing the solicitor shrewdly as he offered civil thanks. Mr Walker had not sat thirty years in his swivel office-chair for nothing; he met the look as blandly as he accepted the thanks, with some comment upon the difficulty of combining high railway speeds with ordinary comfort. He had half a mind to enquire of Mr Luan the meaning of the words which had caught his eye: 'If you would have a dead man's spirit to attend you, and do your bidding in all things, there is a way, how it may be done.' But the clergyman, having stowed the red-covered book in his pocket, seemed inclined to doze, and Mr Walker, who regarded his client's occult studies with the disfavour natural to a priest of the obvious, permitted him to sleep.

Arrived in the northern town, they went direct to the prison. It was arranged that Mr Luan should wait with what patience he could upon an unyielding Office of Works chair, while Mr Walker interviewed his client, and prepared her for the visit to follow. He returned in a short time, shaking his head, with the news (to him not unexpected) that the condemned woman had no wish to see her cousin, and that the matter could not be further pressed.

'One cannot insist,' the solicitor told Mr Luan. 'A condemned person retains certain rights.'

Mr Luan deliberated; then, slowly drawing a note-book from his pocket, wrote a few words, tore and folded the sheet, and courteously requested Mr Walker to deliver the note.

'Pray take it. I believe she will see reason. It is,' said Mr Luan, with an odd smile, the smile of a man thinking of treasure, 'a necessity that she should see me.'

The note was delivered and read. Five minutes later Mr Walker, secretly marvelling, was informing the clergyman that his cousin had changed her mind. Mr Luan showed no surprise, but got to his feet with a kind of clumsy sprightliness and went billowing down corridors at the heels of a wardress to that apartment known to prison officials as the solicitor's room. Lady Paula stood there, a wardress by her, at the other side of a wide table. Her eyes had lost none of their defiance, her hair was black as he remembered it; she still had beauty, but it was contradicted and marred by the line of her mouth, cruel, wholly relentless. She spoke loudly and at once, without greeting.

'Is Ninian coming? What 's the message? Why the hell doesn't Ninian come?'

Mr Luan glanced at the wardress and spoke with the authority his cloth permitted.

'I presume I may speak with the prisoner alone?'

The wardress hesitated, and compromised by retiring to just outside the door, which she left half-open. Lady Paula gave a contemptuous short laugh. Then, seeing the gold chain stretched across her cousin's ample black waistcoat, said suddenly: 'What's the time?'

Mr Luan told her. She began to tap with her fingers on the table, almost as though she were counting, then broke off. 'Well, what's the message from Ninian? You said you had a message.'

'I have none,' answered Mr Luan placidly. 'It was a ruse, to speak with you.' She did not move; but gave him, without turning her head, a hooded look. He continued: 'I have something to say more important than any message from that young man.'

'In two days I shan't be alive,' said Lady Paula harshly. 'Two days and a few hours. I shall know more about it than you, in two days. I don't want to talk about religion, thanks.'

'Nor do I wish to talk about religion,' replied Mr Luan.

Lady Paula stared, gave a half-laugh.

'What sort of a clergyman do you call yourself?'

'Wait,' said Mr Luan, one fat hand raised. 'Listen, if you please.'

The wardress, standing by the door, could see Mr Luan's face. His lips moved without pause. The condemned woman sat, flung sideways on her chair; her expression showed scorn, and later a kind of angry curiosity. The wardress looked away, after a glance at her watch; six minutes yet remained of the quarter-hour permitted. She was a religious woman. The attitude of her charge to the prison chaplain had distressed her, and it was with satisfaction that she perceived the attention with which Lady Paula now heard this stranger clergyman. She began to walk a few steps this way and that, outside the door, to give them an illusion of greater privacy.

Her next glimpse of the pair showed Mr Luan pushing a red-bound book towards the prisoner, and she was about to interfere, for, according to regulations, no interchange of books or papers was permitted; but the prisoner did not open the book, merely laid her hands on it, from which the wardress supposed that it must be a Bible, and let matters alone. The prisoner, hands crossed one above the other, seemed once more to be repeating some formula after the clergyman, and when this was over kissed the red book, though with no very devout expression, and thrust it back along the table. By the wardress's watch it was almost time to interrupt them, but apparently the ceremony was not ended, and it was possible to stretch a point in the interests of salvation. She ceased her march, however, and stood in the doorway as a hint to the two engrossed persons; from this vantage point she heard, with some amazement, Mr Luan recite as follows:

'By which kiss thou, Paula, dost covenant and agree after death to be my servant in the spirit, to go wheresoever I shall bid thee, whether in earth or hell, and to obey me in all things, because by my knowledge I have power to constrain thee. Fiat, fiat. Say, now, after me, Amen.'

'Amen,' said Lady Paula's voice. It was mocking, the voice her husband and lover had both of them known. 'But it looks to me as if you'd made a rotten bargain. I never could do as I was told. And I don't suppose people change much—afterwards.' Mr Luan smiled indulgently. She persisted: 'No, seriously—of course, I mean, it's all quite mad, but just by way of curiosity, what would happen if I turned out to be stronger than you?'

Mr Luan looked at her; at the dominant mouth, the eyes expressionless as those of a snake; and, despite his confidence, felt a little disquieted. She went on: 'After all, I've committed a murder. What have you done? Where does this power of yours come from? You've read a lot of books. I—' She looked at her hands, which had beaten out Alaric Lidyard's life—'I've done things.'

'I must take my chance,' said Mr Luan, and made a curious gesture with his left hand in the air. Paula Lidyard leant back, surveying him with amusement and contempt, as she might have watched an unwieldy animal doing tricks. So thought the wardress, coming forward at this moment. Her prisoner disregarded her entirely, as she had been accustomed for forty years to disregard persons in attendance on her.

'Can't we go on?' said she. 'You take my mind off things. Can't we seal it in blood, do something dramatic?'

'Unnecessary,' said Mr Luan, not smiling at this little joke, and pocketing the red book as he rose.

'You may shake hands,' the wardress told her charge, who laughed and blew Mr Luan a kiss.

'Good-bye,' said she, 'and here's to our experiment. Lucky for you, wasn't it? It's not every day you get hold of a collaborator who's going to be *hanged*.' The word, thus defiantly and loudly spoken, caught her back into nightmare. She went out with the wardress; and Mr Luan heard her outside the door:

'What's the time? There aren't enough clocks in this damn place. Tell me the time, can't you?'

In their hotel that night Mr Walker inquired more particularly if the interview had been a success.

'I think so,' answered Mr Luan slowly. 'Yes, I believe so. Time will show.'

This, Mr Walker's own favourite maxim, had a reassuring sound. He had not been easy in his mind concerning the clergyman. Certain further memories had come back to him, one unsavoury business in particular, with an odour of black magic about it, from the far-off days when Mr Luan had been an undergraduate at Cambridge. He rebuked himself now, and took up the conversation.

'Lady Paula has been something of a problem to the chaplain, I understand. It is shocking,' said Mr Walker, pausing to clip a cigar, 'to consider what she has done with her opportunities, her determination, and her great beauty.'

'Has she then such force of character?' enquired Mr Luan, earnestly.

'That,' answered Mr Walker, pausing deliberately, 'would be

an understatement.' His bright small eyes concerned themselves with the tip of his cigar, but he was well enough aware of his companion's interest to continue: 'She is a woman of one idea at a time, impeded by no scruple that I have been able to discover. She wanted entire control of her husband. That implied the death of her mother-in-law—oh, believe me, I have no doubt of the fact. She has twice done murder, each time for the same reason; that she might have what she wanted.'

'And what do you suppose she may want now?'

'Life,' answered Mr Walker, without hesitation. 'She wants to go on living. The life of the body, I mean, for that has been her sole concern. I should say that what she now deeply wants is a body to dwell in. But there is no way out for her this time, unless'—he regarded his companion with a half-smile—'unless your studies can find her one.'

'My studies?' repeated Mr Luan, quickly for him. 'I am no wiser than my neighbours. What studies do you imply?'

Mr Walker reminded him that one of his published works had to do with thaumaturgy. He did not remind him of that unsavoury affair at Cambridge, whose details still dwelt vaguely at the back of his mind. Mr Luan laughed; disclaimed any practical belief in such matters, and feared that Lady Paula must place no reliance on him.

'A dangerous soul,' then said Mr Walker to his cigar. 'This will sound to you superstitious, Mr Luan, but I cannot imagine so much violence, so great determination, ended by so simple and obvious a process as strangling.'

'It may be diverted, however,' answered Mr Luan, turning up his eyes, 'to other purposes. Yes, to other purposes.'

Mr Walker made no direct answer, for he found his companion repulsive in these occasional sanctimonious moods.

It had been decided that the solicitor and the clergyman should remain at hand in the northern town until Lady Paula could have no further need of their services. During the brief period of waiting Mr Luan betrayed a certain very natural restlessness and discomfort of mind. Occasionally he questioned Mr Walker with notable intensity concerning Lady Paula's character, laying stress in particular upon its ruthlessness and strength. Could it be true that she had committed two murders? Two? Was she indeed so accustomed to have her own way in all things? Mr Walker, having answered, with some impatience, that it was so, Mr Luan would return to the study of his red book. It never left him. Its bulk showed in his pocket, or else he was handling it, not reading, but holding it as though he found it comfortable to his fingers. Once he inquired of his companion if he intended to be present at the execution. Mr Walker replied with distaste that such attendance was no part of his duty.

'It would be interesting'—began Mr Luan; and checked. 'I should be glad to know how my cousin conducts herself.'

'I may tell you this much,' said the solicitor on an impulse, looking at him sideways, 'the interview with you appears to have done Lady Paula some service. She is no longer frenzied at the thought of death.'

'I am happy to hear it,' said Mr Luan, the tone contradicting the words.

'She has swung to the other extreme,' Mr Walker went on, 'as is her wont. She seems to anticipate the hour, almost—I was going to say, almost with zest.'

He observed Mr Luan's cheesy face take on a more absolute pallor at this; and indeed, he personally found the new attitude of the condemned woman disturbing and unnatural. He changed the subject by ringing the bell, and giving precise orders about being called in the morning.

Mr Walker that night slept but ill. So did Mr Luan, if the evidence of his neighbour's ears might be believed. Each time the solicitor woke, and he woke at all hours, he noted a heavy shuffling tread next door, which told him that Mr Luan was awake and troubled. Mr Walker too was by no means indifferent;

and he heard the bells of a church strike the hour of execution, almost with relief.

A minute later, just as the clanging of the bells died down, he heard a different and more sinister sound from the room next door; it was, unmistakably, the sound of a fall. Mr Walker snatched his dressing-gown and ran out into the corridor. Mr Luan's door was shut, but it opened to a turning of the knob. He ran in, pausing to press a bell for help, and looked about him.

Mr Luan lay by the window, grossly sprawled on his back, the red-bound book beside him, open as it had fallen. Mr Walker, in his concern for the man, could not but recognize that same page, that diagram, which he had seen for a moment in the railway carriage two days before. Even as he clasped his fingers upon Mr Luan's pulse his eyes were taken by the clear ancient print, headed with words in larger type: An Experiment of the Dead. He read again, and on, while his fingers noted the pulse's leapings:

'If you would have a dead man's spirit to attend you, and do your bidding in all things, there is a way how it may be done. Get a promise of one that is to be hanged—'

A movement distracted his attention. Mr Luan's large head was moving from side to side, as though to free the neck from some constriction, and as Mr Walker watched, the clergyman's eyes opened and surveyed him; bewildered, yet with a kind of triumph. They rolled once or twice, as the head had rolled, then blinked at Mr Walker; who gently shaking the wrist he still held, asked:

'Are you better, Mr Luan?'

The answer came slowly, in a voice whose words and quality Lady Paula's solicitor heard with the sick certainty of recognition:

'Hullo!' said the voice which was not Mr Luan's, though it came from his throat. 'What—what's the time?'

HELEN SIMPSON

Helen de Guerry Simpson was born in 1897 in Sydney, Australia, where she was brought up on a sheep farm. At the age of seventeen, after her parents' divorce, Simpson was sent by her father to study in France, but with the outbreak of war she travelled to England to stay with her mother. In September 1915 she went up to Oxford to read French, but after two years she left the university and joined the Women's Royal Naval Service, working in the Admiralty as an interpreter and cipher clerk until the end of the war. A competent flautist and pianist, Simpson decided to return to Oxford, this time to read music as she now intended to become a composer. Although she composed a few songs and—in her own words—'fragments for piano', she soon realised that her future did not lie in music and finished without a degree.

While at Oxford Simpson became very interested in the theatre, and she founded the Oxford Women's Dramatic Society. This led to her first book, *Lightning Strikes* (1918), a collection of four playlets including one in which a vampire makes a compact with the devil. She also wrote longer pieces including the fantasy *Pan in Pimlico* (1923) and *A Man of His Time* (1923), a more substantial but episodic work about the renaissance polymath Benvenuto Cellini. As well as plays, Simpson wrote poetry, and a selection was collected in the well-received *Philosophies in Little* (1921), together with some verse translations from French, Italian and Spanish.

Simpson's first novel, *Acquittal*, was published in 1925, having been written in five weeks as the result of a bet after Simpson had described modern novels as being 'written in six weeks by half-wits or persons under the influence of drink'. The book concerns the aftermath of a murder trial, and it sold sufficiently well for Simpson to decide to take up writing full time, always using pen and paper rather than a typewriter which, for her, would shatter 'the peace and quietness necessary to the creative artist', and always working in a room without a distracting view. Her next book, *The Baseless Fabric* (1925), was a collection of strange and sometimes sinister short stories, while the awkwardly titled *Cups, Wands and Swords* (1927) took her back to Oxford.

Around this time, Simpson married Dennis Browne, a fellow Australian and a children's surgeon at the Hospital for Sick Children in London, now better known as Great Ormond Street. She also met the writer Clemence Dane. The two became firm friends, so much so that Simpson named her daughter after Dane, and they collaborated on three novel-length detective stories, two of which— *Enter Sir John* (1929) and *Re-Enter Sir John* (1932)—feature Sir John Saumarez, an actor-manager. They also co-wrote a stage play and the screenplay for *Mary* (1931), an atmospheric thriller directed by Alfred Hitchcock, whose film *Murder!* (1930) had been based on *Enter Sir John*. Simpson also wrote another crime novel, but without Dane. This was *Vantage Striker* (1931), described by one critic as 'the jolliest murder case we've had for a long, long while'. Her next novel, *Boomerang* (1932), drew on the history of her mother's family and won the prestigious James Tait Black Memorial Prize.

Among Helen Simpson's many hobbies was the study of witch-craft and demonology, which were the subject of the many rare books that formed the 'Library of the Devil' in her London home, where she also made her own wine. In 1932, she and her husband travelled to France and Hungary to research sightings of were-wolves and vampires as well as to investigate the alleged involvement of satanists in the brutal murder of a typist in Strasbourg; Simpson would draw on this research for a radio talk, 'On Witchcraft Bound', which made headlines when it was first broadcast by the BBC in 1934 for its frank discussion of ritual murder. She also presented radio programmes for the BBC on homecraft and cookery, and she took part in several celebrity panel shows. Simpson also continued to write. Her other novels include *The Woman on the Beast* (1933), a long triptych fantasy set partly in 1999, as well as two historical novels: *Saraband for Dead Lovers* (1935), about the doomed romance between Sophie Dorothea of Celle and Count Philip Christoph von Königsmarck, and *Under Capricorn* (1937), about Australia's early settlers. As well as the libertarian organisation PEN, Simpson was a member of the Detection Club and she contributed to two of the Club's round-robin mysteries and to *The Anatomy of Murder* (1936), in which Dorothy L. Sayers and others explored notorious real-life crimes—in Simpson's case, the murder of Henry Kinder in 1865.

In 1937, Helen Simpson embarked on a lecture tour of Australia and made various broadcasts for charity. In 1939, she was chosen as a parliamentary candidate for the Liberal Party, but the General Election was postponed because of the Second World War. Her final novel, *Maid No More*, a strange story of slavery and Caribbean beliefs, was published in March 1940. At this time, Simpson and her husband were living in a flat above the hospital where her husband worked and, on 9 September 1940, the hospital was hit by a bomb during an air raid by the Luftwaffe; together with nursing staff and air raid wardens, they helped to extinguish the flames and move the sick children to safety. Just over a month later, the hospital where Simpson was recovering from a cancer operation was bombed and she died of shock. Her last literary assignment had been a series of articles giving a woman's perspective of the war in response to views expressed by an American columnist.

'An Experiment of the Dead' was first published in *The Tatler*, 19 October 1938.

WE ARE SORRY, TOO

Patricia Highsmith

Rita sat beside Midge on the faded blue brocade settee in Mrs
Barton's living room. Mrs Barton was the landlady of the house
in Beacon Street, recommended, said the discreet but quite a
legible sign on the front steps, by 'Motel Tourist's Service'. Here
they had established themselves that morning upon disem-
barking from the New York to Boston nightboat. They had
found Mrs Barton's home not only clean, respectable and homelike, but she had asked them to take tea with her and her sister
in case they should be in around four.

Mrs Barton, a white haired, fragile old lady in a coat sweater,
sat on the blue settee opposite theirs on the other side of the
fireplace and gave her attention to the tea-things.

Midge cleaned close to Rita. 'Beans,' she whispered ever so
softly. 'Ask her about the beans.'

Rita nodded with an admonitory glance.

The fire crackled quietly in the grate, toasting Midge's right
side. The corn on her little toe began to smart, and slowly she
tucked her right foot under the settee and eased it halfway out
of the spike-heeled pump.

Rita shook her head and frowned.

'They *killin'* me!' Midge whispered back.

Mrs Barton handed the first cup of tea to her sister, Mrs
Heminway, who sat in a rocking-chair facing the fire. It was the

first time Midge and Rita had seen Mrs Heminway. She had acknowledged their introductions a moment before with a rigid nod. She sat rather removed from the glow of the fire that enveloped the settees, yet in the central position of the room. Her black dress, relieved slightly by a little lace collar, blended into the shadows behind her.

'You must be quite chilled through, being out in the rain all day,' Mrs Barton said as she gave the tea to the girls. 'I hope this will help thaw you out.' Her small, bony hands were transparent like the china teacups, through which, against the light of the fire, one could see faintly the design of the border, as one saw the veins through her skin.

Rita and Midge smiled and looked down at their cups which they were rather chagrined to find only half full. They handled the saucers carefully in their red-nailed, thick fingers, as though they were sacred symbols, incomprehensible but commanding an unquestionable reverence.

Mrs Barton then passed the silver salver with the china cream jug and sugarbowl, omitting Mrs Heminway who took nothing.

While Mrs Barton prepared her own tea, Mrs Heminway continued to stare silently into the fire, or up at the portrait of the man in the clergyman's collar over the mantlepiece. Had the room being less shadowy, Rita might have remarked that her mouth was much like that of the man in the portrait. But there was no light except that of the fire, and the gloom of the room grew deeper as the logs burned down and the twilight fell outside. Mrs Heminway said nothing and the pressure of her lips suggested that she was repressing something she might have said to her sister, had they been alone. Both of the girls on the settee had the feeling she was waiting for them to finish their tea and leave.

'Of course, staying only two days in Boston, one cannot see everything,' said Mrs Barton, lifting a straw caddy from a china plate, as if the luxury of hot scones were not so rare she could not think of other things, too. 'But tomorrow is Sunday, and you might visit the art museum and the Christian Science Gardens. They are lovely.'

Midge looked at the four toasted half-biscuits the lifted caddy revealed, each with a tiny dot of butter in its centre, bubbling faintly in the heat.

'Oh, yes,' Rita said. 'We intend to do *that*.'

Mrs Barton rose on her slender feet and offered the scone plate to Mrs Heminway, who shook her head in the negative. Midge and Rita each took one biscuit half, and Mrs Barton, returning to her settee, replaced the caddy.

She said nothing for a while as she sipped her tea. The pale blue eyes behind the spectacles looked out on to the olive carpet or down at her lap or at nothing at all. She did not really once look at the girls. The dim light removed what colour there was in her face and her old, well-worn clothing. She was, like her brocade settee, faded and fading still more. Her body was so thin and stiff that sitting on the edge of her seat appeared less of an effort than leaning back would have been. But wasted though she was, she seemed to be trying to kindle within herself a little more warmth and geniality for her two guests.

Rita and Midge sipped at their tea and peered curiously about the room. They could see a few details, however, a heavily framed picture or two, a grand piano draped like a bier in a fringed shawl. The corners were impenetrably black. The ormolu clock on the mantelpiece ticked on. Discreetly Rita bit into her biscuit, muffled the rude sound with her lips, and chewed carefully.

Mrs Barton cleared her throat with a dovelike sound. 'My sister and I like to ask all our guests to tea at least once during their stay with us.'

'It's very nice of you, Mrs Barton,' Midge said. Then to round off her remark properly, 'I'm sure.'

'Of course,' Mrs Barton continued, 'we've been taking in

guests only about a year now, but we've had just the finest sort of people come to us . . . Just as nice as *can* be.'

Midge and Rita's biscuits were gone now and so were their half cups of tea.

Midge looked at Rita. 'The beans. Don't forget,' she said in another feathery whisper.

Rita opened her mouth, but Mrs Barton rose at the same moment with the teapot. She held one hand beneath it, as though its shapely weight were too much for her. The biscuits were passed once again, and Midge and Rita took the other two.

When they were all settled, Rita lifted her biscuit as if to arm herself, and asked, 'Do you know of any place we can get real Boston baked beans tonight, Mrs Barton?'

The vulgar question hung in the air while the old lady reflected. One of the logs on the grate gave an indignant pop.

The last bit of Rita's biscuit broke in her fingers en route to her mouth, and crumbled in the hopelessly small and delicious pieces into her lap. She began recapturing them covertly, depositing them in her saucer, looking at Mrs Barton all the while.

Mrs Heminway had not moved. The vague rustling of her rocking, the ticking of the ormolu clock, the soft breathing of the fire were the only sounds in the room.

'We always recommend the Elizabeth tearoom or the Old Crock Restaurant,' Mrs Barton said finally. 'Almost all our guests ask us about Boston baked beans,' she smiled. 'I do believe New York people eat more baked beans on Saturday night then we Bostonians.'

Mrs Heminway rocked on, oblivious of beans and broken biscuits.

'We'll remember those two places,' Rita said.

'I can give you the exact addresses from the telephone directory,' Mrs Barton said, setting her cup and saucer down. 'They are both not far from here. I daresay you young people could walk.'

She left the room and went into the hall.

Midge smiled at Rita, relieved that the bean problem was about to be solved.

Mrs Barton was gone some moments, and Rita at last ventured to say to Mrs Heminway, 'You people must have been living here a long time.'

Mrs Heminway continued to rock and to stare into the fire, and she was so long replying that Rita decided she was deaf and gave up on receiving an answer.

'Two hundred years,' Mrs Heminway said, without looking at her interrogator.

Rita swallowed and glanced, with the ghost of a smile, at Midge. Midge was nodding with polite interest, though Mrs Heminway could not possibly have noticed. The silence re-established itself.

Mrs Barton returned soon with a piece of yellowed paper on which she had written something in pencil. 'Here are the directions,' she said, giving the paper to Rita. 'And I hope you have a pleasant evening in spite of the rain.'

Rita rose then, and so did Midge, but her cup slipped off the saucer and broke like an eggshell on the floor. The carpet absorbed the bit of tea in a thirsty green splotch.

'Oh, I'm *awfully* sorry, Mrs Barton!'

Mrs Barton smiled imperturbably. 'That's quite all right. I'll get you another.' And she passed out of the fire's light, steadied herself on the piano with the fringed shawl, and went to the cabinet with the glass front in the corner. She returned with an identical cup and saucer which she set on the tea table. 'There's just plenty of tea if you'd like some,' she said, though both girls were on their feet now.

'Oh, no, thank you, Mrs Barton, it was very good.'

'Yes, it was,' Midge agreed, thinking she should say something else about the cup.

'Well, you mustn't hurt yourself on the pieces,' she said, peering about on the floor.

But Midge had recovered the shards, and laid them now with a faint but terrible broken sound in the empty saucer.

Mrs Heminway did not appear to have seen the accident before her, nor to be aware that the girls were leaving.

'We were most happy to have you with us,' Mrs Barton said, as they edged to the door. 'Perhaps if you have time tomorrow before your boat leaves, you both might come again.' She glanced behind her at her sister, as if half expecting, half hoping she might have risen, too.

But Mrs Heminway was still rocking with her cup and saucer in her lap. Her indifference was now tantamount to hostility, and while not speaking to her contributed to the girls discomfort, approaching her demanded more courage than they had. They backed out into the hall.

Upstairs in the room, Midge sat on the high-posted spool bed and removed the painful pumps.

'Gee, two hundred years!' she said.

'Um-m.' Rita unbuttoned her blouse preparatory to washing.

Midge stumped over to the basin in her stocking-feet and began combing her hair in the mirror.

The enamel basin was the only new thing in the room. It was conspicuous there in the corner for its hard, white newness. The rose-patterned wallpaper had been torn away to fix it against the wall. The faucets worked like those in a public lavatory as long as one held them on. It was out of place in the general comfort of the other furnishings.

Rita watched her friend idly. She looked quite short and dumpy with her black hair falling to her shoulders.

'Listen, Midge, that was pretty awful breaking that cup.'

'Yeah?' Midge turned with the comb stuck halfway in her hair.

'Yeah. You don't know how old that was.'

'Gosh.' Then combing again, 'She didn't seem so upset though. I guess if it was so old she'd of said something. She might put it on the bill though . . . Hey, do you think she'll put the *tea* on the bill?'

Rita thought. 'I think she just serves tea anyway.' She went to the window and lifted the green shade. The rain, falling in fine particles, brightened the green of the backyards below. The wooden fences, separating the yards, streaked that morning, were now quite dark with the wet, as were the tar roofs of the woodsheds adjoining the houses. Nevertheless, the few lamplights in the windows were cosy looking and the grass plots were clean and untrammelled.

'Don't it look peaceful?' Rita said.

'Yeah.' Midge put her arm around about Rita's shoulder, and for long moments they stood filling their eyes with the delicious unfamiliarity of the scene.

Then there was a knock on the door.

Midge said, 'Come in.' But no one came until she went and opened the door.

It was Mrs Heminway with the bathtowels over one arm. She laid them over the knobby footboard of the bed.

'Thank you,' Midge said, falling back a step.

Mrs Heminway turned without replying. Her face was exactly the same as it had been downstairs at tea while she rocked and stared into the fire. She closed the door behind herself.

Midge stood still a moment before she took one of the towels. 'She's a funny one,' she said to Rita, and she went to the basin again and began washing.

Rita got out her toothbrush and took the second towel.

'Gosh,' Midge said, with soap all over her face, 'she gives me the creeps!'

After their dinner of baked beans and brown bread, apple upside-down cake and coffee, Midge and Rita went to a movie, because it was too rainy to do any sightseeing. And since it was their last night in Boston as well as their feet, they took a taxi home.

Rita said at the house door, 'Got the key?'

'I thought you were going to take it.'

Rita tried to see you through the curtain behind the top half of the door. There was no light apparently. There was no light at any of the windows either. It was just after midnight.

'Ring,' Midge said.

Gently Rita pressed the bell. They waited a long while.

'Ring again. Nobody heard that.'

Rita rang again, louder, almost at the same instant as the door opened and Mrs Barton appeared in white nightcap and kimono.

'I . . . We forgot our key, Mrs Barton,' Rita explained. 'I'm sorry we got you up.'

'Why, that's perfectly all right, Miss Amanti. Did you enjoy your evening?' Mrs Barton's white face blended against her slightly whiter nightcap. She was like a fragile little ghost.

'Yes, we did, thank you.'

'Yes, we did.'

'Well, that's fine. I'll see you both at breakfast then. Is nine o'clock too early?'

'No, that's fine, Mrs Barton.'

They tiptoed up the creaking staircase. And they went to bed and fell asleep.

A couple of hours later Midge jiggled Rita's arm.

'Rita!' she whispered, shaking with fear. 'Rita, wake up!'

'Um-m? . . . What?'

'There's somebody at the door!' Her eyes were wide in the Cimmerian darkness.

Rita didn't waken completely. 'You're dreamin' . . . Go back to sleep.'

'No, listen!' She raised on one elbow while her heart pounded. 'Now! . . . Hear it?'

Rita listened. She heard a squeak as if the doorknob were being turned cautiously.

Midge gulped. 'You think it's the wind?'

Rita waited. The squeak came again. 'Sure,' she said hollowly.

'There isn't any wind,' Midge said. She clung hard to her friend's arm.

Rita had the awful feeling that someone was standing right outside the door. 'Somebody probably mistook the bathroom, that's all.'

'There's nobody stayin' in the house but us, Rita!'

'Did . . . did you lock the door?'

'I didn't see any key . . .'

The doorknob was turned firmly. Ten feet away as it was, they could not be sure whether the door was open or not. Rita struggled between an impulse to duck under the covers or to get up and try to lock the door.

She scrambled out of bed in a fleeting moment of courage. 'Come hold the door!' she whispered to Midge.

Midge obeyed rather than be left alone in the bed. Rita could feel no key, so they grabbed the knob and pulled hard.

'Do you do you feel anything on the other side?' Midge asked.

Rita was pulling till her arms trembled with the strain. 'No,' she said honestly, 'do you?'

'No.'

Still they pulled. The firmness of the door gave them courage.

'Maybe we only thought we heard something,' Midge said more cheerfully.

Rita swallowed across a dry throat and relaxed her hands somewhat.

'Rita,' Midge said rapidly, 'should we call Mrs Barton and tell her somebody was trying to get in our room? . . .'

'This is my room,' said a voice behind them.

They spun around. Midge's nails sunk into Rita's hands. They saw nothing. Not even a shadow could they discern against the window. Midge felt the doorknob press into the small of her back, and the two girls gripped each other with icy hands.

'My room . . . not yours,' said the voice, with the suggestion of a smile in it.

'Mrs Heminway?' Midge said in a quavering whisper.

They heard the creak of a floorboard, and imagined rather than saw the tall figure approach them. They felt that she was armed, with a dagger, a pair of scissors, with something.

Midge slipped to one side of the door and Rita to the other. The black-clad figure came closer and grew visible. It passed between them as a galleon between two guideposts, and opened the door. The doorknob gave one last squeak and was still.

At breakfast Mrs Barton presided at the white linen table with the coffee urn on her right hand. Rita sat at the opposite end of the table, while Midge was across from Mrs Heminway, who wore her black dress with the white lace collar once more.

Mrs Barton's mouth was in a straighter line than they had seen it the afternoon before at tea. It was now very like a more delicate copy of her sister's. She poured the coffee and passed the cups silently.

'Which place did you dine at last night?' Mrs Barton asked either of them, as she poured into her coffee the judiciously thinned cream.

'The Old Crock . . .' Rita said hoarsely.

'Oh, yes, that's a charming place.' And she lifted the same straw caddy from the four thin pieces of toast with the tiny dots of butter.

Mrs Heminway declined, and took instead one of the soda crackers from the saucer before her.

Mrs Barton kept her pale blue eyes down on the saucer that held no piece of toast, and her old hands fluttered about, adjusting plates, stirring her coffee many times. Among the four people at the table grew the realization that each knew and that each knew the other knew.

'We hope that you will visit us again,' Mrs Barton's voice

cracked on the last word. Her voice was like the strings of an old harpsichord, half musical, half broken. 'We enjoyed your visit and we are sorry that you must leave so soon.'

Mrs Heminway, sitting tall and dominating the table even from its long side, bit into her cracker with the dry sound of a parrot's beak.

Midge rubbed her perspiring hands together in her lap. She could not look up, for Mrs Heminway was sitting opposite. Then her eyes met Rita's and in that instant was exchanged between them the understanding that they would not tell what had happened here to anyone at home. They could not tell anyone, but they did not know why.

Rita drew a red thumbnail upon along the stem of her silver spoon on which was engraved a B in handsome scroll. 'We are sorry, too,' she said.

Mrs Barton proffered, with feeble but hospitable smile, the untouched plate of toast to Midge. It was the first time Midge refused to eat something that was free.

PATRICIA HIGHSMITH

Mary Patricia Plangman, the writer best known as Patricia Highsmith, was born on 19 January 1921 in the home of her maternal grandparents Daniel and Willie Mae at 603 West Daggett Avenue in Fort Worth, Texas. Twelve days earlier, Highsmith's parents had been divorced, and in June 1924 her mother Mary Coates Plangman remarried, on this occasion to Stanley Highsmith, who like her was a commercial artist, as was her former husband, Jay Plangman.

In 1927, Mary and Stanley Highsmith moved to New York where they found work providing cartoons to magazines and newspapers as well as technical illustrations for private companies. They had little time for their daughter, Patsy, who returned each January to Texas where she was taught to read and write by her grandmother. During her annual stay in Fort Worth, Patsy attended Jennings Avenue High School where her talent for writing became apparent, and in 1927 she was among the cast of *Spring Follies*, a dance presentation to raise funds for the Fort Worth Star-Telegram Free Milk and Ice Fund. While Mary Highsmith's memories of her daughter cannot be assumed to be entirely accurate, she would in later years describe fondly the letters that Patsy had written from Fort Worth, some of which were published in *Woman's World* alongside Mary's illustrations.

In her mid-teens and influenced by books on psychiatry that

she found on her parents' bookshelves, Patricia Highsmith began writing what she called 'weirdo stories'. On leaving school, she went up to Barnard College where she studied English Literature, while in her spare time painting and writing book reviews and stories for the *Barnard Quarterly*, of which she would eventually become the editor-in-chief. These early stories included comic stories as well as more suspenseful tales like 'Eel in the BathTub', which appeared in 1940 and features an early version of Tom Ripley, the character for which Highsmith is best remembered.

After Highsmith graduated in 1942 she wrote stories for comic books which she later described as 'not the best work in the world but it pays good money'. In 1945, her first professional short story, 'The Heroine', was published in *Harper's Bazaar*. It had been written when she was just seventeen and, in 1946, it would win a prestigious O Henry Memorial Award.

Throughout college, Highsmith maintained a difficult relationship with her parents. The attitude of Highsmith's mother was at best neutral; in later years Highsmith said that her stepfather had abused her. Nonetheless, she said in an interview that it was while walking with them along the bank of the Hudson river that she got the idea for the novel that would make her name. She abandoned a gothic novel she had been working on and began instead to flesh out the story while on board a freighter sailing from the Italian city of Genoa to Philadelphia. She redrafted and finalised the novel at Yaddo, a residential writers' retreat in New York. On its publication, *Strangers on a Train* (1950) was acclaimed for its 'ugly, fascinating' plot in which an ambitious architect and a psychopathic playboy agree to carry out a double murder. The film rights were bought by Warner Brothers and given to Alfred Hitchcock who reportedly described it as 'the freshest murder situation I've ever encountered'. To Highsmith's regret, she was not asked to adapt her book, nor did Hitchcock seek her advice, even though Highsmith was paid as a technical advisor on the film.

Instead, while the film was being made, she toured Europe, visiting the Festival of Britain and spending time in Munich in West Germany, where she completed her second novel, which would be published the following year under a pseudonym, Clare Morgan. With its then controversial theme of bisexuality, *The Price of Salt* (1952) was moderately successful but, while some work was done on a screenplay in the early 1960s, a film of the book, entitled *Carol*, did not come out until 2015.

In the summer of 1953, Highsmith returned to Fort Worth, where she stayed in an apartment at the Coates Hotel for three months working on her next book in the kitchen with 'a beer at five in the afternoon and plenty of quiet', which at that time she considered the best recipe for good writing. This book, another novel of uxoricidal suspense, would be published as *The Blunderer* (1954) rather than as *The Man in the Queue*, the title she had originally intended. And when not writing, Highsmith gave talks on various literary themes, including one to the B'nai B'rith Little Theater Workshop, which seems surprising given the appallingly antisemitic views she voiced on occasion to friends and in her private writings.

For her next book, *The Talented Mr Ripley* (1955), Highsmith created the character for which she is best known, Tom Ripley, who appears in five novels and in one short piece, an untitled contribution to *The Greatest Mystery Round the World*, an unfinished and unpublished round-robin novella for which chapters were written by some of the greatest names in crime and mystery fiction, including Len Deighton, Helen McCloy, Ngaio Marsh and Christianna Brand. Highsmith's episode is set in Ripley's home in France and echoes a bizarre real-life stunt in which Highsmith disrupted a dinner party by releasing snails onto the table and studiously ignoring them as they moved among the plates. Highsmith often claimed to prefer animals to people and she adored snails, not as food but as pets. On one occasion, she smuggled some through Customs inside her brassiere. Snails feature in several of her books, including the short story collection *The Snail Watcher* (1970) and the novel *Deep Water* (1957), in which the central character is a snail-breeder. While she enjoyed writing novels and short stories, Highsmith was always happy to be distracted, and the director Billy Wilder hired her to add humour to the script for his 1970 film *The Private Life of Sherlock Holmes*, which chimed with her love of the 'Baker Street atmosphere and settings' of Conan Doyle's stories.

While writing was her first love, Highsmith shared her parents' artistry. In the late 1950s, she provided comic illustrations for *Miranda the Panda Is on the Veranda* (1958), a children's book by her friend Doris Sanders. The following year, she took part in an exhibition to raise funds for Rockland County Center for Mental Health in Orangetown, New York. As well watercolours of Trieste and San Miguel de Allende in Mexico, her contribution to the exhibition also included humorous and mildly unsettling pen-and-ink sketches such as 'Pumpkin and Toothbrush', which pictured a disintegrating jack o'lantern, and 'Cat and Fish', which one reviewer described as 'repellent'.

Around the beginning of the 1960s, Highsmith abandoned America for Europe, living in Positano in Italy, and also at Bridge Cottage in the village of Earl Soham in Suffolk, England. In 1967, she moved to Fontainebleau in France, and later to Switzerland. While continuing to write novels, many of which were filmed in English or French, she also completed *Plotting and Writing Suspense Fiction* (1966), even though Highsmith was not entirely comfortable with the notion that she was a writer of such fiction.

Throughout her life Patricia Highsmith drank and smoke heavily and, on 4 February 1995 she died from leukaemia at La Carità Hospital in Locarno, Switzerland. She left her estate to Yaddo, the retreat where she had completed *Strangers on a Train* nearly fifty years earlier. There are several biographies, including Andrew Wilson's *Beautiful Shadow: A Life of Patricia Highsmith*

(2003) and *The Talented Miss Highsmith: The Secret Life and Serious Art of Patricia Highsmith* by Joan Schenkar (2009).

One of only a handful of uncollected stories, 'We Are Sorry Too' was first published in the Winter 1942 issue of *The Barnard Quarterly*. I am grateful to Martha Tenney, Director of the Barnard Archives and Special Collections at the Barnard Library, for drawing it to my attention.

VEX NOT HIS GHOST

John Dickson Carr

NARRATOR: Appointment with Fear!

(*Theme*)

This is your storyteller, the Man in Black, here again to bring you another tale in our fireside series, *Appointment with Fear*. Tonight, good friends, I find myself in a somewhat grim mood; and I have chosen a dark and lonely background— both of the place and of the soul. Is innocence *always* vindicated, as out comfortable theory is? Men's lives have been saved at what some call the last moment. But can a man's life be saved even after he has been strapped into the electric chair? And so, while we watch the last frantic moments of a murderer, we trust we shall keep our promise to bring you . . . an *Appointment with Fear*.

(*Music up. Narrator speaks through*)

New York, nineteen thirty-five.

(*Fantastic music through next voices, which are those of men; newspaper-sellers, and a suggestion of street noises*)

FIRST VOICE: Extra! Read all about it! Harry North dies tonight!

SECOND VOICE: Appeal denied! Dockside killer faces chair!

FIRST VOICE: Extra! Read all about it! Harry North dies tonight!

THIRD VOICE: (*woman, as though reading*) 'New York, August

tenth. Still declaring his innocence, Harry North, aged twenty-eight, former schoolmaster who was sentenced to death a year ago for the murder of Alvin Conyers, heard this morning that Governor Lehmann had declined to intervene.'

FOURTH VOICE: (*woman*) A year ago! Lord pity him!

FIFTH VOICE: (*man*) He did the guy in, didn't he?

THIRD VOICE: 'Long and bitter has been North's fight to save himself from the last mile at Sing Sing and the ministrations of the famous executioner, Riley. North, now little more than a walking skeleton, told me today: "I'm innocent. I swear to God I'm innocent. But I think I'm glad it's all over."'

(*Music up and down, then backing narrator*)

NARRATOR: And so, on that close August night with heat-lightning flickering in the sky, there is tension in the little town of Ossining, some thirty-odd miles out along the banks the Hudson. Here is Sing Sing Prison, city of the lost. But no one inside those walls does the chill of death strike more closely than to a certain girl now driving a motor-car—driving recklessly, almost blindly—along the dim-lit main road which leads from New York to Ossining . . .

(*The music comes out on 'motor-car', and is picked up by car-noise continuing underneath. Dorothy Lake is in her late twenties, of a pleasant voice, but now in a condition bordering on hysteria*)

DOROTHY: (*muttering, to herself*) A quarter to ten . . . that's an hour and fifteen minutes. A quarter fifteen minutes. (*slight pause; bursting out*) I can't *do* it, Harry! I *can't* watch them burn you to death! I . . . I . . . (*sharply*) LOOK OUT!

(*There is a grind as of brakes applied, and a crunch of wheels skidding to an abrupt stop. A man's voice speaks from a distance. Though a rather strong voice, it is mild, middle-aged, and almost humble, with a quick pleading intonation and a very faintly Irish accent. The man seems not ill-educated, and anxious to please*)

MAN: (*off*) Just a minute, miss! Please!

DOROTHY: (*calling*) What on earth do you mean, jumping in front of the car?

MAN: I'm sorry, miss! I didn't mean any harm. But I had to stop you!

DOROTHY: If you're a hold-up man . . .

MAN: I'm not a hold-up man! Honestly I'm not! May I—come closer?

DOROTHY: I suppose so. But . . .

MAN: (*approaching, humbly eager*) That's my car over at the side of the road, miss. I ran out of gas. But I've got to get to Ossining. I've just *got* to get to Ossining!

DOROTHY: (*sharply*) What's that you've got in your hand?

MAN: Only a bird-cage, miss.

DOROTHY: A bird-cage?

MAN: It's a canary, miss. Billy, his name is, after a cousin of mine. He had distemper, and I took him to Redfern's on Forty-Seventh Street. But he's a fine little singer, when I take the cover off the cage. See?

(*The canary sings*)

(*apologetically*) I'm a lonely man, miss; and he's company for me.

(*Dorothy suddenly sobs*)

(*quickly*) Wait a minute, miss! You're crying! What's wrong?

DOROTHY: (*fiercely*) I am *not* crying!

MAN: Sorry, miss. I didn't mean to upset you.

DOROTHY: But I *am* going to Ossining, and I'm in a hurry. If you're going to get in, then please *get* in!

(*Car door opens and closes. Car starts up. Man speaks after its hum settles steadily*)

MAN: We're very grateful, Billy and me.

DOROTHY: That's all right.

MAN: May I ask what part of Ossining you're going to, miss?

DOROTHY: I'm going to the prison.

MAN: (*amazed*) To Sing Sing prison, miss? A nice young lady like you?

DOROTHY: (*through her teeth*) I'm not a 'nice young lady'. I'm a newspaper reporter.

MAN: A newspaper reporter?

DOROTHY: Dorothy Lake of the *Morning Record*. I used to know Harry North. We went to the same college in the old days. So the city editor thought it would be a good human-interest story . . . human-interest story! . . . If *I* covered the execution. If *I* had the last interview with Harry before they . . . (*stops*)

(*The man's voice perceptibly hardens*)

MAN: I wouldn't waste any sympathy on that fellow. miss.

DOROTHY: Why not?

MAN: He's as guilty as hell.

DOROTHY: That's not true!

MAN: (*fiercely pleading*) Listen to me, miss! Please listen!

DOROTHY: (*quickly*) Have you been drinking?

MAN: (*humbly*) Only a little bit, miss. It's my nerves. And—I haven't been well. I'm not drunk, or anything like that.

DOROTHY: Never mind. It's all right.

MAN: Excuse me if I mop my forehead. It's—my nerves.

DOROTHY: (*on edge*) It's all *right*, I tell you!

MAN: This fellow North . . . I read all about it in the papers . . . held up an old man in a car, and battered his head in, and robbed him and then drove the car off the edge of the dock into the East River.

DOROTHY: It wasn't Harry! It was somebody else!

MAN: That's what they proved, miss—Have you *got* to accept this assignment?

DOROTHY: When I was eighteen years old, I thought I was in love with Harry North.

MAN: Then—?

DOROTHY: He was the great man of the senior class, and I

was the little worshipper. I want to see him! I've *got* to see him!

MAN: See him if you like, miss. But—don't go to the other thing!

DOROTHY: Why not?

MAN: Have you ever seen an electrocution?

DOROTHY: No!

MAN: It's that hum, growing louder and louder, when the dynamos start. It's the way their bodies jerk against the straps. It's the smoke that comes up from them—a little bit of singeing—where the electrodes meet the flesh . . .

DOROTHY: (*hysterically*) For God's sake, stop!

MAN: (*changing tone*) I'm sorry, miss. I didn't mean to upset you.

DOROTHY: You seem to know a whole lot about this.

MAN: I do, miss. I'm the executioner.

  (*Long pause. The canary sings above the sound of the motor-car*)

DOROTHY: (*dazed*) You're . . . what did you say?

MAN: (*bitterly*) I'm the executioner, miss. The man they call 'Butcher' Riley.

  (*The car stops abruptly*)

DOROTHY: (*in a strangled voice*) Get out of here!

MAN/RILEY: I beg pardon, miss?

DOROTHY: Get out of this car!

RILEY: (*pleading*) Oh, please, miss! I've *got* to be at the prison by ten o'clock!

DOROTHY: Get out of this car!

RILEY: The execution is scheduled for eleven. If it doesn't take place at eleven, the state law rules that the man's legally dead and there's nothing they can do to him.

DOROTHY: (*struck by a thought*) Do you mean . . . ?

RILEY: (*softly sinister now*) But if you're thinking of stranding me out here, and making me late for my duty, I'd better tell you it won't work.

DOROTHY: Why not?

RILEY: They'd get somebody else to do it. Any electrician can throw a switch. And you'd only make me lose my fee for the job.

DOROTHY: (*with loathing*) Your fee!!

RILEY: I've got to live! The same as anybody else; (*bitterly*) You're just like all the rest of them, aren't you?

DOROTHY: How?

RILEY: They think I'm a good man, a decent man, until they her 'Butcher Riley'. Them I'm a leper, and they'd be contaminated if they touched me. But why?

DOROTHY: Do you expect me to pity you?

RILEY: Am I any worse than the jury that condemns a man, or the judge that passes sentence?

DOROTHY: I don't know.

RILEY: The state makes you callous; and what does it pay for that? It takes away your friends; and what does it pay for that? It makes you the loneliest man on God's earth; and what does it pay for that? Less than enough to live on! (*humbly again*) Drive me to the prison, miss. Please drive me to the prison!

DOROTHY: (*slowly*) All right, Butcher Riley. I'll take you to the prison. But . . .

RILEY: But what?

DOROTHY: How many executions have you handled, Butcher Riley?

RILEY: I don't know, miss. Must be over a hundred, by this time.

DOROTHY: (*very sharply*) Then why are you taking this one so badly?

RILEY: (*just as sharply*) I'm not taking it badly! Who says I am?

DOROTHY: I do. The perspiration's running down your face, and you've started to reach twice for that bottle in your side pocket.

RILEY: It's my nerves, miss. I'm not well.

DOROTHY: Or do *you* think Harry North is innocent?

RILEY: It wouldn't make any difference what I thought, miss. I'd have to throw that switch just the same. But he's not innocent, miss; don't waste any sympathy on him. (*passionately*) He's as guilty as hell!

(*Music up and down sharply. Narrator speaks through*)

NARRATOR: Condemned Row, Sing Sing Prison.

(*The music fades, and is replaced by the ticking of a clock which backs the Narrator's speech*)

Less than an hour, now, before the current is turned on. Condemned Row is a narrow stone corridor, dimly lighted by green-shaded electric lamps, with a line of heavily barred cells—like open cages—along one side. Several of the cells are occupied. And the beasts in these cages are restless tonight: more restless with every tick of the clock. The heat of the August night, the antiseptic smell of the corridor, all have sharpened nerves to a breaking point, when a uniformed guard approaches with a certain girl . . .

(*The guard has a heavy middle-aged voice. Both he and Dorothy speak in low tones*)

GUARD: (*warningly kind*) Don't look at 'em as you go by, miss. They don't like it, much, if you look at 'em.

DOROTHY: Which cell is . . . ?

GUARD: Harry's? Last one down. The one with the very bright light over it.

DOROTHY: That's in case he tries to . . . ?

GUARD: Yeah. We got to keep an eye on 'em.

DOROTHY: How long can I have?

GUARD: Ten minutes, Miss Lake.

DOROTHY: (*blurting it, in a normally loud voice*) Ten minutes? Only ten minutes until . . . ?

GUARD: Sh-h-h!

DOROTHY: (*muttering*) Only ten minutes until the executioner comes.

GUARD: Riley don't go into the cell, Miss Lake. Only the warden and the chaplain and the guards who . . . (*embarrassed*) . . . You know . . . shave his head, and the rest of it.

(*As he speaks, an accordion begins playing very slowly and softly in the background. The tune is 'Swanee River'. It continues under*)

DOROTHY: (*nervously*) What's that?

GUARD: The accordion, you mean?

DOROTHY: Yes!

GUARD: That's Jake Diefer. The one who killed his girl. He's due for it Monday night. (*calling*) Hey, Jake! *Jake!* (*calling*) Cut it out for a minute, will you, Jake! (*The music stops*) That's a good guy! (*in a low voice*) That's Harry's cell, miss.

DOROTHY: (*bewildered*) Where?

GUARD: You can see him through the bars. Sitting on the bunk, with his hands over his eyes.

DOROTHY: That's not Harry North!

GUARD: (*embarrassed*) His hair's kinda grey, miss. I expect you don't remember him like that.

DOROTHY: (*frozen*) No. No, I don't.

GUARD: (*raising his voice, with artificial heartiness*) Look, Harry! Come on, old man; snap out of it! I've brought a friend of yours to see you. (*breezily*) I don't have to tell you who she is . . .

(*As he speaks, there is a noise of unlocking, and a rattle as of a heavy barred door being rolled sideways*)

. . . because you know already. Go on in, Miss Lake. I'll have to lock the door after you; but you won't mind that. Ten minutes, and I won't waste any more of 'em.

(*Door rolls shut; lock turns. Slight pause*)

DOROTHY: Hello, Harry.

(*Harry North is. in his late twenties. His voice is slow-speaking and educated: strong, but a little hesitant and very tired*)

HARRY: Hello, Dolly.

DOROTHY: Don't get up. Please!

HARRY: I—I didn't answer your letters, Dolly. I thought it was better not to.

DOROTHY: That's all right. I only wanted you to know I was thinking about you.

HARRY: Will you sit down?

DOROTHY: Thanks.

(*There is a heavy air of constraint on both*)

HARRY: (*slowly*) I *didn't* do it, you know. I didn't kill that man Conyers.

DOROTHY: You don't need to tell *me*, Harry.

HARRY: (*unheeding*) I've said that so often I wake up from sleep saying it. Always, when I dream, I'm in the courtroom. And they take me straight from the courtroom to the electric chair. That's where I wake up.

DOROTHY: Please, Harry!

HARRY: I wasn't trying to kill Conyers. I was trying to save him. But nobody believed that.

DOROTHY: Except—your friends.

HARRY: (*intently*) I *saw* the murderer, Dolly. He was on the running-board of the car after he'd beaten in Conyer's head. He started the car for the edge of the dock, and then jumped off. I thought I could stop the car and save Conyers. I jumped on the running-board, and that was where the policeman saw me. But I saw the real murderer's face. I saw it under a street-lamp, as plainly as I see yours. Nobody believed that, either.

DOROTHY: Does it do any good, Harry, to go round and round in the same old circle?

HARRY: No. I suppose not. (*blankly*) 'Conyers is dead; vex not his ghost.'

DOROTHY: Please!

HARRY: (*rousing himself*) And I'm forgetting *you*, Dolly. Can I get you anything? A cigarette?

DOROTHY: (*through her teeth*) If you want to break me in little pieces, Harry, just go on being polite!

HARRY: I'm sorry.

DOROTHY: You were always like that.

HARRY: Was I?

DOROTHY: Yes. (*groping*) Can't we talk about—other things?

HARRY: (*half-smiling*) The old days?

DOROTHY: Yes! The old days!

HARRY: Have you forgotten?

DOROTHY: Not a day! Not an hour! Not a minute!

HARRY: Two Yankees—

DOROTHY: (*half laughing*) They called us 'damn Yankees'.

HARRY: —at a college in the Deep South.

DOROTHY: I loved it, Harry.

HARRY: We were going to do great things. Remember?
(*Accordion-music fades in very softly under. The tune is 'My Old Kentucky Home'*)

DOROTHY: I remember how the hill looked at dusk. And the fireflies under the trees—

HARRY: And the scent of magnolia-blossom—

DOROTHY: And the river as warm as water out of a tap—

HARRY: And the white pillars of East Hall—

DOROTHY: And the singing on the steps—

HARRY: (*suddenly*) Remember old Ken, the janitor at East Hall?

DOROTHY: And his cat, Fatima?

HARRY: Ken was very proud of that cat.

DOROTHY: Remember the time you and Jimmy Westlake turned that cat into an eight-foot snake made out of stockings?

HARRY: I heard from Jimmy about eighteen months ago.

DOROTHY: Did you, Harry?

HARRY: He's a doctor now. He worked and worked and worked until he got what he wanted. He worked his way up; he's done great things; he . . .

(*Music stops abruptly. Harry breaks down*)

(*bursting out*) Oh, God, Dolly, I don't want to die!

DOROTHY: Can I come over and sit down beside you?

HARRY: No.

DOROTHY: Why not?

HARRY: They'd think you were trying to sneak some poison to me. Or a knife . . . Dolly!

DOROTHY: Yes, Harry?

HARRY: What time is it?

DOROTHY: I don't know!

HARRY: You've got a wrist-watch on. Tell me! What . . . ?

GUARD: (*interrupting, urgently*) Oi! Miss Lake! Look!

DOROTHY: What is it, guard? What's wrong?

GUARD: You've got to duck out of there, miss! Hurry! The door's just opened! They're coming!

DOROTHY: Who?

GUARD: (*still more urgently*) The warden and the chaplain and the two guards who . . .

DOROTHY: But it's not *time* yet! It's barely half-past ten!

GUARD: Look, miss; I *told* you! They . . . well, they got preparations to make. Come *on!*

(*Door unlocked and is rolled back*)

HARRY: (*unemotionally*) Good-bye, Dolly.

DOROTHY: (*wildly*) I *won't* say good-bye. Maybe the Governor— at the last minute—

GUARD: (*anguished*) For the love of Mike, miss, pipe down! (*anxiously*) Look, Harry. Are *you* all right?

HARRY: Nothing wrong with me, Joe. Just a little light-headed. And I keep seeing that face.

GUARD: (*sharply*) What face?

HARRY: The murderer's face. But you don't believe in it.

GUARD: (*flurried*) Sure I believe it, son. But I got to get this lady out—I tell you I *got* to! Before . . .

(*As he has been speaking, we hear footsteps approaching along a stone floor. The warden of the prison speaks. He has a deep, rather well-spoken voice; of great authority, and rather slow)*

WARDEN: (*fading on*) Stevens!

GUARD: Yes, Warden?

WARDEN: Any visitor to this cell was to have left some time ago.

GUARD: I'm sorry, Warden! I—

WARDEN: Never mind. That's all.

GUARD: Yes, sir.

WARDEN: (*quietly*) Hullo, Harry.

HARRY: (steadily) Good evening, Warden. Good evening, Padre. Is this it?

WARDEN: Yes, Harry. I'm afraid this is it.

(*Music up. Narrator speaks through*)

NARRATOR: Will you come, now, to watch a man die?

(*Pause*)

A bare room without windows, like a stone tank. Don't look too closely at the famous chair or at the high-tension wires running from it past the little booth where white-faced Riley peers out beside a switchboard. Facing the chair are several rows of wooden benches, like pews in a church, reserved for the witnesses. There's the doctor with his stethoscope. There are the fidgeting death-house guards, their eyes on the clock. There are the witnesses, members of the Press in various stages of sobriety, as . . .

(*A confused murmur of voices, speaking rapidly, through which we hear a sudden hysterical laugh which is shushed. Sadie Billings speaks: she is young, tough, but not unsympathetic*)

SADIE: (*not loudly*) Dolly! Dolly Lake!

DOROTHY: (*unnerved*) Who spoke then?

SADIE: It's me, kid! Sadie Billings of the *Bullet*. Don't you even recognise me?

DOROTHY: Oh! Yes! Of course,

SADIE: Look, kid. You're not gonna pass out, are you?

DOROTHY: I don't know. I want to get out of here!

SADIE: Then for Pete's sake hurry up, before . . . ! (*stops, defeated*) You can't do it now, kid.

DOROTHY: Why not?

SADIE: The Warden's coming in!

DOROTHY: Are they bringing Harry?

SADIE: Not for a minute. This is the Warden's pep-talk.

WARDEN: (*fading on*) Your attention, please!

(*The murmuring dies away*)

(*with measured emphasis*) Now, gentlemen . . . and I see there are several ladies too . . .

MAN'S VOICE: (*muttering*) Ladies! *That's* a hot one!

SECOND VOICE: Quiet!

WARDEN: You have given me your word that you carry no concealed cameras, and that you will not attempt to speak to the condemned man when he comes in. If any of you are here for the first time, I want to add a word of warning.

MAN'S VOICE: (*muttering*) Come on! We know all that!

WARDEN: The condemned man will enter by that door— there—between two guards. He will be strapped into the chair, and the electrodes adjusted. Then you will hear a certain humming noise. This is NOT the sign that the switch has been thrown. It is the dynamos generating full power before the current is applied. This will go on for several seconds, until you see me give the signal to the executioner. During that time I want absolute silence. No one—do you understand?—is to speak until . . .

GUARD: (*low voice, quickly*) Warden!

WARDEN: Yes, Stevens?

GUARD: They've started the march.

SADIE: (*under her breath*) This is it, Dolly.

DOROTHY: I *can't* watch it! I—

SADIE: Put your head down, kid! Down low! Don't start yelling in front of the Warden.

WARDEN: *Silence, please!*

MAN'S VOICE: (*muttering*) Where the hell's my notebook?

SECOND MAN: What do you want a notebook for?

MAN'S VOICE: 'Harry North, pale but erect, and walking without assistance, entered the death-chamber at exactly ten fifty-two—'

SADIE: 'He walked straight across towards the chair, past the booth where Riley, the executioner, was watching him . . .' (*sharply*) Wait a minute!

HARRY: (*a little off, crying out*) Warden!

WARDEN: What is it, Harry? Easy, now!

HARRY: Warden! *That's the man!*

WARDEN: What are you talking about, Harry? Grab his arms, boys!

HARRY: Warden, listen! Who is that man? The one standing by the booth where the wires run? An I dreaming again, or do I see him? Who is that man?

WARDEN: That's Riley, the executioner.

HARRY: He's the man who killed Alvin Conyers!

(*A rising mutter*)

MAN'S VOICE: The guy's gone nuts!

SECOND MAN: Crazy as a loon!

HARRY: He robbed and killed Conyers! I saw him under the street-lamp! And I'm *not* dreaming!

WARDEN: Get Harry across to the chair, boys. If he won't stop talking, gag him . . . I'm sorry about this, Harry. I thought you weren't going to give any trouble.

HARRY: (*frantically*) I tell you—

WARDEN: Gag him, boys!

SADIE: (*muttering*) If you don't keep your head down, Dolly, I'll bat you one! This is the foulest thing I ever saw, even in the death-house.

DOROTHY: But . . . it's true!

SADIE: What's true?

DOROTHY: That's why Riley was so upset tonight! *He* killed Conyers! And they're going to electrocute Harry for it!

SADIE: Quiet, kid!

DOROTHY: He did it! Riley did it!

SADIE: (*reasoning, desperately*) Look, kid! Your boyfriend is nuts! It takes 'em that way sometimes.

DOROTHY: He did it! Riley did it!

SADIE: They've got Harry in the chair now. The straps are on.

WARDEN: (*calling*) All right, Riley. You can go ahead.

(*As Dorothy cries out 'Harry!' this is drowned by a high-pitched, intense humming noise which gradually deepens and continues in intensity for about fifteen seconds. Nobody speaks during this time, except for the Warden, who at intervals can be heard whispering*)

WARDEN: Five hundred volts . . . One thousand volts . . . two thousand volts . . . three thousand volts . . . NOW!

(*On the word 'NOW!' there strikes across the humming a fierce crackling sound, the striking of the electricity, which continues for only a second or two. A sudden uproar from the witnesses, and then dead silence*)

MAN'S VOICE: (*aloud, awed*) What in the name of . . . ?

WARDEN: Silence, do you hear!

DOROTHY: (*strangled*) Sadie!

SADIE: (*stupefied*) Yeah, kid?

DOROTHY: Look at Harry! Look at him! He's—he's *all right*!

SADIE: Sure, kid. *He's* all right. But . . .

DOROTHY: But what?

SADIE: Look over at Riley's booth! Look at Riley!

DOROTHY: Riley?

WARDEN: (*calling, steadily*) Everyone in this room will remain still. No one will touch anything. Where's the doctor?

GUARD: He's right here, Warden!

WARDEN: This execution, for a few minutes at least, must be postponed, It may be certain death to touch any of the electrical fittings here. I don't know where the hitch occurred! I don't know what went wrong! But you can look over there and see for yourselves what happened. Riley has been electrocuted.

(*Music up. Narrator speaks through*)

NARRATOR: And once again . . . Condemned Row.

(*Slight pause*)

NARRATOR: In the same cell which he left only a few minutes ago, Harry North leans back on the same bunk in a state of near-collapse. An open door to the cell . . . the rigours of prison discipline relaxed . . . Dorothy Lake with him . . . and the same guard who was on death-watch duty . . .

(*Music fades*)

DOROTHY: Harry! Harry!

GUARD: Better let him alone, miss:

DOROTHY: Why?

GUARD: He's fainted. It's better that way. A guy can stand just so much.

HARRY: (*suddenly*) Dolly! Where am I? Have I been asleep?

DOROTHY: It's all right, Harry!

HARRY: I know. I was dreaming again. I thought—

GUARD: Sure, son. But you're not dreaming now. Easy, Miss Lake! Here's the Warden!

DOROTHY: Warden! Please! Can I talk to you now?

WARDEN: (*slowly*) Talk as much as you like, young lady. That's why I'm here.

DOROTHY: Has the doctor discovered what killed Riley?

WARDEN: Yes. He's discovered it.

DOROTHY: I suppose it wasn't—what they call an Act of God?

WARDEN: No. It wasn't that. But I could almost believe in an Act of God, after tonight.

HARRY: I had a funny dream, Dolly. It almost makes me laugh. I dreamed it was the other man who died instead of me. I could see every detail as plainly as though I'd been awake.

DOROTHY: You weren't dreaming, Harry.

HARRY: I—wasn't dreaming?

DOROTHY: No. Riley died.

HARRY: But that *happened* to him?

WARDEN: Tell me, Miss Lake. They say you drove Riley to the prison tonight?

DOROTHY: Yes! That's right.

WARDEN: Had he been drinking pretty heavily?

DOROTHY: Yes! At least, I thought he had.

GUARD: Riley never touched the switch, Warden, and he never touched the high tension wires behind the booth.

WARDEN: He didn't need to, Stevens.

GUARD: Didn't need to?

WARDEN: A hot, close night . . . the body soaked with sweat . . . alcohol, as a perfect conductor of electricity . . .

DOROTHY: Will you *please* tell me what this means?

WARDEN: It's very simple, Miss Lake. The current jumped.

GUARD: Wait a minute! I think I get it!

WARDEN: The doctor says he's seen it happen to workmen employed near high-tension cables that aren't insulated. You don't have to touch the wires to die.

GUARD: Riley was close to 'em. But he *didn't* touch 'em!

WARDEN: When a man's in that state, the current's apt to jump like a lightning-bolt if you come near. A foot! Six inches! Three thousand volts strike across that gap, and . . . (*enunciating*) . . . do you understand what I'm saying, Harry?

HARRY: (*slowly*). Then it wasn't a dream!

WARDEN: It wasn't a dream, Harry. You're back in your cell now.

HARRY: For how long?

WARDEN: I don't understand!

HARRY: That man—whoever he was—killed Conyers for a wallet full of bank-notes . . .

WARDEN: That's not my business, Harry! I don't know anything about that!

HARRY: No. Of course you don't. That's what's so funny. (*laughs*)

DOROTHY: Please, Harry!

HARRY: You say he died. That's very queer. He went through his own door. And now you can finish the real execution in peace and quiet. I've waited long enough for it, Warden. When do I go back there?

WARDEN: (*startled*) Go back there?

HARRY: Yes! Yes! Yes! For the second time!

WARDEN: (*quietly*) You're not going back there, Harry.

HARRY: Don't make fun of me, Warden! For the love of heaven, don't make fun of me!

WARDEN: You're not going to the chair, Harry. Now, or any other time.

DOROTHY: (*crying out*) Wait! I did hear about it! Riley himself said something . . .

WARDEN: What time is it, Miss Lake?

DOROTHY: Half past eleven.

WARDEN: Right. Half past eleven. (*slight pause*) I don't know whether you killed Conyers, or whether you didn't. But, according to the law of this State, you've been legally dead for just under thirty minutes. And there's nothing on earth they can do to you now!

(*Music up to curtain*)

JOHN DICKSON CARR

John Dickson Carr was born in Uniontown, Pennsylvania, on 30 November 1906. As a child, he attended Uniontown High School where he took part in several theatre productions. Fired up by his father's extensive library and the ghost stories he had been told as a boy, Carr's first short story was published in the school magazine. More stories appeared and, despite being written by a teenager, all are immensely enjoyable. After school and in the holidays he hung around the offices of the *Uniontown Daily Herald*, which his father had at one time edited. He managed to secure ad hoc employment reviewing sporting events and theatre as well as what would now be styled an op-ed, in which he expressed some-times controversial opinions on anything from politics to spiritualism, even the Darwinian theory of evolution.

Journalism and the pressure to meet deadlines gave Carr invaluable experience but his real love was storytelling. From Uniontown High School he went to the Hill, where he wrote detective stories and ghost stories, an adventure serial and essays on political themes like the value of supranational leadership through the League of Nations. On leaving the Hill, Carr went up to Haverford College in Pennsylvania, where unsurprisingly he quickly began writing for the college magazine—mysteries, historical romances, ghost stories, poetry and humorous stories, including one that advocated raising babies on a diet of beer. He was soon appointed editor of

The Haverfordian and sat on the board of *Snooze*, the college humour magazine.

In the autumn of 1926, Carr created the character of Henri Bencolin—a French investigator who owes something to Aristide Valentin, the anti-companion of G. K. Chesterton's Father Brown—who would appear in several novels and short stories. In the early 1930s, Carr created his best-known character, Dr Gideon Fell, whose intellect and physique were inspired by Chesterton himself. Over the next thirty-five years Fell would appear in short stories, radio plays and twenty-three novels confronting Carr's hallmark mystery, the impossible crime: murder behind locked doors, in the middle of a snowy street or in plain view of spectators when no murderer can be seen; death in the centre of an unmarked tennis court, on top of an inaccessible tower or during a séance when everyone in the room is holding hands. Carr's ingenuity was boundless.

Carr also started writing under other names. As 'Carter Dickson', the best known of his pseudonyms, he created the ebullient and eccentric British peer Sir Henry Merrivale, known to one and all as 'H.M.', who was based on Carr's father but also has something in common with Sherlock Holmes' brother, the intelligent if indolent Mycroft Holmes. The Merrivale mysteries are also concerned with impossible crimes, although the problems are, if anything, even more incredible than those encountered by Dr Fell: in one book someone disappears after diving into a swimming pool; in another, a man is apparently ejected from a roof by invisible hands; victims are shot or stabbed within locked rooms or found clubbed to death within a building that is surrounded by unbroken snow. 'H.M.' appears in twenty novels and a few Merrivale short stories.

As well as several standalone novels, Carr collaborated on one mystery with his friend John Street, who wrote as 'John Rhode', whom Carr used as the basis for another detective, Colonel March of *The Department of Queer Complaints* (1940). Carr was passionate about history, which led to *The Murder of Sir Edmund Godfrey*

(1936) in which he investigated a crime that had taken place almost 300 years earlier, the mysterious stabbing of a magistrate close to Carr's London home.

In 1939, Carr joined the British Broadcasting Corporation, primarily to write morale-boosting propaganda plays for the radio like *Britain Shall Not Burn* and *Gun-site Girl*, to highlight bad behaviour at home in docu-dramas such as *Black Market* or to expose Nazi atrocities in thrilling dramas like *Starvation in Greece*. Of course he also wrote mysteries, including one with an extraordinary 'least likely suspect' solution that Agatha Christie herself would have envied. Carr *loved* writing for radio and he has a good claim to be the most important author of Golden Age radio mysteries. He is certainly the only person to do so on both sides of the Atlantic, with plays in two major, long-running series— *Suspense* in the US and *Appointment with Fear* in the UK. Carr also created the series *Cabin B-13*, scripts from which are to be published by Crippen and Landru. While working for the BBC, as well as writing original plays and adapting his own short stories, Carr adapted the work of some of the writers who had most influenced him, including that of Sir Arthur Conan Doyle (whose biography he wrote in later years), along with a series of pastiche adventures, *The Exploits of Sherlock Holmes* (1954), co-authored with Conan Doyle's son Adrian.

After the Second World War, Carr turned to historical mysteries as a means of escaping post-war austerity, including the excellent *The Devil in Velvet* (1951) and *Fire, Burn!* (1957). In 1958 Carr and his wife left Britain for America, where they set up home near Fred Dannay—half of the 'Ellery Queen' partnership—and the magician Clayton Rawson. Both were luminaries of the Mystery Writers of America, of which Carr had been made President in 1949 and was the only person to hold that position as well as Secretary of the Detection Club in Britain. Carr continued to write and he also undertook a lecture tour, but his health was beginning to decline and in the spring of 1963 he suffered a stroke, which paralysed his left side. Even after this he did not stop writing, now using only one hand, although his later novels do not compare well to the superbly plotted mysteries he produced in the 1930s, '40s and '50s. For several years Carr also reviewed books for *Harper's* and *Ellery Queen's Mystery Magazine*. He died of lung cancer on 27 February 1977.

'Vex Not His Ghost' was originally broadcast on 6 January 1944 on the BBC Home Service as the seventh episode of the fourth series of *Appointment with Fear*. It was first published in *Rendez-Vous avec la Peur* (2006), edited by Roland Lacourbe, under the title 'Certains Fantômes Sont Susceptibles' in a translation by Daniele Grivel. This is the first publication of Carr's original script.

WRITER'S WITCH

Joan Fleming

Amyas gave a loud cry of pain and held his head in anguish; Mrs Pegg looked round the door.

'Anything wrong, sir?' she asked with concern. It being a weekday she was not wearing her teeth and, for the same reason, upon her head she wore her husband's old cap, round the edge of which her curlers bobbed playfully. Her face took on a look of shocked disapproval at what she heard. 'Anything wrong?' she asked again, sharply.

Amyas stopped cursing and looked up, but the apparition which he saw through watering eyes in no way mitigated his pain.

'Yes, everything's wrong!' he shouted. 'I've just knocked myself nearly senseless on that blasted beam again!'

Mrs Pegg made a curious sucking noise with her gums, intended, no doubt, to convey sympathy. 'Tch! Tch! Your poor forehead! 'Ow about a spot of marg?'

Amyas dismissed the kindly suggestion with a snarl, and Mrs Pegg wisely held her peace whilst the pain wore off.

Her silent sympathy caught Amyas off his guard; for three weeks he had fought against an ever-increasing irritation and an urgent need to ease himself by bursting into angry complaint. Now he ceased to fight any longer.

'I must have been mad, utterly mad, ever to take this lousy

little hovel, and to think I was going to be able to write here! Peace and quiet was all I wanted, but I didn't expect to knock myself silly on these confounded beams every half-hour—'

Mrs Pegg waited; she sniffed, she wiped her nose with the corner of her apron. Then, with great restraint, she said: 'No, you're not yourself, sir.'

Amyas looked sharply at her. Who was she (their acquaintance being of some three weeks' standing) to know whether he was himself or not?

However, his need to talk was greater than his discretion, and he went on bitterly: 'But I've got to be myself, I can't go on like this! Either I sit at the typewriter doing nothing at all, or else I start moving about and knock myself out, and it won't do. As you may know, Mrs Pegg,' he said sternly, 'last year I wrote a best-seller,' pause for effect, 'and this year I must write another. My publisher is waiting for it, thousands of people are waiting for it, and here I am, the stage set, producing nothing, nothing at all! Not one word since I came. It's all here, mind you,' he said, tapping his forehead, 'or was, but I can't get going.'

Mrs Pegg made her sympathetic noise. She was pregnant with talk; Amyas had known it all along; up till now he had taken immense pains to avoid any sort of mental contact with her. She was, however, an excellent cook, so he sighed heavily, and prepared for the broadside.

'It beats me,' she said, 'how a gent like you could take a place like this, though, *mind you*, it's not lousy now! The council 'as been ever so thorough.'

Still nursing his head, but ceasing to rock himself gently to and fro, Amyas asked: 'What did you say?'

'I said the council spread themselves, like, over getting this place what you'd call dee-loused,' Mrs Pegg replied in a louder tone.

'You don't mean it was really lousy!' Amyas exclaimed, sitting up, his pain forgotten.

'But you've just said so yourself, sir; "lousy little 'ovel" was wot you called it, and lousy little 'ovel it was; only tramps 'as lived in it these past 'undred years, till it was condemned.'

'Condemned?'

'For years,' Mrs Pegg went on cheerfully; 'but it didn't fall to ruin like it might of; stone-built, that's why. Then wot with the 'ousing shortage *ex*cetra, the council dee-condemned it for the evacuees, see?'

Amyas nodded. He saw only too clearly. He had spent but one weekend at the *Crown*, seen the cottage, bought it and, at infinite trouble and expense, had had it 'done up'. He looked round the tiny sitting-room, at the uneven brick floor, the eau-de-nil chintz curtains, the dark oak of the bureau, the shining surface of the gate-legged table, and on it the copper bowl with the nasturtiums foaming from it and tumbling over the side to peer at their reflections in the deep polish.

'Condemned!' he whispered.

'But I must say this,' Mrs Pegg went on; 'mind you, it's a nice little job now, apart from the garden, which you naturally 'aven't had time to deal with yet'—she looked out through the open door on to the grass plot surrounded by the high brick wall. On either side of the flagged central path the grass was high and a few gnarled fruit trees grew neither fruit nor leaf, but, bowed beneath a weight of years, they were covered with a soft grey lichen which blurred their aged outline. 'Yes, apart from the garden, it's marvellous, reely, sir,' Mrs Pegg mused, 'what you've done in the short time—'

Amyas lifted his head wearily from his hands and, leaning back in his chair, with a heavy sigh he said: 'Why didn't anybody tell me all this?' But even as he said it he knew it was a foolish question. Had he sought or desired anyone's opinion? Had he ever laid himself open to advice or criticism from anyone in the village? Had he not deliberately avoided the bar of the *Crown* where he might have been given much useful information about the cottage he was buying?

Mrs Pegg, Amyas thought, was brewing for something. She was poking primly about the bosom of her pink woollen jumper, a sign, he had learned, that a subject of importance was about to be broached. She would fidget thus when about to discuss her wages or how much money Amyas proposed letting her have for 'the housekeeping'.

'You wouldn't of found anyone in the village as would of wanted to talk about the place,' she said at last. 'It's unlucky!' And she continued to poke primly, knowing that she had, at last, roused Amyas's full attention. 'Yes, unlucky!' she repeated, mouthing the word with enjoyment. 'The evacs didn't—'

'The what?'

'The evacuees—they didn't stay long, I can tell you, and then the Army used the place, as an ammunition store, they said, and that scared everyone nearly out of their wits and no one dared even mention the place, *in case—*'

'Yes? In case what?'

'*In* case!' Mrs Pegg repeated in a hoarse whisper.

'Is this some sort of joke?' Amyas asked coldly; 'explain yourself, Mrs Pegg.'

A curious look passed over Mrs Pegg's face. 'All right,' she said (rather nastily, Amyas thought), 'I'll tell you and be blowed! It isn't me as 'as to sleep 'ere nights.' Glancing swiftly to right and to left, she moistened her thin lips and leaned forward. 'It's Mary Ann Beehag! She's never left the place, not since she was 'ung at the cross-roads more nor a 'undred years ago!'

'Ah, I see,' Amyas said in his most superior voice; 'a thief, I suppose.'

'No, not a thief. They 'ung her at the cross-roads on the way to Marley because that's where the gallows 'appened to be and that's what caused it. There weren't no gallows here, see? She'd never set foot out of this village since she was born under this very roof, and they went and took 'er 'alf-way to the next village and 'ung 'er!'

'Why, exactly, was she—er—hung?' Amyas asked, hating the misuse of the verb, but keeping in touch with Mrs Pegg mentally.

Again the look passed over Mrs Pegg's face which he could only describe as primitive.

'She was a very bad old woman,' she said, then she wiped her nose once more with the corner of her apron and turned to leave the room.

Now thoroughly intrigued, Amyas called after her, but she did not come back. He got up and followed her into the tiny kitchen, where she was putting the finishing touches to the salad which she was leaving for his supper.

Amyas leaned against the wall with its brightly shining new cream paint and thrust his hands into his pockets.

'In what way,' he asked, 'was she bad?'

'Mary Ann Beehag? She was famous!' Mrs Pegg said. 'The last of her kind in the county, so they say, to be 'ung.'

'"Of her kind"?'

'Aye,' she replied, giving a lettuce leaf a vigorous shake, 'and a good thing too!'

'"Of her kind"?' Amyas persisted.

'See here, sir,' Mrs Pegg said, stopping her work and looking squarely at Amyas. 'Don't a-go stirring up mud. Least said soonest mended, eh? Walls have ears!'

'I simply don't know what you're driving at,' Amyas said, taking out his cigarette-case.

'You will,' Mrs Pegg told him, briskly plucking off her apron and hanging it on a hook behind the kitchen door.

'I'm surprised at you, Mrs Pegg,' Amyas replied, flicking at his lighter; '*you*, with your electric cooker, and your wireless, and your television, and your bus drive into town to the pictures every week, I really am surprised at your superstitions and your innuendos—' He could feel her getting angry; no one likes having long words thrown at them by a superior voice. Amyas was beginning to enjoy himself; goading Mrs Pegg was poor sport, but better than sitting in front of a typewriter clawing at the blank spaces in one's mind. 'Are you trying to tell me that she was hanged for a witch?'

Silence, whilst Mrs Pegg fidgeted with something in her black mackintosh bag.

'If so,' Amyas went on, 'I am not merely surprised but shocked. Do you know'—he was about to say 'my good woman', but stopped himself in time—'do you know that thousands of poor harmless old women were—er—hung or burned for being, as they say, *witches*? Poor innocent women like—er—like yourself; tortured and put to death by hysterical, superstitious crowds—'

Mrs Pegg was eyeing him with dislike and Amyas stopped abruptly.

'Mary Ann Beehag wasn't no pore innercent old woman,' she declared soberly; 'she was an evil witch. Evil as the devil 'imself.' She opened the kitchen door, hung her black bag over her arm, and looked out at the brilliant afternoon, then with her hand still on the latch she glanced back over her shoulder. 'And the sun shone,' she pronounced, '*right through 'er!*'

Amyas gave a shout of laughter as the kitchen door slammed and he heard her feet on the flags outside.

'"The sun shone right through her!"' he repeated, with delight.

Ducking his head carefully in the doorway, he returned to the sitting-room and sat down in front of his typewriter.

Gradually the amusement and the animation of the last few minutes left him and he sat, sulky and dejected, lighting cigarette after cigarette and writing not one word. Dully, he turned over the pages of his notes headed 'Outline of Plot', which were so drearily familiar to him, and then, with sudden decision, he gathered the loose pages together and tore them across.

'Dammit, it's rubbish!' he shouted.

He stood up, tearing the paper across again and again, and, clutching the pieces in his hand, he strode to the door leading out into the sunlit garden.

Crash went his head against the beam across the threshold, and this time it brought him to his knees, half in and half out of the doorway; everything went black, and there were brilliant flashes in the blackness.

Seeing stars, Amyas thought, like the kids in *Comic Cuts* when they bang themselves. But this won't do! It won't have to go on!

He opened his eyes, and there, in the middle of the flagged garden-path, stood Mary Ann Beehag, looking at him.

And Amyas looked at her.

'What are you doing in my house?' she croaked.

'Trying to write a novel,' Amyas answered; 'a best-seller!'

She gave a cackle of shocking, fiendish laughter.

'What's that you have in your hand?'

Amyas looked at his hand, carefully and stupidly, as though he were drunk. It was full of torn scraps of paper.

'The "Outline of Plot".'

Mary Ann Beehag extended a frightful claw; it was misshapen, gnarled and covered with soft grey lichen which could not hide its aged outline.

Amyas snatched his hand away. He was still kneeling on the threshold. A feeling of cold, dreadful horror came over him.

'Look!' he shrieked. 'Look!' And Mary Ann Beehag laughed again, a cold, rustling laugh, like the wind in dead leaves.

Amyas's teeth began to chatter. 'The sun shines,' he mumbled, 'right through her!'

For the old woman stood in brilliant sunshine, and not to the front of her, nor behind her, nor to the sides of her, was there any shadow.

Mary Ann Beehag laughed again, and this time the sound scraped the inner linings of his soul. She said: 'Yes, only the evil cast no shadow, young man! Give me those—*those*,' she repeated impatiently.

Slowly Amyas put out his hand and dropped the torn fragments of his notes into her extended claw, then he watched, fascinated, as she shuffled down the path, a few steps through the long grass, and stooped under one of the dead trees.

'They're buried now,' she shrieked maliciously, and she laughed again—a laugh that reminded Amyas of a certain book reviewer who had slated his last novel. 'They're buried now, and we shall see what grows there—'

P.S.—Amyas and his publisher are still waiting.

JOAN FLEMING

Joan Fleming was born on 27 March 1908 at Horwich, Yorkshire. Her mother was Sarah Elizabeth Sutcliffe and her father David was a hydraulic engineer with the Lancashire and Yorkshire Railway who would in time become manager of the company's Horwich Locomotive Works.

In later years Joan would say that she owed much to her Lancastrian roots and 'the terrible climate' which meant that much of her childhood was spent indoors and fostered her ability to amuse herself by writing dramatic sketches. Joan had wanted to be a writer from childhood and she was encouraged by her father who bought her a typewriter because, she recalled, he said that her handwriting was so large that she 'exhausted all [her] energy in the *physical* business of writing'. Nonetheless, it would be some years before Joan would have the confidence and ability to consider becoming a full-time writer.

After leaving Brighthelmston School in Birkdale, where her greatest achievement was winning an award for gardening, she was sent away to a Swiss finishing school, afterwards attending the University of Lausanne. On completing her education, she returned to Britain and went to London, where she soon secured employment as secretary to a young ophthalmic surgeon, Norman Fleming, whom she would marry in 1932. Theirs was a long and happy marriage and they had three children for whom she wrote the stories that were eventually collected in her first book *Dick Brownie and the Zagabog* (1944). At this time, Joan and Norman were living in Ellerdale Road in Hampstead, North London, and while continuing to write books for younger readers she began attending evening classes in writing fiction, reading her early efforts to an unappreciative professor who made her cringe. Despite what she described as 'the most punishing experience—not a word of encouragement, nothing', she decided to move away from children's literature to writing crime fiction, albeit in a relatively conventional mould. Her 'adult' debut, *Two Lovers Too Many* (1949), features a doctor as its central character and an unusual method of murder.

As the novel was well received, Joan decided to make writing her career and produced a novel annually until she turned seventy. Her practice was to work from 7.30 a.m. to 12.30 p.m., aiming to type at least 5,000 words a day without even waiting to dress; after lunch she would walk her two dogs and indulge her hobby of buying antiques. Joan would often say that she didn't take kindly to interruptions, nor did she take criticism well, claiming to have abandoned three novels because she was asked to make changes. Fiercely self-critical, she also claimed that her worst fault was 'working out a plot and never sticking to it' and that her ambition was to write a successful play and a 'really great novel that everyone would respect as a classic' to stand alongside those of her great hero, Elizabeth Gaskell, author of *Cranfield* (1853) and *North and South* (1855).

While she never achieved those self-set goals, Joan Fleming was at her peak solidly in the top tier of crime writers, frequently name-checked alongside Agatha Christie, Ngaio Marsh and Nicholas Blake. Her best books are the stunning *Young Man, I Think You're Dying* (1970)—her twenty-fourth book—and the earlier *When I Grow Rich* (1962), whose title quotes the same nursery rhyme 'Oranges and Lemons' as Gladys Mitchell had with *Here Comes a Chopper* (1946). Both of these books won Fleming the Crime Writers' Association's Gold Dagger; she was the first woman to win twice, a feat later equalled by Minette Walters and surpassed by Ruth Rendell.

With a few exceptions—notably two books featuring the Turkish philosopher Nuri Bey—Joan Fleming's novels tended to be rooted in the places she knew best, like the Cotswolds and North London, but she showed more awareness of contemporary issues than most other British crime writers of the 1960s and '70s. Such issues included the impact of living in tower blocks, the Irish Republican Army, drug addiction and illegal abortions. In style and characterisation, she has been compared to Patricia Highsmith and also to Christianna Brand with whom she shared a regrettable penchant for jarringly unrealistic character names. And, like Brand, towards the end of her writing career she wrote several gothic novels, which were not as light in touch as her crime fiction.

Following the death of her husband Norman in 1968, Joan's enthusiasm for writing began to wane. With a friend she set up a nursery in her home, aimed at supporting children to read before they started school. Joan Fleming died in London on 15 November 1980.

One of a relatively small number of short stories, 'Writer's Witch' was first published in issue 10 of the *London Mystery Magazine* for June–July 1951.

THE SECURITY OFFICER

Val Gielgud

This happened at Hogsnorton during the first few weeks of the Second German War.

To avoid any suspicion of needless obscurity, let me add at once that this Hogsnorton was not the celebrated fictional creation of Mr Gillie Potter. It was the code name of a large country house in the south-west of England to which various sections of the British Broadcasting Corporation including my own Drama Department, were to be evacuated in the event of the outbreak of war.

I had always understood that the existence, and especially the exact whereabouts of Hogsnorton was very much 'top secret'. For all I know it may still remain in that category on some list in some obscure file. I will, therefore, confine myself to saying that it stood a few miles outside a town principally famous as the scene of a thirteenth-century battle and for its production of asparagus.

Taken by and large, it was a pretty queer place. No doubt the experts who chose it had their perfectly good reasons. Apart from its rambling size, they were not obvious. Glistening parquet floors echoed disagreeably to the rattle of typewriters, and what had been stables did not convert easily into studios for the broadcasting of plays.

There was a wonderful westward view. There was a superb

lawn, on which surely peacocks rather than planners should have walked, and there was a bear-pit in the garden.

The comprehensive explanation of Hogsnorton was the simple fact that it had once been the home of an exiled Pretender to the throne of France, and decorated accordingly. The royal fleur-de-lis was everywhere in evidence, engraved upon the panelling, embroidered upon the wall tapestries.

From my personal point of view the change-over from London was rather a singular experience. I was evicted from my billet in the town because its owners had never before seen a Siamese cat, and thought that mine was some sort of wild animal of ferocious habits. And in Hogsnorton itself—as the first war-time programmes included no radio drama to produce—I found myself doing a variety of odd jobs, which ultimately included, for some 96 hours, that of responsibility for security.

This was, of course, before the days of the Home Guard. But there were curious, and to me incomprehensible rumours that the Irish Republican Army had evil designs upon Hogsnorton. And patrols were organised, wearing vast sou'westers and vaster boots, who made up for having little to do during the day by squelching through the undergrowth of the Hogsnorton garden during the night. They carried immense and unwieldy clubs. and made more noise than any bodies I have ever heard.

One night I was just going out to join one of those patrols when I was told I was wanted on the telephone. But not the ordinary telephone. This was the Special Line to Broadcasting House in London, which was generally kept for the more intimate communications of high-ranking engineers.

'Hello, Hogsnorton—is that Security?'

I thought twice quickly and replied that it was.

'Security London here.'

'Oh, yes. Of course you're—'

'Don't mention names on the telephone.'

'But I thought this was a special tap-proof line.'

'It is. But you ought to know that the first rule of Security is to take no risks of any kind. Of course you're only deputising.'

I meekly admitted the fact and apologised.

'Now listen. It's possible that there may be an accommodation switch. We may be sending the European Service to Hogsnorton—'

'I think it's a good idea,' I interrupted. 'Drama hasn't any work to do, so this hideout seems a bit wasted on us—'

'I didn't ask for comment,' said Security London coldly. 'If the move takes place it will obviously imply a tightening up of Security your end. I am sending down a representative of the European Service to see you tomorrow night—a Frenchman with experience of police methods.

'His visit is not to be advertised. He will arrive after dark by car. Watch out for him yourself, and give him whatever he needs in the way of information.'

'What's his name?'

'Not on the telephone,' said Security London firmly, and rang off.

I went out to my patrol, and watched a splendid display of searchlights flickering over the clouds to the north. I felt puzzled, mildly apprehensive, and more than a little exasperated.

It was a state of mind which did not change for the better during the following day, which was one of continuous rain, and which became intensified after dusk. For more than three hours I hung about in the immediate vicinity of the entrance to the long drive, with nothing to do but smoke and get progressively wetter. No further message had come from London. No one arrived. Nothing happened.

Finally, I assumed the conventional car breakdown, and a little before midnight went back to the canteen for what might charitably have been supposed to represent a meal. I ate it hurriedly, and retraced my steps down the drive, intending to have a final word with the guard on the big gates before turning in.

Then, almost literally, I ran into him. In the drizzle and the dark one could see very little, but I got the impression of a big stoutish man, a pale fat face with side-whiskers, and a heavy caped coat.

He was leaning on a tasselled stick, wheezing heavily. I thought he looked rather odd, but most of us looked a bit odd at that particular time, especially in the matter of clothes, and he was of course a foreigner. His first words by their accent confirmed as much.

'You expected me—yes?'

'Yes, of course, but a good deal earlier. I suppose you've had trouble—'

'That London road is altogether terrible,' he said.

Technically. I should have asked him for his Identity Card, but he must have produced it to have passed the gates, and I was anxious to get the business over and turn in. Also, I was still smarting mildly from Security London's curtain lecture on the telephone.

'What can I do for you?' I inquired.

'I would wish to see everything,' he replied.

I groaned inwardly, but there was no help for it. We went up to the house, and over it from cellars to attics. A few of my colleagues, busy on night work, were about, but they minded their own business with exemplary tact, and, remembering my instructions, I did not advertise my visitor by effecting introductions.

He said very little except that from time to time he made admiring comments on the decorations.

He expressed particular pleasure over the tapestries that hung the length of the big staircase, and a number of steel engravings dealing with historical subjects which I had never bothered to examine in any detail.

Twice he stopped and waved a plump manicured hand towards secretaries' desks with their shrouded typewriters. 'We shall do better, once we are disembarrassed of those things there,' he said and smiled amiably. I said nothing. To have suggested that the European Service would presumably have a use for typewriters seemed in the circumstances merely fatuous.

We continued our tour, and I felt absurdly like a house-agent who shows a prospective client over a property, as my visitor peered, and stood in doorways 'taking lunars' and making wheezing noises to himself while pointing with his stick. French police methods I thought were quite certainly odd.

We were standing in the hall about to go out again into the darkness and visit the converted stables—in which my visitor had expressed particular interest—when the Night Duty Officer ran down the stairs and told me I was wanted on the Private Line. I made my excuses and followed.

'Hello Hogsnorton. Security?'

'Security here,' I said unamiably.

'London Security here just to inform you that a high-level decision was taken today not to shift the European Service after all. Sorry to have bothered you.'

'But look here,' I interrupted, 'the chap you told me about—'

'Won't be coming, of course. Good night.'

And Security London rang off.

I thought of ringing back. Then my imagination began to work overtime, and I bolted down into the hall. It was empty. My visitor had gone. None of my colleagues nor the guard at the gates would admit to having seen him during the time they had been with me. They had simply not noticed him, or they had taken him for granted. Could he have been a real genuine live spy?'

It was an exciting but also an appalling thought, when I began to think what Security London would have to say to me on the subject. I spent the rest of that might very uncomfortably indeed.

Next morning I felt the need of advice. I went to luncheon with a retired don of my acquaintance, who had a charming house not far from Hogsnorton, told him the story, and asked him what I should do. He blinked once or twice over his port, and said the conventional thing about sleeping dogs.

'Or perhaps,' he added, 'I should say "walking ghosts".'

'Ghosts,' I spluttered. 'Rubbish!'

'My dear boy, that place is well known to be haunted by the Pretender's ghost. Does it really surprise you? Coming back on and off to look over the place and see how it's getting on with simple bourgeois tenants. Your set-up must have shaken him more than a little. No wonder he vanished without fuss when he saw an opportunity.'

'But,' I protested, 'no one saw him except me. It doesn't add up.'

'He only appears to the few queer people who even in this day and age preserve French Royalist sympathies. Surely that's natural? And I remember when I tutored you for the History School at Oxford.'

'You ought to remember,' I said, 'that my sympathies were then, and still are, violently Bonapartist. So now what?'

'I fear I can only suggest another glass of port.'

So I think my visitor was the ghost of the French Pretender. And nothing happened afterwards at Hogsnorton to confirm that he had been in fact a spy.

But I walked with him and talked I remember vividly the caped coat, the plump white hands, the tasselled stick, and boots that had curiously retained their polish for all the length and the mud of the Hogsnorton drive.

VAL GIELGUD

Valdemar Henry Gielgud was born on 28 April 1900 at his parents' home, 36 Earls Court Square in South Kensington, London. While he had been named after his uncle, a notable South African pioneer, young Valdemar was known from birth simply as Val. His parents were Kate Terry, a music teacher, and Franciszek—or Frank—Gielgud, a Polish draper with premises in Bond Street. Kate had been an actress (like her more famous younger sister Ellen) but she had retired twenty years after her stage debut at the age of three. In time, Val also became an actor (like his more famous younger brother John) but his career was to be broader and longer than his mother's.

During Gielgud's childhood, the family lived at various addresses in Kensington and, from 1914, he attended Rugby School where he participated in debates, for example on school traditions and pacifism. In February 1916, he took part in a mock session of Parliament, failing to prevent a 'Government' proposal that would require pupils to maintain the school vegetable garden, and in doing so losing to the 'Prime Minister', who was played by Alfred Alexander Gordon Clark, who would in later years become a judge and, as 'Cyril Hare', an accomplished author of detective stories.

In 1918 Gielgud won a History Exhibition scholarship to Trinity College, Oxford. Surprisingly, he did not gain a degree, but he did gain a wife. On 12 August 1921, he married eighteen-year-old

Nathalie Sergeyevna Mamontov shortly after she left Cheltenham Ladies' College. Stunningly beautiful, Tata—as Nathalie was known—was the stepdaughter of the Grand Duke Michael Alexandrovich of Russia who had been murdered by the Bolsheviks.

The marriage foundered and the couple divorced after two years. During the early 1920s, Gielgud worked for a member of Parliament and also sub-edited a comic paper while, in 1924, he published a collection of poems and essays entitled . . . *Ridiculus Mus*, which included an apologia that 'no young man can resist the temptation to see his work in print'. In October 1925 he became stage manager at the Oxford Playhouse and joined the theatre's repertory company of which his younger brother John had been a member between January 1924 and May 1925. Val Gielgud made his own acting debut in *The Circle* by Somerset Maugham, a performance that the *Oxford Chronicle* considered to be 'adequate but hardly distinguished'. Other roles followed, and reviews were more mixed. For example, one reviewer felt he had 'acted well' in J. M. Barrie's *Dear Brutus* in November 1925, and another damned him with faint praise for being 'better than we have seen him before' in G. K. Chesterton's *Magic*.

Fired up by his family's history, Gielgud tried writing for the stage and in July 1926 his first play, *Self*, was produced by a professional company, The Playmates, at London's Court Theatre. The cast included Frances Dillon—who would go on to act with his brother John—and also Frances's daughter Barbara, who would become Val's second wife two years later. By this time he had joined the British Broadcasting Company as assistant to Eric Maschwitz, editor of the *Radio Times*, the BBC's listings magazine. The fledgling BBC offered many opportunities and, encouraged by Maschwitz, Gielgud moved to the broadcasting side. He was first heard in August 1926, on the service then known as London 2LO, when he gave a short talk entitled 'On Eating'. Other talks followed on subjects as varied as women's fashion, Warsaw and 'the possibilities of interstellar communication'.

Away from the BBC Gielgud remained active in the theatre. His second play, *The Job*, was staged in 1928, and he also acted, appearing in, among others, Noël Coward's *Easy Virtue* and the Sitwells' 'social tragedy' *For First Class Passengers Only*. He also had a novel published. This was *Black Gallantry* (1928), a romance rooted in Polish history, in particular the January Uprising of 1863 against Russia and the Polish-Soviet War of 1920. Shortly after, he and Barbara Dillon announced their engagement. They were married in October 1928 and eighteen months later their son, Adam, was born.

At the beginning of 1929, Gielgud was asked to take charge of drama. Never without affectations, he grew a goatee beard and began sporting a monocle. He set about a personal crusade to improve the quality and range of radio drama, creating the BBC Repertory Company and, ostensibly to eliminate the risk of over-familiarity, decided that in future 'the names of actors in wireless plays shall not be announced'. This was apparently intended to place 'the emphasis on the play and not the player' but given the growing celebrity of Val's brother John, some commentators were quick to detect a hint of sibling rivalry. Possibly to anticipate such criticism, the BBC's announcement stated 'There is no other reason for this move'. However, whatever the motivation, the decree was widely ignored and eventually abandoned.

Over the next thirty years, and with various job titles, Val Gielgud would control every aspect of radio drama on the BBC, and in 1958 Queen Elizabeth II made him a Commander of the British Empire for his services to broadcasting. Throughout his career, he took his responsibilities extremely seriously. Through talks and books he sought to demystify the business of writing for radio and he encouraged new writers like Harold Pinter and Tom Stoppard as well as established ones such as Patrick Hamilton, John Dickson Carr and Clemence Dane to write original material or adapt their novels and stage plays for the medium, as he did himself. He also directed many plays, including in 1931 an abridgement of Shakespeare's *The Tempest*, which featured his wife Barbara and his brother John. He challenged conventions, for example by broadcasting R. C. Sheriff's controversial anti-war play *Journey's End* on Armistice Night in 1929, and when it became clear that radio would be complemented by television, he worked to position drama at the heart of the new service, proposing and directing the first televised production of a play. Broadcast on 14 July 1930 as part of the so-called Baird transmissions, this was Pirandello's *The Man with the Flower in His Mouth*, and only illness prevented Gielgud from also appearing in the cast.

Unsurprisingly, Gielgud was appointed the first Director of Television Drama in 1950, a role for which he prepared by visiting America the year before. He held both roles until 1952 when he confined himself to his first love, 'blind radio', where 'the pictures were better'. While working for the BBC, he also wrote many novels as well as short stories, such as the thrilling novella *Dance Hall Hostess* (1937). Among several stage plays were a controversial political comedy *Party Manners* (1950), a whodunit called *Poison in Jest* (1951) and *The Double Man* (1930), a 'true to life' three-act thriller set in London's East End which he co-authored with his *Radio Times* colleague Eric Maschwitz. Though *The Double Man* was not reviewed kindly, the writing partnership worked well. They turned the script into a novel, *Under London* (1933), published as by Val Gielgud and 'Holt Marvell', and they also wrote several novel-length detective stories and various film scripts. One of the most popular was *Café Colette* (1937), a spy comedy drama based on an infamous hoax in which Maschwitz had debunked critics of British musicianship by broadcasting the completely fictitious 'Orchestra of the Café Colette' in Paris. His best-known collaboration with Maschwitz is the fascinating novel *Death at Broadcasting House* (1934) and in their film adaptation of the book, Gielgud played Julian Caird, a BBC drama director clearly based on himself. He also included the character of Caird in *Inspector Silence Takes the Air* (1942), one of two stage plays he wrote with John Dickson

Carr; these were published in 2008 by the American publisher Crippen & Landru.

In contrast to his BBC career and the generally positive reputation of his work as a novelist and playwright, Gielgud's private life was distinctly bumpier. In May 1943, his second wife Barbara divorced him on grounds of desertion. Three years later, in New York, he married another actress, Rita Weill, who acted in dozens of BBC radio plays as 'Rita Vale'. They divorced in July 1952 and Rita never acted at the BBC again. The grounds for the divorce were Gielgud's adultery with Gina Davies, a Welsh milliner, and a year later he was cited by Gina's husband in a divorce suit. However, his next wife was not Gina but Monica Greey, an actress thirty years his junior whom he married in February 1955; as 'Monica Grey' she had created the role of Grace Fairbrother in the long-running radio soap opera *The Archers* and played the eponymous scientist's daughter in BBC television's landmark *Quatermass II* (1955). In March 1960, Monica divorced Gielgud on grounds of adultery, this time with a woman called Helen Scott at a hotel in Banbury. Six months later he married again, this time to another actress, 26-year-old June Vivienne Bailey, who was known to everyone as 'Judy'.

In 1963, Gielgud retired from the BBC. The final radio play he produced was none other than *The Circle* by Somerset Maugham, the play in which he had first acted at the Oxford Playhouse some forty years earlier. His retirement was marked by a massive party at which he was presented with a volume bearing the signatures of more than 300 of the actors and actresses cast in BBC radio drama over the thirty-four years he had been in charge. They included Carleton Hobbs, the definitive radio Sherlock Holmes, Austin Trevor, the first actor to portray Agatha Christie's Hercule Poirot on screen, and Gladys Young, the first actress to play Miss Marple in any medium.

After his retirement, Gielgud continued to write radio plays and mystery novels like *The Candle Holders* (1970) about murder at a polo match. In the mid-sixties, he and Judy moved to East Sussex where they lived in a house called Wychwood in Church Road, Barcombe. They both played an active part in civic life, and Val pursued his hobbies as well as enjoying 'the society of Siamese cats', which led him to write *Cats: A Personal Anthology* (1966) and *My Cats and Myself* (1972), one of several 'fragments of auto-biography'. He died at Springfield Nursing Home in Eastbourne, Sussex, on 30 November 1981.

'The Security Officer' was first published in the *London Evening Standard* on 14 March 1955 as part of a series in which the reader was challenged to guess whether the stories were true or, as in this case, false.

THE FRAUDULENT SPIRIT

Joseph Commings

'Do you expose fake spirit mediums?' asked the woman in the doorway. Her voice was sharp and vindictive.

It wasn't an unusual question, not in the office of the Bunco Squad. Barney Gant, lieutenant, New York Police Department, looked up. He had flat black hair, a ready disarming smile, and a keen grey eye for a pretty woman.

He smiled at this one. 'They're usually fake after we've exposed them. Come in.'

She came in. She was a lush brunette dressed in a Dior suit designed for spring, for this was June, and she draped her rhinestone-studded veil up from her cobra-like cheekbones. Gant held the back of a chair for her and she sat down and carefully crossed her legs. 'I'm Lieutenant Gant. Your name, miss?'

'Suzanne Dittner,' she said impatiently. She put one grey-gloved hand, curled up into a tight fist, on Gant's desk and leaned forward.

'Do you know Mme Olympe?'

From the other side of the room came a gusty grunt, as if somebody had thrown a sea-lion one of his favourite fish. Startled, she turned her head to look.

Seated in a leather-backed chair reserved for very important people was a huge fat individual with a blowsy outdoor complexion. Senator Brooks U. Banner, He had a rather soiled Panama hat pushed back from his name of grizzled hair and he wore a baggy, wrinkled suit of Congo cloth. She stared vacuously at the rolled-up publication in one of his coat's kangaroo pockets. It was Science Fiction Comics. On his feet were grubby looking white tennis shoes and in one hand he held a shish kebab skewer. It was exhibit A in a recent Armenian stabbing case. He took an unlit 75¢ cigar out of his mouth and scowled at the wet ragged end.

'That,' said Gant, is Senator Banner.'

'Meetcha!' Banner doffed the Panama. 'Somehow,' he continued in a bullfrog voice, I got the reputation of going around and setting fire to old people's wheelchairs. But that ain't the real me. The real me is—'

Gant hastily interrupted. 'He's an authority on spiritualists.'

'Yass,' said Banner dryly. They're all phoneys.' He put the *shish kebab* skewer down and forgot about it. The chair creaked dismally under him as he leaned back and remained silent, which was in itself unusual.

She was saying: 'I'm engaged to Mr Fergus Leslie. His wife died last January and he needs someone sensible to take care of him. Everything was all right until Mme Olympe came and—'

Banner lunged forward in his chair. 'Wait a minnit! I gotta suspicious mind. How'd Mrs Leslie die?'

Suzanne half turned her head away from Gant. 'Fergus lives in a penthouse on Park Avenue. It's twenty stories up with a large outdoor terrace. One night his wife fell off the terrace . . .'

Into the grim bit of silence that followed, Banner tossed one word. 'Suicide?'

'No,' said Suzanne. 'It was an accident. She kept flowers in boxes along the edge of the terrace. When they found her in the street she had gardener's gloves on. And there was a trowel lying on the terrace. She must have reached out too far and lost her balance.'

'I remember hearing about that one,' mumbled Gant.

Banner scraped his broad thumbnail thoughtfully along his ruddy jowl. 'Tending flowers at night in the middle of winter?'

'Jasmine had a mania for flowers. She was pulling out some of the frostbitten plants and discarding them . . .'

'Did you meet Leslie after his wife died—or before?'

'Several months before.' She stopped. 'But that's not it. It's Ferg. He's a successful funeral director and he's got a lot of money.'

'That's a good combination,' rumbled Banner.

'I think,' said Suzanne sharply, 'that Mme Olympe is trying to play him for a sucker. She got in touch with him somehow after his wife died. Mme Olympe said she was starting a new movement called the New Spiritual Dawn Society. She claims to have powers that no other medium ever had. But she needs money to finance the Society. If she can convince Fergus, he'll supply her with unlimited funds. I don't want him to throw away a fortune on her. She has to be stopped.' Suzanne sat there petulant.

'What sorta tricks has Mme Olympe been up to?' asked Banner.

'Some of the things are almost too shuddery to think about,' said Suzanne, allowing her fine tailored shoulders a twitch. 'For one thing she lays claim to greater levitation powers than somebody named Homes.'

'D. D. Home,' corrected Banner. 'He floated in and outta upper windows of a house on Jermyn Street in London.'

'She lives at Rhinebeck on the Hudson. Last month we went up there for a séance. She pretty nearly convinced Fergus that time.'

'What happened?' said Banner.

'We were locked in a room, just the three of us. In the dark I could hear sounds above our heads. There was a strong scent of jasmine fragrance in the room. Jasmine always wore that.

Then I heard a plunk in the middle of the table we were sitting around. We were all holding hands now, so I know Mme Olympe didn't move hers, but when Fergus lit the lights again, we saw one of Jasmine's earrings lying on the table. It was a distinctive earring, black and white cameo with pearls. Fergus swears that was one of the pair she was buried with. Then we looked up and saw the name Jasmine written across the ceiling in red!'

Gant gave Banner a significant look. 'To all appearances,' he said, 'Jasmine has come back from the grave.'

'That's what Mme Olympe is trying to suggest. But I don't believe it. I've got to keep Fergus from believing it. Tonight she's going to put herself to the supreme test. Something that's never been done before.'

Banner pricked up his ears. 'Tonight? Where?'

'At Fergus's penthouse. She's come to town especially for the séance.'

Gant had been jotting notes on a pad. He glanced up and asked her for the address. 'Invite us to attend, Miss Dittmer.'

'Yass,' beamed Banner. 'If Mme Olympe claims to be genuine, she can't balk at a strict control put on her. That'll give us a chance to take a gander at her mumbo-jumbo. Okeh?'

Suzanne hesitated for a moment. 'Then you'll tell Fergus how she does those tricks?'

'Sure thing, honey,' grinned Banner.

Suzanne looked frigidly at him. 'My name is Miss Dittmer, if you don't mind!'

'Yass,' said Banner pleasantly. 'But ain't you been in showbiz?'

He prodded his blunt forefinger at her as recollection came back. 'A few years ago. Didn't you do a devil-devil dance? You put on some class since then.'

Suzanne stood up stiffly, dripping icicles. 'I beg your pardon! I was never in showbusiness in my life!'

'No?' said Banner suspiciously. 'You're the image of the devil-devil gal. She sure fried the customers.'

Suzanne turned rigidly to Gant. 'If that's all. I'll see you tonight.'

Gant nodded and watched her walk out, then he looked at Banner. 'When she first mentioned Mme Olympe I thought you'd bust. What do you know about that medium?'

'The last time I saw Mme Olympe she was dressed in a leopard-skin, leading a carnival parade on the biggest elephant at the Minnesota State Fair. She was duping the yokels with palmistry then. Somebody—I'm not mentioning any names—' he chuckled '—gave her a hotfoot right inside her mitt joint.' He paused, looking more serious.

'Sounds like she's promoted herself since then.'

'I can cope with an ordinary spook racket,' said Gant, 'but this sounds big. Mme Olympe may be beyond my depth. Do you think you're still a match for her?'

Banner got up and announced unblushingly: 'Anything she can do I can undo better!' He lumbered to the window and peered out into the bright sunshine on Centre Street. 'Spooks ain't the main dish, Barney. What you didn't tell Suzanne is that I'm an even bigger authority on murder. I'm interested in the murder.'

Gant spun around to face him. 'What murder?'

Banner leered at him. 'Notice how skeery everybody is about that word? When you and Suzanne discussed Jasmine's death you mentioned accident and suicide, but you steered away from any other probability. I happened to read about Jasmine's death too in the papers, while I was sitting down there on the Potomac, only I kept my yap shut just now.'

'Why?'

'To see how much she'd tell us. Lemme ask you something. How's Homicide got that listed officially?'

'Accidental death.'

Banner rolled his eyes up to heaven. 'Cripes! I thought the police could take care of New York while I was gone!'

'Is that supposed to be funny? Listen here, Banner—'

'Lissen yourself, Barney. If I remember right, Jasmine had gardening gloves on when she fell, and there twas a trowel left on the terrace. Only there was a high wall that she'd have to tumble over—'

'The police considered that. The terrace wall is three feet high and Jasmine was hardly more than two feet taller. There was no one else in the penthouse at the time, no witnesses, so suspicion began and ended there. What else have you got?'

'A hunch,' said Banner softly. 'Nothing else.' He plodded back from the window again. 'She must have been an unrecognizable pulp. How'd they identify her?'

'For one thing, by those earrings that Suzanne mentioned.'

Banner had a sudden thought. 'Was she insured? Yeah? Who benefits by that?'

'I think it all went to her brother who's a crippled war vet in a Pennsylvania hospital. We can check, but I'm sure I'm right.'

Banner looked disappointed. 'I thought her husband might have money to gain . . . Wal, we'll see. The séance tonight'll give us a chance to look for something more than a cheesecloth ghost . . .'

Promptly at eight o'clock that evening Banner and Gant rang the doorbell of Fergus Leslie's penthouse. Leslie opened the door himself. He was a tall, spare man in his fifties, with opaque eyes behind rimless eyeglasses and a comfortable paunch. The greying hair on his large head lay like a thatch. In his dark, pressed business suit and black bowtie he looked more like a merchant prince than an undertaker.

His smile, showing expensive false teeth, looked as if it had been moulded there like sculptor's clay. He waved Banner and Gant in and took their hats.

Banner glanced around. 'No servants, Leslie?'

Leslie's speech was precise. 'Liz the maid is here only in the daytime. She's gone home now.'

'Is Suzanne here?'

'In the sitting room. This way.' Leslie escorted them through the apartment. It was furnished in the best modern taste. Cubist paintings hung on the walls.

Leslie was saying: 'Suzanne told me you'd be coming tonight, gentlemen. Frankly, I wouldn't have minded if she'd invited the American Society of Psychical Research. The more rigid the controls, the better. If Mme Olympe can convince me at this séance, I'm prepared to open my purse.'

Mme Olympe hadn't arrived as yet. Banner asked Leslie if she had ever been in this penthouse before.

'No,' said Leslie.

They walked into the sitting room, its walls panelled in Philippine mahogany. It was large and there were restful chairs in it. Suzanne was sitting in the most restful one, only she sat somewhat on the edge of it. She wore a black taffeta dress with a lot of sweep from the hips and nothing at the shoulders. Her long scarlet-nailed fingers toyed with a Suissesse cocktail. A phonograph was playing South African Veldt music. She looked anxious.

'When'll Mme Olympe get here?' asked Banner.

Leslie glanced at a wafer-thin gold pocket watch. 'In about half an hour.'

'That,' said Banner with a wink at Gant, 'will give us time to frisk the entire apartment.'

'I see,' nodded Leslie slowly. 'You want to see that nothing fraudulent has been prepared. You have my permission. Allow me to conduct you.'

During the next twenty-five minutes Banner and Gant skilfully probed rooms and closets. If there had been a mousehole, Banner wouldn't have overlooked it. At last he mopped his florid face with a red bandana. 'Clean!' he said.

He was standing with the other two men in a sort of foyer just outside the sitting room. The foyer had a French door leading to the terrace. The door was almost closed and it had a sliding bolt on it. Banner closed the door completely and shot the bolt.

He then shagged into the sitting room. Suzanne was still sitting there, still toying with the cocktail glass, empty now. This room had two entrances; the one through which Banner had just come and another leading in from the terrace. Another French door.

Without stopping, Banner plodded across the tapestry rug and out onto the terrace. The others dawdled after him.

The terrace was bathed with the light of a full moon. Stone squares made up the flooring. Wrought iron tables and chairs looked spidery in the moonlight and some of them were crowded against the three-foot wall that embraced the three open sides of the terrace. Banner, glancing up, tripped over a 25-foot hose with an outside connection. Above, the only canopy was a cloudless sky needleworked with bright stars.

Ample room out here, thought Banner, for an open-air dance. He shuffled to the wall to look at the dazzle of the city by night. Spaced along the top of the broad-topped wall were half a dozen 60-inch flowerboxes made of cement. They were a foot tall and as wide as the wall they squatted on. Planted in them were petunias, begonias, violet nasturtiums—whorls of colour in the moonlight. Jasmine's garden. Banner leaned far out over the wall. Twenty dizzy stories straight down was the street. 'Whew!' He jerked his reeling head back.

He poked his forefinger into the soil of one of the flowerboxes, then he whirled around. 'Who's been keeping these posies watered?'

Leslie answered. 'The maid.'

Banner started to amble back.

The doorbell rang imperiously.

'That will be Mme Olympe,' said Leslie, at Banner's elbow.

'I'll answer it,' said Banner. 'From now on we don't dare take our eyes off her.'

He trotted ahead, through the sitting room, through the

foyer, along the hall, and yanked open the door. He glared at the woman who waddled in.

Mme Olympe couldn't have weighed an ounce less than 230 pounds. Her above-average height helped her to carry the weight, with something approaching penguin-like dignity. She wore a long black floor-reaching cloak, which she pulled off her fat shoulders and tossed at Banner.

'For a butler,' she said scathingly, 'you look pretty sloppy.' She reached up and patted delicately her bright yellow hair, set in a series of mechanical waves.

The cloak clung across Banner's front. He clawed it out of his way and dropped it on the floor. His look would have withered anything less substantial. 'Being a gennelman,' he snorted, 'I won't reply to that remark. But I'm sure thinking!'

She was dressed tightly in a dark green velvet evening gown with a high neck and long sleeves. It was glossy where she sat down and there was a rip at the seam in one armpit. On her awesome bust rested a gadget to hold her spectacles around her neck. The capillaries in her nose were a network of tiny crimson threads. There was Pernod on her breath. In Banner's own crude poetry: 'Mme Olympe is built like a blimp!'

Her eye was scalding as she pointed down. 'Pick up that cloak!'

'Pick it up yourself!'

This could have resulted in a draw, for neither of the leviathans would have dared to bend over in close quarters. Mme Olympe looked around for something to throw at Banner's head when Leslie rushed up. At once her demeanour became more spiritual and she purred.

Gant plucked the offending cloak from the floor to hang it in the clothes closet. He took this opportunity to search the garment, for hidden pockets and smuggler's hemlines. There was nothing.

Everybody trooped into the sitting room, Mme Olyrmpe

joggling on open-toed sandals. As Suzanne continued to play more music—Peter and the Wolf—she appealed to Gant with her eyes to start taking some of the hot air out of Mme Olympe. Banner intercepted the glance.

But he waited till he had accepted one of the miniature brandy snifters that Leslie was passing around on a tray. Augustly he saluted everybody and then sipped.

Mme Olympe had lowered herself into a chair sturdy enough to hold her. Banner stationed himself opposite her. He said: 'I heard about that demonstration you gave these people. It was mighty thin.' He propped up one big fiddle-sized tennis shoe. 'About as much ectoplasm emanates from you as there is in my big toe!'

Mme Olympe nearly choked on her brandy.

Leslie started forward. 'Jasmine might have been in that room. We smelled the perfume she used to use.'

Banner looked sour. 'Mme Olympe gave you a sniff from a concealed atomizer.'

Leslie's knuckles were white on the tabletop. 'Jasmine wrote her name on the ceiling!'

Banner made disagreeable chewing sounds. 'Mme Olympe wrote it! How—when she didn't get outta her chair? She had a red crayon stuck on the end of a reaching rod!'

'But Jasmine's earring!' cried Leslie. The earring that landed in the middle of the table!'

Quizzically Banner raised his blacklead eyebrows. 'Telekinesis? You'll notice that rapport is always done with small objects. I've never heard yet of a medium who's done it with a grand pianna. Mme Olympe has an electrically controlled rotating wall-panel that lobs small objects like those earrings out into the room!'

Leslie still looked doubtful. 'How do you explain that it was one of the earrings that was buried with Jasmine? I had them especially made for her!'

'Duplicated somehow, said Banner with a wave of the hand.

He looked at Suzanne and waggled his thumb at Mme Olympe. 'Take her into one of the bedrooms and fan her.'

Suzanne's eyes popped. 'Fan her?'

'Search her. I think you'll do a good job.'

In her chair Mme Olympe's blubbery face had been growing brick red, her hands were clutching like long crusty talons, and she was puffing with hostility. As she struggled to her feet, helped by Suzanne, she choked: 'Doubters! You won't doubt me after tonight! I'll be the greatest medium that ever lived!'

She and Suzanne lurched out of the room.

Waiting, Leslie paced back and forth, worriedly smoking a cigarette. Gant sat, only half listening to the music, trying to keep his wits sharp for whatever might happen next. Banner was humming along with the record in the manner of a man who is completely tone deaf.

Yet his eyes were restless, not missing anything.

Suzanne came back. 'Al I found out,' she reported, 'is that she needs a new girdle.'

Mme Olympe trailed in, smoothing her bolster stomach. She sneered: 'Satisfied, dearie?'

Comical as she is, thought Gant, there's something sinister about her.

Mme Olympe resumed her chair. 'Turn off that phonograph,' she ordered. 'Find seats, everybody.'

Leslie and Suzanne took places near each other. Gant sat back gingerly. It was ready to begin.

Banner lugged a chair around to the doorway. Anyone trying to get out of the room and to the rest of the apartment through the foyer would first have to stumble over him. From where he was he could also keep an eye on the French door that he'd bolted.

'The lights,' said Mme Olympe in a graveyard voice.

Banner was nearest the electric switch on the wall. He clicked it off.

Opalescent moonlight flooded the terrace outside and spilled in through the partly open French door. The five people sat beyond the patch of light, in the darkness. They weren't in the conventional circle and nobody held hands. Except, thought Gant, Leslie might possibly be holding Suzanne's, but for another reason.

The scent of mignonette floated in on the warm night air. Somebody fidgeted. Gant's dollar watch ticked loudly. After a while Mme Olympe began to make sounds that were suspiciously like snoring.

Gant's own eyelids felt heavy. He was drowsy. He yawned silently once. Sitting, doing nothing in the dark. This was pure foolishness, he thought.

And then he saw it.

A shadow moved on the terrace. It rippled across the curtains on the French window, making goblin shapes. It came slowly, slowly, and paused in the doorway.

It was a woman, moonlight on her blonde hair, dressed in something flowing and diaphanous.

My God! thought Gant. This could be the real thing! I might be all wrong!

There was a stirring in the room and a hoarse croak. Leslie's voice. 'Jasmine! Jasmine!'

Gant could smell the jasmine fragrance now, coming in to overpower the mignonette. He was frozen in his chair, watching with opiated fascination every move of the almost transparent figure in the terrace doorway. She seemed to be turning her head as if seeking somebody.

'Nobody move!' snapped Mme Olympe's voice. She wasn't asleep after all.

The figure stood there silhouetted, wavering, fluttering small hands, summoning up the power to communicate.

A small reedy voice pitched upward toward the ceiling. 'I was pushed! I was pushed!'

Banner's voice barked: 'Who pushed you?'

The figure struggled with itself, hesitated, then stepped back, pulling the French door closed with her. Her moving shape flickered on the curtains.

For several long pulsebeats the room remained in stunned silence, then noise erupted. In spite of Mme Olympe's warning not to move, Gant bounded out of his chair. He winced as he banged his shin against an invisible coffee table. Before he could reach the French door he had to wrestle a fat unwieldy body out of the way. If it was Mme Olympe, she must have moved with great speed.

Then the darkness vanished as Banner turned on the lights.

Gant glanced briefly around, orienting himself. Everyone was standing. Leslie and Suzanne were together, looking bewildered. Mme Olympe was in a half crouch by her chair. Banner was lumbering forward, ready to take charge.

It was he who yanked open the French door and led the scramble out onto the terrace. Mme Olympe was the last to waddle out of the sitting room.

Banner floundered among the wrought iron table and chairs.

'She's gone!' breathed Suzanne.

That was true. The terrace was empty. As empty as it had been when they first searched it.

Buffaloed, Banner looked up and around. Nothing. He trotted to the 14-inch wide terrace wall and peered down that abysmal drop to the avenue. Only a fly could have climbed up or down that.

'Look here!' said Gant with excitement. He was pointing to one of the massive cement flowerboxes a few feet away. The violets growing there had been freshly crushed and some of the earth was disturbed.

Banner bent closer. Clearly imprinted in the soil was the impression of a small naked foot, the toe-marks facing the very edge.

Banner said huskily: 'The next step outward would be twenty storeys down!'

'Or over there!' rasped Leslie.

He was standing tensely, looking across the broad avenue to a similar penthouse terrace opposite.

They all looked. On the distant terrace a female form in a diaphanous drape waved her arm sadly at them. She fluttered in and out through the shadows and vanished inside through a dark doorway.

'By the great eternal!' gasped Banner. 'She made it!'

'You'll believe me now!' wheezed Mme Olympe. She seemed completely done in.

Awe was in their faces. Scepticism crept back in Banner. He wheeled toward Gant. 'Barney, nip across the street and see who's in the other penthouse! I'll hold things here!'

Gant turned and ran out.

A weird giggle bubbled out of Mme Olympe's bloated body. 'He won't find anybody there. You saw the miracle. You saw it with your own eyes.'

She staggered back inside. Then she collapsed in the middle of the sitting room rug.

Suzanne and Leslie hurried in to help her, Suzanne reaching her first.

Banner, more calmly and leisurely, advanced behind them, stumbling heavily.

'Brandy,' said Suzanne. 'She's passed out.'

Leslie held a snifter under the prostrate medium's veined nose. Quite suddenly Mme Olympe opened her eyes, tilted the glass, and drank greedily. 'You didn't obey me,' she muttered. 'You broke into my trance. The shock might have killed me.'

With difficulty they lifted her into a chair and gave her more brandy to nurse.

The phone in the sitting room begin to ring. Banner reached out and grabbed it up. 'Yass? Banner!'

This's Barney. I'm in the apartment across the street.

'Any trouble getting in?'

'No. The door was open, inviting like. There's nobody here.'

Banner turned away from the phone for an instant to glower at Mme Olympe. 'Anything else?'

'I have found a few interesting things.'

'Like what, frinstance?'

You'll see yourself when you come over.'

'Stick there, Barney. I'll see you later.' He hung up and turned to the others. 'The séance is over. Everybody better go home.'

Mme Olympe whined. 'I'll never make it back to my hotel alone. I'm bushed.'

'Mebbe you'll take her,' suggested Banner to Suzanne.

'No,' said Suzanne, 'not me.' She looked rebellious.

'I could,' said Leslie.

'I want you to stay with me,' retorted Banner. 'Lemme see.' He prowled around the room, once going out into the foyer to check the locked French door. Still bolted.

Suzanne was preparing to leave when the apartment door opened and closed. Banner peered along the hall to see who was coming in.

'Liz,' said Leslie with a sigh of relief.

Liz Chamberlin, the maid, was one of those timid-looking women. She had a monkey face, drab brown hair, and lead-coloured circles under her eyes. Dressed in a mousy suit, she wore tall-heeled pumps in an effort to increase her height to average. She stared at them with a perpetual worried expression.

'Thank heaven you're here, Liz,' said Leslie. 'We need someone to help Mme Olympe.'

Liz gave him a befuddled nod.

'Good night,' said Suzanne, brushing past.

'Nighty-night,' said Banner. 'I'll be getting in touch with you. Sweet dreams.'

Suzanne closed the door loudly on her way out.

Banner turned to the maid, who was fussing around Mme Olympe. 'How long've you worked here, Lizzie?'

'She—' began Leslie.

'Let her answer,' said Banner sternly.

'I was hired by Mrs Leslie about a month before she—er—died.'

'So you were her maid.'

'In a way, yes.'

'Did you sleep in then? I noticed a maid's room.'

'Yes, I did sleep in. But I didn't think that it was quite—er—proper to remain alone with Mr Leslie. So after the funeral I got a room outside.'

'Were you here the night Jasmine fell off the terrace?'

'No, sir.' She swallowed. 'I went to a movie.'

Banner gave her a ferocious look and she cringed. If you work here only in the daytime, why'd you return tonight?'

She glanced helplessly around. 'Only because I heard there'd be a séance, sir. The apartment would need a little tidying up afterwards. I'd rather do it tonight then let it go till morning.'

Banner muttered: 'Things could do with a little tidying up. Okeh, Lizzie. Will you see that Mme Olympe gets to beddie-bye all right?'

'Yes, sir.'

'Good gal.'

Mme Olympe leaned heavily on the frail maid as they went up the hall, got the long cloak fitted on the medium's beefy shoulders, and went out.

'That leaves us, Leslie,' said Banner impatiently. 'Let's go. I'm rearin' to find out what's across the street.'

Jamming his Panama on his shaggy head, he went downstairs in the self-service elevator with Leslie.

The avenue was quiet. They marched out through the entranceway toward the kerb.

'Look out!' screamed Leslie.

Banner instinctively bunched forward.

Something heavy hurtled down from above, jarring the ground when it hit, cracking the sidewalk. Thick chunks of smashed cement shot through the air, whizzing past Banner.

'Missed us by yards!' he grunted and swore.

Scattered on the dented sidewalk, its soil spread wide and thin, was one of the massive flowerboxes from the terrace wall!

'Somebody up there tried to kill us!' panted Leslie.

Banner was bracing himself at the curb, wiping cold sweat from his face. 'But there's nobody up there!' he said in a hollow voice.

Leslie looked pale but determined. 'I'm going back to see!'

'I'm right with you!'

They sped up in the elevator. They hurried through the apartment to the terrace, not missing anything on the way. There was a lonesome gap in the evenly spaced flowerboxes on the wall.

But there was nobody in the whole apartment.

Strain showed on Leslie's face when they went down again. Banner was frowning and silent. He had to admit it was a narrow squeak.

They remained silent until they entered the other penthouse. Gant was nervously waiting for them.

Banner made an attempt at humour. 'Ketch any spooks, Barney?

'No,' said Gant. 'Smell anything?'

Banner sniffed the air. 'Yass,' he growled, 'Jasmine's been here all right. What else?'

'In here. I haven't touched it.'

The apartment was neat and furnished as if someone were living in it. A woman. In one bedroom Gant pointed to the floor. On it lay a black and white cameo earring with pearls.

Leslie sucked in his breath. 'That's the second one of the pair I gave Jasmine!'

Banner stooped over with a fat man's grunt and picked it up. 'She's a little careless with 'em,' he said sourly.

'She used to drop them often when she was alive,' explained Leslie. 'Her ears weren't pierced.'

Banner slipped the earring into his pocket. 'But this doesn't mean—'

Gant had pulled out a dresser drawer. He lifted up a pink silk nightgown. 'This has been worn,' he said. 'And look at these other things. There're labels on some of them. Size nine.'

'That was Jasmine's size,' whispered Leslie.

Banner looked gloomy. 'Sweet Marguerite! Are you trying to talk yourselves into it? Mme Olympe materialized Jasmine and then had her ghost hop from one roof to another, twenty stories up! Is that it? Use your head, Barney. Find out from the renting agent who's been paying for this joint!'

'I did,' said Gant. 'Had a little trouble reaching him. He's been notified to call back.'

Banner shuffled around, angry. 'That big fat fraud's trying to gull us with a lotta talk about astral bodies and levitation and—'

He was cut short by the ringing of the phone.

He jumped at it and snatched it up. 'Hallo? . . . Who? The renting agent? This's the party in the penthouse. I wanna know— Whuzzat? Huh? . . . Yeah, I got it . . .'

He put down the phone slowly and turned. 'That blows my fuse,' he snarled. 'This place was taken on a six months' lease last December. The person who paid the rent was Mrs Jasmine Leslie!'

Banner and Gant dawdled out into the warm night, 'Since I can't explain it,' said Banner, 'I'm almost ready to believe it myself. There're only three ways off that terrace, up, down, or straight across. Wal, we'd stationed a cop on the penthouse roof as a precautionary measure before we went into Leslie's tonight. The cop says nobody or nothing used the roof for a Peter Pan flying apparatus. So that's out. Nobody ever went down the face of the building either. It's a sheer drop. That leaves straight across.'

Gant shook his head. 'There was nothing like a tight wire stretched across the avenue. I looked.'

'I looked too. It would've been a hellova stunt for even a pro wire-walker. So,' he finished with a windy sigh, 'if seeing's believing—'

They were on the street in front of Leslie's apartment house again. A porter had swept up the smashed flowerbox and the soil. Banner inquired about the sweepings. He was told that everything was in a refuse barrel in the alley.

Banner went blundering into the alley, fumbling a flashlight out of his junk-filled pocket. Reaching the refuse barrel, he peered down into it, lifting up some of the pieces of the shattered flowerbox and looking.

'That's interesting,' he mumbled. 'Mighty interesting.' He dropped the cement shards into the barrel again, switched off the flashlight, and let a puzzled Gant trail him out into the street once more.

'What was that?' asked Gant.

Banner looked absently at him. 'Where's Mme Olympe staying, Barney?'

'Plaza Hotel.'

'Let's go visiting.'

Mme Olympe was her old bouncy self again. She invited them into her large room with a double bed. On the table was the Pernod bottle and a huge Provolone cheese. She helped herself to a long Russian cigarette, offering the box to the two men. Gant liked to experiment, so he accepted one, which he regretted. Banner shook his head and jabbed one of his corona cigars into his mouth to gnaw on it.

Mme Olympe landed heavily in a damask upholstered

armchair with a foam rubber pillow. 'Sit down,' she said. She
was obviously pleased with herself.

Gant sat on the edge of the bed. Banner headed for a rocking
chair. He stopped short when he saw a big black tomcat curled
up on it.

'That's Lucifer,' said Mme Olympe. 'Just lift him off and put
him on the floor. Laziest thing. He'll curl up and go to sleep
wherever you put him down.'

Banner carefully transferred the cat to the floor. He creaked
backwards in the rocker. 'You came straight here, didn't you?'

'Where else would I go?' she asked.

You sure you didn't double back to Leslie's apartment after
we all left?'

'Of course not,' she said shortly. 'That maid came all the way
with me. Ask her.' Little puffs of smoke belched from her cigarette.
'What do you want?' she asked querulously.

Banner looked pleasant. 'I came to make a request. Tomorrow
night there's gonna be another séance at the penthouse. You're
gonna be there and—'

'Not so fast! Who says I will? You can't turn me on and off
whenever you feel like it. I need psychic inspiration. I need—'

'You,' said Banner alarmingly, 'need a swift boot in the pants.
And that's what you're gonna get.' He waggled one enormous
shoe perilously in the air. 'I'm wise to the whole racket. If I
don't get any co-operation from you, I'll bust you wide open!'

'You're trying to bluff me! You can't bluff me!'

'I ain't bluffing,' sneered Banner. 'I know. I know where it all
went. Down the incinerator, There was no other way to get rid
of it.' This last remark made no sense at all to Gant. But it must
have struck home to Mme Olympe, for she blanched and her
talon fingers gripped the arms of the chair. Her cigarette
dropped, burning a hole in the rug.

The two behemoths glared at each other, unmoving. At last
Gant had to reach down and retrieve the smouldering cigarette.

'All right,' said Mme Olympe briefly. 'I'll be there tomorrow night.'

Grinning, Banner got up. 'Bye-bye,' he said. He took Gant by the arm and steered him out.

Downstairs in the lobby, Gant said: 'What was all that? What went down the incinerator? The ghost?'

'Nah,' said Banner. 'Not the ghost. Something else.'

'Then you still don't know the answer to that.'

'I do know the answer, Barney. You can figger it out with simple mathematics, The ghost,' he said solemnly, 'displaces about 10,000 cubic inches and—'

'10,000 cubic inches!' queried Gant. 'What kind of a monster is that?'

'And,' resumed Banner, 'a weight of approximately 225 pounds.'

Gant's eyes gleamed. 'That's closer to something human. The only one who tips the scales that much is Mme Olympe.' Then he stared around wildly. 'But how can she be the ghost?'

Banner looked serious. 'Let's not forget,' he said, 'that the murderer wants to find that ghost too. She's a witness from another world.'

'What's the next move?'

'We have to wait till tomorrow night. If I'm right, you'll not only see the ghost—but you'll ketch a murderer!'

They were all there again in the modernistic sitting room, waiting. Banner had sent Gant on ahead to keep them all herded together till he arrived. He was a little late tonight. Even Mme Olympe was there ahead of him.

Banner plodded in with a mysterious black bag which he didn't let out of his hand. Gant wondered what he was going to do with it. He saw Banner go out on the terrace through the French door in the foyer, then come back, bolt the door carefully, and enter the sitting room. At last he set the bag down by the wall.

Gant, his curiosity getting the better of him, circled till he reached the bag. Secretly bending down, he opened it for a moment. There was nothing in it.

He had no further time for minor details, for Banner loomed behind him and drew him aside for a whispered consultation.

Banner had a glint in his eye. 'The killer hasn't made a move all day. Waiting to see what shows. But I been communing with the spirits and I found out a few things.' His voice sank even lower. 'Jasmine was nowhere perfect as a wife. She nagged, for one thing, she had grasping fingers. She didn't love Leslie either, considering the underhanded way she planned to relieve him of his money.'

'Who told you all this, Banner?'

'Never mind. You'll know later. Jasmine knew Mme Olympe before she died. Yass, that's an important point. To convince Leslie Jasmine and Mme Olympe cooked up a big levitation stunt that would make D. D. Home's aerial antics look sick. Jasmine was going to fly from this penthouse to the one across the street.'

Gant had difficulty keeping his voice down. 'That happened last night! Jasmine's been dead six months!'

Banner gave him an odd look. 'D'you think that'd stop her?'

'For the love of Mike, Banner—'

Leslie, his claylike face set in a grim model, his eyes as opaque as ever behind the gleaming eyeglasses, approached. 'What's the delay, gentlemen?'

Banner grunted something and started getting everybody seated. The arrangement was the same as last night, except that Banner seemed to edge his chair closer to Suzanne's.

'Ready?' said Banner at the light switch.

Mme Olympe nodded drowsily.

Out went the lights.

There was a greater tension tonight, an almost palpable vibration of nerves in the air. Gant knew that there were forces of good and evil about to clash in the dark. He had a healthy respect for Mme Olympe now—and Banner.

Clouds scudded over the moon tonight, alternately shading the terrace and the room. The flower scent crept in. Gant tried not to think of flowers on a coffin.

Gant didn't know how long they waited. The phosphorescent hands of his pocket watch seemed to stand still.

Then somebody made a hushed exclamation. Among the moving cloud-shadows on the curtain, another shadow fell. The ghost was on the terrace again!

She stood in the opening of the French door, blonde-haired, filmy, as if seen through a veil.

'Speak, Jasmine, speak!' It was Mme Olympe's falsetto.

You could see the figure struggling to make itself heard. Again the chilling reedy voice pitched upward. '*I was pushed! I was pushed!*'

'Who pushed you, Jasmine? Who?' Mme Olympe asked again.

'*I—I—it's hard to tell,*' wavered the voice. You do know, Jasmine?'

'*Yes!*'

It was then that Gant heard Banner's voice, in deadly earnest, whispering to somebody: 'If you value your life, don't go back on that terrace!'

Light! thought Gant. *Why don't they turn on the light?*

The figure had edged forward until it was partly inside the room.

'Who pushed you?' grated Mme Olympe.

''*Twas—*'

That's where sanity ended and madness broke loose!

There was a terrible wail, like a lost soul, on the terrace. Something screeching and spitting shot in through the open French door. Something black and evil, claws slashing. Gant felt it land squarely on his chest. It gave a demonical yowl, then it tore straight up in the air. Gant's chair went over backwards.

Somebody screamed hysterically: 'It's the devil himself!'

Gant rolled over and got his feet under him. He was in time to see a gauzy apparition flit out to the terrace again.

'It's getting away!' he yelled above the pandemonium.

He heard pottery crash to the floor and Banner's muffled curse. The lights came on, blinding all of them by their brilliance.

Gant took one swift look around at the destruction. Banner was standing at the light switch, scowling like an archangel come to judgment. Mme Olympe sat dazedly, her yellow transformation askew on her head. On top of the phonograph cabinet crouched Mme Olympe's big black tomcat. Its amber eyes were full of resentment, its tail was bushy with rage and its claws were still distended. Lucifer had joined the party.

Gant was amazed to see Liz Chamberlin, the maid standing in the room. She hadn't been in the apartment when the lights went out. And there was somebody else missing.

Banner wasn't waiting to see. Shouting something about the terrace he went howling out. The others streamed after him.

Someone, tumbling among the iron chairs, was making an infernal racket. Gant tried to see who it was. Wrapped in yards of ghost-like material, the person on the terrace rolled over and over towards the wall.

The creature rose, untwisting the confining cocoon of georgette silk. They all stared at Fergus Leslie.

'Stop right there!' trumpeted Banner.

'Is that the ghost?' cried Gant.

'That,' said Banner sharply, 'is the murderer!'

When Liz Chamberlin faced Leslie and told him that she'd seen him push his wife off the terrace, he gave up. After he was taken away, Liz admitted herself that she actually didn't know who had pushed Jasmine.

'Y'see,' said Banner, taking over, 'on the night of the murder Lizzie was in the penthouse across the street, where she's been living all along. Accidentally she was a witness to the murder. She could see Jasmine cutting out the frostbitten plants, but she couldn't identify the shadowy figger who crept up behind Jasmine, hit her hard enough to stun her, then shove her over. Lizzie knew it was murder, but not knowing who the murderer was, she wisely kept her mouth shut.'

'But,' asked Gant, 'what's all this business of the apartment in the penthouse across the street?'

'I got the whole story from Lizzie today,' said Banner. 'I told you that Jasmine and Mme Olympe were in cahoots to nick Leslie. To do the levitation trick required a bit of preparation. Jasmine rented the other penthouse in December—a month before she was killed. At the same time she acquired a new maid, Lizzie, who had worked closely with Mme Olympe for years, faking spirits, What was important was that Lizzie and Jasmine were of similar build. That there was no facial resemblance didn't matter. We know that Jasmine was about five feet tall, since you, Gant, remarked yesterday afternoon that Jasmine was hardly two feet taller than the three-foot terrace wall. We can see that Lizzie wears high heels to bring her up to average size, which would put her normally about five feet. The size is gonna be important.

'Jasmine's original plan was to work like so: They would have a private séance up here with Mme Olympe, Lizzie being absent. In the dark Jasmine would slip outta the room, go downstairs, across the street, and pose on the opposite terrace. Her place at the séance would be taken by Lizzie, who would be dressed exactly like Jasmine. Leslie would see what looked like Jasmine get up, go out on the terrace, and when he followed a minute later, the terrace would be empty and Jasmine would yoo-hoo from across the street. Conclusion: she'd been levitated across!'

Gant interrupted: 'Where would Liz go?'

Banner chewed his cigar. 'I'm coming to that, all in good time. Unfortunately for Jasmine, Leslie was planning destinies of his own. He'd fallen for Suzanne. Her young charms appealed to him. How to get rid of a nagging wife who holds onto you like grim death? A simple way that might be interpreted as an accident. One quiet night in January the situation was perfect. He stalked her on the terrace and sent her over . . . Yunnerstand the development now? Jasmine was gone, but the set-up to rake in Leslie's dough was as potent as ever. Mebbe more so. Now Mme Olympe could bring Jasmine back from another world with comparative ease. She had the props for it. She knew all about Jasmine's personal life. She had Lizzie planted right here on the premises. She had a pair of duplicate earrings that Jasmine had made unknown to Leslie. She had, finally, the whale of a levitation trick soiling to be used. All she had to do was bring out the props at the right time.

'We know about the first get-together at Rhinebeck, where she palmed off the first earring, the ceiling writing, and the perfume. Last night's séance was to be the clincher to win Leslie over. Lizzie, in a blonde wig and transparent dress, would impersonate Jasmine. The spook would appear from an empty terrace, then wind up across the street. We came to the séance, so we were slapped in the kissers with it too.

'You gotta consider Lizzie's frame of mind. Remember that she knew Jasmine had been murdered. She didn't know who'd done it. This séance was a peachy spot to toss in some vital information, yet Lizzie herself would be entirely out of it. That's why she said she'd been pushed. Even Mme Olympe didn't expect that ad lib.'

'I didn't,' admitted Mme Olympe, sitting lumpily, stroking Lucifer's crackling fur smooth again.

Banner continued: 'You can see the spot I was in—and the murderer. This spook had information for the police. How do we find her? No matter which way you looked at it, the ghost really did fly away. But last night I got thinking. Jasmine was five feet tall and size nine. Lizzie was about the same size. Lizzie was the only one physically able to impersonate Jasmine. Where could a small woman conceal herself on the terrace? Hey? There's something out there that measures an exact five feet in length too. Only it's fulla something else.' He chuckled. 'While we searched the apartment last night, Lizzie was planted here.'

'Planted?' said Gant.

'Actually planted! In one of those cement flowerboxes!' He waved his hands in their excited faces. 'Don't everybody talk at once. There'd be plenty of room once most of the dirt was removed. Who'd have had the time to excavate one of those boxes? Lizzie again! She took the earth out bit by bit and spilled it down the incinerator. The only safe way to get rid of it. When the box was practically empty she constructed a false lid, with about an inch of soil and flowers on it, under which she could conceal herself until it was time to materialize. Got it now? Lizzie, as the ghost, merely came outta one of the flowerboxes and slipped back in again, leaving her bare footprint on the soil of a neighbouring box to point us off into space!'

'Who'd we see on the opposite terrace?' asked Gant. 'Another double?'

'Right! Another of Mme Olympe's faithful followers in the same guise. The distance was too great to distinguish any features.'

'I still don't see how Liz escaped from the terrace to return later as the maid. To get out of the apartment she'd have to pass through the sitting room, full of people, since we saw you bolt that foyer door to the terrace earlier.'

'That,' said Banner, 'is where Mme Olympe scored on me. You'll remember that when we all rushed out after the ghost last night, Mme Olympe was the last to leave the sitting room. She'd skipped into the foyer and pulled back the bolt. Then she distracted everybody's attention, including mine, by throwing a phony faint, giving Lizzie the chance to exit through the foyer door, bolting it again on the inside after her. She changed clothes outside the apartment and re-entered.'

'There's one thing I can't understand,' said Gant. 'Leslie was with you when somebody tried to kill you by dropping a flowerbox on you.'

'Wrong! To cabbage somebody that way you'd have to be an expert bombardier. We just chanced to be close by when it came down. The spiritualists did that, knowing that if I examined the terrace further I might come across the gimmixed box. Lizzie, supposedly going home with Mme Olympe, sneaked back and got rid of the box by simply heaving it over into the quiet street. She had no intention of killing anybody with it. But it was that that led me to the ghost's hiding place. I told you that the ghost displaced roundly 10,000 cubic inches and 225 pounds. I got the measurements by multiplying the known dimensions of the flowerbox, 60 inches long by 12 inches high by 14 inches wide. The weight of the soil in such a box should be about 225 pounds and that's a heap of soil. Yet you'll remember that after the box struck the pavement and smashed, there was only a thin spread of earth, and when I examined the sweepings in the refuse barrel, I had to look down into it. There wasn't enough dirt.'

Gant glanced at Lucifer on Mme Olympe's broad lap. 'Tonight you had that cat in the black bag. That's obvious now.'

'Yup. It was part of a trap for the murderer, with Mme Olympe and Lizzie joining forces with me. Leslie wasn't quite sure who the ghost was, but I knew that if she appeared again he'd try to silence her. All he'd have to do was push her off the terrace and get away with it in the dark and confusion. It'd look like another unfortunate accident. At the séance the killer would slip out the foyer door to intercept the ghost on the terrace. I had to set some sort of alarm to know when the murderer was out there. Mme Olympe said that her tomcat was so lazy that it went to sleep wherever you put it—so I put it down where the murderer would step right on it.'

Banner chuckled. Lucifer came straight outta hell. But Lizzie was in real danger at that moment. I warned her not to go back on the terrace. Yet she had to show something of herself for Leslie to make a grab at. I borrowed a trick from Mme Olympe when I had Lizzie skin outta that georgette silk drapery, hang it on a coat-hanger to give it shape, and poke it out the French door on a reaching rod. Leslie dived for it. And before he could untangle himself we had him.'

Then, with a dramatic flourish, Banner beckoned to Gant: 'And that, m'boy, is that. C'mon, Gant, let's get out of here.'

'What about Mme Olympe?' Gant queried.

'You mean as far as her little racket is concerned? I imagine that when she appears before the bar of justice, the good judge will deal mercifully with her. After all, she was instrumental in helping us crack a murder case. For the present, I wouldn't even bother booking her.'

So, with a deep, almost foppish bow to Mme Olympe and the others Banner retired to the door, dragging Gant with him. As the pair waited for the elevator, the Senator was expansive: 'I'm leaving town tomorrow, Gant. Let's hope that you can take better care of our town while I'm away this time.'

Gant laughed openly. 'We'll try, Banner we'll try.'

JOSEPH COMMINGS

Born in New York in 1913, Joseph Commings is today almost forgotten outside a diminishing circle of aficionados of impossible crime fiction. After a brief spell as a journalist, he began his sporadic and very varied writing career during the Second World War on overseas postings with the US Air Force. Initially, he wrote to entertain his comrades and, on being demobbed, he must have been delighted to find a ready market in the so-called 'pulps' such as *Western Trails*, *Hollywood Detective*, *Mystery Digest* and *Killers Mystery Story Magazine*. His crime fiction is characterised by undeniably improbable situations, unfeasibly trusting witnesses and extraordinarily clever solutions. In one story the murderer might appear to be a vampire and in another a giant, but what truly lifts his work out of the run of the mill is Commings' sense of humour.

Commings' best-known character is Brooks Urban Banner, a Senator in the Democratic party who is also a criminal lawyer and a practising magician. Banner is modelled very much in the style of John Dickson Carr's heroic sleuth Dr Gideon Fell (himself inspired by G. K. Chesterton) and is 'extra large' in every sense: he weighs nearly 300 pounds, has a mop of shaggy white hair and dresses loudly. Fond of tall tales, the Senator claims to have had all manner of careers—including hobo, locksmith and comic book enthusiast—which provide some of the arcane knowledge that allows him to unravel the baffling mysteries with which he is confronted. While he doesn't appear in any novel-length investigations, there are over thirty Banner short stories. Fifteen of these were gathered together by the late Bob Adey, the authority on impossible crime stories, and form the collection *Banner Deadlines* (Crippen & Landru, 2004); a second volume is forthcoming from the same publisher. Commings' non-Banner stories—of which there are at least forty, some written under pseudonyms—are mostly mysteries, sometimes with an unusual setting, but none captures the eccentric genius of the Banner canon.

As a writer, Joe Commings is sometimes criticised for an overly frivolous approach to the business of murder. That was of course quite deliberate. In a letter to the *New York Times Book Review*, published in 1941, Commings protested that the vast majority of publishing houses were uninterested in publishing anything humorous and therefore unwilling to accept his 'whimsical wares'. As he was unwilling to write in any another way his work remained largely confined to the pulps while a few novel-length manuscripts also failed to find a publisher.

In his fifties, Commings supplemented his income from crime fiction by writing pornographic paperbacks with titles like *Man Eater* (1965), *Operation Aphrodite* (1966) and *Swinging Wives* (1971), as well as a study of sex crimes whose aim seems to have been titillation more than education.

In the early 1970s, Joe Commings suffered a stroke and his writing career came to an end. He moved to a care home in Maryland where he died in 1992.

'The Fraudulent Spirit' was first published, as by 'Monte Craven', in *Mystery Digest*, September–October 1960, and I am grateful to the collector Edward Jones for drawing it to my attention.

THE LINE WENT DEAD

Leo Bruce

For the occurrences of a true ghost story there must be no explanation. As soon as the scientist talks of psychic phenomena or aural illusions, there ceases to be a ghost story. An old silk dress may be found under the floorboards or a few bones discovered in the brickwork of the chimney but these satisfy no one except the addict who accepts them as the conventional origin of events, though in reality they can mean nothing. So I must warn you that for what I am about to relate I have no explanation to offer.

The facts are these. Some years ago Miss Ursula Redcar was alone in her flat in Edward Street, Bloomsbury, on Christmas Eve. She was in her fifties, an intelligent woman independent mind, assertive in her opinions but in no way eccentric.

During that year she had lost her only sister Cecilia, with whom for many years she has lived. They had been born and brought up in the New Forest where their father had a large doctor's practice, but they had moved to this flat on his death 20 years before and had never known another home.

Cecelia had died of heart disease (a family failing) in the same flat, and Ursula and her brother Robert, a doctor like his father, had been with her at the last and had attended her simple funeral.

Ursula was always considered the more strong-minded of

the two; Cecelia though not frivolous had a rather irresponsible nature. While Ursula had been called 'handsome' as a young woman, Cecilia was 'pretty'; in the opinion of Mrs Rogers, who had been their daily help for many years, she had made 'a lovely corpse'.

At about eleven o'clock that Christmas Eve, when Ursula was about to go to bed, the telephone rang. Ursula, feeling depressed at her first Christmas in solitude, was disinclined for cheerful conversation or good wishes from one of her many friends and at first thought of ignoring it. But it is always difficult to let a telephone ring itself out, and after a few moments she answered it.

The voice she heard, without any question, was Cecilia's. It was gay; there was, Ursula said afterwards, an echo of Cecilia's characteristic giggle. It sounded as voices on the telephone sometimes do, peculiarly close at hand.

'I've just rung up to wish you a happy Christmas,' it said. '*Joyeux Noël*, my dearest.' This Gallic greeting the two sisters had brought back from a winter in Paris and always used between themselves.

Ursula found herself a trembling and chilled as though the room were an ice chamber. The first words she spoke were banal if not idiotic.

'But . . . you're dead!'

'I know, dear. I thought . . .'

'Cecilia!'

This time Ursula's voice had risen towards hysteria.

'Yes, dear?'

Calm, cheerful, commonplace, she sounded.

'Cecilia, *where are you*?'

As she asked this, Ursula pictured her sister as she had seen her last, serene in death, prepared for burial.

'This line's so bad,' said Cecilia's voice. 'I can scarcely hear you. What did you say?'

Ursula explained afterwards that the very ordinariness of every word added to the horror she felt.

'Oh God! I said where *are* you, Cecilia?'

It seemed that she was slightly misheard.

'I'm all right dear,' came the everyday tones. 'How are you?'

Ursula's voice rose to a scream. She was fighting off a fainting fit.

'Cecilia!'

'That's better. I can hear you now. Well, dear, *Joyeux Noël* and everything you wish in the New Year.'

Again Ursula, trying to control her voice, could only manage to enunciate her sister's name. Still the voice at the other end was cheerful and natural.

'I must run along now. Till this time next year! Goodbye. Goodbye, dear!'

The voice was succeeded by the metallic buzz of a disconnected line.

For more than a minute Ursula stood there holding the receiver. She was sensible enough to recognize that whatever this call had been, however it had been made, it was over, and the buzz she heard was real enough. She did not, as a more weak-minded person might have done, call into the instrument or jab at the receiver hook. She replaced the receiver, then crumpled into a chair.

She did not move for nearly half an hour. Afterwards she would say that for that space of time she had been little short of insane. Her mind was too clouded to seek or invent explanations. She gave herself over to horror and dread. Then, pulling herself together a little, she dialled her brother's number.

Robert lived in Bayswater with his good noisy wife and two talkative children. He was as practical and sound as Ursula had always prided herself on being. There was no nonsense about him.

'Robert,' said Ursula, trying to keep her voice steady, 'could you please come over at once?'

'Is it something urgent?' asked Robert.

'Urgent? Yes, Robert! Please come immediately!'

'It's Christmas Eve,' Robert pointed out. 'The children are in bed and we've got to fill all their stockings.'

'This is a matter of life and death!' said Ursula—and not until afterwards did she realise the horrible aptness of her words.

They were so uncharacteristic of Ursula that her brother was impressed.

'I'll come,' he said, though he still did not sound too willing. 'I'll get the car out and come over.'

'As soon as you can! Please, Robert, come at once!'

'All right. All right. I will.'

When he reached the flat in Edward Street, Dr Redcar found his sister in a violent state of nerves. Had it been anyone else he would have feared for her sanity. He gave her a tranquillizer and told her to take her time, but in a moment she began to recount what had happened.

Robert listened with a grave and sympathetic expression.

'What a terrible illusion,' he said at last. 'You should have come to us for Christmas. I'm so sorry.'

Ursula stared at him.

'This was no illusion,' she said. 'I only wish it were. If I could persuade myself that it was an illusion, I should be so relieved. A telephone bell can be no illusion. When you're sitting in the same room you either hear it or you don't. I heard it distinctly. I was in a perfectly calm state of mind and about to go to bed when it rang quite normally.'

'But the voice?'

'The voice was Cecelia's.'

'My dear Ursula, I'm very sympathetic but you must not be absurd, you know. Cecilia is dead.'

'I know. That's what I told her.'

'You *told* her?'

'Yes, Robert. I was so horribly startled. It was a ridiculous thing to say because she obviously wasn't dead, or how could she be telephoning me?'

'My dear, must I remind you that we have seen and touched her dead body and watched it committed to the earth?'

'I tell you it was Cecilia. Do you think I could be deceived? She used our little private Christmas greeting—*Joyeux Noël*. Even you have never heard us say it. But apart from that I knew. I could hear her chuckle. She sounded . . . just ordinary, as though she were away for Christmas and had rung up to give me good wishes.'

'Some wicked trick, Ursula. Some woman with a gift of mimicry. It can have been nothing else.'

'I should have known. Do you think I shouldn't have known whether or not I was speaking to my own sister?'

'A recording then!' said Robert triumphantly. 'Cecelia had a strange sense of humour. She must have made it before her last illness and somebody . . .'

'Robert, I know you mean to be kind but it's no good. It wasn't just Cecilia speaking. It was a conversation between us. She *answered* me.'

Robert thought for a moment, then must have reverted to his original explanation that Ursula, alone in the flat she had so long shared with her sister, had been a victim of illusion or auto-suggestion.

'Whichever it was,' he said, 'it's over . . .'

'But that's the awful thing, Robert. It's not. She distinctly said, "*Till this time next year!*"'

'Well, it's over for tonight,' said Robert comfortingly. 'Now you get your things together and come back with me. I'll phone Julie to say you're coming for Christmas after all.'

Still dazed and a little resentful of Robert's sceptical common sense, Ursula obeyed.

Ursula changed greatly in the following year. The confidence had gone from her manner and she habitually wore an expression of anxious expectation as though she awaited some blow and did not know how or whence it would come. Her brother, ever practical, wanted her to see a psychiatrist.

'Even if it was something more than an illusion,' he argued, 'the effect on your health is the same. I'm sure psychotherapy would be helpful to you.'

But Ursula was obstinate.

'My mind is perfectly clear and I want no specious explanations for something that cannot be explained. A psychiatrist would be looking for the cause of this in *my* brain. If the cause is to be found it's not there.'

'Where then?' asked Robert, but received no reply. He had taken what he called all practical measures, had been into the matter with the telephone authorities, who had no record of an outside call coming to Ursula's number that night but could not of course say how many times it had been dialled from the London area. He had made tactful but fruitless enquiries to find anyone who had known the two sisters and who had a gift for mimicry. He has tried to persuade Ursula to see a colleague of his who specialised in psychiatric illusions. He was worried about his sister's state of mind but felt there was nothing else he could do.

As the next Christmas approached, however, he insisted that Ursula should spend it with him and Julie and the children in Bayswater.

'No, Robert. I can't do that,' said Ursula. 'Don't you see, *it might be worse*?'

He grew a trifle impatient then.

'What on earth do you mean?' he asked.

'She said, "*Till this time next year.*"'

'Don't be absurd. We'll have the phone disconnected.'

'That's what I mean. She would find *some other way.*'

'Really, Ursula? I know you've had an unnerving experience but you mustn't talk this kind of wild nonsense. Cecilia is dead. To suggest what you do is . . . positively blasphemous. Come to us and forget the whole episode.'

Ursula shook her head.

'No. I must stay here. She wants me to be here.'

Robert was about to ask who '*she*' might be when he saw his sister's face, white and rather tragic.

'Then we shall come and spend the evening with you,' he announced. 'We couldn't possibly leave you alone. We can make arrangements for the children. I shall tell Julie today.'

Ursula said nothing. Ungrateful, Robert thought, but he decided that he must make allowances. Ursula's state of mind was not normal.

So on Christmas Eve the three sat in Ursula's flat and Julie struggled heroically to keep the conversation cheerful. She was a kind soul, and although secretly she had always thought Ursula an overbearing person she was ready to give every sympathy to her in her present affliction. She and Robert privately referred to it as 'this extraordinary mania of Ursula's' or 'this nonsense Ursula has got into her head.'

But despite Julie's best efforts conversation flagged, and after they had eaten a meal and were sitting round the fire the silences grew longer. However sceptical Robert and Julie might profess to feel, all three were quite unconcealedly waiting.

When at last, towards eleven o'clock, the phone rang, Ursula seemed for a moment unable to move.

'Would you like me to take it?' asked Robert.

'No. I'll go,' said Ursula rising unsteadily.

'Remember, my dear, we are both here with you. Whatever it is there is nothing to fear.'

They watched as she crossed to the telephone and with slow uncertain movements put the receiver to her ear. They could hear nothing but they saw her face become transfixed with an ashen and wide-eyed look of sheer dread as she listened.

But what she heard they never knew. For in that moment of violent stress the family weakness betrayed her, and her heart ceased to beat.

LEO BRUCE

Rupert Croft-Cooke, who wrote detective fiction under the pen name of Leo Bruce, was born in 1903. He was brought up in south-east England, an aesthete in a family of athletes, and attended Tonbridge School and what is now known as Wrekin College in Shropshire, where he did well both academically and at the game of darts, at which he excelled.

Croft-Cooke published his first work, a slim booklet of verse entitled *Clouds of Gold*, at the age of 18. Aged 19, after a brief period working as a private tutor, he decided to go in search of what he would later describe as 'adventure, romance and excitement'. He secured a teaching post in Argentina and travelled throughout South America, taking in Brazil and even the Falkland Islands. After two years he returned to England, and began working as a freelance journalist and writer, as well as broadcasting on 2LO, one of the first radio stations in Britain, which would go on to become part of the BBC.

In 1940, Croft-Cooke enlisted in the Intelligence Corps, serving first in Madagascar and later in India. On returning to civilian life, he settled in Ticehurst, Sussex, where he continued to write. In 1953, as part of a 'war on vice'—defined as encompassing prostitution and homosexuality—initiated by the then Commissioner of the Metropolitan Police, Croft-Cooke and his Indian companion and secretary were charged with indecency and convicted. After serving his sentence, he sold up and moved to Tangier, where he spent the next fifteen years writing and playing host to visiting writers including Noël Coward.

Over a career lasting more than fifty years, Rupert Croft-Cooke was amazingly prolific. He authored nearly thirty volumes of auto-biography, including *The World is Young* (1937) on his experiences in South America, as well as collections of verse, memoirs of his extensive travels and biographies of Lord Alfred Douglas—Oscar Wilde's Bosie—and of the entertainers Charles 'Tom Thumb' Stratton and Colonel 'Buffalo Bill' Cody. Croft-Cooke also wrote widely on subjects that interested him, including his beloved darts and the circus, as well as the importance of freedom of the press and the problems caused by 'petty' regulation. After his conviction and subsequent imprisonment, he argued for greater tolerance of homo-sexuality and in support of improvements to the penal system. His writing was highly regarded by critics up to the early 1950s, but after his conviction, reviews tended to be more negative and even favourable ones were marred by obscurely worded but plainly homo-phobic allusions.

As well as his extensive writing under his own name, Croft-Cooke also wrote detective stories using the pseudonym of Leo Bruce. His first mystery novel, *Case for Three Detectives*, was published in 1936. While the titular detectives parody Lord Peter Wimsey, Hercule Poirot and G. K. Chesterton's Father Brown, the case is solved by a cockney policeman, Sergeant William Beef, who would go on to appear in seven other novels. In the early 1950s, Croft-Cooke abandoned Beef and created another amateur sleuth, Dr Carolus Deene, a history teacher who would appear in more than twenty novels. As Bruce and under his own name, Croft-Cooke wrote many short stories including a round-robin novella with Beverley Nichols and Monica Dickens, author of the *Follyfoot* series of children's novels. His last book was published in 1977 and Rupert Croft-Cooke died in 1979.

'The Line Went Dead' was first published in *The Tatler*, 21 December 1960.

THE HOUSE OF THE LIONS

Desmond Bagley

In the year 1887, in the town of Totnes in the County of Devonshire, a man bought a house. His name was William Cooper Johnson and he was a retired clergyman; the house was called Mount Elwell.

William Johnson was in his middle age and he had spent much of his life in Africa as a missionary. The climate of that continent and the agues induced thereby had, however, caused his early retirement and encouraged him to dwell in a more salubrious environment, of which none better can be found in Devonshire. And so he bought the house known as Mount Elwell in the ancient borough of Totnes.

The house was in the style of the last century, having been built in 1791, and was but a simple dwelling and sorely lacking in that elegance of ornamentation which has become the pride and hallmark of our civilisation. Yet the rooms were large and stood foursquare, the walls were thick and the house was warm, there was a small wing attached for the housing of an abigail, and so William Johnson was content.

He had married young and his children were adult and gone into the world, except for his youngest daughter, Alice. And so there dwelt in Mount Elwell William Johnson; his wife, Elizabeth; his daughter, Alice; and the abigail, one Susan Beer who was but a poor half-witted girl, the only child of a farm labourer who was the best servant Mrs Johnson could obtain because there seemed to be a curious reluctance on the part of the lower classes of Totnes to offer themselves or their daughters in the service of this kind and holy man. The Johnsons found this unaccountable and, at first, put it down to the natural conservatism of an isolated folk to whom a traveller from even the next county was a foreigner. It was only later that the truth was to be made terribly apparent.

William Johnson was determined in his early retirement to write an account of his experiences in Africa which he believed would be of use to his fellow men. However, he discovered that the room most natural to use as a study and library was to the rear of the house and faced north, thus being very cold. His wife insisted that, due to his precarious state of health, it would be impossible for him to work in that room, and it was decided to adapt the dining room as his work place. It faced to the south and on to the walled garden and was flooded with sunshine for many hours of the day, both in summer and winter.

There were odd features about this room. It had only three corners—as we generally regard the corners of a room. The fourth corner swept in a curve which Mrs Johnson found to be a nuisance since it inhibited the placing of furniture. Next to this architectural curiosity was a tall cupboard which was even more curious, since its doors opened, not to the room, but to a passage off the hall. It was a tall and unusually narrow cupboard with split doors of the Dutch or stable variety, and it projected inconveniently into William Johnson's new study. He was in half a mind to tear it down but let it stand because his wife found it convenient to have such a cupboard close to the kitchen.

Being a prudent man Johnson decided to insure the house against fire or other disasters and so he made the journey to Exeter where he consulted Mr Frederick Milford of the West of England Fire and Life Assurance Society, obtaining very good terms—thirteen shillings and sixpence premium against a capital sum of £800. It was in the course of this transaction that Mr Milford remarked, 'Ah! Mount Elwell! I believe the property has been standing vacant for some time.'

'That is so,' said Mr Johnson. 'I cannot understand why, because it is a very good property.'

'Just so,' said Mr Milford and said no more on that score, but a little while later he said apparently apropos of nothing, 'The last owner of the house was Captain Hampson, a military man. He died four years ago. Captain Hampson was a very strange man—or so I am led to understand.'

'Would it be he who extended the house—who built the servants' wing?'

'That is so.' Mr Milford paused. 'His servants were black.'

'Black!' echoed Mr Johnson in astonishment.

'Just so,' said Milford. 'Captain Hampson had a great deal to do with Africa, so I believe. He was an explorer and when he retired to England he brought his own servants—heathen black fellers from the jungle. It caused quite a bit of talk, I must say.'

'So I can imagine,' said Mr Johnson. 'I wonder if it was he who was responsible for the lions?'

Milford started nervously and his eyebrows crawled up his scalp. 'Lions?' he said doubtfully.

'Yes. Each bracket supporting the roof guttering is decorated with the head of a lion.'

'Hampson did a lot of reconstruction on Mount Elwell,' said Milford cautiously. 'Lions, eh! A curious man was Hampson—in every way, including his death. There was a lot of talk about that too.'

'In what way?'

Milford shrugged. 'Just a lot of gossip. I didn't listen closely.'

He said no more about it, and Johnson did not pursue the matter although he was curious. All the long journey home the next day he pondered over it and decided to consult the

Reverend Burrough, the Vicar of St Mary the Virgin, which was the fine church in Totnes. Johnson was a man who did not like mysteries.

Over the teacups that evening his wife said, 'I'm sure there's a cat in the house, William, although I can't find it. I have heard it mewing and thought it was locked in the cellar—or the attic, perhaps; but although I have searched, I cannot find it anywhere.'

'But I've seen it,' said Alice unexpectedly. 'It was in the garden—and a very strange animal it was.'

'How was it strange, my dear?'

Alice frowned. 'It had a curious colouring; light brown with a black—or dark brown—head and paws. What was most startling were the eyes—they were a bright sapphire blue.'

Johnson smiled tolerantly. 'Your imagination is running away with you,' he said. 'Whoever heard of a blue-eyed cat? It was probably an ordinary tom-cat—a stray.'

He thought no more about it, but that night he was awakened by a whispered conversation at the door of his bedroom and discovered his wife and daughter in the midst of an agitated argument.

'What is the matter?' he demanded.

'Nothing, dear,' replied his wife. 'Alice had a bad dream, that is all.'

'It was not a dream,' protested Alice . 'A cat did run over my bed. I felt the paws distinctly.'

Johnson calmed down his daughter and they all returned to bed, but just before falling asleep he thought he heard the mew of a cat, although whether that was his imagination or not he was afterwards unable to tell.

Two days later Johnson went to the vicarage of St Mary the Virgin and saw the Reverend Burrough who was an old man, failing in health and not long for this world as Johnson judged. After a few minutes of small-talk he said, 'I've been hearing some strange tales about my predecessor at Mount Elwell. I understand that he was in Africa.'

'That is correct,' said Burrough. 'He was an Army man in East Africa, engaged in putting down the slave trade, and was invalided out of the Army because of a recurring ague of the kind the Italians call the malarin.'

'I know the disease,' said Johnson grimly.

Burrough said, 'What tales have you heard?'

'Nothing definite. How did he die?'

'Dreadfully!' said Burrough somewhat forcibly. 'He was killed by an animal.'

'Thrown from his horse?' queried Johnson.

Burrough appeared hesitant. 'No,' he said at last. 'He was deliberately killed by a . . . a predatory animal.'

'My dear sir,' said Johnson in astonishment, 'This is nineteenth-century England. What kind of predators have we here capable of killing a man?'

Burrough shook his head. 'We could but go by the evidence of his body. I have never seen anyone die so bloodily. The whole of his torso was ripped open and there were dreadful claw marks on all limbs.' His voice wavered. 'It was as though . . .'

'As though . . . ?' prompted Johnson.

'As though he had been killed by a . . . let us say, a large cat or member of the cat family such as a tiger or a leopard.'

'Or a lion.' mused Johnson.

'Just so . . . a lion,' agreed Burrough. He appeared ill at ease.

'And was such an animal found and destroyed?'

Burrough shook his head. 'No,' he said sombrely.

Johnson smiled. 'I really cannot believe that in this day and age such a thing could happen. Cats and lions indeed! Even my daughter is seeing cats and feeling and hearing them when they are not there.'

Burrough sat up straight. 'Your daughter saw a cat! Tell me, did it have blue eyes?'

'Why, yes,' said Johnson. 'Don't tell me there is such an impossible animal hereabouts.'

Burrough seemed disturbed. 'So it has been seen again,' he said softly and then looked Johnson straight in the eye. 'We are both churchmen—do you believe in the physical power of evil?'

'I doubt if the Devil moves among us in physical shape,' said Johnson. 'But that he has spiritual power cannot be denied.'

'I think you are wrong,' said Burrough, folding his lean hands together. 'Captain Hampson was the most evil man I have ever met in my stewardship of this parish—and I have been vicar for nearly fifty years. I am certain he dabbled in the Black Arts—arts he learned in Africa. And he brought devils to Totnes; his servants were black men of abnormal height, scarcely human in appearance. Not one of them was less than seven feet all were thin beyond belief.'

Johnson said thoughtfully, 'I have heard of a strange tribe in East Africa in which the natives are of such a nature. I believe they are called Watusi.'

'That is the name!' cried Burrough. 'They worship lions.' He lifted a hand. 'Strange things happened at Mount Elwell; curious sounds—the beating of drums and the roar of savage beasts—and an odd flickering glow used to appear in some of the rooms. None of the townsfolk would go near, nor will they do so to this day.'

'That I have reason to know,' said Johnson, somewhat morosely. 'But you cannot really believe that . . .'

'. . . that Hampson was worshipping the devil as he had been taught by those savages? Indeed I do. I was on the point of writing to the Bishop for guidance when the tragedy happened and Hampson was torn to pieces by the awful Power he had invoked.' Burroughs' eyes gleamed fanatically. 'And after it was over none of those black devils were ever seen again. It was as though they disappeared from the face of the earth.'

That was certainly an odd circumstance, thought Johnson; a seven-foot blackamoor would find concealment difficult in South Devon. He cleared his throat nervously. 'And what of the strange blue-eyed cat?'

'It is well known that witches and warlocks have their familiars,' said Burrough slowly. 'And the Devil cannot be stupid. Would he appear in the form of a lion in this quiet English town for all to see? But many people have seen the blue-eyed cat and my parishioners know it for what it is.'

The old man was now becoming excited and it took all of William Johnson's powers of persuasion to calm him. Johnson judged Burrough to be senile and failing in intellectual capacity and dismissed his strange story as the maunderings of an old man. All the same, he did not pass on this odd happening to either his wife or his daughter.

The year 1887 drew near to its close and certain events occurred which weighed heavily on his spirit. Alice saw the cat several times although William Johnson never did, nor did his wife. But Mrs Johnson complained continuously about the animal's incessant mewing, and three times she woke up her husband in the dark of the night to tell him that the cat had jumped on the bed. Yet there was nothing there when he looked.

He worked in his study during the dark evenings and was conscious of a brooding spirit which seemed to hover in and around the house, pervading the atmosphere with a dankness that chilled his bones. There was also a heavy scent which seemed to drift about the place and which, at first, he could not identify, but then he recalled his visits to a zoo and could compare it to the musty smell of the lion house.

He became nervous and was strongly aware of being watched and would glance hastily over his shoulder only to see shadows.

Then he would go and turn up the gas lights to their full strength and say a prayer before resuming work on his manuscript.

The Christmas of 1887 was not a happy one for the Johnsons. Since they had spent most of their lives in Africa they had no friends in England, and none of the local people, of high or low degree, would visit the house. Even Susan Beer gave notice just before Christmas, saying that her father forbade her to be in that house at that time of the year. There was no other explanation offered.

It was on Christmas Eve that they began to hear the noises—a faint but persistent drumming sound. 'It seems to come from the attic,' said Mrs Johnson, so William went upstairs, but from the attic the sound appeared to come from the cellar, yet the cellar was quiet apart from that eerie distant rhythmical beat.

'We've heard that before,' said Alice quietly. 'In Africa.'

During the week that followed—between Christmas and New Year—life became very difficult at Mount Elwell. The noise of drums became gradually louder and reverberated through the house. All the Johnsons heard the drums although William Johnson could never determine whether he had actually heard the noise with his ears or whether it was purely in his mind, and when he consulted his wife and daughter he found them in like difficulty.

At last he could bear it no longer. 'You must leave,' he said firmly to his wife. 'You and Alice must stay at the Seven Stars Hotel for a while.'

'And you, William?' asked his wife.

'I will consult the vicar,' said Johnson.

And so he did. Burrough nodded gravely when he heard of the manifestations in the house.

'It is coming time,' he said. 'Hampson died on the first of the year.' He clutched Johnson's arm. 'I tell you, sir; I tell you this house is accursed and must be re-dedicated to God. We are churchmen—and we both know what to do in a situation like this.'

Johnson thought of the ancient rituals of exorcism; he had learned them before he had been ordained into the priesthood, but he had never expected to use them. Burrough said briskly, 'I will come and keep vigil with you on New Year's Eve together with Alfred Earle, the archdeacon. We will drive the Devil from Totnes.'

So it was that on New Year's Eve Johnson, Burrough and Alfred Earle gathered in Johnson's study at Mount Elwell. Burrough lit the two big candles, laid out the brass-bound Bible, and placed the brazen bell conveniently to hand. Earle, a normally bluff and hearty Devonian, was subdued and quiet.

He carried with him an axe of which Burrough said, 'You will find no target for that, Alfred. There is no physical enemy here. Put your faith in the Lord God.'

But Alfred Earle stubbornly clutched the haft of the axe and would not be parted from it.

The clamour of the drums almost deafened Johnson so that he had difficulty in hearing what the others said, but strangely they seemed to be unaware. 'Can't you hear them?' he demanded wildly.

Burrough cocked his head on one side. 'I hear nothing— nothing at all. But wait . . . yes, I hear a faint throbbing. Could it be coming from your attic?'

Johnson set his teeth. 'It begins like that. If you stayed in this house as long as I have your ears would resound with nothing else.'

Time crept by and the three men knelt and prayed incessantly but Johnson, distracted by the drumming and the unexpected yowling of a cat, could not get the words right and made many mistakes.

At last the big grandfather clock in the hall struck the first stroke of midnight, and the tremendous racket suddenly stopped. There was the thick animal scent heavy on the still air, and another smell of putrefaction. The three men looked at each other in wonder, and Burrough made the sign of the cross.

At that instant a voice spoke, at once dry and glutinous, and it spoke words in a language none could understand. It came from the strange cupboard that opened on to the hall, and there was a scratching noise as though something were trying to get out. William Johnson uttered an inarticulate cry and, seizing the axe from Alfred Earle, he swung it at the cupboard in a great blow. The wood splintered under his onslaught, and he swung again and again, chopping the cupboard to matchwood.

Something loomed tall in the opening he had made and fell slowly forward. It was the figure of a giant of a man, seven feet tall—a corpse long dead and mummified which had been concealed in the false backing of the cupboard. It fell forward as a tree falls, but with the lips writhing and incoherent words spouting forth—a tall African dressed in skins and feathers and bones.

Alfred Earle shouted in terror but Burrough and Johnson were struck speechless as a cat, a strangely coloured, blue-eyed cat sprang from the cupboard to crouch on the fallen corpse, its ears flattened and spitting in rage. Johnson looked upon it in horror as it began to change. It seemed to grow subtly and fluidly and in no time at all it was transformed into a huge black-maned lion. He stared into those eyes, now lambent and yellow, and had no time to even shout as it sprang directly at him.

They found them the next day. Burrough and Earle were both dead and there was not a mark on them, but their faces were dreadfully contorted. The medical evidence was that they had died from heart failure. William Cooper Johnson, however, had been torn limb from limb as though by a great cat and his blood lay red and thick across the open Bible. Lying across the corpse was a barbaric necklace of lions' teeth.

*

All that happened a long time ago. The house is no longer called Mount Elwell—it is now Hay Hill—and the cupboard has been torn down and the opening bricked up, although its doors are still there as you can see to this day.

And if you talk to the old men of Totnes as they drink their pints of cider in the Kingsbridge Inn they will tell you their reckonings of these strange happenings. They will tell you that the house is quite safe for the normal run of men—but if the blue-eyed cat is seen again, and if the house is again occupied by those who have lived in Africa, then the drums will be heard and the lion will walk again to rend and tear with claws and fangs.

Because no one who has not lived in Africa has been touched—save for dying of fright at the awesome things they have witnessed—but those who have lived in the Dark Continent, and come to Hay Hill at this time of the year . . . beware!

DESMOND BAGLEY

Desmond Bagley was born on 29 October 1923 in Kendal, a market town in the heart of England's Lake District. His mother Hannah had been a mill worker and his father John a coal miner who rose to become a pit manager. In 1929, after John Bagley suffered a nervous breakdown, he relocated his family to Bolton in Lancashire where Desmond attended St Peter & St Paul School and, as he recorded years later, his parents 'alternat[ed] between boarding houses and fish and chip shops'. In a 1975 interview, Bagley reflected that he had been 'hopeless' at school and something of a loner, largely he felt because of his stammer.

When the family moved to Blackpool in 1936, Bagley moved to a new school where he discovered the work of H. G. Wells, which kindled his literary ambitions—and on leaving school at the age of fourteen he began his working life with a publisher as an apprentice or 'printer's devil' while undertaking training in air raid defence. With the advent of the Second World War, he joined an engineering firm and worked on the manufacture of components for the gun turrets of Spitfire aircraft and he joined the factory's fencing club.

After the war, like many of his contemporaries, Bagley wanted a fresh start. In 1946, he made what would be the first of many visits to Iceland and, in 1947, decided to emigrate to South Africa, leaving Blackpool in the middle of a blizzard—or what passes for one in Britian—as part of an organised group of like-minded young emigrants. The party travelled through Algeria—an experience that would in part inform his first published novel *The Golden Keel* (1963)—and the group crossed the Sahara by truck—which would inform his twelfth, *Flyaway* (1978). Bagley struck out on his own in Uganda where he got a factory job and by night worked as a nightclub photographer. After contracting malaria he travelled south, taking brief jobs in Kenya, at a Rhodesian asbestos mine and in a goldfield in the Orange Free State. Eventually, he reached Durban in South Africa where he had various jobs, including writing for the South African Broadcasting Corporation, working as an import clerk and as warehouse superintendent for a paper mill where he edited the in-house magazine, the bizarrely named *African Gunshots*. In his spare time Bagley wrote what he described as 'bad poetry [and] indifferent short stories', and in 1955 he had a short story published for the first time. This was 'My Old Man's Trumpet', a story inspired in part by the work of Ray Bradbury. The story appeared in the *Johannesburg Sunday Times*. The experience of writing order for *African Gunshots* fuelled Bagley's ambition to be a journalist and over the next five years he would write and review for various South African newspapers, covering a huge variety of subjects anonymously as well as under a number of pseudonyms including 'John Reid', 'Anthony Cantrell', 'Simon Brockhurst' and 'John Lackland'.

Away from work, Bagley continued to write short stories and he also began writing at length, working on two unpublished novels, *Clare* and the unfinished *Ex Machina*. He also continued to pursue his hobby and joined a fencing club in Johannesburg. It was here that, in 1959, Bagley met a young South African woman called Joan Brown. He introduced himself to her as 'Simon', a wartime nickname coined by an unimaginative acquaintance who called several of his friends after Leslie Charteris's character Simon Templar. It stuck. Simon and Joan were captivated by each other and when he proposed, ten days later, she accepted. They were married the following year. By this time, and as well as working as a journalist and writing in his spare time, Bagley was scripting advertisements for products like Johnson's floor polish 'Pledge'. More short stories were published, some under the pen name 'Simon Bagley', until Joan encouraged him to try his hand at 'a Collins novel'. She worked in a bookshop and was well aware of the enormous popularity of adventure stories of the kind written by Alastair Maclean and Hammond Innes, as published by William Collins Ltd. With Joan's support, he began to craft a plot around the real-life mystery of the disappearance of an enormous cache of gold, jewels and currency that had been looted by the Italian leader Mussolini. The resulting novel, *The Golden Keel*, was accepted and published in 1963 by . . . Collins. Bagley would never look back. He had found love and he had, at last, found a career.

While Simon and Joan loved South Africa they were disgusted by the brutal and immoral apartheid regime. As he put it, 'You either stay and fight—which means going to prison—or you go; I went.' After a brief attempt to live in Italy they returned to Britain and settled in the Devon town of Totnes. The Bagleys loved Totnes and supported various charities, including the local branch of the Royal National Lifeboat Institution for which Bagley funded the construction of a five-metre replica lifeboat that could convert into stalls from which RNLI gifts could be displayed and sold; the 'boat' was formally launched by Lecia Hall, Joan's sister, and named by her *The Golden Keel*.

Bagley's second novel was initially rejected but the third was published as *High Citadel* (1965). Over the next twenty years a dozen more novels followed and Desmond Bagley became one of the most popular writers of adventure novels. Modestly, he ascribed much of this to the ingenious gimmicks dreamed up by his publishers, which included installing a seven-metre 'streamer' in London's Euston station and arranging with a coffee producer for millions of 'Bagley book tokens' to be given away in jars of their product. Bagley considered himself to be 'an entertainer [and] a craftsman', basing his books on thorough research and striving for accuracy. Alongside Alistair Maclean, Hammond Innes and Geoffrey Jenkins, he defined the adventure genre but also broadened its appeal, not least by making his female characters significantly less one-dimensional than was customary at that time. He was praised in particular for the authenticity of his settings, the majority of which he and Joan had explored, including Ross Island where they stayed at McMurdo, the largest US station in Antarctica. Four years before that visit, Bagley had sketched out a plot centred on a devastating avalanche and after witnessing one on Ross he returned to the idea which eventually formed the basis of his novel *The Snow Tiger* (1975).

While he would spend a considerable part of the year on research, he would work solidly for three to four months—eight hours a day from Monday to Friday—drafting and re-drafting on an electric typewriter: 'second finger of my left hand only—I'm thinking of getting it insured'. At the end of the day he would often unwind in a local pub such as the Kingsbridge Inn in Totnes and the Cott Inn at Dartington, to which he dedicated *The Vivero Letter* (1968).

It was a relaxed lifestyle but by the mid-1970s levels of taxation in the United Kingdom had become very high. In common with other popular writers, especially those who did not have children to whom rights and royalties could be assigned, Bagley became a tax exile. He and Joan went to live at Câtel House in Les Rohais de Haut in St Andrew, the sole land-locked parish of the island of Guernsey. It is now known as Bagley Hall.

In 1983, Desmond Bagley collapsed at home after suffering a stroke. He was flown to Southampton Hospital where he died on 12 April at the age of just 59. At his death, several novels remained unfinished, some of which had been started decades earlier and abandoned when he had become confounded by an aspect of the unfolding plot. Two were completed by his widow, Joan: *Night of Error* (1984), which Bagley had begun in the early 1960s; and

Juggernaut (1985), whose working title had been *The Road*. To Collins' dismay, an atypically negative newspaper review of *Juggernaut* convinced Joan to down tools. However, more than thirty years later, another of the unfinished novels, *Because Salton Died*, was completed by author Michael Davies and published by HarperCollins as *Domino Island* (2019), the first of a trilogy also comprising *Outback* (2023) and *Thin Ice* (2024).

'The House of Lions' was written to entertain Christmas house guests at Hay Hill, the Bagleys' home in Totnes, in December 1966. It is anthologised here for the first time, and I am grateful to David Brawn for drawing the story to my attention.

THE HAUNTING MELODY

Christopher Priest

When Waddle and I first moved into the cottage, we congratulated ourselves on having found a bargain.

It was only after we'd been in there about month, did we begin to suspect it wasn't such a snip, but by then we were settled and it didn't seem to matter.

Anyway, Waddle and I quickly grew used to the idea of the few disadvantages. Waddle's my dog. I call him Waddle because when he runs he, well, waddles.

People in the village a mile away talked of subsidence under the cliffs, how each year another few feet slipped down into the sea.

Many houses had gone down the cliffs in their time, and no one in the village gave our cottage more than five years before it joined them.

Obviously, this alarmed me at first, but I walked all round the garden and couldn't see that I'd much to worry about. There was at least fifty yards between the cottage and the cliff-edge, and I planned on being there only as long as I needed to be: certainly no more than a year.

Then there was the music . . .

We didn't know anything about it for the first four weeks, then one night there was a strong wind off the sea, and we caught the faintest strains of piano music. It was so faint that at first I thought I was imagining it. Just below the threshold of hearing. I could make out the faint tinkling of notes and chords. No melody that I could recognise, but I felt that if I could hear all the notes there would be.

Waddle heard it too, cocking up one of his floppy ears, and looking as me quizzically.

The next day, I went round the outside of the cottage looking for cracks and crannies, and knocking out old birds' nests from the eaves. There was no other house within half a mile . . . if there was a noise, reason told me it could only be caused by the wind.

That same night, the wind again whipped around the house, and Waddle and I listened to the distant strains of a half-heard piano.

In the end, I got around to mentioning it down at the Anchor in the village. The locals all glanced at each other in the way people do when you've said something they know about, but no one would say anything.

Later, I asked the innkeeper. Like myself, he had come originally from London.

'A piano, you say?' he said as he dried the glasses and put them away on the shelf behind him.

Like the others, he played coy for a while. But in the end, he told me what he knew. It turned out that at one time there had been a house a few hundred yards from my cottage. Until about forty years before, a concert pianist had live there by himself after his retirement from public life.

One night, during a really violent storm, the cliff had subsided and his house had fallen into the sea.

The pianist had been in bed at the time, and his body had never been recovered.

Ever since, people who lived at the cottage had claimed to hear his piano when the weather was rough.

To be honest, it didn't worry me, I'd never believed in ghosts— nor disbelieved in them for that matter. Waddle and I stayed on at the cottage, and whenever the wind rose we heard the piano playing gently. And neither of us minded.

Time passed and the winter deepened. On the cliffs many nights were cold and windy and several times a week I would fall asleep in my bed, with the ghostly music in my ears . . .

One night, during one of the worst gales of the winter, I awoke to find Waddle pulling at my pyjama sleeve. I turned on the light and saw that the hair on his back was up and that his tall was well down between his legs.

'What is it, boy?' I said.

Waddle put his head on one side. I listened.

The sale blew around the cottage like a blast from Hell. The windows rattled, the door banged in its frame, the chimney howled.

I reached out and patted him.

'Steady on, Waddle,' I said. 'It's only the wind.'

But then I realised . . . The piano was silent.

In the same instant, Waddle put up his muzzle and let out the eeriest wail heard. I had ever heard. I jumped out of bed and went to the window.

Outside the sky was clear and there was a full moon. But the few trees around us were bent by the wind, and every now and then grit or pebbles would rattle against the side of the shed in the garden.

I looked towards the cliff-edge the with a sudden shock of surprise. At my side, Waddle began to growl.

There was the black bulk of a house, silhouetted against the sky. I stared at it for nearly minute, my mind refusing to accept what my eyes saw.

'The house,' I breathed. 'The pianist's house . . .'

Then I saw that one of the windows was glowing faintly with light.

Then the music stopped. Apart from the sounds of the gale, I could hear nothing.

With abrupt decision I reached for my clothes, pulling over my pyjamas a pair of trousers and a sweater, and getting into my rubber boots.

I looked down at Waddle.

'Coming, boy?'

He put his head on one side for a moment, then walked to the door. I opened it, and we both walked out into the night. The house was still there, a few hundred yards away along the cliff. I decided to walk along the edge itself, where I knew there was a path.

Far below me, heavy white surf sucked at the base of the cliffs.

We drew nearer the house, seeing the glow of the window grow steadily brighter. Then, literally in the blink of an eye, it vanished.

I stopped, and Waddle came and leaned against my legs.

'It's gone, Waddle. Did you see that?'

Behind us, I beard a deep-throated rumbling that was louder than the sound of the wind of the surf. In the dark, I couldn't see what caused it. It grew louder, and became a thundering roar.

Suddenly the part of the cliff where my cottage stood collapsed like a pack of cards, throwing up a vast cloud of rubble that was picked up by the wind and sprayed like hail against me. I put my arms over my face, and ran.

When the spray of dirt had passed, I turned back again. A whole section of the cliff, my cottage with it, had rolled down into the sea.

Just then, I heard the faint strains of piano music . . .

CHRISTOPHER PRIEST

The author and critic Christopher Mackenzie Priest was born in Cheadle, Cheshire, on 14 July 1943. His parents, Millicent Haslock and Walter Priest, were cousins and his father worked as a commercial traveller for a manufacturer of weighing machines. Christopher attended Cheadle Hulme School until 1959 when his parents returned to Essex, the county where they had been married in 1936. The family lived at Willow Close in Doddinghurst and, rather than continuing his education, Christopher started work for an accountancy firm. At the age of fifteen, he had discovered the work of Brian Aldiss, with whom he would in later years appear at conventions, and in his spare time at work as well as in the evenings he would write short stories. The first to be published was 'The Run', which appeared in *Impulse* magazine in May 1966, and others were carried by *Tit-Bits* and *New Worlds SF*; the majority of this early work, including some previously unpublished stories and a fascinating autobiographical essay can be found in the collection *Ersatz Wines* (2008).

In 1968, Priest married Christine Merchant, a student teacher. Shortly after completing his first novel, the couple moved to a flat in Ortygia House at Harrow-on-the-Hill in North London. Despite a hostile landlady, Priest would live at the house until 1985, completing many of his novels there, from *Fugue for a Darkening Island* (1970) to *The Glamour* (1984).

In *Indoctrinaire* (1970), which Priest produced by merging two short stories, a British biologist is abducted from an Antarctic research station and taken through space and time to face the consequences of his own actions. While Priest appreciated the freedom that the genre gave him to produce 'thought-provoking and radical entertainment', he was uncomfortable with being labelled a science-fiction writer. For him, the proliferation of low-budget films and 'junk' fiction had led critics and readers to undervalue the genre. He saw himself as a writer of 'SF and not Sci-Fi', and preferred to be considered as someone who 'looks into the future and sees possibilities' in the manner of Aldous Huxley, George Orwell and H. G. Wells. For his second novel, he turned to the possibilities outlined in Enoch Powell's hateful 'rivers of blood' speech. The result was *Fugue for a Darkening Island* (1971), a deliberately ambiguous novel that deals with the response of a right-wing government and ordinary, more liberally minded people like Priest himself to a massive influx of refugees. Contemporary reviews found the novel 'terrifying' and 'chilling', and it won third prize in the first year of the John W. Campbell Memorial Award for the Best Science Fiction Novel of 1972. When not writing, Priest was a keen amateur film-maker and in 1972, he helped 25 young people to make a ten-minute film—'a series of interlinked dreams'—financed by the British Film Institute and shot largely on the banks of the river Mole and in the Casson Room in Leatherhead's Thorndike Theatre. Priest enjoyed the experience which, as well as similar work with the Roxeth youth club in Harrow, inspired him to write a manual for young film-makers, *Your Book of Film Making* (1974).

Throughout his life Christopher Priest also supported aspiring authors, for example through appearances at the British Science Fiction Convention and, at a more local level, speaking to groups such as the Harrow Writers' Circle, to which in 1974 he described his approach to writing: 'I start each of my stories by looking inside myself and asking two questions. First, I wonder what would happen if . . . And, secondly, does it really matter to me? Can I make it matter?' For him, 'science fiction did not really predict future events, but it did try to consider the effects of science'. Thus, as *Fugue for a Darkening Island* had centred on a migrancy crisis, the extraordinary *Inverted World* (1974) was inspired by the idea that fossil fuels would eventually run out.

In 1972, Priest's marriage came to an end and he threw himself into work. While books came out under his own name—including the collection of novelettes *Real-Time World* (1974)—he also wrote a dozen pseudonymous paperbacks for New English Library, three of which appeared as by 'Richard Harrington' and nine as 'Petra Christian', a house name which Priest shared with another writer, Peter Cave. The tongue-in-cheek 'Christian' titles, with titles like *The Sexploiters* (1973) and *The Bust-Up* (1974), feature a journalist called Sally Deenes who encounters nefarious goings-on at a nudist colony run by the Whancus family. Fortunately the return on these was not so great as to divert Priest from more serious fiction. Dedicated to H. G. Wells, *The Space Machine: A Scientific Romance* (1976) is set—initially—in 1893 and blends elements of Wells' two great works *The Time Machine* (1895) and *The War of the Worlds* (1897).

With *A Dream of Wessex* (1977), Priest returned to the Dorset location of his childhood holidays and created a Wellsian heroine caught between worlds of reality and fantasy, a theme to which Priest would return in novels like *The Affirmation* (1981) and *The Extremes* (1998) as well as in the multi-award-winning *The Separation* (2002), an alternate history of Britain in the Second World War. Priest's interest in alternates, almost an obsession, also led him to create the Dream Archipelago, a world that features in numerous stories and whose mythos the author developed to encompass its own language, currency and culture. As discussed by Paul Kincaid in his masterful study *The Unstable Realities of Christopher Priest* (2020), duality—in various forms, and across space and time—can be seen as the hallmark of Priest's work and it is the central theme of *The Prestige* (1995), the novel for which he will probably be best remembered.

In 1981, Priest married Lisa Tuttle, an American writer of science fiction. They divorced in 1987 and the following year he married the author Leigh Kennedy with whom he would have two children, Elizabeth and Simon. In 1983, the Book Marketing Council included Priest in a list of the Ten Best Young British Novelists, much to the bemusement of the 39-year-old Priest. This recognition led to his being invited to pen a regular column for *The Bookseller* on various aspects of publishing and judging short story competitions. It also helped to raise his profile and for a while to increase sales. Over the next twenty years—discounting pseudonymous novelisations of films such as *Mona Lisa* (1986) and *Short Circuit* (1986), and one-offs like *Seize the Moment: The Autobiography of Britain's First Astronaut* (1994)—Priest wrote some of his best books. Foremost among these, at least in terms of popularity, is *The Prestige* (1995), an intriguing and suspenseful story of battling magicians, described by Michael Dirda in a review for the *Washington Post* as 'a dizzying magic show of a novel' which he compared to the best of Agatha Christie and Ruth Rendell's work as 'Barbara Vine'. The novel won the James Tait Black Memorial Prize for 1995 and was filmed ten years later by Christopher Nolan with a cast including Christian Bale, Sir Michael Caine, Hugh Jackman and Scarlett Johannson. Priest enjoyed the film and marked its release with an offbeat interview in which he gave a recipe for 'Prestigious Summer Delight'. He also wrote *The Magic: The Story of a Film* (2006), which he described as a 'an appreciative and nuanced study of how a serious and complex feature film is conceived and made by a young film-maker at his peak'. As well as *The Prestige* (1995) and *The Separation* (2002), other memorable books from this period include *The Glamour* (1984) and *The Quiet Woman* (1990), which was inspired by the murder of the peace campaigner Hilda Murrell. The former is a modern take on H. G. Wells' *The Invisible Man* (1897) for which Priest wrote an alternate ending, to date unpublished; and in the latter novel the death of an elderly woman leads her son and her neighbour to create competing narratives about her life.

In 2011, Priest was divorced for a third time and he began living with the author Nina Allan. The couple moved to Devon and from there to the Isle of Bute where they continued to write and were married at Eaglesham House in Rothesay a matter of weeks after Priest had been diagnosed with a form of lung cancer. Mercifully, his illness was brief and, on 2 February 2024, Christopher Priest died—in Nina's words, 'completely peaceful and surrounded by love'.

One of a small number of uncollected stories, 'The Haunting Melody' was published in the *London Evening News* on 14 May 1970.

THE LAST WOLF

Reginald Hill

It was one of those over-ripe Autumn nights when the sky sags low and stars stream across the firmament like angels' blood. But it was the lights below which held the traveller's eye as he came down the hill. The events of that momentous day had kept him lingering from the high fells longer than he intended. Tracks familiar as the streets of home had become smudged and blurred under the rub of slush, and marker cairns which ran like furling posts round a racetrack in daylight were smoothed into the earth by the pressure of the dark.

So, the lights of the village in the distant valley were a reassuring light as he descended the mountains' gentle eastern flanks. Behind him, he thought he heard something move. Twice already he had startled, and been startled by, recumbent sheep which had risen almost beneath his feet and lumbered protesting into the night, so he felt little alarm.

He glanced back, saw nothing, and swore violently as the momentary distraction made him miss his footing on a patch of shale. A sprained ankle could leave him benighted, and though he had spare clothing and a flask of coffee in his rucksack and did not doubt he could pass a night up here safely, if uncomfortably, his mind was already ahead by a tap-room fire with a strong whisky in his hand.

The noise came again. This time he stopped before looking

back. A few yards behind him, something moved. 'Baaa!' he cried, letting the exaggerated tremor of his mock bleating conceal a real tremor of his fear as his mind quarrelled with his eyes, which told him that he briefly glimpsed a shape that looked nothing like a sheep. It moved too swiftly, with a loping predatory motion. A fox, perhaps? Though it had seemed too large. A dog, then? Yes, that seemed more likely. A dog.

Or a wolf.

Wolf!

How had such a crazy thought slipped into his mind? The last wolf in Britain had been killed somewhere near Loch Monar early in the eighteenth century, and there'd been no reports of any in England for two hundred years before that! It was only the previous night that he had pushed up these nuggets of

information when, restless as only past failures and future uncertainties can make a man, he had padded downstairs to the hotel lounge and found himself between some sensational novelettes and the last volume, dog-eared, in flashing leather, a Victorian Encyclopaedia of Natural History.

That, of course, was why this absurd notion had occurred to his always over-suggestible fancy, having tracked it to its lair, he could smile at himself and focus his attention on picking his way down the rock-strewn fellside.

Behind, stones clicked as something else passed over the stretch of loose shale he had just traversed. Once more he stopped and turned. This time he definitely saw something: its long grey shadow, slinking close to the ground. Then it was gone.

'Hey, hey!' he called. 'Come, hey! Stop, stop! Heel, hey, heel!'

He whistled and clicked his fingers and made all the re-assuring, summoning sounds he could. There was no response. It was hardly surprising. These sheep-dogs (and that, of course, was what it must be, a sheep-dog somehow separated from its master and wandering lost amongst the hills) were trained to respond to only one voice and to one specific set of sound signals. He'd often stood and watched the farmers working them north in the hills and down by the lakeside. It was truly marvellous to see the communion between man and beast!

Now, something else he had read or heard came into his mind. Those useful and unapplauded sheepdog skills were man's retirement of instinct, astute and lupine. That clever collie working the sheep along the hillside was but a long echo of its wolf ancestors out on the hunt. Once this was understood, all became clear to the watcher. See how the hunter swings inside to get into position, then approaches steadily to avoid causing alarm! Now come the little rushes forward to get the herd on the move; the freeze to perfect stillness, with ever the savage growl held in the throat, when the animals threaten to panic; the earth-hugging, quiet, dartingly runs to manoeuvre the herd to ground at maximum vantage. And so, at last the hunter is ready, the individual prey is chosen; one last dash separates it from the protection of its fellows! Now the only road to join them is blocked by those eyes, that jaw! To turn and run from them is animal instinct, against rationality! You run, you must, though now too late! You turn and flee but the sudden shark of this ocean of forest and hill is already alongside and his terrible teeth ripping up at your unprotected throat . . .

Aghhh!

He jerked sporadically, as if from sleep. He was still standing looking back up the shadowy hill, and his body was hot with sweat, as though the damp air was heavy with tropical heat, rather than touched with the chill threat of northern winter. But there was nothing to see behind, though even that *nothing* looked hazier than before. He raised his eyes to the heavens. The great atrium of stars was smeary now as if a hand had brushed across it in an attempt to staunch a wound. And when he looked once more into the valley, the lights there, which earlier had prickled like soda bubbles, now gleamed indistinct, like the half-glimpsed scales of an unknown fish deep in a weedy, dark pool.

Well, there was nothing for a man of his experience to fear in the mist. He knew exactly where he was. Not much more than a half hour of steady walking would see him onto a level track and then his long stride would eat up the ground along the valley bottom to the welcoming inn. Hefting his rucksack on his shoulders, he took a step forward. Below him the hazy lights of the village vanished for a moment as a shape moved across them. Once more he opened his mouth to call, but despite the damp air, his throat felt constricted and dry. Before he could muster it, he heard in the dark a long, rumbling growl and his mind saw the red, wet jaw from which this was issuing, and he lost all desire to speak.

The light-eclipsing shape moved again, first to the left, then to the right, swinging silently across the hillside in a pendulum motion. It was making no direct approach, but each loping swing brought it a few feet closer.

And each time it stopped and become once more part of the ground it rested on, he heard its separate existence reaffirmed by the deep growl.

He stopped and seized a jagged lump of rock. Instantly the growl ceased.

'So you know what this means, you brute!' he yelled. The silence and the feel of the rock in his hand gave him new assurance, but not so much so that he ceased to feel the attraction of discretion. So, abandoning his precious line, he turned half left and began to move on a descending diagonal.

He hadn't covered more than a couple of yards when the mist ahead swirled and condensed, and for the first time he saw it clear, head held low and perfectly still, red gleaming eyes fixed unblinkingly on his throat, as it came gliding straight towards him. Shrieking with terror, he hurled the rock. He did not stay to check his aim, but turned at once and fled. Grey as he scrambled and climbed back up the fellside, he knew this was stupid. Unless a man can outrun his hunter, he must stand and face it! This way, all he was doing was exposing his back to the terrible teeth. He imagined them tearing at his hamstrings and then, as he collapsed in helpless agony, slashing irresistibly across his unprotected throat.

In the end, it was fatigue that performed what reason commanded. Exhausted, he staggered to a halt and turned around.

Behind him there was nothing. Only the swirling mist which had now completely drowned all the valley lights. He dragged rasping breathfuls of the grey vapour into his lungs as if by devouring it, he might rekindle those distant friendly lamps. Nothing appeared, nothing moved. Slowly he recovered, though his body still trembled from exertion and fear. He tried to gauge how high up the fellside he had run, but without any point of reference above or below it was impossible. Not to worry, he had matches in his rucksack, with a compass and a map.

He put his hands to his shoulders. The straps were not there, and the familiar weight was absent from his hands.

'Oh Christ!' he swore, or prayed, as he realised that at some point in his mad panicking flight, he must have slipped out of his rucksack and let it fall to lie among the boulders, somewhere below.

He tried to make his mind work for him instead of against him, conjuring up a picture of the fell and its neighbours. Even without the contents of his rucksack, he was confident he could survive. The night did not threaten to turn cold enough to bring the risk of death from exposure. He was wearing weather-proof anorak and thick walking trousers, though the latter were already damp from the all-pervading mist. It would be best to keep moving at a steading pace, to keep his blood circulating.

If he kept going uphill, leaning always to his right, he must eventually reach the northern shoulder of the fell. Once across this, the descent into the next valley was rough, but manageable. It was southward that the ground become dangerously uneven and precipitous.

He noted, almost as an uninvolved observer, that his review of the situation did not admit even the possibility of simply retracing his footsteps. Whatever he had fled from was still down there somewhere. In his over-wrought mind, he imagined, much more real than the swirling mist, teeth and claws ripping up the rucksack in a fury of bloodlust. Shuddering, he turned and set off uphill, bearing diagonally right.

He had been going for only a minute when even further to the right, he heard a noise. He slowed down and listened. It slowed too, but now it was unmistakable; the steady padding of huge paws on turf as something loped in parallel with him, its rhythm varied from time to time by the clink of small stoned being moved, or most frighteningly of all, the nerve-rasping screech of claws scrabbling for purchase on smooth rock.

For a while, he straightened up and the noise faded. But as soon as he bore right again, it recommenced. This time he persisted, and, for a time, it seemed that his bestial shadow was content to keep its distance. Then, though still he saw nothing, the sound of its loping paws was added a rhythmic animal breathing growing perceptibly louder, 'til he realised their lines were no longer parallel, but converging.

His nerve broke, and he swung away 'til he was going straight uphill once more, and he did not attempt to diverge again. A little later, his throat constricted with fear, as a shape loomed out of the darkness before him. But almost immediately he recognised it as a marker cairn, and beyond it another, and he realised he had re-joined the tracked by which he had started to descend; it seemed a lifetime ago.

He felt no fatigue, just a little lightness of the head. Was this, he wondered, how the hunted animal felt as it began to acknowledge that, though the end might still be far, control had passed, irretrievable, to the implacable hunter?

The track was climbing less steeply now, and soon it was almost level. He must be back on the summit plateau. Follow the track straight ahead and eventually the larger cairn, which marked the fell's highest point, would pyramid before him. But this was to be his time, it seemed. From the darkness to his right came a low threatening growl. Obediently, he branched left. Fear had left him now, though he guessed it had only run a little way ahead to prepare a special welcome. But for the moment he was imperious to danger. He even began to play a kind of mad game, deliberately pausing from time to time. Soon from behind him would come allow warning growl. Then, if he didn't move at once, he would hear those savage paws patter closer in a short, menacing rush.

That's when the game stopped and he moved on, even though he knew he was being driven far wide of the safe track into a danger land of sudden gullies, shattered boulders and sucking mosses, which ended in the sharp, crumbling cliffs of the mountain's southern face. Here was terrain to be treated with caution in broad daylight. By night, in mist, only a fool or a madman would venture here. Or a man driven by a ravenous beast to an appointed spot.

For here was the perfect killing ground. Here was a plane of concealment, safe from interruption, where a hunter could dispatch his prey, knowing that any attempt at flight would merely save him the bother of killing.

And here the bones of a slaughtered animal might be forever, unsought and unguarded by the distant herd grazing in complacent safety on some gentler ground.

Despite the darkness and the rough terrain, he was walking with scarcely a hesitation, obeying without demur each nudge and hint of the following beast. It was right at his heels now. He could hear every rasp of its breath. But he never turned to look at it. What need? He knew what a wolf looked like.

Finally, he came to a halt. Before him a huge fractured boulder, darker against the dark, barred the way. Others hulked all around, forming a rough circle. This, he knew, was the place. Behind him the beast had stopped too. He could hear its rasping breath. In his mind, he saw its terrible large teeth and felt its gleaming eyes travelling over his body to pick their spot. This, then, was how it felt to be here and know your death was here with you; to know that no amount of pleading, no appeals to the past or passions for the future could divert that ending, the sharpness from your constricting throat.

Soon. It must be soon.

He could hear those tremendous paws behind him, scraping and scrabbling at the earth, scratching onto earth and stones, as if preparing for him a grave. Oh gentle beast, he wants to bury him! It was time to face it. Where there is no hope, there can be no fear.

Slowly, he turned.

A shepherd, out before dawn the following morning, was attracted by the howling of one of his dogs. He found it standing over a rucksack, which had been dropped by the track not far from the foot of the fell. Puzzled, he opened it up. It contained a cagoule, a sweater, a map, a compass, a flask of coffee and, wrapped in a piece of hand-stained cloth, a ring of gold. He went back to his farmhouse and rang the police who in their turn contacted Mountain Rescue.

It was midday through the morning when the rescue team and the accompanying policeman found him. He was sitting in a little clearing among a scatter of shattered boulders, with his back against one of them, and at his feet, a shallow grave. In it lay the body of a woman with her throat savagely cut. A blood-stained knife lay on her breast, and also the severed ring finger of her left hand. Scattered around were the rocks and earth which had been used to cover up the body.

As the onlookers stood in intent horror, the shepherd who had been following their progress with an attestation of indifference, began to approach. His dog, an ageing border collie, ran ahead, its tail wagging in friendly excitement.

At the sound of its approach, the man started up with a cry of fear and put his hands over his eyes. For the first time, the rescuers saw that his nails were splintered and broken from tearing at the rock and earth and, when he took his hands away, where the skin and torn fingers had touched his brow, fresh droplets of blood gleamed like stars in a pale dawn sky.

REGINALD HILL

Reginald Charles Hill was born on 3 April 1936 in West Hartlepool, a town in County Durham in the North of England. His father, Reg Hill, played football for Hartlepools United, and it was his Scottish mother, Isabel Dickson, who kindled her son's love of crime fiction.

At the outbreak of the Second World War, his father became a storeman with the Air Ministry and the family moved to Cumberland. Hill attended Stanwix Primary School where he devoured Richmal Crompton's *Just William* books and started writing stories of his own. In 1947, he passed the eleven-plus examination and transferred to Carlisle Grammar School. After leaving school, he undertook National Service with the Border Regiment in Göttingen, Germany. He was demobbed in 1957 and the same year went up to St Catherine's College, Oxford, to study English Literature.

In 1960, Hill married Patricia Ruell whom he'd known since he was fourteen years old. The couple moved to Essex where Hill worked as a teacher until the mid-1960s when he got a job back in the North of England. While Pat stayed in the south to arrange the sale of their house, Hill moved up to Doncaster and into a house with only a bed, a card table and a kettle. With 'no social life to speak of' he began writing—or rather typing—and, according to his neighbours, 'the sound of Reg hard at work was almost constant'. Eventually, after 'a bottom drawer of first chapters', he completed a thriller in which two friends find themselves accused of being involved in a murder case. The novel was set in the Lake District and would finally be published as *Fell of Dark* (1971). However, this was a year after the publication of *A Clubbable Woman* (1970), the novel that marked the first appearance of the enduring partnership of two police officers, Dalziel and Pascoe.

Hill had decided to become a full-time author in 1970 and after he resigned from his position as a senior lecturer in English he and Pat moved to Oak Bank in the village of Broad Oak in Ravenglass, Cumbria. Over the next forty years, in a study that looked out towards the Isle of Man, he wrote dozens of books and short stories, as well as a radio mystery, 'Ordinary Levels', broadcast in 1984.

Foremost among this prolific output are the more than twenty increasingly complex novel-length mysteries and several short stories featuring Dalziel and Pascoe. In a 1999 interview, Hill explained that the younger of the two, Peter Pascoe, had been inspired by the thought of what his own life would have been like 'if I had had an academic background at university but, instead of taking up teaching as a career, I had gone into something completely different like the police'. Originally, he had seen Andy Dalziel, named for one of Hill's Oxford friends, as no more than 'a foil to the younger, more educated man . . . a big, fat slob against whom Pascoe could score points and shine', but as he wrote that first novel it became clear that—almost uniquely within the genre— Dalziel and Pascoe were a genuine and credible partnership. Eventually, the novels were adapted, first in 1990 with Philip Jackson and Donald Gee in a radio adaptation of Hill's novel *Exit Lines* (1984) written by Betty Davies. In 1993, there was a television adaptation by Robin Chapman of *A Pinch of Snuff* (1978), starring Gareth Hale and Norman Pace, best known as the comedic partnership Hale and Pace. While Hill found them 'nice chaps [who] approached it very seriously', the approach taken by the producers simply did not work for him. Boldly, he took the difficult decision to exercise his veto over any further productions but, in what he later called 'the fastest comeback since Lazarus', another production company—Portobello Pictures—bought the rights and sold them to the BBC. Starring Warren Clarke and Colin Buchanan—actors rather than comedians—the result, *Dalziel and Pascoe* (1996–2007), was enormously successful, running to forty-six episodes over eleven series. Hill was delighted with the casting, even though he felt Clarke needed to 'put on another seven stone to get it right'. However, he objected to changes made to the character of Peter Pascoe's wife Ellie, which led him to write the novel *Arms and the Women* (1999) from her perspective so that it was effectively unadaptable for the screen.

In addition to the Dalziel and Pascoe books, Hill wrote many standalone thrillers including *A Spy's Wife* (1981), *The Long Kill* (1987) and *The Woodcutter* (2010). There is also a series of novels featuring Joe Sixsmith, a black private eye who lives in Luton, plus a variety of other books written under three pseudonyms. As 'Patrick Ruell', named for Pat, he wrote non-series thrillers including *Urn Burial* (1975), set largely in Cumberland, and the Buchanesque *Death Takes the Low Road* (1974), in which a balding, bespectacled university administrator finds himself on the run in the Isle of Skye. Of his 'Dick Morland' books, the best is *Albion! Albion!* (1974), a 'soccer shocker' written when football hooliganism was at its height and amounting to a horrifying exploration of how bad things might get. Hill's third pseudonym was 'Charles Underhill', which he used for a pair of historical adventures about Carlo Fantom, a duplicitous and surprisingly unpleasant Croatian mercenary who fights on both sides during the English Civil War.

Reginald Hill was a member of the Crime Writers' Association, which awarded his novel *Bones and Silence* (1990) the Gold Dagger for Best Crime Novel of the Year and him the prestigious Diamond Dagger for Lifetime Achievement in 1995. His books are characterised by humour and plausible characters while delivering ingeniously constructed, satisfyingly complex plots. He was kind to aspiring writers and was always ready to lend his support to the CWA's fundraising anthologies. When not writing, he enjoyed spending time with friends or walking on the Fells with his golden labrador. He also took part in several episodes of Simon Brett's radio panel game *Foul Play*, solving 'The Body at the Book Launch' with Lady Antonia Fraser in 1996 and 'Murder at Matins' with Liza Cody in 1998.

In his seventies, Reginald Hill was diagnosed with a brain tumour, and he died at home on 12 January 2012. Most of his shorter fiction has now been collected and published posthumously by HarperCollins in *Dalziel and Pascoe Hunt the Christmas Killer & Other Stories* (2022) and *A Candle for Christmas & Other Stories* (2023). Omitted from those volumes, 'The Last Wolf' is published here for the first time in English, although it was translated into Japanese for *Hayakawa's Mystery Magazine* in November 1987. I am grateful to Shunta Kakuyama and Shunichiro 'Suigan' Futono for drawing it to my attention.

ACKNOWLEDGEMENTS

'A Good Place' by H. C. Bailey copyright © the estate of H. C. Bailey 1922.

'Exactly as it Happened' by E. C. Bentley reproduced with permission of Curtis Brown Ltd, London, on behalf of the Literary Estate of E. C. Bentley. Copyright © 1926 E. C. Bentley.

'Dispossession' by C. H. B. Kitchin copyright © the estate of C. H. B. Kitchin 1951.

'Modern Antique' by Milward Kennedy copyright © the estate of Milward Kennedy 1936.

'We Are Sorry, Too' by Patricia Highsmith first published in *The Barnard Quarterly*, 1942. Copyright © 1993 Diogenes Verlag AG Zürich, Switzerland.

'Vex Not His Ghost' by John Dickson Carr copyright © John Dickson Carr 1944.

'Writer's Witch' by Joan Fleming copyright © Joan Fleming 1951.

'The Security Officer' by Val Gielgud copyright © the estate of Val Gielgud 1957.

'The Fraudulent Spirit' by Joseph Commings copyright © the estate of Joseph Commings 1960.

'The Line Went Dead' by Leo Bruce (1960) reprinted by permission of Peters Fraser & Dunlop (www.petersfraserdunlop.com) on behalf of the Estate of Leo Bruce/Rupert Croft-Cooke.

'The House of the Lions' by Desmond Bagley copyright © HarperCollins Publishers Ltd 2009

'The Haunting Melody' by Christopher Priest copyright © the estate of Christopher Priest 1970.

'The Last Wolf' by Reginald Hill copyright © Reginald Hill 2024, reprinted by permission of United Agents.

Every effort has been made to trace all owners of copyright. The editor and publishers apologise for any errors or omissions and would be grateful if notified of any corrections.